Mary Noailles Murfree

His Vanished Star

Mary Noailles Murfree

His Vanished Star

ISBN/EAN: 9783337028749

Printed in Europe, USA, Canada, Australia, Japan

Cover: Foto ©Andreas Hilbeck / pixelio.de

More available books at **www.hansebooks.com**

HIS VANISHED STAR

BY

CHARLES EGBERT CRADDOCK

BOSTON AND NEW YORK
HOUGHTON, MIFFLIN AND COMPANY
The Riverside Press, Cambridge
1894

HIS VANISHED STAR.

I.

IT was a great property, reckoned by metes and bounds. A day's journey might hardly suffice to traverse the whole of his domain. Yet there was no commensurate money value attaching to these leagues of mountain wilderness, that bore indeed a merely nominal price, and Kenneth Kenniston's was hardly the temperament to experience an æsthetic gratulation that, his were those majestic domes which touched the clouds and withstood the lightnings and lifted up an awesome voice to answer the thunder, or that his title-deeds called for all the vast slopes thence down to the unimagined abysses of the abandoned mine in the depths of the gorge. It was the spirit of speculation that informed his glance with a certain respect for them, as he turned his eye upon the mountains, and bethought himself how these austere craggy splendors were calculated to impress the shallow gaze of the wandering human swallow. He even appraised, in the interest of possible summer sojourners, the rare, pure, soft air with which his lungs expanded. Science was presently set a-prying about the margins of rocky springs, hitherto undiscovered and unnoticed save by oread or deer; a few blasts of dynamite, a great outgushing of exhaustless mineral waters, a triumphant chemical analysis ensued, and an infusion of enthusiasm began to pervade his consciousness. Such resources — infinitely smaller resources — elsewhere in the world meant a fortune; why not here?

He was an architect by profession, and the aspect of the world seemed to him parceled out in available sites. It cost his imagination, trained by study and enriched by travel, no conscious effort to perceive standing in fair proportions, turreted and terraced, finished to the last finial, the perfected structure of his projected summer hotel, on that level space above craggy heights, facing the moon and the valley, with the background of still greater heights, ever rising, heavily wooded, to the peak towering above. He saw it, as a true architect, in completion; as the wren sees his builded nest, not as the single straw or wisp of hair. Yet the day of small things must needs be overpassed, — of straws and wisps, — of struts and purlins, plates and tie-beams. His day of small things was full of wrangling and bitter bafflings, heart-burnings and discouragements. His partners in the undertaking had not been induced to cast their lot with his save by the exercise of infinite suavities of crafty eloquence, overpowering doubt and fear, and indisputable demonstrations of disproportionate profits in the very air. One was a seer in a commercial sort, an adept in prognosticating unexpected expenses for which no covenant of provision had been entered into, and he beheld full-armed disaster menacing every plan save that of his own preference. The other had no imagination whatever, architectural or otherwise. He recognized no needs which required adornment, and measured the taste of the public by his own disposition to spend money to gratify it. That Kenniston's plans should have come through the ordeal of their councils, with the ever lopping-off incidents common to the moneyed non-professional, retaining any element of symmetry or grace or beauty argued much for their pristine value. He regarded them for a time with a sort of pity and affronted tenderness for their maimed estate, but little by little the original intentions faded from his mental view, and he could see with renewed satisfaction the flag flying from the tower without remembering that he had held this octagonal gaud upon the building by main force, as it were, against the iconoclastic grasp of the practical men.

Nevertheless he was relieved to be free from their presence. He felt that it was well that their legitimate business — one as a stock-broker, the other a real-estate agent — held them to their desks in the city of Bretonville. The manifest purpose of their creation, he thought, was fully served in their furnishing forth their quota of the sinews of war. He was much younger than either, but he had learned

something beyond their knowledge in this interne-
cine strife, and when it became necessary to provide
for them occupation, to prevent further interference
in the venture which had come to be of most hopeful interest to both, he wrote to them touching the
finding of a suitable man to keep the hotel when built,
certain that in this quest for a Boniface he had set
them by the ears, and relying on their different
temperaments to keep them wrangling together and
to leave him in peace.

Every sylvan detail of the scene pleased his artistic and receptive sense, as he stood on the great
natural terrace, the site of the future building, and
surveyed the landscape. It was a phenomenally
felicitous opportunity. This plateau projected from
a lateral spur of the Great Smoky chain, and faced
the southeast. Thus the main body of the mountain range, diagonally across the Cove, seemed
strangely near at hand ; one could study its chasms
and abysses, its jungles of laurel and vast forests,
as it were from mid-air; it was the point of view of
a bird. Through a gap lower down, the parallel
lines of the eastern ranges became visible, elsewhere
hidden by the great boundary ridge, — a wonderful
fantasy painted in every gradation of blue, from
the slaty grayish hue near at hand under the
shadow of a cloud, the velvet-like tones of ultrama-
rine beyond, and still further the metallic hardness
of tint as of lapis lazuli, till the most delicate azure
outline of peaks faintly obliterated its identity
against the azure eastern sky. All unflushed the

sky was here, although to the right the clouds were
red above the western mountains. They closely
hemmed in the Cove, heavy, massive, purple and
bronze and deeply green, in such limited latitude of
color as their lowering shadows would permit. Far
down their slopes the river ran, threading the deep
forests with elusive steely glimmers. He could not
hear its voice, but from great cliffs hard by the
silvery melody of the mineral springs beat upon
the air with a rhythm inexpressibly sweet and wild
and alluring. So definite it was that it seemed
odd that one did not " catch the tune." In an
open space some scattered sheep were feeding, — the
effect pastoral and pictorial. The whole scene,
with its blended solemnity and beauty and dignity,
would well accord with the castellated edifice his
fancy had set in its midst. It might indeed be a
mediæval world upon which the windows should
look, instead of the prosaic nineteenth century, so
far it would appear from sordid to-day, so well
would the fashion of the building aid the illusion,
were it not for a section of the foreground immediately below the cliffs of the terrace, where there
stood, bare and open and unsheltered, a primitive
log cabin, a stretch of cornfields, a horse-lot, a
pig-pen, and all the accessories of most modern
and unimpressive American poverty and ignorance.
Being near, and bearing human significance, the
prosaic little home seemed the most salient point,
in its incongruity, in the whole magnificent landscape. The methods of the mountaineer furthered,

too, the effect of antagonism. Along the side of one of the ranges near at hand, a great gaunt blackened area bore token of a "fire-scald." Kenniston's eyes rested frowningly on this deep burnt scar upon the face of nature. It came from the pernicious habit of "setting out fire in the woods" in the autumn, to burn away the undergrowth and dead leaves, in order to give freer pasturage to wandering cattle. Here, as is not unfrequently the case, the fire, instead of merely consuming leaves, twigs, and shoots, had gathered strength and fury, burning the giant trees to great blackened, deadened skeletons, bleakly standing, and had devastated some hundred acres. He could see in the sparse shadows the cattle feeding on the lush herbage, and he ground his teeth to reflect upon the alarm any future conflagration would spread among the autumnal lingerers of summer sojourners and the catastrophe that might ensue to the chateau on the rocks.

"We *must* buy him out," he muttered. "He *must* be made to go."

Kenniston's heart was as heavy with presage as if his flimsy chateau stood on the cliffs behind him; for it was not to be mediæval in point of strength of materials.

The project of buying out Luther Tems seemed hardly so feasible as when first presented to the minds of the company. The proposition to this effect had already been made to the astounded mountaineer, and rejected with a plump No. A second and better considered effort, coupled with a disproportionately large pecuniary consideration, had fared no better. There Luther Tems was, and there he meant to stay, as his father and his grandfather had before him to a great age, till Death bethought himself at last of these loiterers in so obscure a corner of the world, and, although belated, gathered them in. The company was now at its wits' end. The place was an eyesore, a trail of the serpent in this seeming Paradise. It was, too, a source of danger and discomfort, and to seek to remove it was one of Kenniston's errands here, as well as to confer with the contractor, in his dictatorial character as one of the company rather than the architect. His visit was so timed that he was on the ground a day or so in advance of his coadjutor, and in furtherance of his project had asked for quarters in Luther Tems's house.

Far was it from Luther Tems, the fear of being over-persuaded. He was a lugubrious presentment of obstinacy, as he sat at his hearthstone. The immovable determination expressed in the lines of his face and the curve of his lips was incongruous with the other characteristics of his aspect. He was not of the gigantic build common among the mountaineers. He was singularly spare and alert, and there was something in his movements and in the lines of his figure which betokened that when endowed with more flesh it had expressed an unusual grace. His features were absolutely regular, and although the eye, sunken amidst a multitude of wrinkles and half hidden by the beetling eyebrow, no longer showed the fine lines of its setting and its pristine color and brilliancy, and his jaw was lank from the loss of teeth, and his well-cut lips were contorted over his quid of tobacco, he still exhibited to the discerning gaze of the architect enough traces of the beauty of his younger days to justify the feminine sobriquet of " Lucy." A good joke it had been in the Cove forty years before, but custom had dulled its edge and hallowed its use, and now he would have had to think twice before he saw aught incongruous in the appellation. It was a convenience in some sort, too, and averted misunderstandings, for his son bore his name of Luther. Although inheriting a share of his father's good looks, it had been admixed with the "favor" of the Tates, his mother's people, who were a tall, burly folk. He was heavier far than his father, and slower at twenty-four than " Lucy " Tems would be at eighty. The strong resemblance in their faces ended there, for naught could be more unlike the elder than the meditative composure with which the younger man sat and smoked his pipe, and now slowly rose and replenished the fire and seated himself anew. He had nothing in look or motion of the panther-like, dangerous intimation that informed the old man's every gesture and glance. But this expressed itself with a certain supple, feline effect in his daughter, a tall girl, in whom the beauty of his youth was duplicated. She had the chestnut hair, the exquisitely fair com-

plexion with its shifting roseate suffusion, the large
beautifully set dark blue eye, the high narrow
forehead from which the hair grew backward, but
lying on the temples in delicate fibrous waves, —
all the fine detail that had graced her father's
youth, and that had seemed so wasted on the wild
scapegrace boy of the mountains, merely attaining
the recognition of ridicule among his fellows, and
unvalued by its possessor. She wore a dark blue
homespun dress that enhanced her fairness, and
she sat in a low chair in the firelit log room and
busied herself, with a monotonous gesture and a
certain sleek aspect, in carding cotton. Kenniston
had seen her previously, and in his preoccupied
mind she roused no interest, neither then nor now.

He sat down by the fire, among them, much nettled to observe that there was a stranger, a man
whom he had never before seen here, ensconced
on the opposite side of the hearth. The shadow of
the primitive mantelshelf obscured his face, and
even when the fire flashed up it barely sufficed to
show his burly figure in an attitude of composed
waiting and observation.

His presence added an element of doubt and difficulty to the already troublous negotiation, and
Kenniston, accustomed to civilized methods, and
having expected to carry all before him, felt a
sinking of the heart out of proportion to the value
of the property he coveted. He had, in his experience, conducted delicate and difficult negotiations,
involving large considerations, many parties in in-

terest, and conflicting claims, to a successful issue. And yet, what enterprise so unpromising as to buy from a man who will not sell! So did the half-masked presence of the stranger in the shadow shake his confidence that he did not at once open the subject nearest his heart. A short silence ensued upon the greetings, and he was fain to lay hold upon the weather as a subterfuge.

" It holds fair, colonel," he said.

He used the title in secret derision, as the usual sobriquet of men of dignity and substance in the lowlands. He had scant faith in the existence of any discerning perceptions and delicate sentiments in the minds or hearts of people in homespun ; it had served to amuse him at his first meeting with old Tems, when he had not dreamed that so uncouth a character had a part to play upon the elaborate stage of his own future, which was a-building with such care and thought and hope, and he had laughed in his sleeve to observe the simplicity and acquiescence with which the fine title was accepted. He intended its use in no military sense, and he did not learn till afterward that old Tems bore a veritable title, which he had earned on stricken battlefields, and had later commanded a band of guerrillas whose name was a terror and a threat.

Tems took his pipe from between his lips. "·It holds fair," he echoed drawlingly ; then, " Dunno fur how long," as if to admonish any speculator in the weather to be not too happy in a vale of such incertitude.

"All signs favor!" A sudden singing feminine tone pervaded the conversation.

Kenniston glanced up. In one corner, a stairway from the attic above came down into the room. A young girl, whom he had not before noticed, was sitting on the steps midway. From this coigne of vantage she overlooked the room, and participated in the conversation when moved to do so.

Kenniston fancied that from some real or affected rustic shyness because of his presence she had sought this retirement, for she flushed deeply at his glance, and bent her head over a piece of rough mending which she seemed to be perpetrating on a jeans coat with a gigantic needle and a very coarse thread. She could hardly have seen very well to set the stitches, and as her side was toward him he could ill distinguish her face for the shadow and her industrious attitude and her falling hair.

Julia Tems looked up at her with a laughing glance, half raillery, half sneer. But the brother took up the question with an air of contention; he wanted rain for his corn crop, and he believed the clouds must surely hold it in trust for him.

"The fog war a-getherin' along the mountings this evenin', an' I seen 'bout a hour ago a thunder-head a-loafin' round over Piomingo," he averred with a certain bitterness, as if to protest against the arguing away of these prospects.

"Waal," the singing voice, curiously vibrant, broke forth once more, "we air likely ter git a good full rain, ez would holp up the crap 'fore long, but we ain't goin' ter hev no steady set o' bad weather now.   Signs don't favor it."

The old man again took his pipe from his mouth.

" Ye-es.   An' a body mought b'lieve from yer talk that ef Satan war ter cotch us by the right leg this week, he'd be mighty likely ter turn us loose by the lef' leg nex' week."   He laughed sarcastically.   " All of us air s'prisin' apt ter be suited, no matter how things turn out."   He replaced his pipe, adding, with the stem between his teeth, " That's Ad'licia's notion," and then smoked imperturbably.

The little optimist looked at him with an indignant, affronted gaze for a moment, then bent once more to her sewing.

She had forgotten Kenniston, and her face was fully revealed in the moment that she had turned it on her critic, — an oval face, with a little round unassertive chin, a thin, delicate, aquiline nose, a small mouth with full lips, the indenture in the upper one so deep as to make it truly like a bow, and widely opened gray eyes that resembled nothing so much as moss agates.   They were veiled by long, reddish lashes, and the hair that hung curling down about the nape of her neck was of a dull copper hue.   Her complexion was exceedingly white, and she had that thin-skinned look which is incompatible with freckles as annuals; in those milk-white spaces about the eyes were sundry tokens of the sunny weather which even the dark days of winter would not obliterate.   Her figure was slender, and she did not look strong. She wore a brown home-spun dress, and she bit the coarse thread with a double row of small perfect white teeth as she addressed herself to threading her big needle anew.

" Studyin' 'bout the weather, an' gittin' onhappy 'bout yer buildin'? " demanded old Tems of his guest.

There was a slight twist of the lips, suggestive of covert ridicule on his part, as he asked the question.

Kenniston was totally unaware of furnishing in his proper person amusement to the mountaineer, but to his host he seemed a fool more bountifully endowed with folly than any other specimen of the genus with whom Tems had ever been brought into contact, and the projected hotel was accounted a ludicrous impossibility. It was Tems's secret persuasion that most of the population of this country had been slain in the war; he had himself seen much slaughter in its grim actuality. The idea that there were people who would wish to come long journeys to fill that vast projected structure seemed the most preposterous vaporing of imbecility.

" Ain't they got nowhar ter bide? " he would demand, in incredulous pity for the homeless summer birds.

He had come at last to treat it in his own mind as a bubble, a mere brainless figment, and only his courteous instincts prevented this from becoming apparent, although now and again it was perilously near revelation.

"Well, no; I think the weather won't affect my building for a good while yet," answered Kenniston. Then, with a sudden afterthought, and perceiving the opening, "I'm troubled, though, about the blasting for the coal cellars and wine cellar. There will of necessity be quite an avalanche of fragments of the rock falling into the valley, and I wanted to give you warning of it before it begins."

The look of attention deepened on the old face. The thin old head suavely nodded.

"Thanky, sir. I feel obligated." And old Tems relapsed into silence.

Kenniston was baffled for a moment, but presently he returned to the charge.

"You and your family could leave the premises while the blasting was in progress. It might be inconvenient, but " —

"Yes — ye-es — ef so minded," the ancient householder acquiesced.

"By all means," Kenniston pursued with more energy, stroking his brown whiskers with one hand, while he looked, keenly interrogative, at his interlocutor. "There might be danger, positive danger, in remaining." Then, seeking an ally, and taking hope from the quiescent silence of the stranger in the corner, "*You* agree with me surely?"

The stranger laughed, a round, vigorous, elastic tone.

"Waal, I reckon old Cap'n Lucy is about ez good a jedge ez ter the dangers in dealin' in gunpowder ez ye'll meet up with this side o' Jordan. I'd be willin' ter leave sech ter him."

"Of course — of course," Kenniston agreed hastily. "Only I am anxious to have no sort of responsibility, — moral responsibility, I mean, — in case of an accident to members of his family."

He reflected that two of these were feminine, that the sex is to a unit a coward by open confession, and he sought to play upon their fears.

But once more Adelicia interfered to show the more hopeful side of things.

"It's toler'ble fur from hyar, a right good piece," she turned her head to say before she again bit the thread.

"Not from the site of the first blasting; the wine cellar will be under the billiard-room, which will be in the pavilion at this end of the bluffs." He had waxed warm, excited. "The rock could easily be flung as far as this, and even if no human life were endangered, might kill horses or cows, or crash through the roof, or break down the chimney."

"Waal, the comp'ny is a good, solid, solvent comp'ny, ain't it?" said the man in the corner unexpectedly, — "respons'ble in damages?"

Kenniston recoiled suddenly, and Tems pricked up his ears, like the old war-horse that he was. The prospect of conflict in whatever sort was grateful to his senses, and he snuffed the battle from afar. In this, too, he saw his defense and his opportunity. Kenniston would hardly have conceived it possible that, with such inconsiderable adversaries, he could be routed in diplomacy. It was not, however, to bring matters to this point of view that his schemes were designed.

"I hope there will be no need for a demand for damages," he said stiffly. Then, driven back upon his last resource, the simple truth, he continued, turning toward the man in the corner, " It has been partly to avert all dangers and troubles that the company has been trying to buy out Mr. Tems, at his own price."

"My h'a'thstone hain't got no price," said old Tems acridly.

Kenniston had thrown himself back in his chair with a dogged exasperation of manner. His hands were thrust into the pockets of his short flannel coat. His square chin, glimpsed in the parting of his full beard, was deeply sunken in its lustrous fibres. His lowering blue eyes were fixed on the fire, all aglow, for at this altitude the chill summer nights cannot dispense with the smouldering back-log. His legs, in their somewhat worn integu-ments of dark flannel and long boots, — for there are penalties to footgear and garb in clambering about these rough mountains, — were stretched out before him, and Adelicia's cat found them conven-ient to rub against, as she arched her back and purred in the dull red light. He felt at the mo-ment irritated beyond measure. This idea of a lawsuit, craftily interjected by the stranger whom he himself had called into the conversation, might seriously embarrass the proceedings of the com-pany. It could be held *in terrorem* at every point. Nay, it might incite Tems to seek out occasion to make a pretext of injury. It added a prospect of indefinite discomfort and jeopardy to the already harassed present.

"I kin b'lieve that, Cap'n Lucy, — I kin b'lieve that," said the stranger, with a sudden outpouring of his full, mellow, rich voice. Its sonorousness and sweetness struck Kenniston only vaguely then, but he remembered it afterward. "Ye want yer *home*, an' the company wants yer *hut.*"

"I don't want thar money, — ain't got no cur'osity 'bout the color of it," old Tems said tartly.

Neither of the younger Temses uttered a word. Luther smoked imperturbably, and Julia, as sleek, as lithe, as supple as a panther, bent her beautiful, clear-cut, distinct face above the cards, which she moved with a flexible elasticity that made it seem no labor. Every line about her was sharply drawn; the very plaits of her glossy hair showed their separate strands, over and under and over again, in the coil at the back of her head. Against the dark wall, she had a fixity, a definiteness of effect, like a cameo, in contrast with the somewhat tousled head which Adelicia held back to observe her completed industry. She lifted the mended coat in both hands before her, and contemplated the patch, set on indeed as if it should never come off again, but with what affront to the art of fine needlework!

She was not so absorbed, however, as to be unmindful of the disaffected state of feeling in the room below, and she must needs seek to improve it.

"We ain't so mighty easy tarrified, nohow," she

remarked, suavely addressing the information more directly to Kenniston's pretended fears for their safety. "An' ez ter rocks fallin' an' sech," — she turned her head askew to better observe the effect of the flagrant patch, — "I hev tuk notice ez trees streck by lightning mostly falls whar thar ain't no house."

" 'Kase thar be mighty few houses whar the trees be lef'," observed old Tems, whose contradictory faculties were called into play every time she spoke.

"Waal, fower hev fell, lightning-streck, sence we-uns hev been a-livin' hyar, an' nare one teched us," she argued.

Kenniston caught his breath. "How long have you been living here, colonel?" The secret gibe came back to him with the sudden secret renewal of his hope.

"Five year, or thereabout," growled old Tems.

"Five year this comin', fall," put in Adelicia, with exactitude. "We-uns lived then nigher sunrise, on the flat o' the mounting, over thar." She nodded with her wealth of bronze curls toward the east to indicate the direction of the locality.

"And if you would move then, colonel, why not now?" demanded Kenniston.

It seemed as if old Tems would not reply. So deep a scowl had corrugated his face that in its wizard-like aspect not the faintest vestige of his famous ancient beauty remained.

"Burnt out," he growled at last.

"The fire-scald, ye see," explained Adelicia, turning her oval face upon Kenniston.

It had an old-fashioned, even a foreign cast, was his superficial thought, as he gazed up at her in the dusky shadows of the staircase; it reminded him of some antique miniature. But his recognized idea was expressed in the words, echoed in surprise and with a touch of dismay, "The fire-scald!"

"Fire war set out in the woods ter burn the bresh; but the wind sprung up, it did, an' the fire tuk the house an' fence an' all. Ye mus' hev noticed the fire-scald over yon?" Once more she nodded her head in intimation of the direction. "Then we-uns moved hyar an' raised this house."

Old Tems's surly, disaffected look caught her attention. "But this hyar house air a heap better 'n the burnt one; that war old, fur true, an' I tell ye the wind used ter shake it whenst stormin'. Roof leaked, too. Roof war so old that the clapboards war fastened on with wooden paigs stiddier nails. My great-gran'dad — Cap'n Lucy's gran'dad — did n't hev much modern improvemints, leastwise in blacksmith's gear, when he kem hyar ter settle from old Car'liny."

She glanced down, smiling. Her strangely old-fashioned little face was lovely in smiling, but Kenniston did not heed; he did not even hear her words; he was absorbed in a train of thought that came to him as she talked.

She looked slightly ill at ease for a moment, perceiving the defection of his attention; then, as if to make the best of it, she turned her head and glanced over her shoulder at the man in the corner.

"Ye hev hearn that?" she said.

He nodded. She saw the gleam of his full blue eye. "They called East Tennessee the 'Washington Deestric',' arter them days," he said, his big voice booming out. Then he went on to tell of an old house which he knew, in which wooden pegs also served as nails, as a set-off, it might seem, to the ancient dwelling that perished in the " fire-scald," and presently he was wrangling with old Tems as to the precise route that certain early settlers were said to have taken through the mountains, in which discussion even the silent Luther joined, and Kenniston was left undisturbed to his thoughts.

These thoughts were significant enough. He had seen this vast property of his only once before in all the years that it had been in his possession. It had descended to him in due course, with the rest of the paternal estate, at the death of his father, who had been a successful merchant of Bretonville. He had had some little but well-restrained inclination for speculation, and these miles of mountain fastnesses were a single instance of it, looking to the future development of mineral resources. The abandoned mine in the gorge expressed the failure of hopes of silver and lead, which had led him only for a little while and only a short distance. He himself had never laid eyes on his purchase ; but once, in a college vacation, the son, on a pedestrian tour, had explored to some purpose the woods up and down these steeps and across the line. Kenniston remembered now for the first time how the face of the country had impressed him then, for the fire-scald had so altered its aspect. The slope where the quaint little ante-Revolutionary house was perched had then seemed high and steep. In building anew, Luther Tems had selected a site on more level ground, considerably removed from the area of the burnt district. Possibly the fear of disaster when those blackened and decaying trees should finally complete their doom and fall, or the vicinage of springs for the essential water supply for man and beast, had served to influence his decision; but he had certainly made a very considerable journey from his former situation, and cut a large cantle out of the Cove in his present settlement.

Kenniston's mind was hard upon the trail of the boundary lines, as his absorbed eyes dwelt on the red fire. They were ill defined in his memory, for when the great body of a man's land, numbering thousands of acres, bears a merely nominal price, a few furlongs amiss here or there in the wild jungle of the laurel are hardly worth the counting. In this particular instance the accuracy of metes and bounds made a difference all apart from actual values. It was his recollection that his lines included all those slopes to the " backbone," a high craggy ridge that ran like a spinal column adown the mountain mass. If this were the case, old

Tems had inadvertently set up his staff of rest on his neighbor's land, was himself a mere trespasser, and might be ejected without difficulty in due process of law.

Kenniston stirred uneasily as he contemplated this possibility. In its extreme unpopularity there was a very definite menace. He could ill afford to antagonize the whole countryside. The lawless, illogical mountain population would be arrayed as a unit against his interests. Even single-handed, old Cap'n Lucy seemed formidable, when active aggressions were contemplated. And he could appreciate, too, the seeming injustice, from the rustic standpoint, that, for the frivolous and flippant desire of keeping the landscape sightly for the fastidious gaze of the gentlefolk, an old man and his family must be turned out of house and home. Kenniston knew that although he might pay the full value of Cap'n Lucy's improvements, the popular censor would account this naught if the mountaineer were forced to quit his home against his will.

Nevertheless law is law, and Kenniston could easily forecast the triumphant result of a legal arbitrament. Tems had not been ensconced here, within his own inclosures, claiming as his own, long enough to acquire any title under the statute of limitations, even if he could establish adverse possession. The property was his own, and he would satisfy even every moral claim upon him in paying the interloper the full value of his improvements. At all events he would have the line run out, and perhaps the land formally processioned.

At the idea of prompt action in the matter, his full red lips, only partially visible through his beard and mustache, were pressed together firmly; his teeth met with a certain stiffening of the jaw into a hard, determined expression; his eyes were cast up suddenly over the primitive humble interior of the cabin with a certain impatience of its uncouthness, so at variance with the gala trim of modern comforts, so homely, so American, so hopelessly, desperately, the presentment of the unprogressive backwoods. Built five years ago, said they! It might have graced the " Washington Deestric'." His white teeth showed, as he half sneered and half laughed. He would, if he might, with a wave of the hand, have swept it and all it represented out of existence; nay, into oblivion. As his eyes came once more to their former point of rest, the fire, they suddenly encountered the intent gaze of the man in the corner. It discomfited Kenniston in some sort, although he could not have said why. His glance fell; he nervously uncrossed and recrossed his legs, and thrust his hands deeper into his pockets. A vague sense of sustaining covert enmity had begun to pervade his consciousness. He could not say whether this were induced by the mere inception of the unpopular idea of eviction, or whether it were a subtle perception of something antagonistic in the mental attitude toward him of the composed, watchful man who sat in the corner. It was not a furtive observation. It dwelt upon him openly, deliberately, steadily. It held no element of offensiveness; it was so calm, so incidental, so apparently, so naturally, the concomitant of the thoughtful, contemplative pipe, which now and again his hand steadied, or removed to release a wreath of the strong tobacco smoke which pervaded the apartment. Yet Kenniston felt, oddly enough, that it was not an incidental observation. It was charged with much discernment. A discriminating analysis was, he instinctively knew, coupled with it. He began, on his part, to more definitely gauge the two or three fragmentary contributions which the stranger had flung into the talk. The allusion to the solvency of a company and its responsibility in damages savored of a knowledge far beyond the ken of the Cove, this region of primitive barter where there is neither currency nor commerce; where the operations of far-away courts are but faintly echoed, as of retribution overtaking some reckless and unwary criminal, and the provisions of the law seem merely futile and disregarded devices of lawyers who seek to live upon the people by their enforcement. Then the crafty contrast of the differing estimates of the house, the one as a home, the other as a hut, intimated some definite capacity to play upon the springs of human emotions. He wondered if he had ever before seen this man. He had a good memory, but he did not charge it with the various mountaineers he met, and sometimes he forgot their names and occasionally their personality. He was restive under this slow, reflective gaze, and he pushed back his chair suddenly and walked away to the door. It was open and widely flaring, and he stood there as if scanning the weather signs.

For so long he had seen the castellated walls of his new building rise upon the great natural terrace of the mountain, above the series of crags, that he experienced a sort of subacute surprise to mark the loneliness and melancholy of the landscape. Only the pinnacles of the mists glimmered in the moon, as unsubstantial as the turrets of his fancy. Below were all the darkling spaces of the night-shadowed forests. Above, the heavily wooded slopes loomed vaguely in the dim light, for the moon was in her first quarter, here showing the gaunt face of a crag, and there a ravine made visible by thronging spectre-like vapors. The stars were bright. Near the great dome he marked the scintillating circlet of the Northern Crown; its splendors seemed enhanced, he thought, by the vicinage of that towering densely dark mass beneath. So still it all was! He heard the silvery tinkle of the liberated mountain springs near his own site sounding with such freshness, with such elfin spontaneity, with such flexible fantasies of cadence, that one would have imagined he must surely have bethought him how featly the chorusing oreads were singing; it only brought to his mind anew the chemical analysis, and the hordes of valetudinarians waiting to bring all their ills, real and imaginary, to lay them, with more valuable considerations, at the shrine of his Spa.

His sense of difficulties and discouragements took on a new lease, and as he turned impatiently away from the door he almost ran against young Luther Tems, who had come to gaze upon the clouds with that humble, expectant wistfulness characteristic of those votaries of the weather, the farmer class.

" Would you-uns jedge thar war rain in that batch o' clouds settin' ter the south ? " he drawled seductively, as if he sought to influence favorably the unprejudiced opinion he asked.

" I 'm no judge of weather signs," Kenniston returned succinctly, although in another mood it would have suited well his satiric bent to invent and promulgate a formula of fictitious barometrical science.

As he glanced loweringly toward the fireside group, thrusting his hands into his pockets and advancing with long steps to his former chair, he was quick to observe that the man in the corner seemed to have determined on a leisurely departure. He had risen, and was returning to his pocket a brier-root pipe, taking the sedulous care to knock all the ashes out of it on the jamb of the fireplace, which betrays him whose pocket linings have more than once been the scene of an incipient conflagration. Kenniston regarded him, as he stood in the full light, with a disaffected interest, a sort of re-

sponsive enmity. And yet there was nothing of itself inimical in this man's bearing. On the contrary,
suggestions of good fellowship predominated in his
open manner and clear blue eye. He was exceedingly tall, not judging by Cap'n Lucy's elegant and
slight proportions, nor by the burlier Luther's
height, but by actual measurement. It had been
long since he had shaved, — his full yellow beard
hung like a golden fleece far down over the breast
of his brown jeans coat; his long, straight yellow
hair, of the same tint, had its edges upturned in the
semblance of curl by the obstacle of his collar. He
had a large, bony, hooked nose, which gave a certain strength to his countenance. The fashion of
the feature was such as to suggest sagacity in some
sort, as of keen instinctive faculties, but its expression was as ferocious as that of an eagle's beak.
His mustache hid his lips and was lost in his
beard. He wore great spurred boots drawn high
over his brown jeans trousers, and a wide-brimmed
black wool hat. A faded red handkerchief about
his neck now and again showed amidst the hirsute
abundance, for he turned his head quickly and vigi-
lantly. He had an air of self-confidence which was
somewhat imposing. It constrained in his interlocutor a sort of reluctant acceptance of his own es-
timate of himself. Kenniston, looking at him with
an unacknowledged respect for the untrained natural
forces his personality expressed, felt him to be formidable; how, or why, or when it was not manifest,
nor in what sort his conciliation might be com-

passed, nor how it should be worth the effort. His bland phrases of departure set the man of etiquette ill at ease. Kenniston was accustomed to uncouthness in the mountaineers, even to lowering looks and open expressions of enmity when he or his plans impinged on their prejudices; polite duplicity, the native of drawing-rooms, seemed strangely out of place in this region of paradisaic simplicity of feeling and manner. His own acute social sense and his valued commercial acumen had given him an intuition of this man's aversion to him or his projects, or both; but his hand was feeling yet the stranger's cordial grip, and the sonorous invitation, "Obligated ter hev a visit over at Lost Time," was ringing in his ears.

"Who is that man?" he abruptly demanded of his host, as soon as the jingle of the spurs and the sound of the horse's hoofs were silent on the air. Then, seeking to make his question more incidental, he added, "Seems to be a friend of yours,"

Cap'n Lucy and Luther looked at each other, exchanging a grin of derision. The two girls seemed unaccountably embarrassed.

"Waal, stranger," said the old man, "he's a widower, a sort of perfessional widower."

Luther broke out laughing with a hearty joviality. It surely was not he who had been deluded by the clouds and made the sport of the winds; it hardly seemed possible that he could take so much pleasure in aught save good prospects of the fruits of the earth.

" He hev gin me an' Luther a heap o' trouble, an' we-uns hev tuk a power o' counsel tergether ez ter what we-uns war goin' ter do 'bout it," old Tems continued.

Kenniston, conscious that. he had roused some standing joke, cast his slightly satirical glance from one to the other, and with a sort of scornful patience waited their pleasure to enlighten him.

Adelicia, with heightened color and an affronted aspect, was making a great show of inattention; while Julia, with her sleek, deft grace, went on impassively carding cotton.

" He kems hyar a-visitin' the whole fambly, an' thar he sets an' sets; an' Luther loses his sleep, till, follerin' the plough nex' day, he dunno the share from the ploughtail, nor Gee from Haw; mighty nigh fit ter fall in the furrow, jes' walkin' in his sleep."

Once more Luther's crude boyish laughter rang against the rafters; this was at all events no somnambulistic demonstration.

" Ef thar was jes' *one* gal in the fambly, Luther an' me would git off gyard jewty : but ez fur ez he lets on he jes' kems ter visit us all, — *all ;* an' hyar we hev got ter set, an' watch him cast sheep's-eyes fust at one gal, then at t'other, till Luther an' me air plumb cross-eyed, looking two ways at once."

It was a great mutual possession to have so witty a father and so appreciative a son.

" A' fust," continued the old man, when the filial hilarity had somewhat subsided, " I jes' felt like I

could n't spar' either o' the gals. Whenst my darter was born, the fust thing I done war ter buy me
a shootin' iron, express fur the fust feller ez kem
a-sidlin' round, talkin' 'bout marryin' her, an' takin'
her away, an' tryin' ter make her b'lieve ez he was
a finer feller 'n her own dad : an' I did n't know —
the insurance o' some folks is powerful survigrous
— but he *mought* set up ter purtend ter be *better
lookin'!* ”

His daughter might seem to have shown her
appreciation of his famous good looks by adopting
them all. As she lifted her eyes and smiled upon
the narrator, the brilliant and spirited beauty of her
face might indeed be a welcome reminiscence of the
time when he, too, wore so fair a guise, and might
impart a zestful relish of the resemblance.

“ An' then Ad'licia, she kem hyar when her mother, my sister Amandy, died. My sister hed married a second time, a mighty mean man, an' whenst
I tuk Ad'licia — she war 'bout three year old — I
jes' said, ‘ Yer mam did n't hev much jedgmint in
marryin', an' I reckon ye 'll take the failin' arter
her ; an' ye 'll show sech jedgmint ez ye kin l'arn
in marryin' nobody.’ An' she agreed : she war n't
very young at three, jes' sorter youngish ; an' though
people mought think she hed n't hed a chance ter
view the world on sech a p'int, she hed her senses
powerful well in hand. So we made a solemn promise. An' I felt plumb sot up till lately. I don't
want narc one of 'em ter marry. A fust-rate man
ain't wuth a fifth-rate woman, much less a fust-rate

woman," he declared chivalrously. "Leastwise, ye can't git the gals' daddies ter think so. An' now, jes' ez we air all so sot an' stiddy in our minds, hyar kems this widower, this *perfessional* widower; fur he don't show no signs o' bein' nuthin' else! An' we dunno whether he kems ter listen at Julia hold her tongue, or Ad'licia talk, or hear Luther praise God fur the weather, or ter git my best advice on politics. We'd do ennything ter git shet o' him. He mought hev air one o' the gals, ef he'd only say *which*."

And he chuckled as he gazed into the fire.

"What's his business? Farmer, I suppose?" suggested Kenniston.

"Naw; he hev got a leetle store, — powerful leetle trade, 'count o' the cross-roads store at the settlemint, though he trades right smart. Liberal, too. He'll take ennything, — load o' corn, load o' wood, sech like heavy truck ez thar ain't no sale fur ginerally, 'count o' the wagonin' an' roads bein' so heavy. Whenst you-uns git yer railroad put through," — he gave him a rallying wink at this aberration, as he esteemed the projected narrow gauge, — "ye'll mend all that."

"Oh, yes; you'll be in touch with the markets of the world then," said Kenniston, with his satiric laugh. "Only a little question of freight rates between you and New York."

This sarcasm did not cut so deeply as one might imagine. It would have been impossible to insert the idea — save with an axe — into old "Lucy"

Tems's brain that New York was more important
and metropolitan than Colbury, or essentially more
remote.

" This Lorenzo Taft ain't been so sociable till
lately. That 's what makes me call him a *perfessional* widower," old Tems went on, with a peculiar
relish for the designation. " He hev two childern,
gal an' boy, an' the gal hev been with her gran'mam
down in Blount County till the old woman died;
an' now he hev got ' Sis,' ez he calls her, with him,
an' he wants a step-mammy fur her! He ain't
a-courtin' a wife fur hisself; he 's courtin' a step-
mammy fur ' Sis.' An' in course his sheep's-eyes
would go cornsider'ble furder with the gals than
they do, ef they did n't know that he air jes' out
a-trappin' fur ' Sis.' "

" Waal," said Adelicia suddenly, " I dunno ez
folks oughter think hard of him fur that, 'kase ' Sis '
did look powerful lonesome an' pitiful, settin' up all
by herself 'mongst all the men at the store."

" Thar, now! " exclaimed Cap'n Lucy triumphantly, " makin' excuses fur folks agin! I told ye
ez ye could n't hold out till bedtime 'thout excusin'
this one fur that, an' t'other one fur which."

" Waal," said Adelicia, " it 's a mighty late bedtime."

She was rolling up the coat as carefully as if a
first-class triumph of needlework had been accomplished upon it.

" ' Sis ' did n't 'pear ter me ter need enny lookin'
arter whenst I seen her," said old Tems heartlessly.

" She 'peared ter be some fower or five hunderd year old, an' stiddy an' settled ter accommodate."

" She be 'bout ten year old," said Adelicia gravely.

" I wonder," said Cap'n Lucy, with a twinkle of the eye, " I *do* wonder ef that thar pernicious way o' makin' excuses fur folks's faults would hold out ef Ad'licia war ter set out ter be somebody's step-mammy ! "

Luther suddenly held up his hand with an intent look, bespeaking silence. The rain was coming. From far away one could hear the steady march of its serried columns, now amongst the resonant woods, and now through open spaces, and again threading narrow ravines. A bugle blast of the wind issued suddenly from a rocky defile, and was silent again, and once more only the sounds of that resistless multitudinous advance pervaded the mountain wilderness. Already the influx of air from the open door was freighted with dank suggestions commingled with the odor of dust. For a panic was astir in the myriad particles that lay in heaps in the sandy road ; they seemed to seek a futile flight in some inadequate current of the air, and were wafted a few paces along, to fall again upon the ground, and finally to be annihilated by the vanguard of the great body of the torrents. · A tentative drop here and there on the clapboards of the roof, increasing presently to a brisk fusillade, and then all individuality of sound was lost in the tumultuous downpour under which the cabin rocked.

Perhaps it was because he had seldom been brought into such close intimacy with the elements that Kenniston found little sleep that night under the reverberating roof. He could touch it by lifting his hand in the tiny shed-room beneath the eaves, which was devoted to his use as a guest-chamber. At arm's length, too, with but the thin barrier of the clapboards intervening, was the wild, riotous rain. He seemed in the midst of its continuous beat and thunderous splash, as its aggregations swept from the eaves into the gullies below, so entirely did its turmoils dominate his senses. Now and again the shrill fanfare of the triumphant wind sounded, and a broad, innocuous glare of sheet lightning illumined the little apartment through the multitudinous crevices between its unplastered boards ; for this addition to the house was not of logs, like the main structure. He could see, too, at intervals, as he lay in indescribable discomfort on the top of the big feather bed, the landscape without through the open door ; for the heavy, close air had induced him to set it ajar. He found a certain interest for a time in these weird illuminations : the great mountains, slate-tinted in the searching yellow glare, with clouds of white vapor hanging about them ; the rain, visible in myriads of fine lines drawn perpendicularly from zenith to valley, apparently stationary, as if it were some permanent investiture of the atmosphere ; the little porch, low-browed, on which the door of his room opened, and which leaked with a heavy, irregular pattering.

Half a dozen dogs were lying there, having taken refuge from the storm. A scraggy cedar-tree close beyond held down its moisture-freighted branches, and amongst them he saw once a great owl, business interrupted for the nonce, staring at him with big yellow eyes, as it ruffled up its feathers against the rain.

He was conscious of sustaining the steady, sedate gaze of the nocturnal fowl even when the whole world would disappear as with a bound into the depths of darkness. As if the sound had been restrained by the presence of light, the tumult of rain would seem redoubled upon the roof. The unmannerly elements evidently disturbed no one else in the house. It was as silent as if no life beat within the walls. The very dogs were still. One of them, a fat, callow fellow, with an ill-appreciated sense of a joke, roused them once by facetiously snapping at a sleeping confrère's tail, set wagging by the propitious happenings of dreamland. Whether it was that he had interrupted the gustful gnawing of a visionary bone, or simply that his elder was of a vicious temperament, he was soundly cuffed, rolled over on his fat, round sides, and sent shrieking under the house. He came out after some indulgence of vocal woe on a piercing key, and, perceiving Kenniston, sought to make his acquaintance. Being a shaggy shepherd, his rain-laden hair diffused a peculiarly canine odor throughout the little room ; he was used to rebuffs, and it required but a single tweak of the ear to send him, depressed and discouraged, to prosaic slumbers among his kindred.

The lightnings failed.   The world was plunged into unbroken gloom.   The hours wore on into the deeps of the night.   Once, as Kenniston was on the point of losing himself in sleep, he heard a shrill blood-curdling cry, searching out every nerve of repulsion in his body, — a panther shrieking from the terraces of his castle in the air.   Even the fierce dogs, lifting their heads to listen, only whined and huddled closer together.   When at last he dreamed, his mind clung close to the theme that held his waking thoughts.   It was of processioning those wild acres of mountain fastnesses, and the serpentine lengths of the surveyor's chain seemed alive as the chain-bearers dragged it writhing through the grass. And again he was taking off the hospitable roof beneath which he slept, and riving off the doors, and somehow Cap'n Lucy was curiously helpless to resist this desolation of his roof-tree.   But the man in the corner was plotting against him, and seeking to excite public animosity ; and while he was busy in counterplotting, suddenly Julia appeared, with a strange face, subtle and insidious and sinister, leading the panther which he had heard filling the night with terror.   And he was frightened, and awoke.

II

LORENZO TAFT met the rain halfway to his own dwelling. He pulled his hat over his eyes and bent to his mare's neck before its fury, and although the animal now and again swerved from the bridle path at the glare of the lightning, she carried her master steadily and fleetly enough; and it was not far from his reckoning of the hour that they should pass the Lost Time mine when a broad illumination of the skies revealed the great portal, gauntly yawning in the side of the range, where a tunnel had been made in the search for silver, and abandoned. He pulled up his dripping steed and seemed to listen. Water had risen within, evidently, from the infinite enmeshment of the underground streams and springs that vein the great range; he heard it lapping upon the rocks, as it came pouring along its channel in the tunnel. It played around the mare's fetlocks, and now and again the animal fretfully lifted her forefoot. Another flare of the weird, unearthly yellow light, more lingering, brighter, than the last, showed the swift clear flow of the current, the great bleak beetling rocks of the oval aperture, the trees on the mountain side high above it, and beyond, three hundred yards or so, a little log cabin set upon the

slope, which was a gentler declivity here, surrounded by a few acres of cornfield, and the appurtenances of beehives, hen-house, and rickety barn
common to the humbler dwellings of the region.
He could even see, between the house and the steep
ascent immediately behind it, the far-away crags,
as the range rounded out, glimmering in the lightning down the vista thus formed.

It seemed the simplest of domestic establish-
ments, and a forlorn little family group met his gaze
as he opened the door and stepped within.   The fire
had dwindled to a few embers; a flickering flare
from a handful of chips flung on in anticipation of
his return, heralded by the sound of the mare's
hoofs, showed the unplastered log room of the region, more unkempt than is usual, and betraying the
lack of a woman's hand.   The slight preparation
for his reception was not the work of a boy of
twelve, who sat soundly sleeping in a splint-bot-
tomed chair, his whole attitude one of somnolent
collapse, as if he had not a bone in his body, his
round face white and freckled, his curly red hair
growing straight up from his forehead, his slightly
open red mouth of a merry carelessness of expression even in unconsciousness.   On the opposite
side of the fireplace a little girl was staidly seated.
She had a narrow, white, formal little face; thin
light brown hair, short and straight and smooth,
put primly back behind her ears; a small mouth,
with thin, precise lips; a meek eye, with a gentle
lash.   Her father looked at her with a sentiment

of awe rising in his stalwart breast. "Consider'ble older 'n the Newnited States, an' I hed ruther keep house for a regiment o' pa'sons," he commented silently.

She wore a checked homespun dress, spotlessly clean, a dark calico apron, high-necked, buttoned to the nape in the back, shoes and blue stockings, which are rare among the children in the mountains at this season; and despite her limited inches, she was as formidable a spectacle of perfect precocity and prim perfection as ever a man who liked to go his own gait had the pleasure of looking upon. Miss Cornelia Taft was entirely competent to see all that might be going on in her small world, and she had brought her own unalterable standards with her, in her pocket as it were, by which to judge.

There was a little unacknowledged weariness in her expression, and a certain stiffness as she got down out of her chair, which intimated that she was not quite equal physically to her resolution to sit up for him. He was about to requite this after the usual manner of those favored with this feminine attention, but she had begun to rake out some Irish potatoes roasting in the ashes, and Lorenzo Taft's remonstrance was subdued from his original intention.

"Look-a-hyar, Sis," he said, "why n't ye go ter bed? Ye must n't sit up waitin' fur me this time o' night. I don't eat no second supper, nohow."

But he was presently disposing of the refection

of potatoes, corn bread, and buttermilk in great gulps, while she looked on with her inexpressive, unastonished eye.

"Why n't ye make Joe go to bed?" he demanded, his mouth full, as he nodded at the sleeping boy.

The vaguest expression of prim repudiation was on her face. "He 'lowed he war n't sleepy," she said, with some capacity for sarcasm. She would have mended Joe as if he were a rag doll, but for his stalwart resistance. She did not expend herself in vain regrets. She had cast him and his tatters off forever, unless indeed he should come some day and sue to be made whole.

"Waal," said Lorenzo Taft, bending a perplexed brow upon her, "jes' let him be, an' ye go on upsteers an' go to bed. Ye 'll never grow no higher ef ye set up so late in the night."

She turned obediently toward the stairs, or rather a rude ladder that ascended to the loft, while Lorenzo Taft paced back and forth in the room with a long, elastic stride, troubled and absent, and only conscious at the last moment that it was a look of the keenest curiosity that the little girl's placid eyes cast down upon him as she disappeared amongst the shadows of the loft.

He stood still, disproportionately perturbed, it might seem. Then he sought to reassure himself.

"I reckon I ain't much similar ter old Mis' Jinaway, nohow; an' ez she air useter a quiet, percise old 'oman's ways an' talk, I mus' seem toler'ble comical, bein' so big an' hearty, an' take big bites, an' talk loud, an' ride in the storm." He paused in the midst of his sophistry. Her look was so intelligent, so keenly inquisitive. " She's mighty leetle, but" — his caution had returned — " a ca'tridge o' giant powder ain't so powerful bulky. I hev got ter git somebody ter take keer o' her, — or ter take keer o' *me*, sure ! "

If the small Cornelia Taft's curiosity had been excited by what she had already observed, she would have thought his subsequent proceedings very strange indeed, could she have supervised them. But her placid little eyelids had closed at last upon her calm little eyes, and a very few gentle homesick tears for a place where they washed the dishes, and swept the floors, and slept in an airy room with the firelight flickering, and mended their garments ; if amusement must be had, what gay times she and her grandmother had enjoyed, to be sure, when they raced as they knit their stockings, pausing twice or thrice in the evening to compare speed and measure the accomplished hose ! A very strange man she thought her father, and she would have thought him stranger still if she could have seen him presently take a lantern and cross the open passage to the other room of the log hut, which served as store. There were embers here as well, and as he locked the door again they showed the array of gear needed for a country trade, — knives, shoes, shears, saddles, harness, rope, a little calico, sugar, coffee, salt, and iron. There was a counter at one side, on which stood the scales. It seemed a very commonplace structure, unless one should see him open a door into it on the inner side. This was not a cupboard, which might have been convenient; it gave upon a door in the puncheon floor, which, lifted, showed a ladder leading to the cellar. He went through, feet foremost, closing the counter door after him as well as the other. He lighted his lantern, not with a coal or flint, as is usual, but with the more modern and progressive match, and then down the ladder he went very warily, for it was a somewhat slight structure, and he was a heavy man. It could be removed, too, in a moment, which added to its insecurity.

And still there was naught apparent which could justify so much caution. The lantern, now fairly alight, revealed empty boxes and barrels, and a scanty reserve of stock similar to the goods which the shelves above showed. He pushed a few boxes aside, took down a board or two of the wall in the rear, and in another moment was in one of the tunnels of the abandoned mine, the wall replaced behind him.

Surely, a man was never more ingeniously secure, he thought, as he went at a brisk pace into the depths of the mountain, and it would all be jeopardized by the influx into the Cove of a horde of tourists and summer sojourners that the projected hotel might bring. No exclusive aristocrat was ever more jealous of his seclusion from the roving of his kind than Lorenzo Taft. And then this danger of his own household, his own hearthstone; this silent, disapproving, prying, perfect little primness!

He crossed water once. He never crossed it without remembering the instinct of the deer pursued to put a running stream between its flight and the hunter. The rivulet, very narrow here, flowed in a rocky bed at a swift rate. This was a tributary of the larger torrent that had flooded the mine, and, together with the small output and the inadequate prospect, had caused the work to be abandoned. Two of the miners had been drowned in the catastrophe, and this circumstance had doubtless contributed to the solitude of the locality. It was a place of strange sounds, with the forever-echoing rocks, and few curiosity seekers had ever ventured farther than the great outer portal of the Lost Time mine. Into this tunnel, with which Taft had joined a tunnel of his own secret workmanship, the water had not risen, albeit the lower excavations were all submerged; and as he went dryshod, he heard the deft patter of his tread on the well-beaten " dirt " path multiplied behind him by the echoes into the semblance of many a following footfall. This illusion might have jarred less accustomed nerves, but Taft had heard this impalpable pursuit so long with impunity that he was hardly likely to heed it now. Something, however, that he sometimes heard, and that was more often silent, he had learned to watch for, to fearfully mark the sound when it came, and to note its absence with a shuddering sense of vacancy and a chill suspense. It was like the sound of a pick continually striking into the earth, not with a hurried or fitful stroke, but timed with a composed regularity characteristic of the steady workman. Sometimes it seemed far away, sometimes immediately overhead, and again just underfoot. Those who heard it accounted for it readily enough. Who had set the ghastly superstition afoot none might say, but the belief widely obtained that the two lost miners thus wrought continually in the depths of the mountain, digging the graves that had been denied them on the face of the earth. To Taft, the familiar of the dark, the weird, and the uncanny, it seemed a likely enough solution of the mystery, and he nothing doubted it. He could not account for another phenomenon, not so frequent, but often enough forced upon his contemplation to bring him to an anxious pause. Sometimes he heard, or thought he heard, voices, loud, resounding, distinct, — hailing, hallooing voices ; and again so uncertain, so commingled, were these vibrations, so repetitious and faint, that he could not be sure that they were not merely echoes, — echoes of the talk and mirth of the group of moonshiners whom another turn of the underground passage showed him at their work in the broader space of a chamber of the mine, where the great timbers still stanchly supported the roofing masses of earth, and the walls of sandstone bore freshly the gaunt wounds that the blasting had wrought in their rugged sides.

III

THE gloom of the place had a unique underground quality which could hardly be compassed elsewhere by the mere exclusion of daylight. The yellow flare from the open door of the furnace seemed chiefly to serve to render visible the surrounding darkness. The masses of shadow were densely black. Where the firelight smote them they merged reluctantly into expositions of the darkest possibilities of umber and burnt sienna and dismal gradations of duskier brown. The clay wall facing the furnace door at one side, however, glowed with the reddest of terra-cotta hues. Against this the group was outlined, motionless, all eyes turning upon the black aperture of the tunnel along which the faint, wan gleams of Taft's lantern had preceded him. The moonshiners had an air of pretermitting work, and the expectant, receptive attention which characterizes the secluded in colloquy with him from the world without.

There is a certain rapacity in this demand for developments. Withdrawn from the scene of action, it seems as if anything definite and decisive might have happened in the interval of time, when perhaps only combinations of causes are slowly and imperceptibly tending toward the precipitation of the event. When the full-voiced greetings were supplemented by the inquiry for the news, Lorenzo Taft stood for a moment at a loss, conscious of a need of caution in the recital of his suspicions and doubts and indeterminate fears. He sat down on the side of a barrel, looking, in the flickering dusk and the vivid gleams from the furnace, like some able-bodied, overgrown Bacchus, with his flowing yellow hair and beard definite against the terra-cotta wall behind him, his reckless, jovial blue eyes full of life and vigor, and his fair and florid complexion wearing already the deeper flush painted by brush whiskey.

"I dunno 'bout *news*, edzac'ly." He hesitated, wiping his mouth with the back of his hand, as if he could hardly summarize so few experiences and impressions for the benefit of the debarred.

"That's always the way," sarcastically exclaimed Jack Espey, a slight, eager-eyed young man, the impersonation of impatience. "'Renzo don't never hear no news in the Cove; leastwise" — he cast a keen, significant glance at the others — "none ez he air aimin' ter tell agin."

The facial expression of the other men changed subtly, unmistakably. Some strong sentiment of disaffection had evidently been set astir in Taft's absence. As he slowly recognized it, a deep, dismayed gravity fell upon his features, which were as incongruous with his expression for the moment as if they were merely component parts of some jovial mask. It was a petrified look, as if he had suddenly beheld the Gorgon Head of Trouble.

The other men said nothing, maintaining a sort of wary attention inimical in its close receptivity. The suggestion had communicated instant fire to certain inflammable suspicions and antagonisms. All the work about the still was given over for the nonce, and Lorenzo Taft had a certain overpowering realization of being brought suddenly to judgment, without a moment in which to take account with himself and his agile duplicities and perfect his defense.

There were four of the moonshiners besides Lorenzo Taft. Their aspect had so little in common that one might wonder at the cohesive property of the enterprise to hold them together, were it not for the opportunity of profit so rare in these mountain communities, and the great and ever-present dangers of the law that served to cement their association when once they had fallen into the toils of the illicit worm. One, in his shirt-sleeves, was somewhat beyond middle age, bearded and grizzled and grave, with a sedate eye, callous hands, and a steady look as if he might be trusted to do a good deal of hard work by sheer force of industrial momentum when once about it. He had distilled much liquor against the law in his time, and even had an experience in such matters antedating the unpopular whiskey tax. His was a sober, trusted judgment in questions of pomace and mash, singlings and doublings, and the successes of the manufacture were his. Another had a downy lip, full, petulant, passionate; a large

blue eye, deeply bloodshot; a tousle of light
curling hair; an overgrown, large-jointed look,
—a mere boy, despite his thickened utterance,
his shaking hand, and his frequent reference to a
jug down amongst the shadows which the others
left almost untouched. A far more dangerous
personality was exemplified in the keen-eyed man,
of about twenty-five, called Jack Espey. He
had a wild, alert, aggressive look, widely opened
bluish-gray eyes, full of reflections of the world
without, straight black hair, a drooping mustache,
a fair complexion, a square jaw, and about him
was the unmistakable intimation of recklessness.
He wore a white wool hat set far back on his
head, a blue shirt, and blue jeans trousers, and he
clasped both his hands across one knee above
his long spurred boot, while he sat on a shelf
of the rock, half in the shadow and half in the
light. The gleam fell on the handle of the knife
in his belt and his pistols, which he did not lay
aside to assist in the work. Yet it was not toward
him that Taft, surprised and overtaken, cast the
first covert glance of anxiety and deprecation. A
smiling, dark-eyed gaze fixed upon his face shook
his confidence, in that moment of detection. The
smile was not one of pleasure, but Larrabee's eyes
were seldom without it. It was tinged with a suggestion of contempt; it was habitually slow; it
seemed rather an unintentional emanation from
the spirit within than a means of communication
with others of his kind. He smiled, as it were, to

himself. He had a pale, clear-cut, intelligent face, with fine straight features, dark eyes, and short auburn hair. He was about twenty three or four years of age, lean but strongly built, and tall, and was dressed in brown jeans, with great rough boots. He had a certain inactive, lounging aspect, and laid aside with a reluctant gesture the worn New Testament which he had been laboriously reading as he sat close to the door of the furnace and caught its glimmers.

"Naw," reiterated the keen, eager Espey, with what he intended to be a sneer, but which was instead a snort of indignation, "ef 'Renzo hears enny news, he ain't rememberin' ter sheer it with we-uns; he keeps it from us, moles o' the yearth that we be!"

He dropped his voice dramatically. The others, with a hot sense of injury, gazed with glowing eyes upon Taft.

"Why, look-a-hyar," Taft felt impelled to defend himself, "what is it I ain't told ez ye want ter know?"

There was a close understanding among the "moles o' the yearth," for the united accusation about to be voiced was withheld as Larrabee fixed his ever-smiling eyes upon him and held up his warning hand.

"Waal, 'Renzo, what *is* the news ye hev tole hyar?"

It was the pride of intellect which illumined Larrabee's face, that ineffable sense of power which a conscious mental superiority bestows. The smile in his eyes extended to his lips; he laughed a little, showing his strong white teeth, and there was something craftily brilliant in his expression as he looked down and turned the Testament in his hands, and looked up and laughed again.

" Yes," exclaimed Espey rancorously, " ye purtend ter go out an' see nuthin' an' hear nuthin'. I reckon ye air 'feared we 'll git skeered too easy, an' light out an' leave the still, an' sech; so ye tell we-uns nuthin' 'bout sech ez ye meet up with. Jes' ondertake ter jedge fur us an' gin us no warnin' nor nuthin' " —

Larrabee broke in suddenly: " *We* 'll ondertake ter tell you-uns the news, 'Renzo Taft, though we do be ' moles o' the yearth '! *Thar 's a stranger in the Cove!* "

A large, imposing personality is at a peculiar disadvantage when overtaken by disaster. Lorenzo Taft felt detected in every fibre, and he was conscious of comprising a good many pounds avoirdupois of culprit as he sat arraigned before them all. He could only look from one to the other in flushed doubt and anxiety as to how much they knew of what he had his own reasons to conceal.

" He air 'bidin' down at old Lucy Tems's house; an' ez ye sot out ter go thar this evenin', ye air 'bleeged ter hev viewed him," persisted Larrabee.

" Oh, I viewed him," said Lorenzo Taft, the steadiness of his fixed gaze beginning to waver somewhat as he sought to assume a more incidental manner, in the midst of his amazement to hear the details of his visit to the Tems cabin from these "moles o' the yearth," miles away in the rain and the mist and the darkness, and locked up in the denser medium of the depths of the solid ground.

"I'll tell ye his name," continued Larrabee, his eyes still smiling, but the curves of his mouth fierce, and his breath coming fast. "His name is Kenn'ston, or sech."

A wild, confusing fear of supernatural agency in this knowledge had begun to pervade Taft's consciousness. Then he caught himself suddenly.

"Ye mus' hev hearn on *him* whenst *he* war hyar afore," he said.

"Hyar afore!" exclaimed the anxious-eyed men in concert.

"He be the man ez 'lows ter build some sort'n tavern in the Cove, or sech like. Ye mus' hev hearn 'bout him."

A silence ensued. "That war 'way las' year," the elder moonshiner said at last.

"He 'pears ter go powerful slow," said the boy, disaffected and incredulous.

As the grizzled elderly distiller pondered on the matter, the perplexed wrinkles and lines of his worn face were painful to see. "Ye be right sure he ain't no revenuer nor nuthin'?" he asked anxiously, subordinating his own judgment.

"Great Gosh, naw!" exclaimed Taft, with a resonant, confident note. This idea, so at variance with his knowledge of Kenniston's plans, had not occurred to him. He broke out into a sonorous laugh at the fears which for the first time he comprehended. "Revenuer!" he cried contemptuously. "Moonshining would be a powerful slick bizness ef revenuers war sech ez him!"

The sense of relief induced a slackening of the tension among the others. They too laughed, albeit a trifle constrainedly, and glanced consciously from one to the other. But Larrabee turned the Testament back and forth doubtfully in his hands, and asked suddenly, without looking up, "Then, why n't ye tell 'bout him a-fust, ef ye did n't want us not ter know 'bout him, — jes' ez news?"

Taft was silent for an instant. But the sense of partial success is a prophetic element in the completion of triumph, and, with an irreflective dash at the nearest means of exculpation without full disclosure, he replied precipitately: —

"News! I did n't count *him* no news. Sech ez him don't count much whenst a man's a-goin' a-courtin'."

The silence with which this was received was expressive of extreme surprise. The crackle of the furnace fuel, the roar of the flames, the rush of the air along one of the unseen shafts near by that had some immediate communication with the outer atmosphere, and sustained a strong current through the connecting drift, even the continuous dripping from the worm, each made itself conspicuous in the absence of other sound.

Jack Espey had suddenly lifted one spurred

boot to his knee, and was affecting to examine the rowel. " Who be ye a-courtin' thar at old Cap'n Lucy's ? " he gruffly demanded, but with an obvious effort to assume an off-hand manner.

The steady look which Larrabee fixed upon Taft was, evidently, not incidental. The blood rushed to Taft's head. He had not dreamed of this complication. He saw that his answer meant far more to each of them than to him. And yet it was a difficult answer to give. He could not even seem to hesitate, and he must needs decide his fate at chance medley.

" Ad'licia ! " he blurted out at a venture. Then, as the recollection of the handsome, silent Julia came over him with the inevitable sense of comparison, a pang seized his utilitarian heart ; for since an excuse for his silence as to the 'details of his visit must needs be framed, and a stepmother be chosen in such haste, why could he not have bethought himself of the beauty ? The fact that others were touched by this matter, of which he had so suddenly a subtle perception, rendered his decision extra hazardous. His own natural interest, his swift regret for his choice, which was likely to ensue in any event since his feelings were not involved, dulled his observation for the moment. It was the least fraction of time which he had failed to improve, but when his discerning, covert gaze sought the faces of the other two men it could tell him naught of what he wished to know. Jack Espey still sedulously examined the rowel of his

spur lifted to his knee, and Larrabee's eyes were
fastened upon the worn book which he turned in
his hands.

" I reckon I 'm mighty welcome ter my ch'ice
of Ad'licia," Taft said ruefully to himself. " Ad'-
licia 'd stand no sort'n chance with young fellers
sech ez them, alongside o' sech a lookin' gal ez
Julia."

The instinct strong in ambitious human nature
to enter the lists for a prize stirred within him,
albeit it was merely his own fancy that rated Julia
at this phenomenal value. Fictitious though it was,
it belittled Adelicia in his estimation. However,
the die was cast.   He had openly avowed his preference, and it was hardly to be presumed that the
arrogant Julia would suffer herself to be second
choice to one of her own household. The possibility of defeat from any objection to him on the
part of the lady never occurs to a man of that
type. In his bluff vanity, a concomitant of his
other hardy attributes, he thought he had only to
choose. And he had chosen. He began to seek
to reconcile himself to his selection. It would not
be judicious to have a rivalry in a matter of this
sort — of which young men are apt to make so
much — between himself and members of his
gang; more especially Espey, who was dangerous
because of his hot head, and Larrabee, who was
dangerous because of his cool head. And then
Adelicia was of an easy, acquiescent, optimistic
temperament, and was likely to put up more readily

with the two children, Joe and Cornelia. He astutely reflected that it would probably require all the optimism attainable in the Cove to put up with " Sis." He began to feel that he was very lucky, or rather instinctively and intuitively sagacious, to have made such a choice at a snap shot. A troublous household would the determined and doubtless exacting beauty make of it. "Sp'iled ter death, I expec', by Luther an' old Lucy ; nare one of 'em dunno *how* ter say 'no ' ter nuthin' Julia sets her head ter, I reckon. An' I ain't no young feller, nohow, to go danglin' arter the purtiest gal in the kentry, pickin' out a second ch'ice fur a wife. Ad'licia hain't got no home, bein' jes' Cap'n Lucy's niece, an' I reckon she 'd be glad an' pleased ter hev a house o' her own, with nuthin' ter do but ter keep blinders on Sis 'bout'n the still an' sech, an' set her a-sewin' or a-hoein' till she gits some growth an' jedgmint." He began to pluck up. " Purty is ez purty does. Air one o' them boys is welcome to Julia ! "

Then a sudden thought smote him.

" 'Pears ter me I oughter hev a cornsider'ble gredge agin you-uns," his big voice boomed out with all its sonorous confidence once more. "I kem hyar arter goin', ez ye knowed, ter Tems's, an' durned ef ye don't haul me over the coals like ez ef I hed hearn suthin' ez I did n't want you-uns ter know."

"So ye did, so ye did ! " said Espey eagerly. " Ye did n't 'low fur we-uns ter know ez that man

war hyar agin surely settin' out ter build his tavern or sech.   'Kase ef sech a many folks war stirrin' in the Cove, we-uns would be 'feared they'd
nose us out 'fore long, an' quit the still."

Lorenzo Taft's face once more grew stony, as if
he beheld some petrifying prospect not included in
the range of vision of the natural eye.

" I reckon I hev got ez much call ter be 'feared
ez you-uns," he protested.   " I dunno ez enny o'
you-uns hev sarved out a prison term fur illicit distillin' but me."

The others stirred uneasily at the mere mention
of the possibility, their faces, stricken with a deep
gravity, all illumined by the brilliant flare of the
flames springing up anew ; for the grizzled elderly
man was busying himself in replenishing the fire.
The wall of red earth on one side, on the other the
wall of dark gray rock, alternating with lighter
tints, where the blastings had riven its close texture ; the heavy supporting timbers made of great
tree boles (what sordid translation from the noble
forests without, where the unstricken of their kindred still towered toward the stars, and sang with
the winds, and received glad gifts from the seasons
in springing sap and spreading leaf, in acorn and
cone, and kept a covenant with time registering
the years in mystic rings in their inmost hearts!);
the black aperture of the tunnel on one hand, and
opposite a mysterious recess leading beyond ; even
a rat, and his elongated shadow, which, augmented
into frightful proportions, sped after him in a

mimic chase across the trampled red clay floor, — all became visible in detail. The disorder of the immediate surroundings, the barrels, the tubs, the sacks full of meal, the great woodpile, the rotting refuse of the pomace in heaps waiting to be cast down into the half-submerged shaft close at hand, the copper still, itself, and the spiral worm and its adjuncts made a definite impression hitherto lost in the gloom. The shadows of the mountaineers doubled their number, as they sat, grave and absorbed, and gazed at the deep red and yellow and vivid white flare within the furnace. They seemed to wait in silence until the ill-fitting door clanged again, as if their senses recognized an added safety in the gloom which was not approved by their judgment.

As the door closed the elder distiller spoke.

"I dunno ez I hanker ter sarve no prison term," he said lugubriously. "An' I kin see full plain ez this hyar still will hev ter quit ef the Cove gits full o' valley folks. We-uns will hev ter move, sure!"

"Move whar?" demanded Taft. "I been a-movin' afore. That's how kem I lef' Piomingo Cove, whar the revenue folks knowed me better."

There was another long silence.

"Burn him out!" exclaimed Jack Espey violently, bringing the foot which he had held on his knee down to the ground with a vehemence that made the spurs jingle. "Let *him* move! Burn his shanty every time he gits it started."

Lorenzo Taft recoiled. The glimmer from the crevices of the furnace door made a dull red twilight about him, as he sat on the barrel against the red wall. The suggestion was not new to his mind. He had not intended, however, that it should take root amongst the moonshiners and augment their jeopardy. He thought that, if he were any judge of character, Kenniston would soon have enemies enough here. The stranger was already busy in antagonizing Cap'n Lucy, — an early collision was inevitable. This catastrophe to the building might be presumed to be the natural outcome of their wrangles, and he would fain have silently awaited this interpretation of. the event. As to the old mountaineer he felt no qualms of conscience ; Cap'n Lucy was amply able to take care of himself.

This was the trend of Lorenzo Taft's plan, — the reason of his avoidance of the subject of the stranger. How or why his expectation should have miscarried he could not for the life of him see. The man had before been in the Cove. His presence would soon be an ordinary accepted fact. Fate merely would seem to harass Kenniston and his plans. Fire is a dangerous element in building, nevertheless requisite, in the tinner's, the plumber's, even the paper-hanger's art, and a conflagration in remote places is a terrible thing. Kenniston would become discouraged after a time, and desist.

But Lorenzo Taft had never intended that this

work should be through the united means of moonshiners. Five men were too many to keep the
secrets of arson. The art of moonshining is necessarily worked with numbers, but the fire-bug's
must needs be a solitary trade. He could not see
the rift in his logic. How *had* they taken the
alarm?

He marked with secret fear how the suggestion
fared. Larrabee, who had begun again to read by
the knifelike gleam from the crevice of the furnace
door, caught upon the page on his knee, as he sat
close beside it, looked up with a keen, pondering
face, his finger still on the line along which it was
wont to guide his wavering comprehension. Surely
he found no thoughts in its wake responsive to the
idea now astir in his active, untaught brain. Law-
breaking is a progressive evil. If he had not been
engaged in the crime of illicit distilling, — which
has, however, its apologists from the mere standpoint of economics, who plead the inherent right
of a man to use his own corn and fruit to serve
his own advantage, — this further iniquity of the
destruction of the property of another could not
have found lodgment in his consideration, for he
was not naturally a cruel man, nor wicked. But
in the depths of the earth, working at an unlawful
vocation, in jeopardy of his liberty and in fear
of his life, viewing the world only in transient
glimpses in the midst of a backwoods community,
and sustaining in effect an assumed character,
that of a slothful farmer, an ignorant man's mind,

however good the native essence, is not likely to develop fairly; and he may read the New Testament, as indeed those wiser and better than he have done, as a matter of literary interest and excitement, with not a thought of personal application.

The half-drunken boy pulled himself out of his semi-recumbent position on the floor.

"That's the dinctum, by Gawd!" he exclaimed, his solemn red face swollen and somnolent of expression. "Burn him out! Burn him out! Make *him* move! Kindle up a leetle hell around him!"

He broke out with a wild, hiccoughing laugh, singing in a queer falsetto, —

> " 'Ladybug, Ladybug, fly to yer home!
> Yer house is on fire ' " —

ending in a shrill cackle of derision and a quavering whoop.

"Shet up, sonny!" said Copley, the veteran moonshiner, who seldom interfered save upon a question of work. Even he turned from the examination of the fermentation of a tub of mash which had been in question, his lantern in his hand, and a slow smile of discovery in the perplexed, anxious wrinkles of his wooden face. "I reckon our fire would last ez long ez his buildin' timber."

There was not a protest from among them. Lorenzo Taft, more dismayed than he could at once realize, again marveled how they had taken the sudden alarm.

"Ye ain't never tole me yit how it air ez you-uns fund out, sence I been gone this evenin', ez thar war a stranger in the Cove, an' how ye knowed 't war this hyar Kenn'ston down at Tems's."

There was a sudden volley of laughter, and Larrabee closed his book with a bang of triumph.

"Our turn now! Jack, *he* wants ter hear the news!" he called out to Espey.

"Ye mought ez well s'arch the hen-house fur teeth ez ter kem hyar ter we-uns, 'way down in the ground, axin' fur news!" protested Jack sarcastically.

A frown was gathering on Taft's face. He no longer had the incentive to self-command which the welfare of a plot requires. His plot was shattered; the event was out of his control, at the uncovenanted mercy of the future. It was almost sheerly from the force of curiosity that he pressed the question : —

"How *did* ye know, ennyhow?"

Perhaps he might not have been enlightened save for Larrabee's relish for detailing the circumstances, in the paucity of incident and interest in their underground career.

"Waal," he began in a narrative tone, and they all composed themselves to listen. Even the elderly drudge decanted a jug of doublings into a keg with marked speed of manner, and shuffled up into the circle, where he seated himself on a broken-backed chair, which, since he could not lean backward, rendered him fain to lean forward, his elbows on his knees, — "waal, this evenin', it bein' sorter lone-

some down hyar, — I knowed 't war goin' ter rain,
— I felt sorter like 't would be toler'ble pleasant
ter read in my book."

He paused in pride; the respect of the others for
this accomplishment was visible on their faces; it
might be said to be almost tangible.

"I could n't find it, though, nowhar; an' I
s'arched an' s'arched. An' suddint I 'membered I
hed lef' it on the counter in the store. So knowin'
't war nigh dark, an' nobody likely ter be stirrin', I
went up inter the suller an' listened; an' ez I hearn
nuthin', I went up the ladder inter the room. Ye
know I felt plumb safe, fur I thunk the door war
locked on the outside."

"Waal, war n't it?" asked Taft, with a swift
look of alarm.

"*It war n't locked at all;* fur, ez I stood thar, —
I hed jes' by accident shet the door o' the counter
up an' the suller, — the door of the room opened."

Taft's breath was fast. He had himself unlocked
the door before he came down to the still. He could
have sworn it.

"The door opened, an' a leetle gal kem in,"
Larrabee went on.

Taft's dismayed eyes were fixed unblinkingly
upon him.

"Ye did n't tell her nuthin'!" he exclaimed, for
he recognized the avenging "Sis" without description.

Larrabee laughed at the reminiscence of the hu-
mors of the situation.

"I war fit ter drap down dead with plumb skeer at the sight o' her! But I sorter held up by the counter, an' I say, 'I kem ter see 'Renzo Taft, — yer dad, I reckon.' An' she owned up ter it. An' I say, 'I 'lowed he kep' the door o' the sto' locked.' An' she say, 'He do. I think 't war locked.' 'I reckon not,' I say, 'fur I could n't hev walked in ef he hed locked it.' An' she say, 'I could n't hev locked it *good*, agin. I *onlocked* it this evenin' with my grandmam's key what I brung from her house.'"

Lorenzo Taft gasped. The idea of old Mrs. Jiniway's keys unlocking his helpless doors gave him a sense of the futility of concealment from the prying feminine eye which nothing else could so adequately compass.

"An' then," continued Larrabee, with another burst of laughter, — Taft did not think "Sis" half so funny, — "I axed her what ailed her ter open the door of her dad's store whilst he war gone. She looked like she hed a mind not to say another word. But she tuk another notion, — I reckon she did n't like ter be faulted, — an' 'lowed ez a strange man hed rid by; an' his horse bein' turrible fractious and hard-mouthed, the bit hed bruk in the critter's mouth, an' he wanted ter buy another. So Sis tried ter open the door, and done it, with her granny's key. An' she sold him a bit. She said he war powerful saaft-spoken an' perlite, ez ef she 'lowed *I war n't!* An' that gin me a chance ter ax her what he said. An' she tole his name, an' the word ez he war 'bidin' at Tems's, — fur Sis axed him. He got away with mighty leetle news that Sis hed enny cur'osity 'bout."

Lorenzo Taft listened in silent despair. Disaster seemed closing about him. Certainly this was a field for a stepmother. Adelicia could not take the enterprising " Sis " in hand a moment too soon.

" How much did she want to know 'bout *you-uns* that *ye* did n't tell ? " demanded Taft.

" Waal, I fell in line, an' wanted ter buy suthin', too. I purtended I wanted ter buy a pound o' nails. Sis weighed 'em out fur me, — gin me mighty scant measure, — an' then I 'lowed I would wait ter see you-uns, an' I sot down in a cheer. An' she sent Joe ter set with me, — ter see I never stole nuthin' o' the gear, I reckon, — an' went off in the t'other room ter spinnin', ter jedge by the sound o' the wheel. An' Joe drapped off ter sleep, an' arter a while I croped down hyar agin. I reckon she 'lowed, when she missed me, ez I got tired an' went away."

Taft, anxiously canvassing the probabilities, could but deem this more than likely. He began to breathe freely. The girl was too young to critically observe any departure from the usual routine, or to reason about the matter. He doubted if she would know what moonshining was, or could draw any inference from the fact of concealment should their precautions chance to fall under her notice. Not that he intended, however, to submit them to this jeopardy. The finding and fitting of old Mrs.

Jiniway's key to the door, in order that the sale of the bit might not be lost, savored too much of a precocious intelligence to be needlessly trusted. "Sis will bear watchin'," he said to himself, unaware that this was a mutual conclusion.

For early rising was one of the virtues inculcated in old Mrs. Jiniway's rule of life. Cornelia Taft was awake betimes the following morning, — a dawn full of rain, of gray mist veiling the mountains, of low clouds, of heavy, windless air. She saw its melancholy gleams through the crevices of the clapboards of the roof above her head and the batten shutter close by her bed. She knew that these fugitive glimmers were brighter than the dull day slowly breaking without, from the contrast with the deep tones of intervenient shadow. She lay looking at them for a time with this thought in her mind, and then she leaned forward and opened the shutter. It was as she had fancied: the dusk was almost visible, like a brown mist that seemed subtle and elusive, and always vaguely withdrew whenever the eye would fain dwell upon it. A great elm grew just without the window and hung high above the roof. Its leaves were all lustrous and deeply green with the moisture; the graceful bole and branches were darker and more definite than their wont. A bird's-nest was in a crotch. She turned her head to hear the sleepy chirp of nestlings. She wondered that Joe had not rifled it, — only because he had not observed it, she felt sure. "That boy don't take notice o' nuthin'," she commented acridly upon her senior. The next moment her own powers of observation were brought into play. She heard steps, voices, a loud laugh, and before she could experience either fear or surprise very definitely two or three men passed out of the house, under the elm-tree, and down the road, vanishing in the mist. She recognized one of them as the man who had so suddenly appeared in the store the day before ; another she had never seen; the third was very young and very drunk.

Despite the sanctimonious atmosphere that had characterized Mrs. Jiniway's domicile, the doings of the unregenerate had always been commented upon with the freedom affected by those who are subject neither to the temptation nor the transgression. Few gossips were better informed upon current affairs than she and her youthful charge; and it might be safe to say that, to all intents and purposes, a United States marshal knew no more about the revenue laws as applied to illicit distilling than did Miss Cornelia Taft.

Her small mind received a great enlightenment as she watched the young moonshiner reel down the road with his two companions, and then she leaned forward and softly and deftly closed the shutter as before.

IV.

The day proved of variable mood. The mists clung sullenly to slope and ravine for a time; the clouds hung low, full of menace; even a muttering of thunder afar off now and again stirred their dense gray masses. The veiled mountains were withdrawn into invisibility. Below, the earth lay as if it consisted only of dull levels, limited, silent, comatose, for the dank, drowsy influence pervaded all energies alike of the animate and the inanimate; there was no sound of beast or bird, no stir of wind or rustle of leaf, and a lethargy dulled pulse and muscle and brain.

The sunburst came with the effect of revelation. A vague tremor pervaded the tissues of the gray mists, and all at once a great white glory was on the green mountain sides. The vast spaces to the blue zenith were filled with radiant flying fleecy forms as the transfigured vapor took wing. Far in the south the gray cloudage still held its consistency, and trembled with thunder and sudden elusive palpitating veins of yellow lightning. But the lithe arc of a rainbow presently sprang athwart it, and the wind came gayly piping down the gorge. In the actual perceptible jubilance of the earth, it might seem that the miracles of the goodness and the

gladness of the sun were no common thing.   There
was a visible joy among the leaves as they fluttered
together, and lifted up their dank fibres, and lus-
trously reflected the pervasive sheen, and tremulously murmured and chanted in elfin wise beneath
the breath.   How was it that the plaining river
should suddenly find its melodies again as if light
and song were interdependent?   A tumultuous, rol-
licking stave it flung upon the air; and so, faster
to the valley!   The benignant revivification was on
the very flocks; the dull, submissive sheep, huddled
drowsily together in the gray menace of the morning, were astir once more, and dispersed here and
there as they browsed.   Even Luther was singing
in the barn as he mended his ploughgear.   All day
the swift upward flights of the sheeny white figures
continued at intervals, and when Adelicia set forth
to drive the cows home, in the afternoon, only the
more radiant aspects of the world gave token of the
storm of the night.   She hardly left the print of
her shoe in the wild woodland ways through which
she wandered, so had the warmth and the light
dried the dank herbage.   She was out betimes.
There was something in the long, meditative strolls
that harmonized with certain moods, and Cap'n
Lucy sometimes sourly commented, " Ad'licia gone
ter fotch home the cows ?   Waal, who be a-goin'
ter fotch home Ad'licia ? "

It might be an hour before Spot would think of
turning her crumpled horns homeward.   The sun
shone aslant through the vast forests, but still hung

well up in the western sky. Through the deeper gloom amongst the gigantic trees the rays hardly penetrated. She stopped once to gaze from the midst of the dark green shade of the umbrageous tangle at the strange effects of the light where it fell into an open space cleared long ago by "girdling" the trees, which betokened collapsed agricultural intentions, for the ground had never been broken by the plough. The enormous dead trees were still standing, and time and rain and wind had worn them to a pallid whiteness. She could see the successive clusters of columns, one after another, rising in the sunlight, until the roofing foliage nearer at hand cut off the view. To Kenniston's cultured experience they were reminiscent of the colonnades of some great cathedral, when he had observed the place and the same effect. She had naught in mind to which she could compare them, but those white, silent, columnated aisles in the midst of the savage fastnesses of the great wilderness always impressed her with a certain solemnity as she passed, and she was wont to pause to gaze at the spot in awe and with a vague sinking of the heart; for, despite her optimism, Adelicia's heart was not always light. She was sensible of its weight this evening, as she wandered on, leaving the still, white sanctuary in the midst of the forest glooms. Her face was wistful and pale. Her dark gray lustrous eyes were dreamy. She walked slowly and aimlessly, her brown dress brushing the undergrowth aside with a gentle murmur, her yellow calico sunbonnet hanging on her shoulders and leaving her auburn head bare. Her errand was far from her mind. She did not even bethink herself to call the cow, until suddenly she noticed how high upon the great boles of the trees the slanting sunlight registered the waning of the day. Then, as she set the echoes vibrating with the long-drawn cry of " Soo, cow ! soo ! " she turned at right angles, following the trend of the mountain stream, invisible in the labyrinth of the woods, but not far distant she knew by the vague murmur of waters borne by the wind. She had looked for no other listener than the somewhat arbitrary Spot, who would heed or not as she listed, and who might now be standing knee-deep in the limpid ripples near at hand, hearkening, but making no response, intending to fare home at her own good pleasure. But the long, musical, mellow call, with its trailing echoes, attracted other and more receptive attention, and as Adelicia turned suddenly into a straighter section of the path she saw at the end of the vista, before it curved again, standing beneath a tree and with his face toward her, a man apparently listening and waiting for her.

He had dismounted from his horse, a light-tinted yellow roan, who stood as still as if he were of bronze, while his master leaned against the saddle, with his hand on the bridle. He held the other arm akimbo, with his hand on the belt which supported a knife and a pair of pistols. They were unconcealed by a coat; he wore a blue shirt and blue jeans trousers, with heavy boots drawn to the knees; and she recognized him rather by his accoutrements than his face, for his wide white wool hat was pulled far over it. From under the broad brim he gazed at her with sullen, lowering eyes.

"I hearn ye callin' the cow, an' I knowed yer voice," he said. "I been waitin' fur ye."

She faltered for a moment; then, with an evident effort, quickened her step and went forward to meet him. She apprehended the anger in his face, apparently, for there was a disarming, deprecating look in her clear dark eyes as she cast them up at him. Her yellow sunbonnet hardly served more for shelter than an aureola might have done, —a background for her auburn head; her dark brown dress and the green shadows of the trees added a pallor to her white oval face with its small delicate chin. He did not heed her appealing gaze. It was with a stern, hard voice that he spoke, and a fiery eye.

"I hev got a word ter say ter ye, Ad'licia," he began, walking slowly by her side and leading his horse, the reins thrown over his arm and his uplifted hand near the bit.

The animal's head was close above his shoulder, and as Adelicia met the creature's large-eyed and liquid gaze it seemed to her as if she were doubly arraigned before them both.

"Ye need n't ter try ter fool me," said Jack Espey between his teeth.

"I ain't tryin' ter fool ye," protested Adelicia.

He looked at her narrowly, taking note of her evident discomposure, and placing disastrous construction upon it.

"Ye 'low ye kin fool me 'thout tryin', I reckon," he said, with a sarcastic smile.

"I ain't a-foolin' ye," gasped Adelicia. "Ye know — why, *ye know* I ain't!"

He hesitated, half constrained to believe her. He still gazed searchingly at her from under the broad brim of his hat. Her wild, agitated look made him doubtful.

"Now, ye jes' ondertake ter·fool me," he continued, with an accession of angry jealousy, "an'" — he laid his hand on the pistol in his belt — "I'll ondertake ter shoot ye dead on the spot."

The color surged to her face. The tears rushed to her eyes. A sharp conflict waged in her heart for a moment, and then she walked on beside him, pale, composed, silent, as if she were alone in the depths of the primeval wilderness.

Only the sound of the stir of the saddle with the breathing of the horse as the animal tramped on behind them, their muffled footfalls barely perceptible on the thick herbage of the cattle path, the light whisper of the wind in the leaves, broke the pause, while Jack Espey's touch trembled on the handle of the pistol as he walked beside her.

Her calmness shook his own composure.

"Ad'licia!" he exclaimed petulantly, but with an evident softening of his fierce mood, "why n't ye say suthin'? Why n't ye say suthin' ter me?"

"I dunno what ter say," she responded coolly.

"Ye know what I want ter hear," he declared passionately.

"'T ain't no use ter say it agin." She turned upon him her eyes, soft and lustrous, like some brownish-greenish moss in the depths of a crystal spring. "I done said it an' said it."

His hand released the pistol, and pushed his hat far back on his dark hair with a hasty gesture of impatience. Then, with a sudden calmness, "Ad'licia, ye ought n't ter git mad with me! Ye ought n't ter git mad so dad-burned easy!"

"Mebbe I ought n't," she said, with a note of sarcasm in her vibrant voice. Her eyes were bright, her cheek flushed.

"'T ain't right," he continued didactically. "'T ain't religious." He looked at her with grave, admonitory eyes.

"Mebbe 't ain't," she responded. She laughed a little, unmirthfully, and her lip quivered.

He strode on a few steps in silence, at a loss for words for explanation. He dreaded and deferred it, and yet he longed for its possible reassurance. As his thoughts canvassed its probabilities, he broke out tumultuously once more: —

"I hev got good reason ter b'lieve ye air foolin' me, — good reason, I tell ye, now, Ad'licia!"

"Good reason agin my word?" she demanded, her pride in her eyes.

He stared at her. "A gal's word!" he said lightly, and then he laughed. As a guaranty it struck him humorously. "I reckon thar ain't many men ez would be willin' ter stand or fall by sech."

"Ye set store by it wunst," she said humbly.

"'T war when ye promised ter marry me," he declared precipitately, unconsciously showing that it was the prospect which he had valued without trusting the promise. "An' I want ye ter 'bide by it, too," he sternly added, suddenly perceiving that it was not policy to adduce too freely precedents as to the friability of feminine promises.

She shook her head, regardless of his keen, fiery eye. "I ain't goin' ter marry nobody, I reckon," she said slowly. "Ye'll shoot me dead fust, some day, in one o' yer tantrums."

"Ye ain't a-goin' ter marry 'Renzo Taft, an' that I tell ye, now. I'll shoot ye fust, sure!" he cried furiously, his eyes blazing upon her.

The look in her face checked his passionate rage. An utter wonderment, a deep bewilderment, overspread it as she echoed, "*'Renzo Taft!* The man over yander at Lost Time mine? War ye a-talkin' 'bout *him?*"

He controlled himself instantly, although his eyes were all ashine and alertly restless.

"Who war you-uns a-thinkin' 'bout, Ad'licia?" he asked gently and incidentally.

"Jasper Larrabee, o' course," she answered innocently.

He could only grind a curse between his teeth, and then he was speechless for a moment.

" I dunno nare nuther good-lookin' young man in the Cove," continued Adelicia, girlishly talking on, oblivious of the significance of her disclosures. " Though I b'lieve Jasper ain't studyin' 'bout sech ez marryin'. He jes' kems thar toler'ble frequent ter read out'n his book ter uncle Lucy. He kin read powerful well. Uncle Lucy 'lows he senses the Gorspel better from Jasper's readin' 'n the rider's, 'kase whenst he don't onderstan' he kin make Jasper stop an' spell it out an' read it over. An' sometimes " — she broke into a little dimpling laugh — " whenst the Gorspel goes agin uncle Lucy's policy an' practice, he makes Jasper spell an' *spell*, an' yit them times he can't spell it out to suit uncle Lucy. But it's plumb heartsome ter hear Jasper read of a stormy night," she added, recalling the one spiritual pleasure of her stunted, starveling spiritual life.

As she glanced at his face, there was something so gruesome, so strange, in its expression that she was fain to remonstrate. " Ye 'pear powerful techy, Jack," she said. " Ez ter 'Renzo Taft, it's jes' old uncle Lucy's foolishness; an' I wish he'd quit it, too! Though 't ain't no harm, nuther. Uncle Lucy jes' makes out ez 'Renzo Taft air arter me or Julia fur a stepmammy fur his leetle gal, an' it tickles him ter talk 'bout'n it, — it's so foolish! Why, Jack, 'Renzo Taft is old enough purty nigh ter be *my* dad; an' — he ain't ugly, edzac'ly — but, but — nowise desirable. Uncle Lucy air always peckin' at me fur puttin' myself out ter obligate other folks, but I ain't so powerful meek-tempered ez ter marry 'Renzo Taft ter be a stepmammy. Though he ain't axed me, nor nobody else ez I knows on. An' I ain't got nuthin' agin him."

He walked on beside her, hardly listening, and scarcely caring what she said or thought of Taft. For him, at the moment, Jasper Larrabee, and his gift of reading the Scriptures and interpreting them to Cap'n Lucy's satisfaction and her humble and incidental pleasure, filled all the horizon. His jealousy had taken a new lease on life with this more promising object, and with the surer foundation of what she said of Larrabee rather than of what Taft said of her. He hardly heeded her presence as he sought to gather together his faculties. He did not even feel the clumsy caress of the horse now and again rubbing his head against his master's shoulder, as he minced along behind him, accommodating his long stride to the shorter compass of the human step. The young man's eyes were hot; they seemed to burn the dry lids, as he gazed down through the cool leafy vistas of the forest; but his voice was calm enough when he suddenly said to her : —

"Ad'licia, ef ye keered ennything 'bout me wuth talkin' 'bout, ye 'd marry me now."

The placidity which her face had resumed as she had talked disappeared abruptly. She was once more anxious, disquieted, on the brink of tears.

"Ye know, Jack," she expostulated, "I can't marry agin uncle Lucy's word."

"Ye would ef ye keered a straw, a bare straw."

"Uncle Lucy jes' say, 'Wait awhile.' It's jes' 'awhile,' else I would go agin his cornsent."

"Ye don't keer," he reiterated dolorously, for her protest was welcome to him.

"Uncle Lucy jes' say," she went on very fast, "jes' wait till that man ez you-uns shot in Tangle-foot Cove gits well. He'll git well, I reckon. Ye said he war powerful hearty an' big. Uncle Lucy say he ain't goin' ter lemme marry a man ez mought be tried fur his life, ef he kin holp it."

"Ef ye keered fur me, ye wouldn't gin *that* fur Cap'n Lucy's word!" he asseverated, as he lifted his arm high in the air and snapped his fingers resonantly.

The horse shied suddenly at the sound, and pulled heavily on the hand that held the bit.

Her eyes were full of tears.

"Jack," she said in deep humiliation, "I can't 'low at this time o' day ez I don't keer fur uncle Lucy's word. I never eat none o' my own bread in my life."

She knew that he had turned and was staring at her, although she could not distinguish him through her tears. If she had never loved him, her heart might have warmed to him now, for the vehemence, the partisanship, with which he protested her independence.

"Eat yer own bread!" he cried in a ringing voice that made her shrink. "Ye never eat nuthin' else! Who churns, an' sweeps, an' mends, an'

cooks, an' milks cows, this many an' many a day?
That thar dough-faced Julia?"

To his amazement she burst out laughing, but
the next moment she was sobbing in good earnest,
and he hardly knew whether she was glad or sorry.

He scarcely paused to wonder. He went tumultuously on to repudiate the obligations that so lowered her pride and her title to self-respect. "Who
hoes, an' sews, an' weaves, an' spins, an' raises the
chickens an' tur-rkeys an' sech, an' answers old
Cap'n Lucy's call ' Ad'licia! Ad'licia!' all day long?
That thar long, lank, limp Julia? Ef I war ter
marry ye an' take ye away from thar, that house
would fall down, I reckon, an' old Cap'n Lucy
knows it."

His well-set bluish-gray eyes had brightened as
he spoke; he smiled genially; his face was handsome and intelligent with this expression. The
next moment it clouded heavily. He could not do
this as almost any other man might, — marry a
wife and take her home. He was a fugitive and an
exile by reason of the jeopardy of the man whom
he had shot in Tanglefoot Cove, and who still hung
between life and death, his own fate involving that
of his enemy. Jack Espey felt sure that he could
have proven self-defense, had he permitted himself
to be apprehended at the time. But from the circumstance of his hasty flight, uncertain what he had
done and animated by ignorant terrors of the law,
the lapse of time, the dispersion of witnesses, he
feared to submit his action to a legal arbitrament
now.

The suspense was in itself a terrible retribution, but it is safe to say that Espey had hardly appreciated its rigors till now, when it hampered his every prospect in life. He had been a man of some substance in his native place, according to the humble rating of the mountaineers, and the lowering of pride involved in his present situation was very bitter to him. He could not ask to be received under Cap'n Lucy's roof, and its hospitalities certainly would not be offered. He repented of his candor in making known his circumstances when he had "asked for" Adelicia, for in the probation on which he had been placed he recognized the crafty hope of her uncle that the affair would soon blow over. He felt it a poor reward for his frankness, and he determined that it should not go without requital in turn. "Jes' lemme fix up that cussed bother in Tanglefoot, an' durned ef Cap'n Lucy ever shell see Ad'licia's face agin!" he often said to himself.

Meanwhile he hung around as best he might, fraternizing secretly with the moonshiners; for here was the best opportunity of earning enough to provide for his simple wants, and to keep him out of the observation of the law, while awaiting the result in Tanglefoot, whence the news had lately become more hopeful.

He had fallen in with Jasper Larrabee at the blacksmith's shop at the cross-roads, where he had paused in his flight for his horse to be shod; the two had "struck up" a mutual liking, and Espey had come with Larrabee to the Cove, where he divided his time pretty equally between his new friend's home and the Lost Time mine. His frankness had not extended to these acquaintances, who knew no reason why he should shun observation except that which they shared with him concerning the still. His utility there and its financial advantages were ample to justify the continuation of his stay in the Cove; and thus, but for his own attack of conscientiousness in revealing his true circumstances to Adelicia and Cap'n Lucy, he might have seemed as advantageously placed as any of his compeers.

"Waal," said Adelicia, unaccountably brightened, "we-uns hev ter 'bide by uncle Lucy's word an' wait awhile, bein' ez he hev tuk keer o' me all my days, mighty nigh. An' ye better be toler'ble perlite ter Julia, too," she added, with a radiant smile. "Julia's cornsider'ble apt ter take notice o' slights."

He promised humbly, swallowing his pride with a mighty gulp; and as they came out from the woods into the more open spaces shelving to the great crags, they encountered Kenniston, a cigar in his mouth, a memorandum in his hand of the boundaries of his land, taken from the calls of his title-deed, a good-humored triumph on his face, and a gay, kind voice as he instantly recognized and greeted Adelicia.

He called her to come and observe the splendor of the view from a certain craggy point where there would be an observatory, and his enthusiasm was not dashed even when she gazed off wonderingly into space, seeing nothing to which she was unaccustomed, and evidently apprehending naught of what he said. He wondered a trifle, subacutely, how much the perception of beauty may be promoted by the sense of contrast. Since she knew no dull levels or discordant scenes, the sublime was merely the natural daily presentment of creation, no more a marvel than the rising of the sun, and thus she was bereft of its appreciation. He wondered, too, if the converse of the proposition were true, — if those to whom nature is expressed in a meadow, or a series of knobs, or a pond, can have no mental conception of the austere splendors of the craggy heights or the stupendous area of infinite detail spread before the eye within a wide horizon piled with mountains. He showed her, too, a small drawing of the projected hotel, which she held awry and almost reversed to gaze upon it. His good humor extended to her companion, whom he had never before seen. Although usually aloof and averse to strangers, Espey found the suave words a salve to his sore heart. He did not know how much less pleasant Kenniston could be when not pleased. Just now even this new acquaintance harmonized most aptly with his gracious mood. Artistically viewed, poor Espey might have graced the romantic stage, as he stood, in his dark blue shirt and trousers and great spurred boots, defined against the yellow-bronze horse which he held by the bit, his belt full of weapons, his broad white hat far back on his black hair, and his defiant face at once wild and eager and wistful. The man of the alert pencil was moved to wish that he had the art to do him justice.

Kenniston's kind and ingratiating manner as he explained his plans and expectations, which could not interest the mountaineer, who was as foreign to such considerations as deer or bear, secured nevertheless Espey's attention and respectful silence. He looked now and again with a sort of reluctant liking at Kenniston's face as he talked, regretting that, since he attached so much hope and consequence to the project, it would be necessary to burn the buildings down as fast as they were erected.

In the plenitude of his access of amiability, Kenniston lagged behind and let them stroll away homeward together, — as pretty a pair of rustic lovers, he thought, as one could wish to see.

. The sun was well down ; the sky was red ; the evening star was in a saffron haze ; the nearest mountains had turned a deep purple, with a vague, translucent, overlaying gray hue like the bloom on a ripe grape ; the distant ranges had vanished in the mystery of night. It was not dark, but the flare of the fire within the door of Cap'n Lucy's cabin was visible as it rose and fell on the puncheon floor in transitory flickers. It was a poor place, but it was home, and to the exile it looked like paradise. Julia had come to the door, and stood there half in the soft outer light, and half in the firelight within. Schooled and docile, Espey remembered his monitor's bidding, and roused his unwilling, flagging energies and his tired, sad heart to evolve some pleasantry as he called out a greeting from the bars. She turned her sleek head and smiled at him. There had never been such eyes in the Cove, except perhaps those which Cap'n Lucy had opened there first some sixty years before, nor such long, dark, curling lashes. She might, however, have been no more comely, for all Jack Espey cared, than old " T'bithy," Adelicia's cat, who arched her plebeian scantily furred back in the door, and surveyed the landscape with her yellow eyes, and yawned from sheer mental vacuity. He got through the interview with what poor grace he could, and from a sense of duty; and as he was about to mount, he offered, unobserved by the others, to take Adelicia's hand. To his amazement, she looked him full in the face with hard, angry eyes, struck down his hand with a petulant gesture, passed him like a flash, and disappeared within the door.

Jack Espey, who had no more recognition of the aspect of jealousy than if he had never felt its power, could but mount and ride away in angry bewilderment; and Kenniston, hearing the furious speed of his horse's hoofs as he went headlong down the dark, rocky road, looked wonderingly after him.

" He 'll break his neck, at that rate," he said.

V.

Kenniston's gracious mood was not of long continuance. He was of the temperament which demands a prerequisite for good nature. Given an adequate reason to be happy, and he could show you a fine article of felicity. But his heart would not bubble with gratitude on general principles for ordinary blessings enjoyed in common by humanity at large. It was not enough for him that the fried chicken was fat; that his cigar was good; that as he smoked after supper on the little porch, the air was so fragrant, so fine, so dry; that the stars were brighter for the great dark amphitheatre of mountains above whose summits, serrated against the horizon, his far-reaching gaze sought them; that Julia, as she sat on the step of the threshold, had an outline and a coiffure that he would have discriminated as classic in marble; that every trace of the battered beauty of old Cap'n Lucy's countenance vanished, leaving it a unique ideal for a gargoyle, when his guest chanced to intimate that he had written to the register in the county town, who had furnished him with the calls from his title-deeds, and that he felt very sure that Cap'n Lucy had inadvertently trespassed on his neighbor's domain. Harmoniously ugly as his countenance was, Cap'n Lucy's conduct was more so.

" Waal, sir," he said, after an interval of stunned dismay, during which Kenniston leaned forward, drawing with his cane an imaginary line on the floor, and repeating the measurements for the boundaries from the paper in his hand, " ye an' the register may go to hell, sir, an' brile, sir ! "

Cap'n Lucy's face was very distinct in the light from the fire within the door, as he sat tilted back in the chair against the post of the porch, and a sudden sensation ensued amongst his household as they gazed upon him, astounded by this unprecedented breach of all the canons of hospitality. There was silence for a moment. Luther stirred uneasily, the legs of his chair rasping harshly on the rough flooring of the porch. Even Julia gave signs of having heard by turning her head slowly, with a certain interest and excitement on her impassive face. Adelicia's eyes dilated with alarm as she half rose from her seat on the step of the porch ; she had grown pale ; her delicate, fine little chin and her lips quivered with the agitation of the moment.

" Oh, uncle Lucy, ye don't mean that, — ye don't mean that, now ! " she urged.

"Oh, I ain't partic'lar ez ter *when !* " the old man blurted out. And then he paused to chuckle in sinister fashion over his play upon the double meaning of the word " now " in this connection. He had a satisfaction, too, in thwarting the ever-ready peacemaker and apologist, and in her look of balked surprise as she cogitated upon his answer.

His grimly jocose pride in his cleverness relieved the tension of the moment. It suddenly became more practicable for Kenniston to overlook his rude rage, when the circumstances rendered it hardly possible for him to take cognizance of it. His indignant repugnance to the situation was sharply manifest in his face, however, which was of an expressive type, but he compassed an offhand manner as he said, —

"Oh, the register and I may be burned indefinitely and to your heart's content, in due course of spiritual justice ; but I fancy it won't be the direct consequence of anything in the nature of muniments of title, and it won't change the metes and bounds of this land by one rod, perch, or pole."

Another voice broke into the discussion abruptly :

"What reason hev ye got ter 'low ez Cap'n Lucy be on yer land ? "

The dull irradiation of the porch from the flicker of the fire within the house barely sufficed to show Lorenzo Taft's burly form standing beside the post. His approach had been unnoticed by the group, but his question apprised them that he had joined them some moments previously, and the pawing of his mare at the gate showed that she had been hitched in anticipation of passing the evening there. In the excitement of the situation the usual greetings were dispensed with, and Kenniston not unwillingly recited anew the calls of the title papers, again sketching the boundary line with his cane on the floor, and even taking from his pocket a letter, and drawing upon the back of the envelope a miniature plat of the irregularly shaped body of land. Even in his preoccupation he could but note the intelligence of the attention which the visitor closely bent upon his exposition and the rude draught, the receptivity of his mind, the pertinence of his questions. Taft stood leaning over the back of Kenniston's chair, his blue eyes fixed on the paper in the slim deft fingers of the draughtsman, his own brawny hand laid meditatively on his long yellow beard.

" Of course," said Kenniston, folding the paper, and by way of concluding the matter, " I am ready to pay the colonel the full value of his improvements. He has only to name his price."

The irate glance which Cap'n Lucy shot at him served to steady him a trifle, to tame his buoyant sense of triumph. He had an ample fund of physical courage ; that is, in his fresh, healthy, normal mental impulses he never thought of fear. But he had seldom been brought into actual personal danger, and the details of sundry lawless and furious feuds that had come to his knowledge during his stay in the mountains were brought suddenly to his remembrance by that swift, scathing look ; he was further reminded that few of these bloody chronicles recounted so definite a provocation as the effort at eviction. Nevertheless, the sense of proprietorship was strong within him, and the active aggressiveness of a man with the coercions of that weapon in his hand, the law of the land, made his blood stir when Cap'n Lucy, wagging his arbitrary old head, retorted, "An' s'pose I say — like I hev said — ez my h'a'thstone ain't got no price! S'pose I won't sell, an' I won't gin in, an' I keep my line whar I know my line hev got a right ter be, — whut then, hey?"

But for his gray head, so did his manner and expression reach the climax of aggravation, it might have seemed righteousness to smite him. Kenniston, held in the bonds of such considerations, controlled himself with difficulty. He was unused to self-restraint, or to occasions that necessitated it. The color had overspread his face; he was hot, impatient, indignant. "Why, then, there's nothing for it but to procession the land and establish the boundary," he declared.

Cap'n Lucy stared in amazement. This possibility seemed never to have occurred to him as a solution.

"Percession my lan'!" he cried at last, as if the extremity of insult had been offered him. "Percession my lan'!" His face was scarlet; his eye blazed; his hand, held out with a gesture of insistence toward Kenniston, shook with fury.

"Or *my* land," Kenniston sneered. "'T is n't capital punishment. Plenty of men have survived the processioning of land, — thriven on it! My land, then; the process won't hurt it. Get the line, — that 's what I want."

Once or twice Adelicia sought, in her agitation, to interpose. Now she rose and came to Cap'n Lucy's side, taking hold of the shaking hand which he brought ever nearer to Kenniston's face, who would not draw back, nor mitigate nor postpone his demand, in the front of this threatening gesture. "Oh, uncle Lucy — don't — don't! Sweet uncle Lucy, don't! Thar's room enough in the mountings fur all o' we-uns! Look at the mountings — how big they air — toler'ble roomy fur sure! Don't quar'l 'bout *lan'*, uncle Lucy, — whenst we-uns hev got all out o' doors fur lan', — an' git in a fight, mebbe, an' git hurt, an'" —

"Ad'licia," snarled "sweet uncle Lucy," with a gasp, pretermitting his attentions to Kenniston to turn upon her his corrugated face, " Ad'licia, I tole that man ez war so dead set ter marry ye ez I would n't let him hev ye. But I hev changed my mind. I 'll tell him he kin cart ye off from hyar ter-morrer, an' welcome, mighty welcome, ef so be he ain't changed his mind; fur I can't abide ye an' yer ' peace talks,' like a Injun, an' yer interferin' with yer elders, an' yer purtenses, no mo'! Thar, now!" he exclaimed in triumph, as she fell back quite speechless because of this disclosure of the matrimonial proposition. " I reckon ye 'll set down now, an' stay set!"

Then he turned to Kenniston with an accession of fury, the fiercer for the momentary stemming of the tide.

" An' I say, hyar I be, an' yer percessionin' don't

tech me nowhar. An' hyar I 'll 'bide, no matter
whut! An' I won't sell out, an' I won't take no
price fur my h'a'thstone, no matter whut!' "

"Then," said Kenniston hotly, "you 'll be ejected
in due process of law, — that 's all."

He changed color the next moment and bit his
lip, for he had put himself in a false position.

"That 's toler'ble tall talk ter a man under his
own roof," said Cap'n Lucy, suddenly cool, and not
without dignity.

Kenniston was out of countenance for the nonce.
He felt that there was scant grace or utility in forcing the matter, which was beyond the control of
either, to this unseemly issue. He had been hurried by his impatience of contradiction and Cap'n
Lucy's illogical and arbitrary temper far beyond his
intention, which was originally merely to propose
to have the surveyor run out the boundary line in
order to demonstrate for the old man's enlightenment the fact that he was a trespasser, and to offer
to pay the full value of the improvements. But he
was not of the type from whom penitents are developed. The acknowledgment of being in the wrong
was inexpressibly repugnant to him. Perhaps he
could not have constrained himself to make it but
that he foresaw the reversal of their mutual position.

"You 're more than half right, colonel. I am
out of place here. I feel that. And, under the circumstances, I think I had better take myself off."

He had intended to get the better of his host.

But his most cruel desire could never have sought to compass the deep humiliation of vanquishment which had befallen poor Cap'n Lucy. The implied reflection upon his hospitality, the consciousness that his own hasty words justified it, the receding and diminishing aspect of the provocation common to the mental vision at such moments, with the magnifying of the offense, all combined to render him a chopfallen and lugubrious old noncombatant in the space of a second. But Cap'n Lucy's talent for open confession and repentance was not more marked than Kenniston's. He sat grum, crestfallen, afflicted of mien, but silent. His keen eye had no longer an alert interest; it was fixed with an absorbed, reflective stare on an intermediate point some two feet from the floor, with the air of insight rather than outward vision. Kenniston was not prepared, either, for the protest from the younger and ordinarily acquiescent members of the family.

"Thar, now!" exclaimed the apathetic Luther, rising to the occasion like a man of this world. "Ye hev actually got ter the p'int o' quar'lin' over yer old land an' worldly goods an' sech. An' what diff'unce do it make? The line is thar, no matter what air one of ye say, an' I reckon the county surveyor air man enough ter find it. Mebbe ye 'low ye air powerful interestin', but I ain't listenin' much, through wantin' to interjuice this hyar plumb special apple-jack I got this evenin' from the cross-roads. Ye 'lowed ye hed never tasted sech, Mr. Kenniston. Now try this, sir, an' ye 'll feel good enough ter set out an' sing psalms an' hymes an' speritchul chunes the rest of the evenin'."

Adelicia took a pitcher which the languid Julia had alertly fetched. She spoke for her, as if Julia were dumb. She looked up at Kenniston, with her delicately tinted old-fashioned oval face set in smiles.

"Ef ye want ter temper it enny?" she suggested.

"Git out'n the way, Ad'licia, with that pernicious jug o' cold water!" exclaimed Luther, shoving her aside. "Take it straight, stranger; don't spile the good liquor."

The feminine members of the family had observed that Kenniston's glass was usually diluted, and in their eagerness to facilitate peace they gave him no excuse. He hardly liked to nullify his bluster of incipient farewell by accepting this show of good fellowship and further hospitality, and yet he could not rudely repel it. He felt that both he and his host had gone too far, much farther than he had intended. Yet nevertheless his was not the nature nor the practice to overlook an affront. He took the glass, with a slight laugh and the outward show of amity, but he was determined to adhere to his threat of departure. Their interests were too adverse to make a longer sojourn appropriate; time would render them even more inimical, and he was under no obligations to put up with indignities at the hands of Cap'n Lucy or any other man. Could he have thought anything humorous that affected his interests, he must have been moved by the serio-comic aspect of the old man, sedulously silent lest his tongue escape him, solemnly sampling the· new liquor, — for his son had filially and with great show of courtesy waited upon him, — a sort of aged pallor upon the wrinkles of his face, where erstwhile his rage had glowed so ruddily. In drinking, Taft had unconsciously a knowing and discriminating air. He was comparing the quality of the beverage with the apple brandy of the Lost Time still. He looked very thoughtful as he lowered the glass, and let the flavor permeate his palate, and once more took a careful, considerate draught. It was more like business than pleasure. Luther himself did not indulge beyond the merest swallow for form's sake. He was occupied in guiding the conversation clear of difficulties and bellicose suggestions; and, considering his limited and uncouth experience, his efforts to reëstablish the decorums of peace were worthy of praise. He evidently considered that he had failed utterly when Kenniston rejoined him in the porch, after the rest of the family had retired for the night, and communicated his intention of immediate departure. "I can make the cross-roads by daylight or breakfast time, no doubt," he said, "if you will let me have my horse; and I can rest there an hour or so, and then ride on and reach the train, the night express, as it passes the tank and stops for water, about sundown."

In vain Luther protested. Kenniston declared

this his original intention. He would save time,
and prevent making both journeys by daylight.
" I don't believe I could stand the sun two days in
succession, at this season. And if I like, I 'll lie
over at the cross-roads, and make another night
ride." He urged Luther to say nothing to Cap'n
Lucy or the other members of the family, as he
did not want to combat any objections to his departure. " The old cap'n will think I bear malice,
and — really I must go."

Luther's hesitation in the matter was a trifle net-
tling to a free agent. He evidently hardly liked
to take the responsibility of acting without the
autocratic paternal concurrence. Kenniston himself felt the irking of leading-strings. " Cap'n
Lucy or no Cap'n Lucy, I 'm going," he said to
himself, making a dash for liberty, as it were. " I
believe the man thinks Cap'n Lucy owns the
earth."

Luther's obduracy gave way presently, although
he persisted in saddling his own horse, also, and
accompanying his guest as far as the cross-roads.
Kenniston was oppressed with the sense of so punc-
tilious a host, and the long ride in the dewy night,
along the deserted roads, under the white silent
stars, would have accorded better with his humor
had he been solitary. But the freshening wind
that came with the daybreak had a sense of liberty
in the broad spread of its wings. Under the slow
revelation of the clear gray skies of dawn, he
marked how far the tumult of its flight extended

in the stirring of the forests on the mountain sides, awakening from the lethargies of the night. He experienced a certain quickening interest in the unrolling of an unfamiliar landscape from the obscurities of the darkness. He had a keen zest for its beauty, the splendid symmetry of its setting amidst a new and strange conformation of the mountains ; he was responsive, too, to that touch of pensive melancholy, that sense of loss, which one must feel in noting the day-star fade, the quenching of that white, tremulous, supernal lustre in the midst of the roseate mists ; but his strong mundane heart stirred to see the sun sail majestically up amidst the full argosy of scarlet and amber clouds, freighted with the future, and the breathless expectation of the quiescent landscape merge into the certainty of largess to the present moment. And he had a yet deeper satisfaction : he noted the inferiority of the magnificence about him to the scene he had left, his own, his very own, and he dwelt upon the recollection of it with a personal triumph, as if he had himself designed and built it. It was with an influx of hopefulness, of content, of renewed interest in the world, that he shook hands with Luther, glad enough to part with him.

The mountaineer looked after him with a certain wistfulness. His experience was too limited, his idea of the world beyond too vague, for his thoughts to follow the traveler. It was only the sudden dim perception of that fresh, vital, alert turning to fields beyond his ken that smote upon him with a sense of deprivation or of discontent, too subtle to be definitely discriminated.

It was, fortunately, fleeting. Luther's satisfaction to discover that old Cap'n Lucy approved of his course, and in fact was secretly pleased to be rid of Kenniston's presence, dominated every other consideration. As the day wore on, the old man's jaunty self-importance returned. From various meditative pauses, in which he evidently argued anew the situation, he visibly derived self-justification. He was altogether at ease and himself again in an indefinitely short time, for the father was hardly more worldly-wise than the son. He considered Kenniston's departure final. He assumed that his taunt and his sturdy resistance had bluffed the man off from the design of processioning the land, which, being a thing undreamed of hitherto, Cap'n Lucy vaguely feared, albeit sure enough' that he stood well within his own boundaries. As time went by without incident or news, he began even to speak of the projected hotel as a thing of the past, a sort of mental mirage of a crack-brained visionary.

It came upon him, therefore, with the force of an unexpected blow when Luther one day burst into the house with a paper in his hand giving notice of the proposed processioning, and blurted out that he had seen the public notice posted, according to law, at the voting-place of the district, which was the gristmill on Tomahawk Creek.

Cap'n Lucy, lapsed in the soft securities of

peace, was stunned for a moment. That valiant essence, his temper, of all his faculties recovered its vitality first. He mounted his horse and rode to Sawyer's Mill, where, confronting the obnoxious notice, conspicuous upon the doorpost, he stood for an instant the centre of a curious group of idlers, frowningly contemplating it; then, with a single irate gesture, he promptly tore it down, in defiance of the law. He silently got upon his horse and rode away, leaving Luther and the kindly miller to patch the fragments together, and to replace the notice as before, where, the fractions not perfectly adjusted, it haltingly and disconnectedly continued to proclaim the date, some twenty days hence, when said Kenneth J. Kenniston designed to cause his land to be processioned, stating the corner at which he intended to begin, to ascertain and establish its boundary line.

Kenniston's absence, however, Cap'n Lucy still appreciated as a boon. He was free to flounder about amongst the dense jungles of the laurel, "huntin' fur the line ez ef 't war hid 'mongst the bushes like a rattlesnake, an' he mought find it by hearin' it rattle," Luther observed, with his first unfilial criticism. Since the full value of the improvements would doubtless be paid, should it be ascertained that the land was Kenniston's, the son could only think it a matter of inconvenience to be obliged to move, and a misfortune to that extent. But he regarded the contingency as untenable as a *casus belli*, having no realization of the reserves of obduracy in Cap'n Lucy's mind,

or of that aversion to change so characteristic of
the home-loving aged. He deemed the surveyor
the fit discoverer of the line, and deprecated his
father's long jaunts up and down the mountain
from one "monument of boundary" to the other;
for since there was no adversary to relish the spectacle, Cap'n Lucy's pride did not preclude him
from daily patrolling the extent of his possessions
so far as his strength and his horse's legs might
serve. But Luther came to think this a frivolous
objection indeed, in comparison with his view of
his father's standpoint later.

One day Cap'n Lucy rode up to the side of the
cornfield, a late planting, where Luther, with a
bull-tongue plough, was industriously engaged in
"bustin' out the middles," since the land had been
planted, in view of the backwardness of the season,
without the preliminary "breaking up." The
young man reluctantly came to the fence, his ruddy
countenance shadowy, glimpsed beneath his broad-
brimmed hat.

"Mount an' kem along straight," commanded
his father.

Obedience, implicit and unquestioning, had been
Luther's lifelong habit. He looked with desperation at his suffering corn. "Why, dad, I ain't got
on no shoes," he ventured to urge.

"I aint keerin' ef ye ain't got on no skin," the
arbitrary elder declared. "Git on yer beastis an'
kem along with me."

The surprised old plough horse was released, and,

with his clanging gear still rattling about him, and
his owner on his saddleless back, began to take his
way, following Cap'n Lucy's lead, up the precipitous slope of the mountain. The dark forests closed
high above their heads. The change from the
glare of the noontide of the open field to the chill
twilight of the shade was grateful to the senses.
The undergrowth and the jungle of the laurel
seemed well-nigh impenetrable, except indeed for
the traces in broken boughs and bruised leaves of
Cap'n Lucy's former transits. They had journeyed nearly to the summit, and Luther was ruefully meditating on the loss of two good hours of
farming weather, when the old man turned his
head, glanced over his shoulder, and drew rein.

"Luther," he said, excitement shining in his
blue eyes and the color rejuvenating his face, "ye
know that Kenn'ston 'lows his southeast corner air
at that boulder, 'known ez Big Hollow Boulder,'"
— he quoted from the notice with a sneer, — "ez
ef it could hev been known ez a peegeon-aig boulder or sech."

Luther nodded in surprise.

"Waal, he gins notice ez he begins thar."

Luther nodded again in assent.

"Waal, sir, that thar boulder hev been moved."

The young man stared for a moment. Then a
blank alarm settled on his face.

"Why, dad, it 's onpossible ! " he exclaimed.

"Kem an' see! Kem an' see." And Cap'n
Lucy rode on as before.

Luther was never sure whether he really came upon the old landmark earlier than he expected to see it, or whether the anticipation of something novel and incongruous colored his mind. There it was, presently, lying on the steep slope in the midst of the wilderness, as he had always known it, — a vast boulder, weighing many tons, with a cavity in it which almost pierced through its bulk, and was large enough to accommodate a man standing at full height. The slope above was bare, for it was near the bald of the mountain, and with outcropping ledges of rock ; athwart these several trees were lying, one apparently old and lightning-scathed long ago, the others freshly storm-riven, for the winds had raged in a recent tempest, and instances of its fury were elsewhere visible in broken branches in the woods.

" The wind could n't hev done it," observed Luther, as his father pointed at the boulder with a wave of the hand.

" Wind ? — ye sodden idjit ! "

" 'Pears like ter me it air whar it always war," said Luther, seeking refuge in conservatism from the hazards of conjecture.

" Luther," said his father impressively, " I know that thar rock war the fust thing my gran'dad viewed in Tennessee, whenst he wagoned 'crost the range ter settle. I hev hearn him say that word time an' agin. He said he camped by it, 'count o' the spring close by, up over thar. I hev knowed it familiar fur better 'n fifty year, an' I

tell ye ez it useter war around the curve o' the bend
o' the mounting up over thar, a-nigh the spring."

" Hev ye viewed that spot lately ?" asked
Luther, drawing his horse to one side, and gazing
blankly at the big hollow boulder.

" Nuthin' ter view, — jes' rock an' laidges an'
sech."

" Why, dad, how could it hev kem down hyar ?"
demanded Luther.

Old Cap'n Lucy broke into a high, derisive
laugh.

" Ax Mr. Kenn'ston ; don't ax me.   I ain't
'quainted with them things he talks 'bout by the
yard medjure, — 'splosives an' giant powder an'
daminite."   (Thus Cap'n Lucy profanely denominated a certain cogent compound.)   " Enny one o'
them would be ekal ter fetchin' the rock ' known
ez Big Hollow Boulder ' down hyar whar he wants
it to be."

" Whut fur, dad ? " demanded Luther.

" Whut fur, ye fool ?   Ter make the line run ter
suit him, ter take my house an' lot an' sech in his
boundary, ter turn me out 'n house an' home ter suit
his pleasure.   He can't buy it, so he 's a-fixin' ter
take it, — take it by changing the corner fur the
start o' the survey."

His eyes dilated with anger, and his chin shook
with the weakness of age and the vehemence of his
emotion.

Luther's face grew grave.   " That 's agin the
law, ain't it ? "

"Ter move corner lan'marks or monimints o' boundaries air a felony, that's whut," said Cap'n Lucy, cavalierly swinging his feet in his stirrups. "Mr. Kenn'ston hed better gin keerful heed ter his steps."

He grinned fiercely as he took up the reins, and, followed by the astounded, dismayed, and ruminating Luther, fared cheerfully enough down the mountain.

VI.

The roof beneath which Jack Espey had found shelter was the readiest expression of hospitality. Its several expansions beyond its builder's original gambrel design were betokened by the incongruity of the additions, and the varying tints and fashion of the warped and worn old clapboards. Two shed-rooms were obviously of a later date than the dank and mossy covering of the main building; a queer projection above a modern porch exhibited an aboriginal inspiration correlated to a dormer window, albeit lacking the aperture; a section of the limited porch itself was boarded up to serve further as house-room; and a valiant disregard of the possibility of leakage characterized the intrepid domestic architect. It further differed from the conventional roofs of the district in its surroundings. In lieu of the bare dooryard and the neighboring fields, or the low tangle of peach and apple orchards, great forest trees loomed above it, the gigantic poplar and white oak of the region; for the space about it was rugged with the outcropping rock that sheered off further down into the great precipice on the mountain slope, precluding the possibility of cultivation. An exhaustless freestone spring burst out from the rocks close at hand, the reason of the selection of its vicinity as a building-site, and the " gyardin spot " and the cornfields were lower down the slope at the side, out of view amidst the clustering foliage. So little industrial were the suggestions that hung about this roof, so allied was it in its rough, gray, mossy aspect to the rugged bark and gnarled boles of the great trees, that it too might have seemed some spontaneous production of the soil, as it rose from the ledges of the rock, mossy and gray and rugged, too, like the rest. It had an intimation, also, of an aspiration toward higher things, as it, like the trees, gazed out upon the environing lofty seclusion of the mountains, the very inner sanctuary of nature; for, save the mystic mist, or the sun and the pursuing shadow, or the vagrant wind, naught ventured into that vast semi-circle of mountains and intermediate valleys that lay before it, refulgent with color, massive, mul-titudinous, illimitable, the compass of the human vision failing to trace further than the far horizon the endless ranges still rising tier upon tier.

Whether the inmates of the house consciously derived aught from the scene, from its calm, its splendor of extent that might serve to widen the imagination, its vast resources of suggestion, one of them spent many idle hours in gazing upon it. Often Jack Espey lay all the forenoon upon the hay in the loft of the little barn, watching through the bare logs, guiltless of " chinking," the shadows dwindling on the hazy indented slopes, blue in the sunshine, amethyst in the shade. The

white clouds would sail when the wind was fair,
or in still noontides would lie at anchor off the
great shimmering domes. Sometimes these loiter-
ings were prolonged till the pageants of sunset-tide
were on the march along the great purple western
slopes, and from the shipping of the skies floated
every pennant of splendid color; the sun, with the
burnished dazzling quality quenched in the great
blood-red sphere, would go slowly dropping down
behind the western ranges, leaving the sky of a delicate amber tint with scarlet strata, amongst which
incongruous gorgeousness the evening star would
shine with a pure, pensive white radiance. The
loft of the flimsy little barn, but now all aglow
with bars of gold alternating with brown shadow
as the sunlight fell between the logs, gilding even
the tissues of cobweb and the masses of hay, would
sink into a dull, dusky monochrome. A shadow
would seem to fall upon his spirit. The anxiety to
which the contemplative, languorous idleness had
granted surcease roused itself anew; the voices
from the house, never silent, were reasserted upon
his attention, and the necessity would supervene of
joining the family circle, — a necessity sometimes
infinitely repugnant to his troubled soul, craving
solitude for its indulgence of woe, and hardly able
to maintain the cheerful disguise which must needs
screen it.

So poor were his arts of deception that perhaps
they would scarcely have served his purpose elsewhere, but here he and his peculiarities were given

scant heed. He could not have found another domicile, in all the length and breadth of the country, where he could have been installed and have excited so little attention and curiosity. And indeed, to Mrs. Larrabee, the head of the house, he was only one more in addition to the rest of the tribe that must be warmed and fed and housed, or, as she expressed it, "tucked away somewhar." She always was equal to the emergency, although whenever Espey entered the large circle about the fireside it seemed to have been recruited somewhere, and more numerous than at his last survey.

"Ye 'pear ter hev a cornsider'ble head o' humans hyar, Mis' Haight," he observed on one occasion to the old grandam who sat in the corner, the stepmother-in-law of Mrs. Larrabee, and whose reproval seemed the natural incident of all that her daughter-in-law did. The world had gone much awry with her, after the mundane manner, and in the evening of her days she had neither the softening influence of religion nor the resources of culture to mitigate the asperities of the result.

"In course, — in course!" she exclaimed rancorously, gazing at him over her spectacles with little dark eyes, the brighter for exasperation. "Thar's me an' my old man, — he's got the palsy," as if this rendered him more numerous; "an' thar's Jerushy, my darter, an' her chil'n, five, an' her husband; an' S'briny Lar'bee herself, an' her son Jasper. An' ez ef that war n't enough, she hearn ez Henrietty Timson's husband war dead, an' they war burnt out an' hed no home, so S'briny Lar'bee jes' wagons down the mounting an' brung 'em hyar ter stay, seben of 'em, — seben with thar mammy makes eight. S'briny jes' tucks 'em away somehows, ez she 'lows, in this hyar leetle house!" She sneered toothlessly, then laughed aloud. Suddenly she leaned forward, and, with her knitting-needle in her hand, pointed at the group of floundering children. "See that thar brat, the leetlest one?"

Espey, turning in his chair, descried a tow-head bobbing not far above the floor. The significant eye of the old woman fixed him as if reciting an enormity.

"He war a infant whenst he kem, — a ill-convenient infant in arms, *with the rickets!*"

As the subject of this criticism scampered out of the crowd, with a single unbleached cotton garment on, very rotund as to trunk, very fat and cherubic as to legs, very loud and blatant as to voice, very arrogant and impudent as to manner, the young man was moved to remark that he "'peared toler'ble hearty now."

"Course he do," she assented, "through a-gormandizin' of so much fat meat; scandalous, impident shoat, — ez well ez a bear!"

She loved a quiet life, did Mrs. Haight. She had been an only daughter. She had had only two children. She had always had her house to herself; and in this congregation of incongruous elements around her widowed daughter-in-law's hearth she beheld only inconvenience, perversity, and an un-

filial disregard of her own very sage advice.   It had
even been advanced to exclude her own daughter.

"Let Jerushy's husband take keer o' her.   She
would marry him, spite o' all.   Let her 'bide by
her ch'ice."

But poor Jerusha's husband was a drunkard, and
the forlorn household had suffered hardship and
very nearly grazed starvation before they made
their happy advent into this populous haven.

There were certain sensitive thrills of pride and
shame in the fugitive's heart, as he listened to this
arraignment of the numbers crowded about the hospitable hearth.   He said to himself, in justification,
that he was only one more among so many, but he
felt that he was an imposition.   There was no such
thought, however, in Mrs. Haight's mind.   She regarded him only as a visitor, a personable young
man, and moreover as possessing a certain unique
interest for her ; for in her youth she had spent
some days in Tanglefoot Cove, and, despite the wide
diversity of their age, occupation, and outlook at
life, they passed sundry companionable hours in
gossiping of the people of that locality, and detailing the various chances that had befallen families
known to both.   During these sessions he was wont
to hold her yarn for her to wind.   She never slipped
the hank across his wrists that he did not bethink
himself of other wristlets destined for him, perchance, and made of sterner stuff.   He was prone
to be silent for a time during the winding of the
skeins, but she improved the opportunity to talk to

an attentive listener; for Sabrina was too liable to
interruptions from her various charges to meet her
somewhat exacting demands as an interlocutor, and
she was at scornful variance with the other elders
of the family.

"Mis' Lar'bee 'pears ter be fond o' comp'ny,'
said Jack, as he leaned forward, with his submissive
hands outstretched for the yarn.

The old woman, peering keenly through her spectacles as she sought to find the end of the thread, —
she had a cautious, skillful, alert air, as of a trap-
per, — paused suddenly, her knotted, withered hand
poised like a claw.

"'Tain't that!" she exclaimed scornfully. " No-
thin' like it! Ye reckon enny 'oman in her senses
likes sech ez that?"

She nodded acrimoniously, and Jack, following
the direction of her eye, glanced over his shoulder
at the turmoil of towheads scuffling together in the
flickering firelight. Supper was in course of preparation, and they were even noisier at this glad
prospect than their wont. One of them, under
cover of Espey's preoccupation, had approached,
and, slipping his hand under the arm held out for
the skein, was venturing slyly to touch the pistols
in his belt, with all the greed of the small boy for
deadly weapons. Espey, his white hat far back on
his head, looked down upon him, his suddenly scowling face all unshaded, and the little mountaineer
fell back affrighted and in dismay; for, despite his
humble estate in life, he had encountered few
frowns.

"Naw, S'briny's reason ain't got no reason in it." Mrs. Haight had begun the winding now, and the red ball was whirling, ever larger, in her nimble fingers. "She jes' hed a son kilt in the wars. Leastwise the tale ez kem back war that he war wounded in a scrimmage, turrible; an' his folks war all on the run. An' he crawled ter a house nigh by, an' the 'oman tuk him in. An' he died in her house stiddier on the groun' or in a fence corner. That war the tale. S'briny never could find out who war the 'oman, nor edzac'ly whar it happened. But sence then, ter pay back her debt, she takes 'em all in, an' whenst they gits too crowded she knocks up a shed or suthin' an' packs 'em in; whenst like ez not the 'oman lef' Alvin ter die on the hard, cold groun', an' mebbe sot the dogs on him ter hurry the job."

There was a silence for a few moments, while the firelight flickered upon Espey's absorbed eyes and intent, listening figure. The wrinkled, parchment-like face of the old woman was partly in the shadow as she sat in the corner, but her spectacles gleamed with unwonted brilliancy as she actively moved and nodded her head under her big ruffled cap.

"S'briny say, too, ez old pa'son Jenks say ez ye mought entertain angels unaware. An' *I* say, then agin ye moughtn't! Fur ef enny o' these hyar that S'briny *hev* entertained air angels, they air powerful peart at hidin' it, sure!"

Once more she cast a caustic glance at the group, and her sarcastic laughter fell upon the air, sharply treble.

If celestial visitants, these were certainly well disguised. Espey glanced at the bloated face of the inebriate husband of Jerusha, tremulous, full of sudden fits and starts; at Jerusha herself, slatternly, slothful, and down at the heel, a snuff brush in her mouth, and her forlorn discontent with life in general on her weak, flabby face; at the old, feeble-minded man dozing and muttering in the corner, — he had once in his life worked in the Lost Time mine, and he sometimes gave Espey a sudden start by bringing out the name with a deep, full, blood-curdling curse. Henrietta Timson's thankfulness had merged into a suspicion that too much gratitude was expected of her, and she was prone to magnify the lighter tasks which she selected, and went about with an overworked drudging air, and with some distinct proclivity for the rôle of martyr. It was a furtive, jealous eye which she cast upon Mrs. Larrabee, at home, competent, and emphatically in command. The children, nevertheless, were disposed to take undue advantage of their protectress; and the smaller they were, the more capable, by reason of her leniency, of imposing upon her. This disposition characterized even an infant turkey, which had contracted some disease by exposure to the inclemency of the weather, and, being put into a basket of cotton to recuperate, found its way out, from time to time, with a cotton girdle adhering about its middle, and, with a fifelike voice, made the grand tour of the hearth, in imminent danger of catching fire in its cotton gear, causing her acute anguish lest it should be baked alive and before its time.

Even Mrs. Larrabee herself, — if there were aught spiritual about her, it must have been in the ends of her fingers. She was much given to wearing a sunbonnet, in the depths of which her thin, pallid face had a look like marble, with its keen, straight features. Her busy eye had not casual observation : she looked at the children to see if they were sick or cold or hungry ; at Jerusha's husband to descry if perchance he were drunk again ; at Jack Espey to discover if he wanted aught, and if he had no want or ailment she noticed him not at all. He could hardly have been more free to come and go as he would, and the long hours when he and Larrabee were away at the still passed altogether without remark. It was nevertheless to her that he resolved to open his heart. The door was ajar, and he could see that the long, loitering summer night had come at last. Through the gap in the trees the stars were visible, glowing white above the sombre mountains in the distance ; he could not distinguish a constellation, — only a whorl of brilliant stellular points of light in the scant interval where the black leaves of the oak, as distinct and as dark as if cut of bronze, failed to fill the space between the threshold and the zenith. It was not long now before she would be at leisure, and sleep would silence the juvenile members of the family, except indeed the turkey, which, though unclassified amongst nocturnal fowl, was wont to pipe lugubriously in the dead watches of the night, necessitating the uprising of the mistress of the house with a draught of water and a light lunch of corn-meal batter to compose it once more to slumber. As Espey observed it gadding about on its long legs, disproportioned to the size of its body even when begirt with the cotton batting, he sagely thought that Mrs. Larrabee's tolerance toward its exacting idiosyncrasies was the result of no sense of obligation to it or its kind. "She's a powerful good-hearted woman, and smart, too," he said to himself; "she's got enough sense ter hev some feelin's."

The evening, passed in winding the yarn, wore slowly away to him after his resolve. He was very taciturn and still, and Mrs. Haight, finding so acquiescent a coadjutor, grew industrious, and hank succeeded hank upon his motionless and submissive wrists. His silence did not discourage her flow of words. On the contrary, it assumed the narrative form in lieu of their usual dialogue; and as the fervor of reminiscence waxed, her small black eyes grew brighter, her parchment-like cheek flushed, and, with her red "shoulder shawl" and big white cap and snowy hair and blue apron, she looked like some fairy godmother. And indeed, as she briskly wound the thread, now blue, now red, and again gray "clouded" with white, it might have seemed that she wielded some sorcery to reduce to this humble fireside utility this wild-eyed, defiant spirit. The young desperado, his belt stuck full of weapons, was oddly at variance with the solicitude which he now and again exhibited when a troublous tangle developed, and the thread perversely knotted and broke. The firelight that flickered on his face, the fairer from his sojourn in the sunless depths of the Lost Time mine, his great boots and spurs, his pliant attitude and submissive gestures, and his aged and incongruous companion served also to show what speed was made in disposing of the youthful gentry for the night. With that perverse disinclination for bedtime which betrays the old Adam in the youngest infant, they severally resisted, each to the best of his very respectable capacity. One or two of tender years, having been hustled up the ladder to the loft, came down again in scant attire, and he who had triumphed over the rickets, and whose bed was in a box, resuscitated himself from amongst the bedclothes whenever he was stowed away, but finally was overtaken, and fell asleep on the old house-dog's neck as he lay snoring on the hearth.

Espey was of that type of man to whom juvenility is neither comical nor alluring. Duty was revealed to him in graduated doses adapted to the age of the taker, and he was disposed to make no allowance to infants for delinquency. It seemed to him that Mrs. Larrabee's patience was much misplaced, and he now and again gazed with disapproving eyes at the group. He was obliged to linger long before she was at leisure and sitting in front of the hearth with the shovel in her hand, ready to heap the ashes over the coals to keep the fire till day. The two beds in the room were edged with the tow-heads of the children, sleeping cross-wise; the baby's box-crib and the turkey's basket had each its wonted occupant; and if the dreams that went up from the conclave could have been materialized, what wild display of phantasmagoria they would have made! The door had been barred up against the possible marauder of the elder's apprehension, and the black bear of juvenile dread. The shadows of the two loiterers were on the red, dully illumined ceiling, two gigantic, distorted heads of dusky brown.

"I war sorter waitin' fur Jasper," observed Espey disingenuously, having noticed that Mrs. Larrabee looked inquiringly at him. "I reckon he be a-visitin' down at Tems's."

"Mebbe so," she acquiesced succinctly, rasping the shovel on the hearth. She seemed indisposed for conversation.

"Mis' Haight's mighty good comp'ny," he continued, leaning sideways in his chair, with his elbow on its back as he supported his head in his hand. . "Talkin' 'bout old times, an' her courtin' days, an' sech."

For, according to Mrs. Haight's own account, she had been a truculent heart-breaker in her heyday. There were few names that one might mention, native to her locality, which she could not have worn had she chosen. She always alluded cavalierly to the husband she had and to the one

she had lost as "toler'ble samples o' the whole
b'ilin'."

Mrs. Larrabee's immobile face was more inexpressive than before, as the red light sought it out
in the depths of her sunbonnet. She had her
secret doubts as to this wholesale destruction of
the peace of youth a half century ago.

"Toler'ble interestin' ter me!" protested Espey
suddenly. "I hev been sorter in love myse'f —
leastwise" —   He did not continue to qualify, for
Mrs. Larrabee turned her face, illumined by maternal interest, upon him. "It 's gin me a heap o'
trouble, too," he broke out impetuously, divining
her sympathy.

She was looking at him tenderly, remembering
her own youth and her own young lover, dead and
gone this many a year. Jacob Larrabee had, in
happier days, laughed retrospectively at his own
lackadaisical woe and wakeful nights and anxious
doubts. "Sech a *funny* fool I war. Thar may
hev been ez *big* fools, but I 'll swar I war the *fun-
niest*."   But his woe had always appealed to her
commiseration, and she was glad she had consciously been no factor in it. "I would n't hev
hed ye so tormented fur nuthin', Jacob, ef I hed
knowed," she would say gently.   .

Jack's young face, worn with fiercer griefs and
turmoils and keener fears, was appealing in its anxious lines; her warm motherly heart went out to
him. He leaned his hands on his knees, and assumed a confidential tone.

"Now, Mis' Lar'bee," he said, "I 'lowed I 'd ax ye what this hyar gal means. I hev done everything I knowed how ter please her,—even whenst she tole me ter go a-perlitin' around another gal. I done *jes' like she ordered*, an' what ye s'pose she done?"

"What?" demanded his partisan confidante angrily, knitting her brows heavily.

"She hit me."

"Did she hurt ye?" exclaimed Mrs. Larrabee sympathetically, dropping her voice in contemplation of the enormity.

Remembering the relative proportions and force of Adelicia and himself, Espey and his woe were out of countenance for the nonce. He laughed a little sheepishly. "Naw," he admitted reluctantly. "She did n't hurt me none ter speak on."

Mrs. Larrabee's brow cleared. "Sonny, 't war jes' love-licks," she suggested, in old-fashioned maternal phrase.

"Naw, sir! Naw, sir!" Espey shook his head with grave protest. "She war too leetle ter hurt me, she war bound ter know. She jes' wanted ter hurt my feelin's. An' she done it, too."

Mrs. Larrabee's face was all commiseration; and suddenly a truly feminine curiosity became manifest. "Whar do the gal live? Hyarabouts or in Tanglefoot?"

However far a man may trust a woman, he never trusts her completely. Jack Espey caught himself sharply. "It 's fur off,—mighty fur, 'pears like ter me," he said mendaciously. "Now, Mis' Lar'-bee, I wants ter git yer advices. What ails the gal ter treat me that-a-way, jes' 'kase I done her bid an' gin the t'other gal good-evenin', full perlite like she told me ter do? What ails her?"

"Pride," said Mrs. Larrabee sternly. She could be severe enough with people whom she did not see, and her mental image of a buxom termagant was far enough removed from the fragile and shrinking Adelicia.

Espey looked at her with doubtful, troubled eyes. "Jes' turned on me an' smit me!" he protested. "I feel like I 'll never git over that lick. I 'll die of it yit!"

"Pride!" fiercely reiterated Mrs. Larrabee. "An' ef ye wanter make her repent it, ye jes' perlite up the t'other gal fur true! Whenst I went back ter Tanglefoot Cove, I 'd show sech manners ez it ain't used ter, — ye 'd better b'lieve I would. That thar gal 'lows she kin git ye too easy, too powerful cheap. T'other gal good lookin'?"

"Waal," drawled Espey uneasily, evidently contemplating apprehensively this heroic treatment for the small smiter, "nobody don't look purty ter me but one, an' she 's plumb beautiful, ter my mind."

"Oh, shucks!" Mrs. Larrabee exhorted him scornfully.

"T'other gal hev got the name of it, though," he said reluctantly, plainly jealous for the preëminence of his lady love. "T'other gal is named a reg'lar gyardin lily fur beauty."

"Waal, then, perlitin' 'round her won't go so turrible hard with ye," said Mrs. Larrabee discerningly. "Though mebbe ye hed better let the 'gyardin lily' inter the secret, 'kase she mought fall in love with ye an' yer perliteness."

But Jack Espey shook his head; he had bitter cause to distrust candor. "I can't go 'round warnin' the gals against me," he said sturdily. "Ef she falls in love with me, she 'll jes' hev ter fall out agin, that 's all."

He sat for a little time gazing moodily at the fire, and contemplating the details of this scheme of reprisal. Then, with a curt good-night, he rose and tramped off to the roof-room, which he shared with Jasper and a delegation of the larger boys; leaving Mrs. Larrabee covering the embers, and pausing now and again, as she knelt on the hearth, with the red light on her statuesque features, to ponder on the lover of her past youthful days, and the sensible advice she had given Jack Espey to reduce the inordinate pride of the arrogant, arbitrary damsel of his heart in Tanglefoot Cove.

But the bars so stoutly made fast against the door were not destined to keep their place that night. The moon had long before slipped from the vaguely illumined limited space of the sky, which her own light had rendered faintly blue, down behind a jutting crag of the western mountains; it glowed a sombre purple as the crescent passed, with a pearly gleaming mist half revealed against the black summits about it. The white stars, whiter still, pulsated in the darkening sky. So pervasive a sense of silence was in their mute splendor that even the benighted mountain wilderness seemed to assert many voices, strange, murmurous, unknown to the light. Espey, stretched upon his pallet in the recess of the dormer window above the porch, with his wakeful, troublous thoughts, languidly sought to differentiate the sounds. He heeded the rustle of a vagrant zephyr, the twitter of a nestling, the murmur of the spring in the rocks near at hand, the never silent chirring of the cicada of the Southern summer night. But what was it in the insensate world of crag and forest and mountain and chasm that drew a long breath, and paused, and once more sighed heavily, and again resigned itself to silence? He could see in the rifts of the clapboards above his head a palpitating white star, — how its heart of fire beat! He felt his own pulses throb heavily, and the next moment they seemed to cease. A new sound intruded into the monotony of the mountain stillness. He heard it once far away, and then silence. He lifted himself upon his elbow and listened, with dilating eyes. Only the sense of the noiseless dewfall, the cracking of a sun-dried clapboard, the swift scurrying of a mouse amongst the rafters, and once more silence, or that mysterious voice of the night which rose and fell in the cadence of sighs. He was about to lie down when the sound came again, — distinct this time, unmistakable, so close at hand that it seemed the very malice of fate

that he should not have distinguished it earlier.
It was the hoofbeat of horses, and they came at a
swift gallop, — so swift that he had hardly a moment to take counsel with himself, in a turmoil of
doubt and fear ; his foot was barely on the stairway when a heavy tread fell upon the little porch,
and a sturdy fist thundered at the door.

Into the dusky red darkness of the room below
— for the glow of the embers could hardly be reckoned as light — a feeble white glimmer was stealing. Mrs. Larrabee, without her sunbonnet for
once, had hustled on her homespun dress, buttoned
all awry, and was striking a light for a tallow dip.
Perhaps its dim flicker revealed the young man
standing high in the deep shadows on the stair that
led to the roof-room, or perhaps she only distinguished his step in the midst of the clamor at the
door, for she called out suddenly to him, " Open the
door, Jack, open the door, sonny, no matter who it
be! Every chile in the house will be a-swarmin'
up d'rectly ef that thar bangin' be 'lowed ter go
on, an' I reckon we 'll *never* git the baby inter bed
agin ! "

The turkey was already awake and alert, its piercing pipe adding to the confusion and nervous stress
of the situation, as Jack Espey, after one irresolute
moment, strode to the door, and Mrs. Larrabee rose
from her knees on the hearth and stood in the dusky
brown background, shading with her hand the timorous flame of the candle.

Perhaps it was well for Jack Espey that the bars

went down with so resolute and hearty a clangor, for, as he confronted the men at the door, they did not doubt that they faced the son of the house.

" Widder Lar'bee lives hyar ? " said a keen, tall, dark-eyed man, with high cheek-bones and a hooked nose, above which his thick black eyebrows met. His soft black hat had a sort of peaked crown, and he wore a suit of plaided " store clothes," as befitted one having access to the towns, but which were much creased, and his boots were drawn, country fashion, over his trousers to the knees.

" Air that enny reason ter bust the door down ? " demanded Espey, looking at the stout battens as if expecting to discern injury as it swayed in his hand.

Mrs. Larrabee interposed blandly, " I be Widder Lar'bee. 'T ain't no use ter talk loud. I got some mighty fractious chil'n hyar 'sleep."

The fractious turkey stood upon the hearth and piped till the end of its tail quivered with the energy of its vocalization. A cricket was shrilling keenly. The trivial sounds seemed to throb in Espey's brain when the visitor said, " I be dep'ty sher'ff o' this county, Mis' Lar'bee, an' I hear ez thar war a stranger in the Cove a-puttin' up hyar."

The two men behind the officer looked over his shoulder, their bearded faces sharply inquisitive.

" Naw, sir, I ain't got no stranger hyar ; not but whut I would take 'em in, — me an' my son hev made a rule o' that, — but we-uns bide too fur off'n the road." She did not account Espey a stranger, so accustomed a figure had he become in the domestic circle.

There was a definite disappointment in the officer's keen, high-featured face.

Mrs. Larrabee turned to Espey. " Ye ain't hearn o' enny stray man hyarabouts, hev ye, sonny ? "

" Thar be a stranger down at Tems's," said Espey ; " though I reckon he ain't done nuthin' agin the law, — saaft-spoken an' perlite an' peaceable."

The high-featured face was contorted in a jocose grimace, to which the meeting of the black eyebrows gave a singularly sinister effect. Espey felt his heart sink as the official winked at him.

" Perliteness would have been wuth mo' ter this man ef he could hev showed manners sooner. War mighty onpolite indeed in Tanglefoot Cove, Mis' Lar'bee, an' shot a man."

" Kilt him ? " she demanded in a bated voice, and turning pale. She held the candle awry, as she spoke, and the flickering light as the tallow melted and dripped heavily on the floor showed only her own straight features and masses of brown hair, dulled with gray, coiled at the back of her head.

Espey's overladen heart thumped heavily. The cold drops stood thick on his face, all in the shadow, white and drawn with suspense.

" In an' about, — a sorter livin' death. An' sence he hev got so much worse his folks want the malefactor apprehended straight. We hearn ez he air hyarabouts or in Persimmon Cove, one. An' ez the constable o' this deestric' air sick abed, — ailin' old cattle like him ought n't ter be 'lowed ter hold office ! — the high sher'ff sent me ter look arter him, ef I could come up with him. Waal,"—he was turning away,—"I 'm sorry I hed ter roust ye and yer son up this time o' night."

Mrs. Larrabee took no note of this misdescription. Her thoughts were engrossed by a sudden hospitable intention.

" Would n't a bite an' a sup hearten ye up sorter, arter so much ridin' in the night wind ? " she drawled amiably.

The deputy, despite his lean, lank, ill-nourished air, was susceptible to the allurements of the pleasures of the table. He hesitated, and a very little urgency sufficed to induct him into a chair by the side of the fire, while Mrs. Larrabee ransacked her stores for the bite and sup, which were more easily promised than provided.

He was new to his office, and disposed to magnify its dignities and difficulties, as he and his two companions waited for the refection, while Espey stirred up the fire and rescued the turkey, which had burrowed into a mound of dead ashes, still permeated, however, with the grateful warmth of the embers.

" Ye 'd be plumb s'prised, Mis' Lar'bee, at the slyness o' sech malefactors, an' the trouble they 'll gin. Now I be a stranger ter this e-end o' the county, an' what with the constable sick everybody sorter holds back 'bout informin' the officer o' the law ; turrible 'fraid lest the folks in gineral takes it out on them, ye know. Some 'lows I be a-trappin' moonshiners ; an' that ain't my business at all. I got no mo' agin moonshiners 'n I hev agin whiskey. It's all one ter *me*. I don't c'lect the tax, an' I don't pay it nuther. I drinks mos'ly on treats, sech ez this." He held up his glass, for Espey had proffered the product of the Lost Time still, and it seemed to him at the moment that the very jug looked conscious. " I could n't git a critter ter kem with me ter-night 'thout reg'lar summonsin' a posse: one man ailin'; t'other man, sick wife; another man, sore foot; another man, lame horse. Course *I* could hev *made* 'em kem," waving the hand with the glass in it with a capable gesture; " but I did n't want ter be harsh an' requirin' with the citizens, 'kase, ye know," with a sudden sly geniality illumining his countenance, " I mought want ter run fur sher'ff myse'f some day, — that is, ef the old man was ter git done with the office," he added, mindful of his tenure through the favor of the high sheriff. " Now this hyar man," pointing out one of his followers, who bore with a sort of wooden equanimity the united gaze of Mrs. Larrabee and Espey, " he be a stranger hyarabouts, too, — kems from my deestric', frien' o' mine, — so o' course he war n't acquainted hyarabout, nuther."

Mrs. Larrabee's perceptions detected something embarrassing to a sensitive nature in this invited survey of the silent, bearded man, who had not opened his mouth except to put a biscuit into it. As amends, she handed him the plate anew, and the second biscuit silently went the way of the first.

" Now this hyar other man," — the officer indi-

cated a short, square-set fellow, — " he war powerful
leetle 'quainted round hyar, though he kem from
neighboring ways, the Gap; so he ondertook ter
p'int out yer house " —

The short man interposed in great haste, and
with his mouth full : —

" Though I hev never hed nuthin' agin you-uns,
Mis' Lar'bee, an' I hope ye won't lay it up agin
me, marm.   I knowed 't war mighty safe, — 'kase
you-uns war n't the sort ter harbor evil-doers 'gainst
the law an' sech ez that, — hevin' been powerful
well 'quainted with yer husband whenst he war a
boy; an' this hyar dep'ty war so powerful partic'lar,
an' I did n't see how ter git out'n it, an' " —   The
crumbs in his throat and the scruples in his heart
combined to choke his utterance, and as the climax
came in a paroxysm of coughing Mrs. Larrabee
turned to the officer.

" I got nobody hyar wuss'n yerse'f, sher'ff," she
drawled, with a slow smile.

" Waal, now, Mis' Lar'bee," said the officer, probably mindful of political hopes, " ef ever ye want
ennything of me, ye jes' lemme know.   I wanter
show ye how I 'll remember this hyar squar meal
ter-night.   I ain't one o' them ez can't remember
dinner till it 's dinner time agin."   He smiled gal-
lantly upon her from under his superabundance
of brows.   Then he turned to Espey.   " I been so
well treated it makes me plumb bold ter ax another
favior.   I want ye ter git on yer horse an' ride with
me ter set me in the road ter Tems's.   Nare one
o' these men air 'quainted with the way."

His dark eyes hardened under his sinister black brows, and Espey, who had taken heart of grace, felt his hope of escape annihilated in the instant. His eyes were fastened with a fixed stare on the officer's face; his nerves were all a-quiver; his heart seemed to stand still; a cold, insidious thrill crept along the fibres of his skin. The conviction seized him that the conversation which had seemed so incidental was merely a blind devised for the purpose of getting him apart from the women and children, that he might be captured with less ado or less danger to the bystanders, perhaps further from the chance of rescue. He thought of rescue, himself, of Jerusha's husband blind drunk in the shed-room, of Jasper away at the Lost Time mine. Through some other sense than that of conscious sight he was aware of the movements of the deputy's comrades : that one, seated in the chair, was carefully examining his revolver; that the other was standing beside the door with his hand on the latch. But Espey's eyes never quitted the face of the sheriff, who apparently took note of this fixed, unresponsive gaze.

"Air he deef?" he demanded of Mrs. Larrabee, and was about to repeat his demand in a louder key, when his hostess interposed.

"No deefer than them in gineral be who ain't willin' ter hear," she muttered. "Go saddle yer critter, Jack. 'T won't take ye long." Then, in a lower aside, "Ye 'll jes' hev ter guide 'em ez fur ez Tems's, ennyhow."

Her insistence constrained him; and indeed no alternative was definite to his mind. He turned with a bewildered, submissive mien toward the door.

The chill midnight air, blowing freshly on his face as he held it open and the draught rushed through, revived him like the very breath of freedom. The obvious opportunity flashed through his mind like an inspiration. He could give them the slip while saddling the horse. He would have the start of them even if by only a few paces. Let him but once get foot in the stirrup again, with the kindly shield of the darkness about him, and he would give them a good run through this pathless mountain wilderness. He caught up his saddle that lay upon the floor, and made for the door again with a sudden eager alacrity.

He heard an abrupt clanging noise, as one hears a sound in sleep, muffled, unreal, distant. It was only when he saw one of the men stoop and rise again and follow him that he realized what had happened. One of the stirrup irons had fallen from the saddle, unbuckled perhaps in the unwarranted juvenile curiosity of the meddling youngsters of the house. The deputy sheriff also followed. " I 'll put that on agin whilst ye air a-ketchin' an' a-bridlin' of the nag," he said.

Espey heard the loud, strident tones of his hasty farewells as he took leave of Mrs. Larrabee, — he evidently intended to return no more, — and then he was by the young man's side in the barn, followed by his two companions. For the horse was not in the pasture lot; he had repaired to the shelter of the barn, and had stretched himself on his bed of straw. At the first indication of the prospect of journeying the roan struggled up, and, with a sound of greeting that was almost articulate, came out from the stall, ready and willing to be saddled and bridled. Espey experienced a sort of animosity toward the creature for his unreasoning alacrity. He was even denied the poor respite which the usual delay in catching the horse might have given.

In his numbing, silent despair as he buckled the girth and slipped the bridle over the horse's head and the bit into his mouth, he took no definite heed of his surroundings, and yet they were all impressed upon his consciousness. He noted, uncaring, how the horse tossed up his head askance at the stranger's touch, when one of the men laid his hand on the powerful shoulder and opined that he must be a " toler'ble good goer." He was aware, somehow, of the blue-black, translucent gloom of the air, and the differing darkness with its effect of solidity, of the fodder stack looming close by, of the fantastic roof of the little log cabin against the stars, and of a vague sense of motion where the invisible smoke curled up from the chimney, faring off into the dense shadow of the foliage of the great trees. The door was still open, and the yellow light fell far out into the darkness; in the interior he could see the gaunt, tall form of Mrs. Larrabee walking back and forth, and in her arms the baby, who had

been roused by the falling of the spur. The child
needed little tenderness, in his robust self-suffi-
ciency, and was elderly indeed for such infantile
coddling. His fat legs stuck far out of her arms,
and his bawling objections to the interruption of
slumber attested temper rather than delicacy. Espey realized how her heart would go out to a real
trouble, — how she would feel for him if she only
knew! Somehow the thought of that fictitious anguish of sympathy soothed him for the moment, and
he was resigned to say to himself that it was best
as it was. She could have done naught. He was
no child like the others to cling to her in a sort of
fervid faith in her omnipotence. No ; resistance
would only have endangered her and hers. And so
he was strengthened to put his foot in the stirrup
and ride away, with the sheriff at his right hand,
and the other men close behind, all looking alertly
forward into the gloom. The roan horse, fresh
from slumber, was beginning to feel his hay and
corn, snuffing the quickening wind, pulling on the
bit, and forging on at a more speedy gait. The
other men noticed this, for now and again, with
a touch of the spur, they closed up, and the roan
horse was in the centre of the squad.

VII.

As they went, the deputy sheriff's manner was little characterized by an official decorum. He seemed rather some bold roisterer who himself might have had ample cause to dread the law that he was sworn to administer. The rough humor of his sallies affected Espey as an incongruous sort of fun, taken in connection with his interpretation of their errand, and his recollection of the keen, sinister, thin face, with its piercing dark eyes, and its sharp hooked nose, and the straight, menacing eyebrows meeting above it. He had this mental vision distinctly before his contemplation, as it had impressed him in the flicker of Mrs. Larrabee's tallow dip, instead of the undistinguishable equestrian shadow that in the black night pressed close to his horse's flank, and now and again laid a sinewy hand upon his arm. For the officer, in a spirit of mock confidence, was detailing, much to that worthy's discomfort, the spectral fears of his friend from "the t'other e-end of the county," a believer in ghosts, and making 'an elaborate pretense of sharing them. Now and again, with a sepulchral voice and an agitated manner, he would conjure Espey to say if he saw nothing flickering, waving white, in some open stretch of the road that

lay vacant and vaguely glimmering in the starlight
before them. Then, hardly waiting for an answer,
he would burst into a whoop of derisive laughter,
startling the solemn silence of the night-bound
mountain wilderness, and rousing strange echoes of
weird mirth from rock and ravine. More than once
the uncanny tumult of these wild, insensate cries
moved the staid comrades of the deputy sheriff to
remonstrance.

In the distance and the night and their repeti-
tiousness, the sounds seemed curiously unrelated
to those that had evoked them.

"That ain't no rocks a-answerin' back," said the
man from the Gap. "I b'lieve somebody is a-hollerin' at ye."

The officer turned alertly in his saddle to look
back over his shoulder. "That would n't s'prise
me none," said the capable deputy, whose large experience would seem to furnish precedent for any
given phenomenon. "I knowed a man out our way,
— mighty loud talker and a toler'ble active cusser,
— whilst callin' hawgs, hed n't tuk no special notice
o' the rocks answerin', till one day whenst he war
'dad-burnin'' an' 'all-firin'' round till the very
shoats looked blue. He stopped ter take breath, an'
he hearn a voice, powerful coarse, out'n the woods
jes' yellin' like sin, 'Fire-burn!' 'Fire-burn!' an'
he knowed that minit who 't war. An' in course
he jes' hed n't no mo' interes' in nuthin', an' jes'
dwindled away."

He paused abruptly.

"But — but — who war it ez said 'Fire-burn' with a coarse voice?" breathlessly demanded the believer in spectral manifestations.

"Why, Satan, to be sure, ye fool," replied the deputy. "I useter hear him myself a-callin' in the woods, 'Fire-burn!' whenst Ad Peters would git ter cussin' his hawgs! Jes' so" — He lifted his voice in a wild, fantastic cadence, and throughout the long stretches of the mountain fastnesses the words, as of some demented incendiary, echoed and re-echoed, varied presently with mocking cries of unpleasant falsetto laughter, set astir when the officer's gravity failed.

The patience of his friend had given way. "Look-a-hyar, 'Dolphus Ross," he broke out angrily, "this hyar ain't no way ter go ter apperhend criminals, a-hollerin' like a plumb catamount through the woods."

"I don't want ter s'prise nuthin'," said the crafty deputy sheriff, "that is nuthin' unyearthly, on its yerrands what no mortial knows about, an' mebbe git s'prised myself plumb down ter the doors o' the pit. Ye know them ez sees harnts either draps down dead or loses thar minds, one. They 'low now'days ez all the crazies kem so from seein' sperits. An' ye know yerse'f, an off'cer of the law needs brains."

"Ef ye don't know yer bizness no better 'n that, I be goin' ter l'arn it ter ye. Ye 'pear mo' like a jay-hawker 'n a off'cer o' the law," retorted the other tartly.

But not even with this rude touch upon the sensitive nerves of official pride could he control the elusive and slippery deputy. " That 's a fac', Pearce. But the truth is, I be all-fired 'feared in these hyar lonesome places, whar humans air seldom an' few, o' seein' suthin' or hearin' suthin' what no mortial eyes or ears air expected ter see an' hear. So I like ter hear the sound o' my own voice, — let 'em know I 'm a-comin'. Even with two or three men with me, it 's so darned fur an' lonesome ! I 'pear less like a harnt myself, an' less apt ter meet up with one, ef I make myself sorter lively. I 'm a mighty quiet cuss in town. I 'm a—   What 's — what 's that ? " he broke off sharply.

He drew rein suddenly, throwing his horse back upon the haunches. The two men behind him, coming forward at the swift pace he had set, collided heavily with the obstacle thus furnished them, a reckless proceeding here on the narrow rocky road, on the verge above the abysses of the valley on one side, and with the inaccessible heights of the mountain rising sheerly on the other. They stood between heaven and earth, on this craggy beetling promontory, with the pulsating white stars above and the dark depths of the gorge below. His sight becoming more accustomed to the night, Espey could distinguish through the clear darkness the fringed branches of a pine-tree clinging to the heights above and waving against the instarred sky, and below a vague moving whiteness which he knew to be the involutions of the mist in the valley. He too had drawn up his horse, slightly in advance of the others, and was looking forward in keen expectation of developments.

"What's what?" he demanded of the deputy, who was managing his rearing horse with considerable skill.

"Something white — beckonin'," gasped the officer of the law.

Espey, with all the ignorant superstitions of his class, felt his blood run cold. Nevertheless he sought to reassure himself and his comrades.

"Jes' these elder-flowers, mebbe," he said, breaking off a great bough from a bush rooted in a crevice of the crag, and so profusely blooming that the black night itself could hardly nullify its whitely gleaming graces. He received full in his face the cool spray of the dew and the sweet breath of the flower, all unheeding, for the officer again protested in a loud, broken voice: —

"Beckonin' — beckonin' — Oh, my friends, somebody in this crowd is a sinner ; somebody hev done wrong ! An' he may be a saint in the church-house, or leastwise familiar with the mourner's bench, — an' he may escape jedge an' jury, — an' he may cheat hemp, — but in the dead o' the night an' in the lonely paths o' yearth he 'll be betrayed by a v'ice, or he 'll see a beckonin'" —

"Oh, shucks !" interrupted the believer in "harnts." "I 'm a-goin' back ter Mis' Lar'bee's." He was essaying to wheel his horse on the narrow ledge.   " 'T ain't my bizness ter go 'long with ye, ter apperhend crim'nals in the middle o' the night. Ef ye can't take 'em in the daytime, go 'thout 'em, I say."

" Some truth in that.   I wisht I could jine ye," said the deputy. " But my jewty lies ahead.   I be bound ter go on ; an' I reckon it can't be so fur from Tems's now, — air it, frien' ? " he asked, turning to Espey.

With a sinking heart, Espey replied that it was not very far, and the wonder as to what lay before him in the unknown scenes to which he sped in such haste reasserted itself in his mind, as the deputy rode briskly up alongside once more.

It required, perchance, only a moment's reflection on the inexpressible loneliness of the miles of mountain woods, that must of necessity be traversed before the shelter of Mrs. Larrabee's house could be reached, to change the design of the deserter from the little party.   The beat of his horse's hoofs annotated his continued presence, which was soon made even more indisputable by his raucous voice again lifted in remonstrance.

" Ye mus' see, now, 'Dolphus, ez n'ise an' ribeldry an' gamesomeness don't purvent ye from viewin' sech ez ye air intended ter view.   Sech goin's-on ain't lawful fur citizens, much less off'cers o' the law."

" Ye ain't gone back, then ? " commented 'Dolphus over his shoulder.

There was no answer to this, and after a pause the facetious deputy went on : —

"*I* ain't fur hollerin' an' rampagin' an' sech. *I* be a mighty quiet cuss in town, like I said, — a mighty quiet cuss indeed. The old man," he alluded thus to the high sheriff, " he sez ter me sometimes, ' I dunno, 'Dolphus, whether ye air in yer skin or no. Ye jes' 'pear ter be settin' thar, 'sleep or dead.' Wunst he tole me ez I war n't mo' lively 'n jes' a suit o' clothes hangin' outside the store door, an' a suit would cost less 'n my pay ez a dep'ty. I tried ter brace up arter that."

He had braced up considerably from the quiescent state he described if the sudden yell that he emitted might be received as evidence of his more stalwart condition. The sharp exclamations of surprise from the rest of the party afforded him intense delight, which was not mitigated by a blood-curdling shriek, as it were in response, set up by a catamount on the opposite heights, so close at hand by the direct line across the spaces above the valley through the air, despite the intervening miles of trackless mountain desert below, that they could hear the creature snarl before it lifted its thin, keen, inarticulate voice shrilling again into the black night.

There was no definite remonstrance, for he forestalled their outbreak, beyond a few words, by declaring tumultuously that he saw it again, — something a-waving, a-beckoning.

"No use talkin'!" he exclaimed. "The guilty sinner is 'mongst us, an' hyar he be!"

He leaned out of his saddle and passed one arm around Espey, pinioning the young fellow's right arm to his side. Espey, startled beyond control, despite his expectation of this contingency, with which, however, hope and suspense had juggled painfully, detected with sharpened senses the dull clanking of handcuffs. He hardly knew how it came there, he had no definite intention of resisting arrest, but a pistol was in the hand over which the rude wristlets dangled; a jet of red light that showed the dark-eyed, laughing, grimacing face near to his own, the whizzing of a bullet so close between the officer's side and arm that the blazing powder singed and burned his "store clothes," an abrupt report, and once more the night, rent by the sound, clamored with echoes.

From the dense darkness the officer's voice, with a changed tone, a sharp note of surprise, was crying, "Look out! Look out!"

The other men were stunned with amazement. They had only a vague sense of struggling mounted figures which the darkness did not suffer them to descry. And suddenly a second swift funnel-shaped glare for an instant invaded the gloom, — it came from the officer's pistol this time, — a second clamorous report rang amongst the rocks. The frightful, almost human scream of a wounded horse, a wild plunging on the side of the rocky bridle-path, and Espey and the yellow roan disappeared over the verge of the cliff. The three men standing in the road, hearing with sickening horror the dull thud far below, might judge of the terrors of the fall by the time elapsing before the sound reached their ears.

VIII.

THE household at the Tems cabin were keeping late hours that night. Except for a certain reserve of cogitation, which at times held him silent with a burning thought in his eye, his superficially moving lips framing unspoken words, and occasionally a keen, sarcastic smile irradiating his features with the light of some satiric expectation, Cap'n Lucy had resumed his wonted aspect and mental attitude and the habits of his simple existence.

"Ye fetch yer book out'n yer pocket," he said imperatively to Jasper Larrabee early in the evening, when the young man had joined them on the porch. "The gals ain't goin' ter run away, — leastwise 'thout cornsider'ble mo' incourage*mint* 'n they hev hed. They 'll keep! Ye jes' sot awhile by that thar taller dip in thar an' read yer book, an' I 'll listen out hyar."

The penalties of the acquisition of knowledge, from the days of the Garden of Eden to those of the hero of the horn-book, have not been few. They fell somewhat heavily on Jasper Larrabee, debarred the fresh air, heavy with perfumed dew; the vicinage of dank vines; the glimmer of the firefly in the bosky gloom; the scintillating stars in the sky above the massive mountains; the sweet, low voices of the two girls, silenced now; and the trivial chatter so dear to the heart of youth. The room, with the low red glow of the embers, was warm to-night; the tallow dip melted and sputtered and cast a wan, melancholy, ineffective radiance into the dusky spaces, rendering the aspect of the familiar furnishings strange and spare and dull, instead of all ruddily a-flicker with the dancing firelight in which he was accustomed to see them. Even the dogs had deserted the hearthstone, and went in and out with lolling tongues, and hot, sleepy eyes, and an inattentive manner. Moths and strange winged fire-worshipers, unknown to his observation hitherto, would fly in from the cool darkness without, circle swiftly about the white jet of the candle, and now and then, with a sudden dart, would fall, shriveled cinders but for the convulsive throes of lingering life, on the page of the volume.

He wondered sometimes, as he droned on and on, if Adelicia were listening, or if Julia could see him from where she sat. From the lighted spaces he could not distinguish their shadowy figures, albeit Cap'n Lucy, close at hand and with the red glow of his pipe, was plain enough. Sometimes Larrabee felt the vague sense of a gaze fixed upon his clear-cut face, all etherealized, illumined by the soft pallid white light within against the brown shadows. He was unaware of any valid embellishment of his aspect from the pensive gleam, the irradiated square of the window, the ascetic gravity of his expression, intent and pondering on the longer words, which it was his pride that he need not pause to spell. On the contrary, he was often conscious of cutting a sorry figure when Cap'n Lucy, with the rigor of a most rational reason and all the fervid insistence of a personal interest, would plunge at him, and require him to recant, to spell out syllable by syllable some questioned dogma, and at last, with all the nonchalance of a sophisticated theologian, take refuge in the equivalent of a plea of mistranslation.

"Ye can't haffen read, boy!" he would exclaim roughly. "Ye don't read ekal ter what ye hev done. Keep on goin' back'ards, an' ye'll git thar arter a while. 'Agree with thine adversary!' My stars! ef ye war wuth a grain o' gunpowder, ye could see ez that air obleeged ter be '*Dis-*agree with thine adversary.' It stands ter reason! '*Dis*-agree' with him, early and often, else the dad-burned critter will git up the insurance ter disagree with you-uns. I know thine adversary! Been 'quainted with him this many a year! Read on, read on, Jasper; git shet o' thine adversary."

Thus it was that, with the shadowy, snarling, intent old face vaguely visible in the dusk, just at his elbow, outside the window, ready to spring forward at the first intimation of an unacceptable doctrine; with the sense of responsibility for all the biblical dogmas irreconcilable with Cap'n Lucy's tenets and the tenor of his way; with the spectacle of glamour, lure, catastrophe, and death furnished by the unrestrainable moths, Jasper Larrabee found his preëminence of learning a comfortless pinnacle, and even the wonted sweet solaces of complacence in his superiority were denied him. He was forced to appear before the eyes of his lady love as an ignorant pretender, of ridiculous and inadequate assumptions, — and that by a man who could not read his own name, — humiliated and browbeaten; for how dared he answer Cap'n Lucy? More than once he wished himself back at the Lost Time mine, where he knew Espey thought him to be, and where Lorenzo Taft needed him. The work, unpalatable as he often found it, would be welcome indeed, and his untutored, unquestioning, often inattentive audience there a happy exchange from Cap'n Lucy in the character of polemic. He made some effort to shift the subject, to turn from the preceptive and doctrinal pages upon which he had chanced to fall to the chronicle of events in the nature of historical detail, as less liable to elicit Cap'n Lucy's contradictory faculties. It availed him naught. Cap'n Lucy's interest was fairly roused, and he imperatively negatived the proposition. The guest felt, still later, that it was not hospitality in its truest sense which so flatly declined to heed the suggestion of departure. And thus constrained, he read on, so conscious of the shadowy face at his elbow that he seemed to see it, with the light of excitement in the wide blue eyes, the alertness in

every line, the lips intently parted, the glow of the
pipe dying out as it was supported motionless by
the uplifted hand.

"Hey!" shrieked out Cap'n Lucy suddenly, as
if he had been poignantly pinched. "Ef he takes
yer coat, gin him yer cloak! Jasper, ye air demented! Ye ain't 'quainted with the dad-burned
ravelings out o' the alphabit, let alone the weft of
it! My sakes!" in an outraged falsetto, "ye
tell me that 's sot up ez Christian doctrine in the
Book! Take yer coat, gin yer cloak! Whar 's
the man ez hev done it! Trot him out! Great
Moses an' Aaron! I 'd like ter look at him! Take
yer corner-stone an' monimint o' boundary, an' gin
him yer line an' yer lan'!—ha! ha! ha! Let
him take yer rock known ez Big Hollow Boulder,
an' gin him yer corner-stone! — ha! ha!"

Luther rose precipitately. The significance of
the paternal discovery of the removal of the corner-stone was fraught with great perplexity and
foreboding, and he hardly knew what ill-judged
disclosure was to follow. He had intended to interpose, albeit he scarcely had a pretext. It came
to him at the moment.

"What 's that? I 'lowed I hearn suthin'!"
he exclaimed.

Cap'n Lucy turned upon him with the breathless acrimony of one interrupted in some cherished
pursuit.

"Hearn suthin'? Jes' the rustlin' o' yer own
long ears, — that 's all. I" — He stopped abruptly.

In the midst of his strident raised tones an alien sound smote his attention. There was an approach of horsemen from down the road. Cap'n Lucy's acrimony was merged in curiosity and excited expectation. Still holding his pipe, filled with dead ashes, as stiffly and cautiously before him as if its wonted coals glowed in the cob-bowl, he rose from his chair, and advanced a pace or two nearer the rude steps, peering out into the darkness. The two girls had turned their heads toward the sound. Larrabee was leaning on his arms in the window, and Luther had started down the path to the bars. His deep bass voice sounded in a bated, thunderous mutter, as he rebuked the barking dogs, whose menace subsided into low growls, punctuated now and then by a clamorous yelp. Perhaps the insistent tone of these canine threats influenced the newcomers, for it was at a goodly distance that the party called a halt and hailed the house.

Luther returned the halloo with a ringing response in kind, but Cap'n Lucy added a genial "'Light and hitch" to the unknown guest that the midnight had convoyed hither, his habit of broad hospitality all unmindful of the individuality or intent of the new-comers. "Me an' Luther air ekal ter all sorts," he would sturdily answer to the occasional remonstrance that times were not what they once were, and that he might thus "at sight unseen" be inviting in the marauder or the devil. "Me an' Luther air ekal ter 'em."

The tone of this hospitality seemed a sore-needed encouragement in this instance. Rodolphus Ross had flung himself, metaphorically, upon the fraternal bosom of Luther, as he hastily sought to summarize the misfortunes that had befallen him; the slow young mountaineer, all unprepared for so dramatic a recital, staring, uncomprehending and amazed, at his interlocutor, hardly knowing whether to ascribe his fluent diction to drink or to histrionic talents; as fact he did not take it into account.

"Yes, sir!" the wild-eyed Ross was saying as he came up the steps, "flung over the bluffs, horse an' all, — dead or alive, I dunno! Cap'n Tems, yes, sir; plumb proud ter shake hands," mechanically acknowledging the introduction to the head of the house. "Jes' purtendin' ter handcuff the fool, — jes' fur fun, — an' he fired at me! Yes, sir, fired at the off'cer o' the law! I dunno what ailed him, 'thout he thunk I war in earnest. But Lord! he war bound ter know I war arter another man. I tole him so. I hed nuthin' agin this hyar Lar'-bee. I war jes' purtendin' ter handcuff him, jes' shuck the bracelets at him, jes' fur fun, — ye know, Cap'n Tems, it's powerful dull an' drowsy a-ridin' so stiddy arter malefactors 'thout no sort'n entertainment or enjyemint, — an' this hyar Jasper Lar'-bee jes' ups an' fires at the off'cer o' the law, jes' scorched my clothes." He held up his arm, and caught the pallid light of the candle on his coat and powder-singed sleeve. "Not that I keer fur the josie, 'ceptin' it 's too durned near the meat fur thar ter be enny fun in shootin' through it."

He laughed in a constrained falsetto tone, — his wonted laugh, but with all the mirth eliminated from it. It had a sort of wooden quality, and ended with a nervous catch in his throat. The light falling through the window showed his dark eyes, set a trifle too close together, and the straight black brows meeting above them. His teeth gleamed, for the laugh left his lips mechanically distended. Larrabee, leaning on his folded arms in the window, a mere silhouette upon the pallid lustre of the aureola of the candle behind him, gazed silently on the stranger's face.

One is apt, in thinking of a man of experience, to associate sophistication with the idea. But life presents varied aspects of mental development, and the caution, the silence, the reserve of judgment, with which Cap'n Lucy hearkened might have seemed gleaned from the observation of the juggle of cause and effect in a far wider sphere. The two comrades of the deputy sheriff said not a word, and once more the officer began to elaborate the justification of his conduct.

" It takes a toler'ble stiff backbone ter set on a saddle an' let a man shoot at ye fur nuthin'. It 'stonished me powerful. I war jes' funnin', an' purtended ter be aimin' ter handcuff this young rooster, an' he jes' whurled roun' an' let the bullet fly. I b'lieve he 'lowed I war in earnest, yes, sir. This hyar Lar'bee hev been up ter suthin' agin the law, — moonshinin', I reckon, — else he would n't hev been so dad-burned handy with his fi'crackers."

" Why — why " — blurted out Luther, amazed at the lack of symmetry in the situation, and incapable of the paternal wisdom of silently awaiting developments, with the incongruity of the sight of Larrabee in the window mutely hearkening to the reflections upon the " Larrabee " who took so vehement a part in the officer's reminiscences — " 't war n't Lar'bee, mebbe ; some other fellow."

" Naw, sir," returned the deputy. " This hyar man," laying his hand on his bulky companion's shoulder, " knowed whar Lar'bee's mother, a widder lady, lived, an' we-uns called him ' Lar'bee ' an' ' Jasper,' an' he answered ter 'em both ; an' his mother called him ' Sonny.' He 's a wild-catter, sure. He 's " — He caught himself suddenly, remembering the prepossession against the revenue force which often animates even law-abiding citizens of this region. " But he need n't hev fired at *me !* I got nuthin' agin moonshiners. I b'long ter the County, not ter the Nunited States, — to the County ! "

" Whar 's this man now ? " demanded Cap 'n Lucy circumspectly.

The alert, sinister face of the deputy changed. But he sought to bluff off the anxieties and conscious criminations which crowded upon him. He swung his hat, which had a bullet-hole in it, gayly in his light grasp, and his dark eyes twinkled as he met the gaze of his host.

" Ye air a powerful good hand at axin' riddles, but this 'n air too hard fur me! I *dunno*, an' these men *dunno!* I fired back in self-defense at the miser'ble fool — I hed been funnin' all along, cap'n. I shot his horse, I know, an' the critter slipped, an' the whole caboodle went back'ards over the bluffs — an' — an' — he mought be dead or alive — Air — air that a cheer?"

He had suddenly lost his self-control; he sank back into a seat and seemed gasping for breath.

The details of their immediate errand thus devolved upon his comrades, — a lantern and a guide to search the slope where the victim of the deputy's pleasantry had fallen.

" 'Dolphus air sech a turrible bouncin' wild buck," said his friend from " the t'other e-end o' the county," who had begun to resume his remonstrant air, as of " I-told-you-so." He was a slow and serious-minded man, with a scant appreciation of even the most symmetrical jest, but when the joke seemed furnished with such distortions of sequelæ his gravity grew aggressive. " 'Dolphus kin crack a toler'ble funny joke wunst in a while, but this hyar one air goin' ter make him laff on the t'other side o' his mouth."

" Who war it ez ye war arter, sure enough?" asked Cap'n Lucy.

" A stranger what they 'lowed war puttin' up with you-uns, Cap'n Tems."

" Hey?" cried Cap'n Lucy, with a high quaver of excited delight. " He hev gone; but, my stars!

what a hearty welcome ye mought hev hed with him ! "

"What 's he done ? " demanded Larrabee, speaking for the first time, addressing the friend of the deputy.

"Shot a man in Tanglefoot Cove," he replied, looking somewhat intently at the silhouette in the window.

" What did ye 'low his name war ? " asked Larrabee, placing one hand behind his ear as if he had not heard what indeed they had not disclosed.

"Espey, — John Espey from Tanglefoot, o' course. He hev been hidin' out cornsider'ble time."

There was a sudden significant silence which the stranger felt, but did not comprehend. Then Cap'n Lucy, recovering his poise, remarked : —

" Waal, the stranger ez we-uns hev hed hyar air named Kenneth Kenn'ston, from Bretonville. He air a town man, an' aimin' ter build some sort'n tavern in the Cove."

The three men — for the officer was himself again — looked at one another with the pathetic helpless disgust of hunting dogs on a false trail.

It seemed that their quest was hopeless from the beginning, and in its interests they had deeply involved themselves in the toils of the law which they sought to aid.

" Waal," said the deputy's friend, " we-uns hed better git the lantern, an' take ter the woods agin an' find the corpse," — the deputy winced at the word so palpably that even his sturdy, literal-minded companion was moved to seek some euphemism ; " leastwise find out what 's the damage we-uns hev been an' done."

His stolid, unflinching shouldering of such responsibility in the matter as might fall to his share was oddly contrasted with the nervous excitement and agitation of the man from the Gap, who had served as guide to the party to Mrs. Larrabee's house.

" Waal, *I* ain't done none o' the damage," he protested, nodding his head emphatically. " I thunk I hed ter kem along o' the off'cer o' the law whenst required. I hed no idee o' junketin' 'roun' with the wildes' buck this side o' hell, a-caperin' like a possessed lunatic, an' a-shootin' of 'spectable citizens off'n the bluffs. Jasper Lar'bee done nuthin' ter me, — never laid eyes on him afore. *I* done none o' the damage. I call ye ter witness, Cap'n Tems, ez I hed nuthin' ter do with his takin' off."

Cap'n Lucy, always adorning the opposition, gave a high, fleering laugh. " *Me ter witness!* Me ! Why, man, I been settin' hyar sence dark, a-readin' o' the Holy Scriptur's. I hev no part in yer ridin' an' raidin'."

That repulsion to the idea of taking life, and all its ramifications of moral responsibility, apart from the legal consequence, natural to the civilized man, had yielded in the deputy sheriff to his habitual mental impulses. His wild, fierce, shallow personality was in the ascendant once more.

" I 'll guarantee ye, Bob," he declared, with his wonted swift smile of dark eyes and red lips and lifted meeting eyebrows. " Ef the g'loot is dead, he died resistin' arrest by the off'cer o' the law. Ef he be 'live, I be durned ef he don't hev cause ter resist the off'cer o' the law, fur I 'll swar ter glory I 'll nose out what this hyar Jasper Lar'bee hev been a-doin' of ter be so monst'ous afeard o' the bracelets bein' put onto him, — murder or moonshinin', it 's all the same ter me. I 'll set the bloodhounds o' the law onto him, sure! He hain't gin me sech a skeer ez this fur nuthin' ! "

As the blood came surging hotly along its accustomed channels, his fury mounted higher. It jumped with his humor to threaten as living the man who he feared was dead. He sought to spurn that possibility from his consciousness. It renewed his confidence in himself, too, to protest so jauntily that if the man had lost his life it was in resisting the law legitimately enforced. He reviewed, with a burst of anger, the fright of the other two men and his own anxiety that had suffered this lapse of attention to his own interest, and allowed the true detail of the case to be rehearsed here publicly. Naught could obliterate this; naught could justify him save to prove that the surprised Jasper Larrabee had been guilty of some offense against the law, and was resisting arrest legally attempted.

" I 'll fix him! I 'll follow him like a bloodhound! I 'll nose him out and pull him down!

Bless God, I will!" he cried out with sudden vehemence. Then he turned roughly to his two companions. "Kem on, ye two mud-turkles! Ye got jes' about ez much life an' sperit ez a couple o' old tarripin. Stir yer stumps, bubby," to Luther. "Git yer lantern, an' bring yer slow bones along ter aid the off'cer o' the law! An' ye, too, my frien' in the winder, ez quiet ez a cat stealin' cream; ye 'pear ter be young an' able-bodied. I summons ye ter kem an' aid the off'cer o' the law!"

The tallow dip, which had been for some moments sputtering in the socket of the candlestick, suddenly flared up with a wide illumination, then sunk as suddenly almost to extinction, feebly rose again, and, in a gust of wind, was extinguished, leaving a tuft of red sparks on the drooping wick, and a pervasive odor of burning grease in the room and porch. Perhaps it was because of the brighter light for the moment, perhaps because of the keener observation of the officer, whose faculties were once more well in hand, but no one else had noticed a strange stillness in the figure of Adelicia, as she sat in her wonted place on the edge of the floor of the porch, leaning back against the post.

"One o' yer darters hev fainted, I b'lieve," he said to Cap'n Lucy. "Suthin' ails her." Then, turning away, "Kem on, fellers; mount an' git out'n this. We-uns hev been hyar too long now."

As Jasper Larrabee rode away in the little troop toward the scene of the disaster, to search for the body of the supposititious Jasper Larrabee, his mental faculties began to recover from the torpor of surprise which had benumbed them. That cautious self-control which sometimes seems an added faculty in a certain type of law-breaker had held him mute as he watched the development of events. Now, as he began to take cognizance of the disclosures of the evening, he adhered of sober intention to the policy he had intuitively adopted. He feared the acknowledgment that he had received and harbored Jack Espey, a fugitive from justice, more than the acrimonious search of the deputy sheriff for the misdeeds of Jasper Larrabee. This, indeed, might result in his apprehension for the violation of the revenue laws, and the discovery of the moonshiner's lair, and this would mean many years of imprisonment; but the other might involve him, and possibly his mother as well, in a trial for murder, as accessories after the fact. It might be impossible to establish their ignorance of Espey's crime, and their lack of connivance in his escape. He had that pervasive terror of the law, as of technical and arbitrary construction of crime, common to the unlearned. His heart burned with rancor against his whilom friend. He would not recognize Espey's share in these ignorant terrors of the law. He argued that if his friend had been open with him, he would at least have been a free agent in receiving him, have had some voice in the degree of responsibility he assumed. As it was, his open-handed hospitality had been grossly imposed upon, and as a return he was given the choice of the jeopardy of a charge as accessory to a murder, or of an infringement of the revenue laws. He realized the whole drama as it had been enacted. He understood that Espey, conniving at the officer's mistake, and allowing him to suppose him to be Larrabee, had thus shielded his own identity as the fugitive from justice whom they sought. And this ruse Espey fancied was discovered, when the deputy, in his wild horse-play, had facetiously endeavored to handcuff him; he had therefore strenuously resisted, and thus had possibly come to his death. This possibility did not soften Larrabee toward him; perhaps he did not altogether accredit it at once, for death is difficult to realize even when a certainty. He dwelt upon his own danger, even more upon his mother's possible jeopardy; upon her untiring and laborious hospitality; upon his own labors which had rendered such entertainment practicable, for the money earned without her knowledge at the still went, much of it, to this pious use.

The sharpest sting of ingratitude is often the sense that the giver has been a fool. Larrabee harbored a surly grudge against himself as he rode silently on, and Luther, uncomprehending his friend's reason for not disclosing his identity, and suspecting that Jack Espey was the man they sought, was silent too. The loud voices of the

others in acrimonious criminations and recrimina-
tions accented the stillness of the night, and the
sound of their horses' hoofs as they filed along the
mountain passes, multiplied by rock and ravine,
and far echoes from distant heights, might have
seemed the march of squadrons of cavalry.

The skies had taken on that unfamiliar aspect of
the hours which straitly precede the dawn. Far,
far, on their pauseless way the constellations fared.
Stars were low in the west, which on these summer
nights had seemed the familiars of the meridian.
A strange sense of loneliness, of silence, pervaded
the firmament. The breathless pause that heralds
the miracle of dawn bated the pulses of nature.
No more song of cicada, no more stir of wind.
Once a meteor, with an incongruous irrelevance of
effect, shot athwart the sky with its gleaming trail
as of star-dust; the motion was like a sacrilege in
the holy stillness and breathlessness of the world.

And suddenly in the midst of the myriad scin-
tillations a brilliant white jewel was ablaze, which
Jasper Larrabee could have sworn was not there
before; pellucid, splendid, tremulous, a star of
stars. He knew the skies only as the herder or the
shepherd knows them in lonely, lowly paths of
earth, but even an ignorant man may feel that the
circuit below is narrow and the ways above are
wide, and the heart is lifted up. Not the name of
one of the stellular glories visible to the naked eye
could he syllable, but he had marked them all;
he was wont to dwell for hours upon their contem-

plation; he knew the contour of their most brilliant whorls and scintillating arabesques as he knew the intricacies of the woodland ways in the wilderness. He had drawn his horse hastily back upon the haunches, and again his eyes sought the alignment of the stars as his fancy had marshaled them. There was one more, — one that he had never before seen; one unknown to all the splendid nights that had ever shone upon the earth.

The voices of the men patrolling the slope below the point, where they had paused, rose excitedly on the still air. The horse was found, he gathered vaguely, dead, shot through the brain. The man was gone. The officer, in a frenzy of energy, beat the bushes far and near, lest the fugitive, wounded and disabled, might have crept away in the midst of them, and still lay hidden in the leafy covert. The hour wore away; the dawn came on apace, and, with the quest still fruitless, the officer presently mounted his horse and rode speedily off, fearing less, perchance, the review of his conduct by his superiors in the county town than the arbitration of the few citizens of the scantily settled region, who might take an inimical view of the disappearance of the guide of the jocose officer.

Only when the gray day came with the tremulous wind over the mountains, and the craggy ranges grew darkly distinct, and the unpeopled wooded valley distinct and vaguely drear, and the deep blue sky faded and was colorless, and one by one the stars noiselessly, invisibly slipped away without a trace, like some splendid promise never to be fulfilled, did Jasper Larrabee turn rein, perplexed and disquieted and greatly awed. For in his unlettered ignorance he had never heard of that simple fact known to astronomy as a temporary star.

IX.

In the days that ensued, no trace of the fugitive was developed. Cap'n Lucy experienced a certain relief in the fruitless result of the extended search instituted by the friends that Espey had made in the Cove. In their opinion the conclusion was inevitable that, despite the lack of his horse, he had made good his escape, and did not lie wounded or dead in the jungle of laurel, awaiting their humane succor, or burial at their hands. He was glad that Espey was gone, doubtless never to return, and that the matrimonial problem was gone with him. He was not quite frank with Adelicia in regard to this expectation. Her constitutional hopefulness instantly adopted the general belief of Espey's safety as fact, and she fixed her expectant eyes on the future with such fidelity of certainty that it seemed they must constrain the return she so definitely awaited.

"He 'll find out ez them off'cers 'lowed 't war Jasper Lar'bee, an' never knowed they hed *him*. An' then, uncle Lucy, he won't be 'feared ter kem back," she said many times a day.

"Course not," assented Cap'n Lucy. "He 'll be hyar afore long, jes' ez good lookin 'ez he knows how ter be."

It was perhaps a pious fraud, for the girl's despair and grief had been so wild that Cap'n Lucy was glad for her optimism to be reasserted on whatever terms, and to have the pleasant thing in the house once more.

Luther had necessarily been enlightened by the recent events as to the sentimental phase of the matter; for Cap'n Lucy had hitherto sedulously kept it secret, since he did not favor a fugitive from justice as a suitor for his niece, and was determined to break off the affair at all hazards. Luther looked with disapproval upon his father's crafty methods.

"I dunno what ails ye ter make Ad'licia b'lieve ez Espey will kem back," he once ventured to say aside to his father. "He air sure ter 'low ez they never tuk him fur Lar'bee, else he would n't hev tried ter break away."

"Luther," said Cap'n Lucy, "I hev noticed ez a man air obleeged ter hev a powerful strong stommick ter be able ter tell the truth at all times. An' ez I git old, I hev sorter got the deespepsy."

The son merely gazed at him with a sort of literal-minded bovine stare, as he sought to entertain this statement of the moral effect of debility.

"An' then, whenst I war a leetle boy," continued Cap'n Lucy, "I war bit by a rattlesnake; an' sometimes whenst I hear myself sayin' sech ez air agin the actual fac' it don't s'prise me none, fer I know it air jes' a leetle meanderin' o' the venom o' the sarpient in me yit, 'kase, ye know, he war a deceiver from the beginning."

What impression the strange and unexpected events had made upon the impassive and reserved Julia, none had taken thought to observe. The demonstrative, expressive characteristics of the other members of the household filled the domestic stage. It was only when the poignancy of Adelicia's grief and anxiety had given way to a resolutely patient and hopeful waiting, and Cap'n Lucy's vehement interest had subsided into a trivial occupation with the passing details of life, that it chanced to be noticed that Julia was wont to sit idle at her spinning, the thread in one hand, the other lifted as if to regulate the whirl of the motionless flax-wheel; her wonderful blue eyes fixed upon the distant purple mountains, glimpsed through the parting of the gourd vines above the porch; her head, with its smooth plaits of glossy hair, held up and alert; some unspoken thought upon her marble face that filled every still line with meaning.

"Ye 'pear ter be palsied, Julia," said the unobservant Luther, smoking his pipe on the porch one evening. "Ye hain't moved hand or foot fur a solid hour."

She started slightly at the sound of his voice, fixing her attention on him with obvious effort. Her mind was evidently coming back from distant removes, and Adelicia, with vague curiosity, demanded suddenly,—

"What air you-uns studyin' 'bout, Julia, whenst ye air lookin' like that?"

"Studyin' an' a-studyin'," said Julia, dropping her hands in her lap and leaning back in the chair, her eyes once more turning to the high, massive mountains afar off as if they possessed some magnetic attraction, "'bout'n whar pore, pore Jack Espey kin be now, an' how powerful cur'ous 't war ez ye would n't marry him whenst he axed ye."

The fore-legs of Luther's tilted chair came down to the floor with a thump. With a hand on either knee, and the cinders and burning tobacco dropping from his pipe unheeded to the floor, he sat fixedly staring at his silent sister. To his comprehension she was speaking her mind very unequivocally now. Despite the vaunted feminine quickness, Adelicia heard in it only personal upbraiding, for a certain remorse had made her sensitive on this score, and prone to protest her constraining dutifulness.

"I hed uncle Lucy's word agin it!" she exclaimed, with a rising flush and angry bright eyes.

Julia slowly shook her head, her eyes, her thoughts, far, far away. "I would n't hev keered fur no 'uncle Lucy's' word," she declared iconoclastically. "I reckon, ef the truth war knowed, dad hisself married ter suit his own taste. Leastwise, I ain't never hearn o' no old uncle or aunt or dad, or sech kinfolks, ez ondertook ter make a ch'ice in marryin' fur him."

"Waal, sir," Luther interposed, in a tone of shocked propriety, "settin' up hyar an' talkin' by the yard medjure 'bout marryin' an' men-folks, an' I 'd bet my best heifer that Jack Espey ain't gin air one o' ye a single thought sence he lef' hyar. No, nor nare 'nother man. Ef the truth war knowed, ye hain't got a haffen chance apiece, — without it air 'Renzo Taft, down yander at the Lost Time mine, an' he can't make out which air the hardest favored 'twixt ye! Ye hed both better go ter work. Jack Espey 'll never kem back agin. Dad jes' say he will ter pledjure Ad'licia. An', Julia, ef ye don't spin up that thar truck," — he pointed with fraternal imperiousness at the wheel, — " ye 'll be toler'ble scant o' new clothes, an' ye 'll look wuss like a skeercrow 'n ye do now."

Julia received this taunt to her beauty with the equanimity of one whose title is unimpugnable; but Adelicia, all unheeding any subtler sense than the obvious meaning his words conveyed, protested against even this conjectural banishment of poor Jack Espey. He would come back, she declared. He had doubtless found out by this time that he was mistaken in supposing the officers cognizant of his true identity, and that they were jesting, thinking him still Larrabee. And now that the nine days' wonder had blown over, and people were interested in it no more, and so much was going on in the Cove to usurp public attention, she looked for him any time just to slip back in his old place. " I never kem out on the porch but I look ter see him in that thar cheer whar Luther be. I hev 'peared ter see him thar."

" That ain't the way I 'pear ter see him," said Julia suddenly. " I dreampt he war a-kemin' on his claybank horse, a-lopin' down the road, a-wavin' his big white hat at we-uns like he done that day he kilt the wolf an' fotched home the pelt. That 's the way I view him ever sence I dreampt that dream."

" Then ye hev the nightmare," said Luther, surly and helpless to stem the tide of sentiment, " an' ye hain't got no mo' sense sleepin' than wakin'; fur that claybank roan will lope down these rocky roads no mo', partly through bein' dead, an' partly through old Miser Miggins hevin' gone down the gorge an' tuk off the critter's shoes. Ye better content yer-self with the claybank roan ez a nightmare, fur ye ain't goin' ter view Espey an' the critter a-lopin' round no mo', no matter how much be a-goin' on in the Cove."

For the Cove was indeed in a phenomenal fer-ment. To the astonishment of the leisurely and dilatory mountaineers, the work on the new hotel had begun, and was being pushed forward on paral-lels inconceivable to their ideas of progress.

Cap'n Lucy, his mind recalled to his more im-mediate personal interests, watched it with a sort of avidity of observation from the porch of his own house, where he was wont to sit with his pipe. His sneer, his silent laugh, his acrid enigmatical phrases, grew frequent as the blasting for the cel-lars proceeded, and the flying fragments of rock, which had elicited such formidable prognostication, fell far short of his cabin or his inclosures, indeed seldom coming to the ground beyond the jungle of laurel at the base of the great natural terrace, the site of the work.

" He did n't git the edzact range, Luther," he would say in affected surprise ; or, sarcastically, " This hyar Kenn'ston would hev made a powerful spry gunner in the old war times, — sech a eye for distances ! "

Adelicia, observing the circumstance, also remembering Kenniston's expressions of fear for their safety, only saw cause for gratulation.

" Mr. Kenn'ston 'lowed ez we-uns mought hev ter move an' leave home whilst the blastin' war goin' on ! " she exclaimed. " An' he made a powerful mistake, uncle Lucy."

" So he did," said Cap'n Lucy, with a twinkling eye. " He air a great man fur movin' ginerally. He b'lieves in movin' things."

Luther, remembering the peripatetic corner-stone and the impending processioning, understood the allusion, but he had a foreboding of trouble, and his heart sunk within him. He was glad when the blasting was concluded, which it was shortly; for he feared a premature or ill-advised accusation, and it seemed to him that the meaning of those thinly veiled sarcasms must presently be revealed to others as well as to himself. The foundations were laid, and the framing of the building followed promptly; soon the gaunt skeleton of the hotel, an outline of modern frivolity and summer pleasuring and flimsy vastness, was incongruously imposed upon the silent, solemn mountain behind it, with the rugged, austere crags below it; with the unfamiliar mists shifting through it and drifting along corridor and ball-room and scaling the tower; with its prophetic shadow, like a line engraving, flung by the moonlight on the dark surface of the top of the dense forest below. More than once furious mountain storms assailed it; but its builder's philosophy had taken account of these inimical forces, and it held fast.

The unbroken mountain wind, however, played havoc with the light shanties of the workmen in this exposed situation on the promontory of rock, and when rebuilt the camp was moved below the terrace, down in a sort of gorge, shielded and safe, albeit the distance from the work was a matter of some inconvenience.

They proved civil folk, the town mechanics, and answered gravely many a queer question put from a vast distance in civilization and sophistication, albeit at arm's length from the natural body; for from far and near the mountaineers visited the unfinished structure. Often a wagon with a yoke of oxen would stand, the patient beasts humbly a-drowse, for an hour or so in the sandy road, while the jeans-clad owner would patrol the new building, solemnly stepping from timber to timber over the depths of the cellar, or with the utmost simplicity of assurance make a critical circuit about the whole, and offer suggestions looking toward improvements. Sometimes the visitor was of shyer gentry: a red fox was glimpsed early one morning, with brush in air, speeding along the joists of the ball-room; it might seem they would never know the weight of aught more graceful or agile ; a deer, doubtless a familiar of the springs, was visible once, leaping wildly down the rocks in great elastic bounds, evidently hitherto unaware of the invaders of these preëmpted sylvan wilds. Others, too, of the ancient owners of the soil came on more prosaic quest, but in the dead hour of darkness or the light of the midnight moon. A young bear, who had long harbored predatory designs upon a certain fat shoat, a denizen of that pig-pen of Cap'n Lucy's upon which the owner and Mr. Kenniston looked with such differing eyes, was brought to a pause, in a cautious reconnoitre, by the fragments of food, scraps from the workmen's dinner, which might be found by nosing about among the shavings. Perhaps it was this alone that led him about the angles and turns of the building; but as he went between the sparse substance of the timbers and their scant linear shadows that, in the sorcery of the moonlight, appeared hardly less real, he seemed as censorious a critic as Cap'n Lucy himself. Sometimes he would pause in his clumsy shamble, and, with the moonlight a-glitter in his small eyes, lift himself on his hind feet and gaze about the solitary building, indescribably melancholy in the loneliness and the wan, pensive sheen; grin with his white teeth, a-gleam with a sarcastic, snarling contempt; fall to all fours again; and, shrugging his heavy shoulders to his ears, scud along with the aspect of clumsy sportiveness common to his kind.

It chanced that a light, portable forge had been in use that day, in the process of the work; the foreman had himself looked to the extinction of the fire, albeit the scene of the operation was upon the solid rock, and far from any possible communication with the building. The wind could never have turned over the low apparatus set in the hollow of the ledges, but the bear could, and did. Then he sat down suddenly to lick his singed paw, for the metal was still hot. The fuel had been charcoal; it still sustained heat, and even combustion. There was a steady spark in a few of the scattered cinders, quickening, reddening, as the eager night air touched them. The shavings amongst which they had fallen, further down the slope, were slightly astir for a moment; then a timorous blaze sprang up along the more tenuous, lace-like, curling edges.

How the destructive element fared, whether by slow, insidious, fearful degrees, as of conscious but furtive evil intent, or as animated by a wild, tumultuous, riotous impulse, more and more rapacious with impunity, as of some turbulent, maddened thing escaping control, none but Bruin might say, for, save the impassive, neutral night, the event had no other witness. Before the flames had fairly taken hold of the studs and joists his cowardly fears had gained the ascendency over his gluttony. More than once he paused, in gnawing his trophy of a beef bone, to growl fiercely, his remonstrant, surprised eyes illuminated by this alien flicker. As

the skies began to redden, and the pale moonlight
to fail, and the great massive mountains to appear,
dark and weird, from the deep and silent seclusions
of the night, he left his booty and retreated toward
the verge of the woods, pausing now and again in
the dun-colored shadows, all veined with shifting
pulsations of red and white, to look with eyes aglow,
reflecting the fire, upon its ravages, growling
fiercely at times; then, with his recurrent fears,
setting out once more on a lumbering run.

Perchance the reflection flung upon the clouds,
all lurid and alight, before which the stars shrank
away invisible, apprised the traveler journeying in
far-away coves and ranges, or the herder of the
lofty solitudes of the balds, or the hunter in distant
coverts, of the disaster in progress before the nearest neighbors were roused. The angry glare of the
conflagration seemed to pervade the world, like the
vivid searching terrors of the red day of doom,
when the workmen, down in their sheltered nook
beneath the crags and the dense shadows of the
forest, discovered the untoward fate of their handi-
work. Into the crevices of the batten shutters of
Cap'n Lucy's glassless windows the keen rays at
last pierced, like some sinister, pestilential, dazzling sunburst, illuminating the homely scenes with
an uncanny flare, and displacing the broken dreams
with a terrified awakening.

Naught could be done. It might be accounted
a spectacle in some sort, — to watch the airy acro-
batic feats of the lithe flames leaping from beam to

brace, from joist to rafter, of the three tall stories, seeming of vaster proportions with all their detail illustrated in these living tints upon the subsidiary, flickering night. There was a series of wild, dancing, tangled blazes a-whirl in the lengths of the ball-room, white and red and orange and blue, an uncanny rout. High up on the battlemented turret a vermilion banner flaunted suddenly out to the moon, and then it was struck amidst a myriad of sparks, and the echoes clamored out against the crashing of the tower.

For days thereafter the smoking, charred ruin was the terminus of many a pilgrimage amongst the simple folk of the region, who had never beheld wreckage on such a scale. The idle workmen hovered about it, dispirited and anxious, awaiting orders. There was much mysterious talk of incendiarism, and a rumor pervaded the Cove that the matter had already been reported in this light to the authorities, and that Rodolphus Ross was on his way to the scene of action.

Cap'n Lucy, seated on the rocks about the limpid spring, at a comfortable distance from the hot, smouldering mass, smoked his pipe, as he contemplated it, in more placidity of mind than had for some time fallen to his share. He was not a man who would deliberately seek to injure his enemy in person or property; but Cap'n Lucy was eminently human, and he could but admire the wisdom of the uncovenanted dispensations of Providence, through which Mr. Kenniston's game was, as he conceived it, so handsomely blocked. He had a most buoyant sense of irresponsibility in the matter.

"I ain't so much as once spoke to the Lord 'bout'n that man," he said privately to Luther, as if his prayers must needs have been inflammable.

He was not the only one of the spectators who thought, in view of the magnitude of the ruin, that the whole project was necessarily ended, and who looked on Kenniston's invasion of the Cove as a thing already of the past. It was a matter of very general surprise when the "town man" suddenly reappeared upon the scene in a bounding fury, and, in the metaphorical phrase of the mountaineers, "primed and loaded for b'ar." They little dreamed how literal a reason he had to hold a grudge against Bruin.

X.

THE season seemed full of menace to the troglodytes of the Lost Time mine. The work went on about the still as hitherto, but with added precaution — various and vain, for the limits of their ingenuity had already been reached — and with a heavy sense of presage. The old moods that had prevailed here were gone, whether of brag and bluster, or wild hilarity, or jocose horse-play, or the leisurely and languid spinning of yarns to help the hour to pass. Even the industry of old Zeb Copley, the veteran of the force, was mitigated by sudden long pauses and a disposition to hearken fearfully for unaccustomed noises, and by eager and earnest urgency that the work should be pretermitted for a time. The youngest moonshiner of all felt it a dreary world to look at with sober eyes, and, despite his morose abstinence and surly staidness, a less discerning judgment than Taft's might have foreseen the brevity of this enforced drought and the danger of a relapse, with all his reminiscences at his thick tongue's end, were he free to fare about the world without. Espey's vacant place was ever significant of the reason for it, and Larrabee would sit for hours brooding over the untoward chances of his own fortunes ; his gloomy eyes on the ever-glinting line of light playing through the furnace door, his motionless pipe full only of dead ashes in his heedless hand.

" Ye air a toler'ble dangersome neighbor," Taft remarked one day ; for the complication of the mistaken identity had come to his ears during a sortie from his stronghold, and the threats of the deputy sheriff against the supposed Jasper Larrabee coupled with his suspicions as to moonshining.

Larrabee looked up fiercely. " Move, then, ef ye don't like yer neighbor."

He was like a fox run to earth ; he had no further resource. His one idea of dealing with the law was by evasion and subterfuge and concealment. He had no remote expectation of justification. By a series of deceits he had persuaded his mother to go on an immediate visit to a bedridden great-aunt who lived in an adjoining county. The horse she rode belonged to a neighbor of the aged relative, who chanced to be in this locality, and who was taking home with him a led horse, a recent purchase. Jasper himself was to go after her in the indefinite period when the corn should be laid by and her own horse at leisure. The infant conqueror of the rickets went with her, mounted behind her, his chubby arms stretched at their utmost length clasping her gaunt waist, and with as unchastened a vainglory and pride in the earnest of this great journey and the envious wonderment of the other children as if his bourne were the north pole. Thus Mrs. Larrabee set out, with the grim-visaged neighbor of the aunt in advance, and with a frisky, dapper colt — already *en rapport* with the pilgrim youth by reason of mutual juvenility, irresponsibility, and frivolity — kicking up his admired heels in the rear. And Henrietta Timson reigned in her stead under the queer little sylvan roof that seemed no more made with hands than the cups of a triple acorn.

Thus it was that Jasper Larrabee was roofless for the nonce, save for the strata of the Lost Time mine.

That Lorenzo Taft would fain be rid of him he saw grimly enough, and this he grimly refused to heed. He had incurred the suspicion of moonshining by reason of Espey's choosing to wear his name for an hour or so. He had incurred it through no fault of his own. The infringement of the law was common to them all, and involved a danger which they should share.

At all events, there would be nobody to answer for harboring the fugitive, should Espey's true identity become known to the law, and Rodolphus Ross find his way again to the little house on its airy perch. Taft had thought it wise that Larrabee, already tainted with suspicion in the mind of the officer of the law, and thus a source of great danger, should follow Espey to parts unknown. But the world, to the unlodged of earth, is doubtless of aspect like the face of the waters to the dove when first loosed from the ark, without foothold or friendly sign.

Larrabee replied even to the innuendo : —

"Go whar ? An' leave you-uns a-cuddled down hyar so snug in the groun' that the devil hisse'f will sca'cely nose ye out on the Jedgmint Day ? Naw, sir. I see nuthin' but resk fur me on all sides, but less hyar 'n ennywhars. I hev stood in ez much danger ez enny of ye. I hev tuk my sheer o' the resk 'thout wingin', but I won't be kicked out like a stray dog an' gin up ter the law 'kase you-uns air 'feared 'Dolphus Ross 'lows I be a moonshiner. He can't find or hear o' me hyar. I got ez much right hyar ez you-uns, 'Renzo Taft. I own my sheer in the business, an' hyar I be goin' ter 'bide."

The other two moonshiners, Copley and young Dan Sykes, regarded him askance and with sullen eyes. This minority might seem to be fraught with no small danger. His chief fear lest Espey should be overtaken, and the details of his refuge with the Larrabees be elicited, involving himself and his mother as accessories to the crime, he never mentioned. It so absorbed his thoughts, however, that for a time he did not observe a symptom of the antagonism of his confrères which deeply augured its seriousness.

A shaft hard by the still-room, if such the nook where the apparatus was worked might be called, which was sunk into the very deepest limits of the mine, came near relieving them of their perplexity on this score, one day. Larrabee's foot slipped in the rotting refuse of pomace on the verge while he was handling the bags of grain, and as he came heavily to the floor, barely saving himself, he saw like a flash a sudden irradiation of hope on the flushed, foolish face of the boy, a keen expectation in Taft's eyes, and even in the elderly drudge's wooden wrinkles a sort of disappointed resignation as he scrambled to his feet, that daunted him more than the immediate danger.

His precious book he read no more by the light of the furnace flicker, after this. Not that he now brooded over his cares, but his watchfulness never flagged. Whether the accident suggested the idea to Taft, or whether it were the flimsy fiction of the inimical atmosphere and his own alert apprehensiveness, Larrabee thought that he was given several opportunities to take leave inadvertently of the world. Once, in cleaning a pistol said to be unloaded, the ball in the last chamber whizzed sharply by his head. Again and again he was set to handle the heavy bags of grain on the slippery verge of the shaft. After a time a new cause of alarm was developed. Despite his crafty vigilance in his determination to remain at all hazards, he did not notice, until it became very marked, their unwillingness that he should leave the still at all, and Taft's expertness in disallowing every pretext. The truth dawned upon him at last, with its most valid reason. Although they would be glad were he to quit the country, yet, since his permanent absence could not be compassed, any chance excursion into the Cove or neighborhood was fraught with danger, as he might be seen, identified as Larrabee, and fol-

lowed by the man who had spotted him as a moonshiner to Taft's house, where, spending days and
nights, the mystery would soon be unfolded.

Larrabee came upon this discovery with a suffo-
cating sense as of a prisoner. Instantly he was possessed by a wild urgency for the outer air and the
freedom beyond that seemed as if its own impetus
might break through the barriers of a thousand feet
of the solid ground. He almost felt the wind blow
in the strength of his keen desire ; and when he set
himself instantly to compass his deliverance, eagerness outran tact in his first demonstration.

"Hello, 'Renzo," he said in a cheerful, incidental
voice, strikingly at variance with the gruff tones
that had of late served him in the absolutely essential colloquies between them touching the work.

Taft's keen senses instantaneously apprehended
the difference. He glanced around with a quick
eye, illumined by the feeble white gleam of the
lantern in his hand, for he had but just emerged
from the tunnel. He did not simulate. He looked
as he felt, interrogative, expectant, as he sat down
on the side of a barrel without pausing to extin-
guish the lantern. Its pallid glow suffused his
florid face and yellow beard, and brought out the
tint and effect of translucency in his blue eyes.
They were fixed steadily on Larrabee, who was
suddenly out of countenance. He had intended a
more casual disclosure of his project than the impending interview permitted, — a sort of unpre-
meditated announcement of his determination, as

of being free to do as he would.　He felt that his face had changed, and he knew that the change was noted.　A new rush of alarm seemed to surge through his nerves.　For, guarded as Taft evidently was, he too had betrayed somewhat the importance which he attached to the plans, even the words, of his employee, or his partner, or his prisoner, as Larrabee might be variously regarded.　It daunted Larrabee : the latent ferocity that lurked in Taft's character, repudiated in his burly good comradeship of manner and in his florid face, — save for a certain beaklike outline of the nose that gave a rapacious, cruel intimation, — was instinctively known to the young mountaineer, who was not skilled in the craft of a knowledge of his kind, and had no habit of analysis.　He somehow flinched to be made anew so definitely aware that he was a factor, and a troublous one, in Taft's schemes.　He felt no match for the elder tactician.　He wished he had gone long before, when the moonshiner sought so openly to be rid of him.　At all events, he would go now, and without chicanery or subterfuge.　He blurted out his plan, which he had intended to trench upon with great care and circumspection, and which should have appeared a natural evolution and outcome of the conversation.

"'Renzo," he said, with a distinct abatement of his former genial inflections, but still with a pliable, amiable tone, — and for his life he could not suppress an intonation of appeal, — "'Renzo, I'm a-studyin' 'bout takin' yer advice.　Ye air old'n me an' hev got mo' 'speriunce an'" —

" What advice ? " Taft interrupted succinctly. The sentence seemed very short in his big, mellow, sonorous voice ; it was like a key struck inadvertently on some great organ ; the heavy vibrations in themselves seemed to promise continuity.

" 'Bout goin' out'n the Cove. I been studyin' it all out, an' I 'low 't would be safer fur all consarned ef I war ter cut an' run."

Taft remained silent. His illumined eyes were glassy and fixed ; somehow, the absorbed, introspective thought seemed to eliminate their expression.

" Jes' cl'ar out," said Larrabee, as if in explanation ; he could not repress the manner of asking a permission, although he raged inwardly at himself.

" Whar'bouts ? " Taft's great voice boomed out once more as it were inadvertently.

" Ter Buncombe County in old Car'liny, whar I got some kinfolks a-livin'," said Larrabee. " That 's what I war a-studyin' 'bout," he added, still striving for a more incidental effect.

The furnace door was open, for the fire was low, the still but just emptied, and the work intermitted for the nonce. The bed of red coals filled the place with a dull glow. In its dreamy light he saw suddenly the broad, flabby face of Dan Sykes, the youngest of the moonshiners, distorted with silent mirth, like the face of a caricature. He sat upon a billet of wood in a lowly attitude, frog-like with his upturned head which was supported by his two hands, his elbows resting on his knees drawn high under his chin. His distended grin of evident delight in Taft's answer showed that it was not unexpected.

"Why, law, Jasper," exclaimed Taft, — but the unctuous tone would not mix with the lie of the intent, and floated in its midst like oil on water, — "I could n't make out *now*, jes' *now*, 'thout you-uns. I be short-handed now, 'count o' Espey, an' I got word ter-day from the cross-roads fur two barrels o' corn juice quick ez it kin be got thar. Yer kin in Buncombe," — his eye twinkled, for he suspected the kin in Buncombe to be of that airy folk known only to dreams and deceits, — "they 'll keep. Ye 'll hev jes' ter put off goin' fur a leetle spell, — bein' so short-handed, ye know."

"What air they aimin' ter pay fur them bar'ls?" demanded Larrabee calmly.

Thus he drew the conversation aside to the commercial aspects of the situation, as if he acquiesced in Taft's view, and recurred to his proposition no more. He controlled his voice, but his heart sunk like lead. He had not dreamed but that they would be glad to let him go if he quitted the region. He had not even feared that this resource was in jeopardy. He could not imagine the turn of events which must needs preclude his flight abroad, as well as his familiar appearance in his wonted haunts about the Cove. He cursed his fatuity again and again that he had not escaped when he could. What were the dangers of the world at large in comparison with the mysterious menace that environed him here? He dwelt continuously on these thoughts for a time, and it was only gradually, and chiefly by reason of Sykes's leering grin and secretly gleeful eye, that he became aware that this Benjamin amongst them had been specially deputed to watch him. In the days of his own terrors of the world without, he had ceased to go out for his meals or to sleep. He subsisted on " snacks " which Taft fetched down from his own table, — which abstraction caused no surprise to his small housekeeper, for Miss Cornelia Taft had long since exhausted her capacities for astonishment at any prodigies of food consumption on the part of her father, who took such big bites in comparison with old Mrs. Jiniway's custom, — and he slept at broken intervals, as his uneasy thoughts permitted, on the empty meal sacks in the shadow of the piles of barrels. This life continued now of necessity, as formerly of choice. Larrabee's apparent acquiescence, he had a vague idea, surprised and perturbed the others. They were evidently prepared for resistance and harsh measures. They had lost their balance in some sort; their attitude was like that of one who makes ready for a running leap, and stops short of the jump. Thus, their unsteady, balked surprise bore scant relation to their persistent, unchanged purpose, for their watch upon him was not for one moment relaxed. Even in the network of wrinkles about the sunken eyes of the elder distiller, a sort of staggered, dumfounded suspicion expressed itself, in conjunction with an observant heed of Larrabee's every movement which hitherto would not have been allowed to absorb so much of the attention he was wont to bestow on the still.

At first the discovery came near to breaking down Larrabee's reserve of endurance. His heart thumped so loudly, so heavily, that he sometimes thought they must hear its treacherous clamors as he sat and smoked in the dull red glow, assuming a calm and somnolent, satisfied aspect. Occasionally, with that terrible sense of the key turned, the door closed, the realization of restricted liberty, so overwhelming to the free habit of the mountaineer and the woodsman, with a charter to wander as wide as the wilderness, the blood would surge to his head, the copper boiler spin round and round, his companions slowly wheel about in that dim space of shadow and light; and he thought he lost consciousness at these times. But always when he came to himself he was sitting as before, calmly smoking in his wonted place, seeming a trifle disposed to shirk his work, perchance; and latterly he had begun to drink heavily, as it were upon the sly. He could not have said how the idea had come to him: it was not gradual; the scheme was full fledged in an instant. He knew that his every movement was under surveillance, and that he was under the special guard of the young drunkard, who had been longer sober now, perhaps, than for many a month. Dan Sykes watched with glistening eyes Larrabee's furtive hand reaching for the jug of whiskey, the trick of the hasty swallow aside, and presently Larrabee had a companion in his covert potations. He trembled lest the young fellow's scanty powers of self-restraint should not be adequate to conceal long enough to serve his plan the swift ravages of drink in his recent abstinence. He seemed insatiable and frantically keen of thirst, and the necessity of concealing his indulgence from Taft, who had evidently sent forth some fiat against it, developed an almost incredible deftness of craft. On the day that the liquor was barreled and removed, Sykes had been drinking almost without cessation. His share in the work was scant, his duties as guard serving in substitution. Perhaps for this reason, perhaps because of the absorption in the enterprise, neither of the two elder moonshiners noticed his condition; and indeed he had become singularly skilled in assuming a sort of veneer of sobriety. It passed muster in this instance.

Taft got away early in the night with his load, taking note, apparently, of nothing beyond some extra hazard of the enterprise, as Larrabee gathered from the caution with which he loaded his revolvers and his frequent conferences aside with Copley, who enjoyed his special confidence, being his near kinsman as well as coadjutor. The barrels were to be concealed in the wagon under bags of feathers, dried fruit, ginseng, and other strictly rural commodities of barter. Two barrels of innocent and saccharine sorghum found themselves, too, in the unholy company of those barrels that the still had furnished forth. It was somewhat difficult to make out the load. Copley was eager for it to be off, notwithstanding, but Taft persisted until all the probabilities had been satisfied. There was much passing back and forth in the tunnel; through its long lengths Larrabee could hear the commotion in the room beneath the store. When the preparations were completed at last, he knew as well as if he had seen it how the great white canvas-covered wagon looked, standing with its two stanch mules before the door of the store, under the early dusky night sky and the burly overhanging purple heights, the yellow light streaming out from the open door upon it, and all the cheerful bustle of departure rife as it were in the very air. Taft came back at the last moment for his coat. As he swung himself alertly into it, and crushed his big hat down on his big yellow head, he had all the breezy impetus of one who is about to start on a pleasant and successful journey.

" All loaded ! " he cried cheerfully. " A kentry merchant a-goin' ter buy goods can't be too keerful — oughter take along all the gear he kin ter trade — ha ! ha ! ha ! Good-by ! Take keer o' yerse'fs ! "

And thus he strode out with his light, elastic tread. Larrabee listened as it beat on the dirt path, and then to the echoes that duplicated its progress, till it ceased to sound.

Somehow the void about the circle was not without melancholy intimations, the normal incident of departure, whether it be regretted or cause for gratulation. Perhaps because of the sudden disordered quiet and loneliness in the quitted scene, the unoccupied mind must needs always reach forward into the unknown journeyings, meeting in speculation the varied events denied to the home-abiding. Larrabee sat still for a time in the low red glow of the furnace fire, exchanging now and again an incidental comment with his companions on the subject of the journey and its chances. The intervals of silence grew longer ; the shadows gathered and deepened ; the younger man's head occasionally nodded grotesquely in sleep, but more than once, as Larrabee was about to rise to his feet, he saw in the obscurity the large bloodshot eyes opened and fixed soberly upon him. He had waited long ; long for the certainty that Taft would not return on some forgotten errand ; long for the drunken sleep that must needs overcome the inimical vigilance of the young moonshiner. He could wait no longer. With an abrupt, shrill cry like that of a savage panther, he flung himself upon his elder companion. Copley was a man of powerful physique, and his every muscle was developed by the heavy labor in which it was exercised. In his undiminished strength his age gave no advantage to his adversary, whose slight bulk he might have flung from him with a single arm but for the surprise and suddenness of the attack in which he was borne to the ground. All Larrabee's strength hardly sufficed to hold him there for a moment. There was a fierce struggle ; a pistol ball whizzed by Larrabee's head, and the narrow precincts were filled with the echoes and with Copley's hoarse calls upon Sykes for help. The young fellow rose in response, stupidly echoing the cries of his own name, took one tottering step forward, and fell like a log, flabby, nerveless, helpless, on the floor. Larrabee wondered afterward that it could all be so quickly done. It was by virtue of surprise, desperation, sleight of hand, deftness, and quickness rather than by strength or courage. A meal bag served as a gag, and a rope, used in transporting the heavy barrels up the steep incline to the store, to pinion the arms and shackle the feet. Larrabee was almost exhausted by the capture of the first prisoner, and it was perhaps auspicious for his freedom that the young drunkard, beyond an ill-directed blow or two, could make no resistance. The rope was made fast around the solid masonry of the furnace; and as Larrabee contemplated his work, he felt sure that the two prisoners, one yet vainly struggling, the other already sleeping the sleep of the very drunk, would find no means of deliverance till Taft's return the next day.

Again and again in his durance Larrabee had pre-figured how swift would be his flight along the tunnel to the free outer air. Now he feebly plodded, and trembled, and faltered, and again went groping along the densely black way, essaying to keep a straight line, but feeling himself continually touching the wall, now on the right, and again on the left, in his zigzag course. Once he paused with an alert start. A sound of human voices had struck his ear, and at the merest possibility that his escape was not complete, certain, every flaccid, exhausted muscle was tense again. He lifted up his head, hardly breathing, that he might listen, but heard only the uncontrolled motion of his own heart plunging like an unruly horse. All else was silent in the black stillness of the deeps of the earth, save for the slight purling of the thread of a stream which farther on intersected the tunnel. No stir, no sound from the still-room, his late prison-house, where his jailers lay bound hand and foot ; and yet he had thought he heard voices — human voices — words — he could almost have sworn it. And suddenly the sound came again. This time he recognized it, — louder than its custom, more distinct, for he had heard it before, — the sound of the strange, unexplained voices that at long intervals were wont to reverberate along the tunnel of the Lost Time mine, and that were accounted by the moonshiners echoes from their own wrangles or mirth or talk as they toiled. He was certain that it did not come now from the still ; his fear that his work had been slack, and that his comrades were liberated, was without foundation, but an earthly rational fear is a wonderful exorcist of a ghostly terror. Otherwise, when he thought of it afterward, he felt that he must have been struck dead with the horror of it, when he suddenly heard, close at hand, the sound dulled by the dense medium of the earth, a word of command, as it were, in a

queer, strained, false-ringing voice, and then the
regular strokes of a pick cleaving the earth with a
workmanlike steadiness and precision. His blood
ran cold; for his credulity harbored no doubts.
It was the sound of the drowned miners, lost in
the flooded shafts, still vainly digging the graves
that the niggard earth denied them. The thought
mended his speed; he flew like a shuttlecock from
side to side of the narrow passage, where he could
but grope, for the lack of a lantern; and although
he often put forth his hands expecting to touch the
boards of the partition at the further end, he
thrust into his palms a score of the hairy splinters
of the reverse side of the rude puncheons long before he could have reasonably expected to reach his
goal. He observed none of the precautions and
silence common to the moonshiners in their exits
from the still; and indeed the feat was hardly expected to be attempted in the dense darkness. He
dropped one of the boards, and the deep, cavernous, clamorous echo coming up from the hollow
vaults below almost overwhelmed him, as it resounded again and again. He had lost control of
his nerves. He stumbled over the empty boxes and
barrels in the room beneath the store, tumbled up
the ladder, and as he clambered from the door
beneath the counter he realized for the first time
that the room was built, as were many of the
meaner cabins of the region, without a window,
depending on the door for ventilation and light.
This was a matter of precaution with Taft, and

being a not uncommon feature in the district occasioned no surprise ; but Larrabee trembled as he remembered that it was Taft's cautious habit to lock the door when he himself was not in the store. Feeling that the bars were in place against the battens, he was apprised that it had been thus secured by the worthies down at the still, and perchance the key was now in Copley's pocket. His only resource would be to retrace his way, all the toil and risk of his escape to be repeated. But no, the bolt turned in his hand, and as he stepped into the passage outside his eyes were dazzled almost to blindness by a tallow dip blazing in the hand of little Cornelia Taft, summoned by the noise to investigate its source. Behind her, looking over her head, was Joe's round, careless, plump face. Larrabee was little less staggered by the monition that there might be other persons at hand in the house than by the expression of Cornelia's prim, disapproving, unfriendly, intelligent little countenance. The next instant he cared for neither ; a salient change in the aspect of the cabin claimed his attention. The open passage between the two rooms had been boarded up, and a stout door fitted in, barred and bolted, on which gleamed a strong new lock. There was no key visible. He gazed at the lock with greedy eyes, silent, till the girl's question had been twice repeated.

" Me — doin' hyar ? Oh, I been doin' some work fur yer dad," he said, more at ease, for he had seen her occasionally as he came and went,

presumably in the character of customer, and he
detected recognition in her calm and non-commit-
tal countenance. "I got shut up in thar, — mought
hev been noddin', — an' I war 'feared the door war
locked." He advanced upon the outer door.

"Ye can't git out'n that one," said the little girl
coolly; "hit's locked on the outside, an' dad hev
goned away ter the cross-roads with the key in his
pocket."

Larrabee's first impulse was to try his strength to
burst it open, and once more that salutary monition
of the probable presence of others in the house controlled him. He turned toward the door of the opposite room, partly to settle this doubt, and partly
to discover — it had never before occurred to him
to notice — whether it had a window. The room
was vacant, and his eager eyes ranged the walls in
vain for an aperture.

"It's like a trap," he muttered, as he sunk exhausted into a chair. "What ails 'Renzo ter lock
up the house an' make off with the key, an' leave
you-uns inside by yerse'fs?" he demanded.

The two children had followed him into the room.
Joe stood by the door, holding by the frame, swaying back and forth, attempting some distortion of
attitude impossible to the human configuration;
but the little girl had seated herself staidly in a
chair opposite, and showed herself not averse to
conversation.

"'Kase thar be sech a lot o' strange, idle folks
in the Cove," said the prim Miss Cornelia, with an
expression of strong disapprobation.

Larrabee could not restrain an exclamation of surprise. It was indeed like a new world, the familiar Cove, so long he had been shut out of it.

"What folks?" he asked succinctly.

"Them ez hev been building the new hotel," said Sis. "Them, in course."

"What they doin' now? Ain't they buildin'?" he hazarded tentatively.

"Naw," — the small Cornelia Taft pursed up her lips contemptuously, — "jes' a-roamin' round the Cove in gangs, a-foolin' an' a-idlin', an', my sakes, a-drinkin' whiskey, thick ez bees!"

A new light was breaking in on Larrabee. Taft had at first desired that he should leave the Cove, — slip away quietly; now, since it was infested with a troop of scattered workmen, apparently out of a job, all of whom had doubtless spent an idle hour agape over the story of the supposed Jasper Larrabee, the last nine days' wonder of the Cove, — the facetious freak of the pretended arrest, the miraculous escape of the fall from the cliffs, the mysterious disappearance, the suspicion of moonshining, and the threatened vengeance of the deputy sheriff, — it was scarcely probable that he could get away without exciting notice which might lead to recognition, pursuit, and arrest. He was safer at the still, — this he himself admitted now, — far safer in the depths of the earth; except, indeed, for Taft and his fellows.

"Did you-uns see the fire?" demanded Joe suddenly, still writhing and twisting against the door frame. "*I* did!" in triumph.

"Ye would n't ef I hed n't a-woke ye up," said Sis, with acerbity. "I 'low ye did n't see much nohows, bein' so sleepy-headed."

Larrabee sat looking in surprise from one to the other, his questions anticipated by their eager relish of the subject.

"Dad never seen nuthin'!" cried the boy triumphantly.

"Dad would n't b'lieve thar war a fire till he went an' viewed the cinders of the hotel," said the girl.

The hotel! A sudden suspicion smote Larrabee, a recollection of the threat to burn the building which had originated amongst the moonshiners before a stone was laid in mortar or a timber lifted. He did the craft injustice in this instance; Taft and his associates had no part in the conflagration. But with Espey out of control, and Larrabee touched with the suspicion of moonshining, a chance word might fix upon the distillers this far more serious crime known to them both to have already been broached here. There was much reason for his detention, — too much. He must be going, and that shortly..

"I wonder ye all ain't 'feared o' burnin' up in hyar, locked up," he said suddenly, the catastrophe seeming to render the danger of fire more imminent, although he knew it to be the habit of the country folk to lock small children in when convenient to leave home without them.

The little girl's thin lip curled.

" Ef we-uns hain't got no mo' sense 'n ter set the house or ourse'fs afire, I reckon we 'd be wuth ez much roasted ez raw," she replied.

"Dad, he locked the door so we-uns kin tell them stragglers ez he be gone, an' they can't git in ter trade fur drink," put in Joe.

Larrabee said nothing more. He knew full well that the children were not so alone as they seemed, since Copley, who was their mother's half-brother, was wont to be in the store, in Taft's absence, often enough to be at hand should he be required to suppress any disturbance; and being a near relative, he had a personal interest in their safety. Miss Cornelia Taft was a fine combination of her father's shrewdness and her grandmother's preciseness. As Larrabee felt her small, discerning eyes studying him, he became conscious that he was looking about wildly and with manifest anxiety as to his next step. He made an effort to allay her dawning curiosity.

" Things look powerful nice an' cle'n up in hyar," he remarked casually.

He was unprepared for the effect of his words. If Miss Cornelia Taft had a soul, it was expressed in her housewifely instincts. In a dozen frantic and funny juvenile misconceptions, the precepts brought from Mrs. Jiniway's domicile were put into practice here. The basis of them all, cleanliness and an effort for order, was plainly apparent, and Sis spent the better part of her days in seeking to impress upon Joe's unwilling mind the value of

an occasional dish-washing, and the utility of wood
ashes in scouring. An evil day, Joe considered it,
when she came into his ragged, soapless, happy-go-
lucky life ; but Taft connived at their wranglings
over their primitive housekeeping and Joe's subjec-
tion. "Keeps Sis busy, an' lets me git on her blind
side, — ef she hev got enny blind side," he added
grimly.

Her pallid face flushed, her eyes sparkled; she
cast a glance of triumph at Joe, who had seated
himself in a chair, and was twisting his bare feet
in and out of the rungs in a way painful to witness,
if not to experience, writhing his body to and
fro, and rolling his head from side to side over the
high back of the chair in a restless frivolity of
motion that certainly had no family resemblance
to the staid "manners" which Mrs. Jiniway's
disciple exhibited.

She had entered volubly upon a detail of her
exploits here in reforming Joe's misrule amongst
the pots and pans and kettles.

"Dad 's so 'way from home, an' Joe 's so tur'ble
shif'less," she complained.

The task of redding up the Augean stables was
slight in comparison, one might believe, to judge
from her show of horror now and then, and there
was considerable difference between the size of Sis
and of Hercules. She had succeeded in reaching
some sense of culinary propriety in Joe, or pride,
for he now and again became sufficiently still to
look poutingly sullen, and to ejaculate, " 'T ain't

true!"   "'T war n't!" and similar disaffected negations.

"I l'arnt all that whenst I lived with my granny," she concluded her exposition of the true methods of dealing with the trivet and the skillet and setting the house in order. "An' when we war done, we 'd knit stockings an' tell tales."

"Tales 'bout what?" asked Larrabee, seeking to conciliate her, for he began to have a shrewd suspicion that she could aid him if she would. His interest was the more easily simulated, for he had a literary taste himself.

"Oh," she cried, with a little bounce forward, not unlike Joe's elasticity, "them in gineral we-uns hearn the rider read, — 'bout Sam'l."

"I hev read 'bout Sam'l," said Larrabee quickly, with an air of playing willingly to her lead; and indeed she had struck him on his strong suit. "An' old Eli. Eli war an able man, but he never 'peared ter me ter hev much jedgmint."

"I jes' *lo-o-oved* ter hear 'bout leetle Sam'l an' his mother, an' her a-bringin' of him new clothes. He wore a white shut, an' she brung him a leetle coat every year," continued Sis, with placid eyes shining with the delighted reminiscence of the little prophet's fine gear.

"Eli never could hev led the children of Isrul through the wilderness like Moses done," said Larrabee meditatively, reverting naturally to the elder character; whereas with Sis the *personnel* of the Bible was chiefly juvenile, rarely attaining a greater height than four feet.

"Jes' ter think," she cried, "they put Moses whenst a baby in a leetle dug-out, an' anchored him 'mongst the willows under the ruver bank, an' lef' him by hisself! Don't ye know, he hollered an' hollered! An' he wondered whar all the folks war gone."

"An' Dan'l I hev read about," continued Larrabee.

"In the painters' den! Oo—oo!" The little girl shivered with a sort of enjoyment of the terror of the situation, drawing up her shoulders, and holding both hands over her mouth.

"He war n't 'feared. I reckon he mus' hev been a powerful hunter whenst young. I wonder ef he ever hed enny 'speriunce with wolf an' bar, an' sech?" Larrabee speculated.

"Them bars! War n't that awful, — plumb turrible!" exclaimed Sis suddenly, her scanty brows knitted as she frowningly recoiled into the back of her chair, and her small eyes grew large. "Them two bars what eat them forty childern, — though 't ain't manners, an' it never war, ter make game o' yer elders."

"'T ain't true! No two bar ever eat forty childern. They 'd hev bust!" Joe interposed realistically. "Sis jes' made that up out'n her own head."

"It air true," protested the little Biblical student. "I hearn the rider read it myself."

"Them childern war obleeged ter be sorter sizable ter hev quit bein' bald-headed tharse'fs, ef they war able ter run an' p'int thar fingers. An' shucks!

I hev been sassier 'n that a many a time, an' no bar hev eat me yit," said Joe hardily.

" Ye air savin' up fur Satan, I reckon," retorted Miss Taft, with acerbity. " I hev a heap o' trouble with this boy," she added, turning a dreary, disgusted little face toward Larrabee.

Their unity of literary interest had fostered a degree of sympathy for her. " Ye oughter go down sometimes an' set at Tems's," he suggested. " He hev got a darter an' a niece, though they air older 'n ye be."

" I don't mind old folks," said Cornelia, evidently with no idea of the gradations of age. " I be used ter granny. I wisht dad would marry one of 'em at Tems's," she added.

Larrabee glanced keenly at her.

" What ails ye, ter say that ? " he asked jealously.

" I 'd like ter see a tuck took in Joe," said Sis bitterly.

She obviously spoke without further information or meaning. Larrabee rose restlessly, the interest of the literary symposium at an end.

" I wisht ye could let me out'n hyar somehows," he said, glancing uneasily about. Then, with a sudden recollection, " Ain't you-uns got a key ez would open the sto' door, what ye brung from yer granny's house ? Mebbe 't would open t'other."

" Dad took it ; he did'n't want the sto' do' opened whenst he hed locked it."

" Hain't you-uns got no mo' keys, no kind o' keys ? "

She hesitated, but he had won upon her somewhat obdurate predilections ; his acquaintance with the heroes of the tales that she had learned at her grandmother's home was a pleasing and fresh bond of interest. She divined his sympathy, and had seen his approval of the works she had wrought in the service of order and cleanliness; he saw in her little prim face that she had keys at hand, and presently she nodded brightly.

"Let 's try 'em," he urged, as if the experiment had a mutual interest.

It was a bunch of two or three rusty old keys which she produced, held together with a rough leather string, but they meant liberty and life to Larrabee. He could hardly be still long enough to clean and oil them before the attempt which should be decisive. The little girl rubbed one with a will, while he busied himself with the other. She held the candle as he knelt tremulously on the floor and applied them successively to the lock. One slipped in and turned futilely all round, — too small. The other would not even enter the keyhole.

As he knelt there, the tallow dip showed a white, set face. He was remembering his comrades, bound hand and foot down at the still, and prefiguring Taft's alarm, — which was in itself formidable in its valiant disregard of all but his own safety, — his resentment and revenge, when their imprisoned estate should be discovered to him. Whatever might betide in the world without, it was death, indubitably, to remain. He rose suddenly, almost overturning the child at his elbow, starting toward the door of the store to get some implement to serve to break the lock.

"Try a file," said Sis reasonably, misunderstanding his intention.

She was still holding the candle as he came back, its white light on her precise little face and smooth hair put primly behind her ears, and a tall womanly caricature of her aped her gestures as her shadow stretched up on the new poplar weatherboarding of the partition.

Her suggestion worked like a charm. A few moments of a sharp, rasping noise, while she set her little teeth, a second essay at the lock: the bolt slipped back as if made for the rusty old key that had worked no miracles before save that of opening old Mrs. Jiniway's "chist;" the door swung open. A glimpse of the windy night, the clouds, the tossing woods, and Sis, putting up the bars again, heard the last echo of Larrabee's swift step as he strode away.

XI

The day fixed for processioning Kenniston's land dawned with an element of perplexity all its own to add to the troublous questions which it was expected to decide. The weather was the aptest illustration of uncertainty. The first gray light came with a rolling cloud and a dank wind sweeping along quick gusts of rain; then the sun rose, diffusive, promissory, with a great lavishness of red and yellow suffusions, a range and degree of rank, heavy color that seemed nearer to the hues of sunset than to the luminous purity and delicacy of wonted matutinal freshness. The slate-tinted clouds were massed once more, the beams failed, the wind brought the rain anew, and when it ceased at last, light mists were stealing along the heavy purple mountains, and rising from every chasm and depression; even far away amongst those vague contours, gray and dun-tinted and brown, that were like the first lifeless sketch of the dazzling azure ranges that the sunny days were wont to paint with such brilliant softness upon the fair field of the horizon, these vapors, white, soft, opaque, flocculent, could be seen. So from the furthermost reaches to the nearest limits invisibility was visibly garnered.

As Kenniston, perturbed because of the weather

signs, turned ever and anon in his saddle, as he rode up and up the mountain to the tryst at the Big Hollow Boulder, he saw now the great outward bend of the mountain, with heavily wooded green slopes under the gray sky, all the coloring heightened by the impending tufty white of the masses of silent approaching vapor; the surly crags of the terrace dark with the moisture and the shadow; and the great black mass of the charred wood still sending up a slow, melancholy thread of smoke where the hotel lay in ruins. And again, looking over his shoulder to verify some half-forgotten detail of the scene, the trees twenty feet away were barely visible in the encompassing medium, so fleetly did the impalpable cloud press upon them. To him, unversed in mountain weather, the enterprise of the day seemed impracticable; and he was half surprised to see the surveyor, with his Jacob's staff and his chain-bearers, already waiting at the boundary corner. The figures of the group of men, with their horses picketed hard by, stood out against the inexpressive whiteness about them with the distinctness of sketches on otherwise blank paper. They were easily recognizable even from a distance, and Cap'n Lucy's slim proportions and grace of movement further served to differentiate him from the burlier forms of the others.

" Ah, colonel," called out Kenniston as he dismounted, " you here? "

It might hardly be believed by one who had experienced its causticity, but Cap'n Lucy's tongue was blunted of much of its capacities under his own roof-tree by the exactions of hospitality. Now he felt the franchise of the free outer air.

" I 'm a mighty confidin' young critter, I know," he replied, advancing a few paces with his hands thrust in his pockets, " but this hyar man " — he nodded at the surveyor and affected to lower his voice confidentially — " hev got the name o' bein' sorter tricky, an' I 'lowed I hed better kem along like a good neighbor ter holp ye some, else he mought cheat ye out'n a passel o' lan'."

The surveyor, a tall, saturnine, businesslike body, took not the slightest notice of this fling, but his two young chain-bearers grinned their appreciation, and the other men laughed outright with evident enjoyment, notably a tall, dark-eyed fellow, whom Kenniston presently recognized as the deputy sheriff, with whom he had already had some slight colloquy touching the possibly incendiary origin of the fire that had destroyed the new building. The recollection furnished him with a retort. He had flushed darkly, and his eyes were angry.

" I should n't be surprised to be ill treated in any way now in the Cove — after what *has* happened."

The laughter was checked by his tone. The men glanced at one another constrainedly. Before his coming, the event had promised to the volunteer assistants an episode of sociability affording the interchange of ideas and jocular converse, the interest of the developments sufficiently great to repay them for the hardship of the steep scramble down the mountain side. The significance of the proceeding was reasserted, and the silence was unbroken until the surveyor, busily adjusting his compass, remarked to Kenniston that he had noted one or two blazes indicating an old line, as he came up the mountain.

"Ye won't go a-nigh them blazes!" cried Cap'n Lucy sarcastically, waving his hand along an imaginary line. "Ye take my word fur it, ye won't see them blazes 'twixt hyar an' the mounting's foot."

Kenniston detected a covert meaning in the tone, and glanced keenly around at the speaker. But Cap'n Lucy's face was as enigmatically satiric as his laughter ; and as Kenniston's questioning stare sought out the son, Luther turned away to avoid meeting his eyes, lowering, anxious, and it seemed somehow conscious. Conscious, too, was the hang-dog manner with which the usually bluff young mountaineer spoke to the deputy sheriff Ross, observing that he did not see how the surveyor could get his bearings such a shut-in day as this.

The deputy sheriff had found it easily compatible · with his interpretation of his duty to spare the time to assist as idle spectator at anything promising so much interest and excitement as the processioning of the Kenniston tract. For the antagonism between the disputants had already been noised abroad, and Rodolphus Ross, albeit a "peace officer" within the meaning of the statute,

was not so attached to the service of the white-
winged goddess that he did not cherish a lively
expectation of whatever sport could be extracted
from Cap'n Lucy's and Kenniston's belligerent
idiosyncrasies. He protested now so clamorously
that it might seem he feared that this unique opportunity would be wrested from him, and, assuming the rôle of a trustworthy weather prophet,
maintained that whenever it rained before twelve
o'clock, noon, an early clearance was the certain
sequel. The discussion and the aspect of the
weather diverted the general attention from Cap'n
Lucy's singular words, and from Luther's unwillingness to proceed and surly disaffection.

But Kenniston, whose already keen observation
was whetted by the appreciation of the enmity he
sustained and the magnitude of the disaster that
had befallen him, followed Luther's motion with
an alert, apprehending eye, and hardly lost sight
of him even when the mists swept between them
and gave him but a distorted looming presentment
of the young mountaineer; though thus carica-
tured, Luther never lost for a moment his unchar-
acteristic and already significant demeanor. Small
as the group was, the figures of two or three were
now and again abstracted from it, as if literally
caught up in the clouds, slowly materializing again
as the mists shifted. The horses hard by were
sometimes invisible in the dense white medium,
and anon only their heads would appear here and
there in various attitudes, like studies for a cav-

alry subject. Even the Big Hollow Boulder, the corner of the lines, seemed to recede, and again was near at hand, in a manner altogether inconsistent with its accepted attributes of immovability as a monument of boundary. The great felled trees, lying close by athwart the outcropping ledges of rock, — traces of the mountain tempest, — were obliterated and invisible in the encompassing whiteness. The chilly sound of the rain beating heavily below in the valley rose on the dank air, and more than once the white gauzy suffusions of the encompassing vapor were pervaded with a transient yellow glow, broad and innocuous reflections of the lightning of the storm cloud of the lower levels.

The surveyor was a tall, well-knit man of forty-five or fifty, with a square, short, grizzled beard decorating his chin, high cheek bones, a blunt nose, a far-seeing gray eye, and a quid of tobacco that seemed to render him indifferent to the joys of conversation. His high boots were drawn to the knees over his trousers, — a style affected by the rest of the party; Kenniston's correct equestrian garb being sufficiently dissimilar to give him that air of peculiarity and modishness that somehow seems so unworthy and flippant among plain and humble folk, as if they cared for better things than fashion. It made him a trifle ill at ease, and he had a sense of being out of his sphere, added to the conviction of the vicinage of enemies. He stood with his riding-whip in his hand beside the surveyor as he adjusted his instrument, conscious of sustaining the curious attention of the chain-bearers, two stalwart young fellows arrayed in brown jeans and heavy boots, amply competent for the task of carrying the chain through that rugged wilderness; conscious, too, of Cap'n Lucy's brilliant, laughing, handsome eyes, the doubtful, furtive glances of the others, and Luther's anxious, troubled gaze.

Suddenly, with an infinitely light, elastic effect that permeated all its vast area, the cloud began to uplift; the great grassy bald of the mountain towering above them showed its vast green dome as it were between precipitous white cliffs of still higher cloud mountains. An eagle's wing caught the sunlight as he soared above, beyond rifle range, and as he felt the rising wind his keen, exultant cry floated down to them. A tempered white glister suffused all the clouds about them; the sun was out, and as the illumined masses parted, the blue mountains afar off now glimmered with a dusky section of the quiet valley below, and again were veiled with the gleaming gauze. Between its shining folds a glittering green avenue opened out down the woods, as the surveyor, bending first to take sight, then holding his Jacob's staff stiffly before him, set out from the Big Hollow Boulder with a fair start and a long, elastic step; the two chain-bearers in file alertly followed, alternately bowing down and rising again, while the chain writhed through the grass between them like some living sinuous thing, ever and again drawn out tense and straight, and the echoes rang with the strophe and antistrophe of their sudden short cry, "Stick!" "Stuck!" "Stick!" "Stuck!"

It might seem that all the oreads of the Great Smoky were set to flight by this invasion of their sylvan haunts, so many a flitting white robe fluttered elusive among the dense shadows of the trees, gone ere you could look again; so often a glistening white arm was upflung in the deepest green jungle of the laurel. They sprang up by every shadowy cliff and lurking chasm, by every hidden spring and trickling stream, and fled with tattered white scarfs streaming in the wind behind them. All the way the rout continued as Science came down the slope, led by a compass rather than the sun or the shadow, and with her votaries to mete out the freedom of the wilds, and the grace of the contour of the slopes, and the beauty of herbage and flowering growth, and the largess of the gracious earth, and to reduce all to an arbitrary scale, and judge it by the rod or perch or pole.

The grizzly old surveyor saw naught of this, — not even when, in advance of all the company, he threaded the sun-glinted green glade, and strode almost in the midst of a bevy of white gauze-draped fleeing figures. Nor his chain-bearers, young though they were, and presumably impressionable, — not even when they rose from their alternate genuflections, and their sudden call "Out!" resounded on the air, though they stood idle and looked about them while the surveyor paused to mark the "out."

Nor Cap'n Lucy, as light and swift on his feet as the youngest, fierce, jaunty, with his clear, defiant eye. Nor Rodolphus Ross, finding great opportunity for mirth behind Cap'n Lucy's back as he scuffled along amongst the knot of spectators, keeping up as best they might, skirting the barriers that the surveyor and his chain-bearers, constrained by duty, went over, and tumbling, pulling, and struggling with each other now and then for the best and foremost place. " Look at old Cap'n Tems! " cried Ross. " Ain't he the very model of a game rooster? He ain't big, an' he ain't strong, an' he ain't heavy, but Lord! how he thinks he is! " Nor Kenneth Kenniston, beginning to pause now and again, — albeit he did not flag, despite the hard pull over the impracticable ground, for he was a man of stalwart physique and a practiced pedestrian, — to look instead at the memorandum of the calls of the title-deed, which original paper the surveyor held in his hand, in doubt at first, in growing dismay, then in hot and mounting anger. At the next " out," when the surveyor set down his Jacob's staff, Kenniston strode over and tapped him somewhat imperatively on the shoulder.

" My good friend," he said, with an evident effort at self-repression, " are you not making some mistake? You surely are not following the calls as they are set forth in these papers? "

To the professor of an exact science the suggestion of mistake is an imputation of incapacity.

The claims of the quid of tobacco were disregarded
for the nonce. The surveyor spoke, albeit with his
mouth full, and spoke to the point : — .

"I reckon I know what I'm about, Mr. Kenn's-
ton. If you don't like the way I'm runnin' this
line, run it yerse'f."

"The blazes on those trees on the side of the
mountain, that you called my attention to, indicating the old line, are away over yonder on that sharp
ridge." Kenniston waved his hand with the paper
in it toward a high rocky crest to the left; then he
fixed insistent eyes on the surveyor, and stroked
his full brown whiskers mechanically with the other
hand.

The surveyor followed with perplexed eyes the
direction pointed out. He gave a little puzzled sniff,
as if he sought to smell the line. Then he reverted
to that prop of common sense, his Jacob's staff.

"D 'ye want me to run the line according to the
compass and the calls of the title papers, or by
the old blazes scattered about in the woods on the
trees ? " he demanded. "You don't know whether
they ever were intended to mark the line, nor who
put 'em thar, nor for what. I know they ain't no
kin ter the line I 'm runnin' now, 'cordin' ter the
calls an' the compass."

Once more he took his bearings, and, holding his
Jacob's staff before him, walked steadily forward
into the deeps of the wilderness; the two sworn
chain-bearers, who had listened with indignant,
sullen brows to the wrangle, and reflection on the

work, again began diligently to bow down and rise up, as they ejaculated their "Stick!" "Stuck!" "Stick!" "Stuck!" — the clanking of the chain sounding loud and metallic in the sylvan quiet. The other men, with their shadows, all pressed forward in a close squad, for the pause had given the stragglers time to gather.

Kenniston was aware that Cap'n Lucy carried the sympathies and good wishes of all the company, save perhaps the impartial surveyor, who would suffer himself to be influenced by nothing less just than his compass. He realized that he was looked upon as the "town man," and a rich one, desirous of wresting, by a slight technicality of the law, a very little land from a poor man who had in good faith built his house upon it. He had grown extremely bitter in his sentiment toward the people of the section because of the fire in which so much of value had perished, for he believed its origin incendiary. He was conscious of sustaining much antagonism, and he had fiercely resolved to deserve it. He had, in his first uncontrolled rush of anger, declared that he would punish somebody, — the true culprit, if possible ; but *somebody* should kick his heels in jail for a while, and go to the penitentiary if might be. He did not in reality go so far in feeling as in expression, but his was not a prudent tongue. He earnestly desired success in the matter of the processioning ; the scheme of the new hotel had grown very close to him ; it seemed to him that one log cabin might serve the mountaineer as well as another, and that, moreover, in justice to himself, he should claim his own. He had felt sure, perfectly sure, that his deed called for the land that Cap'n Lucy held. For the first time, as he clambered with the rest down the rugged slopes, a doubt of this entered his mind. It made him wince from the probable result. He was not prepared to occupy the position of having sought to despoil a man, and a poor man, of his own, his very own, and fail. He knew that if he succeeded the countryside would wish that he had failed, and Cap'n Lucy would be a popular and picturesque object of commiseration. But he could not endure the idea of the rejoicings in his failure. To work a hardship to another was bad, indeed, and he had never contemplated it without the salve of an ample money compensation. To futilely seek to work a hardship was far worse. Again and again he knit his brows, as he gazed at the treacherous annotations in his hand, while the interchange of glances behind him commented on his attitude and his evident state of mind. Cap'n Lucy, who could not have read a word of the notes, strode on, apparently indifferent to fate, the " very model of a game rooster," esteeming Kenniston's show of anxiety the merest subterfuge; for would that monument of boundary known as the Big Hollow Boulder have become so nimbly peripatetic, despite its tons of weight, if the line run out therefrom were not to be materially altered for the betterment of the claimant at whose instance the processioning was held ?

And still the chain clanked and writhed its length along the ground, and the cries "Stick!" "Stuck!" of the chain-bearers alternated as before, until the sudden call "Out!" resounded, and the surveyor paused to mark the "out" once more.

XII.

As the surveyor planted his Jacob's staff anew he drew a long sigh of fatigue, and gazed out discerningly at the weather signs from over a craggy, jutting precipice at one side, which in its savage bareness disclosed from the midst of the dense forest a vast expanse of the tremulous mountain landscape below. The uncertain flicker of the sunshine was now on the green of the wooded valley, which presently dulled to the colorless neutrality of the persistent shadow, albeit the summits of the far horizon line gleamed delicately azure, as if the tint possessed some luminous quality and glowed inherently blue. To the right hung masses of vaporous gray; and beneath, fine serried lines were drawn in myriads against the darker tints of half-seen slopes, where the rain was falling. Still beyond, a great glamourous sunburst appeared in the mist, with so rayonnant an effect of the divergent splendors from its dazzling focus that it might seem a fleeting glimpse of the actual wheel of the chariot of the sun. It rolled away speedily. A rainbow barely flaunted its chromatic glories across the sky, and faded like an illusion, and all the world was gray again; from a dead bough starkly thrust out of the wooded slopes half way to the valley a rain crow was calling and calling.

The other men, too, were looking over the valley, so long obscured by the dense forest trees and still denser undergrowth through which they had taken their way. It seemed much nearer than when they had last seen it from the dome, even allowing for the distance they had traversed, and they noted, with that interest always excited by a familiar scene from a new standpoint, the aspect of the well-known landmarks, all changed and strange. Kenniston had drawn near the verge; he stood sharply outlined against the sky, a field-glass in his hand, which again and again he brought to bear upon the smouldering black mass on the cliffs far below that once was the new hotel, only to be located now by the thinly curling smoke from its ruins. The instrument was familiar enough to the mountaineers, who had most of them observed its use during the war; but to a certain type of rustic an affectation of ignorance is the prettiest of jests.

"Say, mister," Rodolphus Ross adjured him, with a show of eager anxiety, "air yer contraption strong enough ter view enny insurance on that thar buildin' ? "

The echo caught his laughter and blended it with the rain crow's call. He was not sensitive himself, and he could not appreciate sensitiveness in others. The fact that the building had perished in the flames, without insurance, was well known to the community; and how could it help or hinder that he should sharpen his wits by a little exercise on the theme ?

Kenniston made no reply, still sweeping the landscape with his glass. As the surveyor bent to take sight, Kenniston suddenly turned.

" Stop," he said ; " you will stop this farce right here. This is a conspiracy ! "

The surveyor, still in his stooping posture, looked at him in amazement.

" Hey ? " he exclaimed, as if he did not believe his senses.

" A conspiracy ! " Kenniston reiterated.

The surveyor, in the course of his brawny career, had been offered few insults, and these he had promptly requited with stout blows. But the sight of a man who has lost reason, temper, and policy together has sometimes a steadying effect on the spectator. Besides, he was in the performance of a sworn duty, and, being a faithful and efficient officer of the county, he had a high ideal of the functions of his office. He was nettled by Kenniston's self-magnifying attitude, but it was obviously in order to give him the correct measurements, not of himself, but of his land, and although he retorted, it was in good enough temper.

" Conspirin' with the meridian line ? " he demanded, with a sneer, thrusting his quid of tobacco into his leather jaw with a tongue grown expert by long practice in thus clearing the way for its own utterances. " Or maybe ye think the points o' the compass have got in a mutiny against ye ? "

Cap'n Lucy came alongside the Jacob's staff, and gave Kenniston a rallying wink, sly, malicious, sarcastic, and altogether unworthy of the fine eye that it eclipsed. " Conspirin' with a monimint o' boundary knowed ez Big Hollow Boulder? " he said.

Luther turned away suddenly, with an accession of hang-dog furtiveness in his manner, and Kenniston's fury was stemmed for the moment by his surprise and doubt and bewilderment. Still with choleric color mantling his face, his eyes bright and wide, his white teeth pressing on the lip which he was biting visibly despite the thick abundance of beard, with all the fire eliminated from the angry facial expression that he yet retained, he stared silently at Captain Lucy, who was scornfully laughing. The surveyor took advantage of the seeming lucidity of the interval to seek to rehabilitate pacific relations.

"I can't help *how* ye expected the line ter run out, Mr. Kenniston.   I'm runnin' it 'cordin' ter the calls an' the compass.   Ye an' Cap'n Tems are here as owners o' the adjoinin' tracts, ter see it done fur yerselves."

" Not me ! " cried Cap'n Lucy.   "I ain't looked at yer durned bodkin " (thus he demeaned the magnetic needle) " sence I kem out.   It mought waggle todes the north pole, like ye sez it do, — 'pears onstiddy enough fur ennything, — or it mought waggle todes the east pole.   I ain't keerin'.   It may know the poles whenst it sees 'em, — though I dunno ef that needle hev got an eye.   My main dependence air in that monimint o' boundary

knowed ez the Big Hollow Boulder — corner rock
— corner o' the lines — oh my! — yes!"

The significance of this was hardly to be overlooked.

"See here, Cap'n Lucy," said Kenniston, suddenly dropping his aggressions even to the unusual
point of giving the old man his accustomed title,
"what do you mean by that?"

Cap'n Lucy gave him a broadside of big bright
eyes.

"Why, don't you-uns know that monimint o'
boundary knowed ez Big Hollow Boulder — corner
mark — been thar so long?"

"Well, what about it?" demanded Kenniston
impatiently.

"Why, it's *known* ez Big Hollow Boulder,
'cordin' ter yer own notice posted up at the mill,"
said Cap'n Lucy tantalizingly.

Kenniston still stared, and the surveyor, seeking
to cut short a futile waste of time, bent once more
to take sight. "The only way ter git things settled
is ter run out the line 'cordin' ter the calls an' the
compass, an' I'm a-doin' of it fair an' square."

"There is something radically wrong," persisted
Kenniston angrily. Then turning to Cap'n Lucy,
he continued vehemently, "I know — and *you*
know — that Wild Duck River is on my land, and
does n't touch yours in any of its windings; and
look there! — Wild Duck Falls!"

He pointed diagonally across a ravine, where,
amidst the dusky depths of green shadows, and

close to a gray cloud that came surging through
the valley, a narrow, gleaming, white, feathery
mountain cataract, with an impetus and a motion
like the flight of an arrow smartly sped from the
bow, shot down into the gorge.

It transfixed Cap'n Lucy. He stood staring at
it, motionless, amazed, it might seem aghast. For
the boundary line that the surveyor was running
according to the compass and calls had thrown
within his tract this mountain torrent, this wayward
alien, which he had known for many a year as the
native of the Kenniston woods.

"It makes no difference, gentlemen, what ye hev
'lowed ye owned, an' what ye did n't," interposed
the surveyor: "this boundary line I'm runnin' out
will show ye the exac' extent o' yer possessions."
And once more he bent to take sight.

Then he rose and stalked forward, his Jacob's
staff held before him, his eyes intent and fixed, the
links of the chain once more dully clanking as it
writhed through the grass, and the chain-bearers,
with their cabalistic refrain, "Stick!" "Stuck!"
bowing down and rising up, as they ever and again
drew it out taut to its extreme length between them.

The spectators followed on either hand, plunging
into the deeper forest, which, as it interposed
before the cliffs, cut off the view of the wide landscape, that seemed lifted into purer light and more
transparent color by the contrast with the bosky
shadows as it disappeared, and again was vaguely
glimpsed between the boles and hanging branches,

and once more vanished, leaving the aspect of the world the bare breadth of the herder's trail through the laurel.

Two of the men — shaggy of beard and of hair, and shabbier far of garb than the others — gazed at the proceeding with the eyes of deep wonderment and reluctant acceptance, as if it were some formula of necromancy which revolted credulity. They were denizens of a deeply secluded cove near by, lured hither by the report of the processioning, and looking for the first time upon the simple paraphernalia of land-surveying, — the chain, the Jacob's staff, and the compass; even the surveyor and the chain-bearers were only the verification of wild rumors that had reached them. They were not unintelligent; they were only uninformed. The knowledge and experience of the commonplace process which the others possessed might hardly be considered an adequate set-off against such fresh and illimitable capacities of impressionability. Few people can so enjoy a day of sight-seeing as fell to the share of these denizens of "Painter Flats."

Kenniston lingered for a few minutes, still sweeping with the field-glass the rugged ravine where Wild Duck Falls gleamed white, swift, amidst the deep, dusky green shadows: disappearing beneath the approaching gray cloud as its filmy gauzes expanded and floated into the larger spaces of the ravine, then piercing its draperies with a keen, glimmering shaft of white light, and vanishing again as the cloud thickened and condensed in its passage through the narrowing limits of the gorge. He turned away at last, the glass still in his hand, following hard on the steps of the surveyor, marking all the successive stages of the proceedings with a keen, alert, inimical observation. He wore a grim, set face, and his manner expressed a sustained abeyance, watchfulness, and a dangerous readiness.

The landmarks were such as were easily common to any line. When the deed had called for four hundred and fifteen poles northwest to a white oak-tree, the chain-bearers had brought up, without a link amiss, at the gnarled foot of one of a cluster of such trees. A half-obliterated indentation upon it the surveyor accepted as the specific mark of identification, although others considered it an old "blaze" indicating an ancient trail, and Kenniston declared it merely a "cat-face." Again, the line, diverging, ran due north eight hundred poles to a stake in the middle of Panther Creek. The chain found the middle easily enough, though not the stake, which was, of course, in the nature of things, a temporary mark, and liable to be carried away in a freshet, or broken down by floating logs or other obstruction. The stream, however, kept an almost perfectly straight line — barring the slight sinuous meandering inherent to a natural channel which did not affect the general direction — for more than a mile through a grassy glade almost free of undergrowth, purling along under the shadow of the great trees and rocks. Thus, if the previous markings were correct, this of necessity depended upon them. The surveyor had a stub driven down, in place of the missing stake, in the middle of the stream, re-marking the line according to the law. Once more the chain-bearers, dripping like spaniels from their excursions into the water, began their series of genuflections and their ringing outcry, " Stick ! "   " Stuck ! "

All had observed Kenniston curiously during the halt, and the doubt and discussion as to the missing mark, expectant of some wrathful demonstration. If he did not coincide with the surveyor's opinion, he made no sign. In one sense, his demeanor balked them of the amusement which they had ravenously looked for. He made no protest, which, reasonable or unreasonable, they would have relished. His attitude, his face, his words, were constrained to a stern neutrality and inexpressiveness. He seemed only grimly watchful, waiting. The change itself afforded food for speculation, an entertainment more subtle and of keener interest than his previous outbreaks, although less alluring to the maliciously mirthful spectator. It seemed, however, to disconcert the surveyor more than active interference and aggression. Submissiveness is so abnormal a trait in a man of Kenniston's type that its symptoms indicate a serious moral crisis. Now and again, the surveyor, pausing to mark the " out," appealed directly to him. To be sure, the remark was in relation to the weather, for the clouds were gathering overhead, a slate-tinted canopy, seeming close upon the summits of the tall trees, till a white lacelike film scudding across it in contrary currents of the wind served to show, by the force of comparison, the true distance of the higher vapors. Kenniston had only monosyllables for reply, and the man of the compass could but mop his brow, and listen anxiously to the distant rumblings of thunder, and wish this troublous piece of work well over, and take his bearings anew. When the call in the deed for a girdled and dead poplar-tree was found to have no correspondent mark on the face of the earth, being, as he observed, a mark bound to be obliterated in the course of time, since the tree was dead when the deed, which was of remote date, was written, Kenniston's silence had evidently an unnerving effect.

" Why, look here," the surveyor broke out in self-defense at length. " I ain't got no sort o' interest in the line except to run it according ter the calls an' the compass. I 'll git my fees, whether or no. 'T ain't nuthin' ter me which gits the most lan', you or Cap'n Tems."

As Kenniston still continued silent, he looked appealingly at Cap'n Lucy, and, receiving no encouragement, set his teeth, addressed himself to his work, and communed thenceforward with naught more responsive than his Jacob's staff.

But what, alack, had befallen Cap'n Lucy? Did ever a gamecock, that had never so much as felt his adversary's gaff, drop his feathers so suddenly? He was all at once old, tired, anxious, troubled. He tugged along at the rear of the party, lagging and flagging as he had never done on certain forced marches that had seemed a miracle of endurance. For Cap'n Lucy's frame had been upborne by his spirit in those ordeals, and now that ethereal valiance had deserted him. For what mystery was this? The moving of the monument of boundary "known as the Big Hollow Boulder" — he thought of it thus for the first time without the sneer of inscrutable offense which the rotund phrasing had occasioned — had, instead of stripping him of his possessions, resulted in throwing much land, which he doubted not belonged to his neighbor, within his own lines. That Kenniston had himself moved the corner landmark or connived at the commission of this felony, if not otherwise preposterous, was thus rendered absolutely incredible. But who, then, could have moved it? When? How? For what unimaginable reason? How strange that he should have discovered the change! And what mad freak of fate was it that it should be he, he himself, who should profit by it, acquiring the legal title to hundreds of acres at Kenniston's expense? Cap'n Lucy was an honest man, and the thought made him gasp. Had it been possible, he would at that moment have flung all the Great Smoky Mountains at Kenniston's feet. No recantation was too bitter, no renunciation was too complete, rather than be suspected, with any show of reason, as he had suspected Kenniston. Not that he cared for the groundless suspicion, but for its justification. This consideration

summoned his tardy policy. He must needs have
time to think. Were he bluntly to declare the
corner-stone to have been moved, it might seem to
criminate himself; for albeit the line was running
to his advantage here, who could say how its diver-
gences might affect his possessions lower down
on the mountain? "Windin' an' a-twistin' like
the plumb old tarnation sarpient o' hell!" Cap'n
Lucy vigorously described it in a mutter to his
beard.

Moreover, even if the later results were also to
his benefit, as it had been notoriously contrary to
his wishes that the land should be processioned at
all, it might seem that moving the boulder had
been his scheme to thus thwart any definite estab-
lishment of the line of boundary,— and this was
a felony.

Cap'n Lucy experienced a sudden affection of
the spine which seemed to him abnormal, and, at
the moment, possibly fatal, so curious, so undreamed
of heretofore, were its symptoms. A cold chill
trembled along its fibres; responsive cold drops
bedewed his forehead. His hand had lost its normal temperature, and was cold to the touch. For
the first time in all his life Cap'n Lucy's nerves
were made acquainted with the shock of fear. He
did not identify it; he could not recognize it. He
was spared this acute mortification. He only felt
strangely ill and undecided and tremulous, and he
doubted his survival. He began to wonder if Kenniston suspected aught. He no longer questioned

the genuineness of his enemy's demeanor earlier in the day, when each unexpected divergence of the line had seemed by turns to perturb and to anger him. Cap'n Lucy noted the cessation of the protestations, the grimly set jaw, the smouldering fire of the eye, the attitude of tense expectancy and waiting. He wondered if Kenniston were " laying for " him now as he had been " laying for " Kenniston. He thought of the intention deferred from " out " to " out " to loudly proclaim his discovery of the removal of the corner landmark, of his relish of his enemy's fancied security in outwitting him. He had only given Kenniston a little line, a little more, as it were, that he might hang himself with it, and now, forsooth, this noose was at his own service.

He felt a moderate and tempered gratulation that he had not been precipitate in the matter, that as yet no one knew of his discovery ; but suddenly he remembered his ill-starred confidence to Luther. For the first time he marked his son's furtive, skulking, downcast manner.

" Like a sheep-killin' dog ! " said Cap'n Lucy to himself, in a towering rage. " What ef he do know it 's been moved : did I move it ? "

He remembered, too, his reiterated allusions to the perambulatory boulder, and Kenniston's amazement, which then he had thought affectation, but which he now believed to be quite genuine. Were they the exciting cause, so to speak, of that grim air of abeyance and biding his time ?

"The boulder can't be put back," said Cap'n Lucy to himself, suddenly on the defensive. "Nobody could make out whar it kem from fust, 'kase it never lef' a trace on the rock; an' a dozen horse could n't haul it up sech a steep slope. It mus' hev been blowed down by dam-i-nite."

It was a fine illustration of a moral descent, impossible to be retraced; but Cap'n Lucy did not think of that. His mind was full of the complications of his position, the dangers of disclosure, and the impossibility to him of accepting the boundary line, thus taking possession of another man's land, even if the owner would compose himself to sleep upon his rights. Judging from Kenniston's looks, it was easily to be argued that he would prove very wide awake in this emergency.

But for the changing weather signs the old man's altered demeanor might have encountered other notice than Kenniston's keen watchfulness. Now and again the thunder pealed among the mountain tops, and the slate-colored cloud had spread until it overhung all the visible world, when they once more drew so near to the verge of the precipice as to have glimpses of the densely wooded cove and the circling mountains. The ranges were all sombre gray or deeply purple, save far away, where some rift in the clouds admitted a skein of sunbeams suspended in fibrous effect over a distant slope that was a weird yellowish-green in this scant illumination which had fallen to its share, rendered more marked by the dull estate of its dun-tinted and purple compeers. Nearer at hand, the shadows were deepening momently in the forest. Once or twice, when the sharp blades of the lightnings cleft them, the lifeless bronze aisles of the woods sprang into a transient glare of brilliant green that was hardly less dazzling, and again the thunder pealed.

Two or three of the mountaineers left the party, evidently with no mind to be drenched. A man with a hacking cough remained, animated by that indisposition to self-denial, that avidity of enjoyment, that determination to seize all which niggard life holds out, characteristic of a type of consumptive invalids. " 'T ain't goin' ter rain," he declared buoyantly. It might seem that nothing less potent than powder and lead could wean from the sight of processioning the land the two denizens of Panther Flats. They patrolled every step that the surveyor took. Whenever he paused, they came up and stared, fascinated, and at close quarters, at the Jacob's staff. They counted the chains from " out " to " out." As one of them observed to the other, he " was just beginning to get the hang of the thing." He could keep under shelter at a more convenient season.

A sudden flash that seemed to pierce the very brain, so did it outdazzle the capacity of vision, a simultaneous deafening detonation, beneath which the mountains appeared to quake and to cry out with a terrible voice, while again and again the echoes repeated the thunderous menace, and then all the air was permeated by a swift electrical illumination, visibly transient, but so instantly succeeded by a similar effect that it seemed permanent, — in this weird glare the surveyor bent once more to take sight.

" Old man sticks ter his contrac' like a sick kitten ter a hot brick ! " cried Rodolphus Ross to one of the chain-bearers.

But the chain-bearers had scant sympathy for the spectators, and visited upon the company in general their displeasure because of the reflections upon the " old man's " work, for which Kenniston alone was responsible.

" Why n't ye wear yer muzzle, 'Dolphus ? " the one addressed retorted gruffly.

Most of the party had now deserted the spectacle, in deference to a timely admonition as to the fate of the horses picketed on the " bald," and their peculiar susceptibility to the fear of lightning. When the progress of the surveying again brought its adherents to the verge of the mountain and an extended outlook over the valley, there remained only the two men from Panther Flats, Rodolphus Ross, Cap'n Lucy, the chain-bearers, the surveyor, Luther, and the owner of the tract at whose instance the processioning was made.

As they looked out over the gray valley, distinct under the sombre sky, as though only color, and not light, were withdrawn, — Cap'n Lucy's cabin, the inclosures, the grim black crags beyond, the smouldering mass of the ruins of the burnt building, even the shanties of the workmen in the gorge at the foot of the cliffs, all perfectly distinguishable in their varied interpretation of gray and brown and blurring unnamed gradations of neutral tones, all overhung by the storm-cloud definitely and darkly purplish-black, with now and again, one knew not how, fleeting lurid green reflections, — Kenniston, brisk and dapper, lightly tapping his spurred boots with his riding-whip, smiling debonairly, but with a dangerous sarcastic gleam in his fiery eyes, stepped up to the surveyor. He carried his field-glass in one hand.

"Now, if you will come a few paces this way, — and you, colonel," in parenthesis to poor Cap'n Lucy, — "and use your telescope, you are obliged to see that if you run out the line seventeen hundred poles to the north, according to the deed, you will go beyond the site of the hotel. I seem to have built my house on the colonel's land. It was *your* house that was destroyed, colonel. Let me beg you to accept my condolences, — ha, ha, ha!"

A flash brighter than all that had preceded it, and his satiric laughter was lost in the roll and the reverberation of the thunder. A sudden darkening overspread the landscape, like a visible thickening of the clouds; the form of a horse darted along the verge of the precipice, so swift, so gigantic, defined against the green suffusions of that purple-black storm-cloud, that it seemed like the materialization of the hero of some equine fable. A wild cry went up that the horses had broken loose, and were stampeding through the woods. A terrible wrenching, riving sound followed another flash, and they could see a stricken tree on the slope below, in the instant before the blinding descent of the torrents. The wind rose with a wild, screaming cry; the forests bent and writhed; no one of the party could discern his neighbor's face; and, despite the pluck of the surveyor, the processioning of the Kenniston tract remained unfinished.

XIII.

Cap'n Lucy enjoyed in his own family an immunity from interference, criticism, and filial insurgency that was truly patriarchal. His word was law; his every thought was wisdom; all his dealings embodied the fullest expression of justice. Until his unlucky disclosure to Luther of his discovery of the strange removal of the Big Hollow Boulder, and the interpretation he placed upon it, imputing to Kenniston a crime of such importance, involving consequences so grave, his son had never entertained a moment's doubt of the sufficiency of his prudence, the absolute infallibility of his judgment, the integrity of all his prejudices, notwithstanding his arbitrary temper, his high-handed methods, and his frequent precipitancy. Such remonstrance as ever was ventured upon usually emanated from Adelicia, in the interest of her pacific proclivities; or to sue uncle Lucy's clemency for some object of his most righteous displeasure; or to prevail upon him to blindly consider some untoward chance a blessing in disguise. Now and then, too, she indulged in some solicitude lest the affluence of his courage should lead him into danger. But to his own children " dad " had always seemed more than capable of coping with all the forces of nature, ani-

mate and inanimate ; and as the day of the processioning of the land wore on, Julia listened, with
her silent smile of sarcastic comment, to Adelicia's
monologue of argument of alternate fears and reassurance for uncle Lucy's sake. First, lest Mr.
Kenniston succeed in unjustly wresting some of
his land from him. "But," she declared buoyantly,
" the surveyor won't let him ! " Then, lest a personal collision ensue, to her bellicose relative's
injury. "But uncle Lucy ain't been often tackled ;
ennybody kin see he 'd hev a mighty free hand in a
fight." And again she was reduced to fear simply
that things in general might fall out to the mag-
nate's dissatisfaction. "But uncle Lucy 's been
mighty mad a heap o' times before, an' 't ain't set
him back none," she argued blithely. And so the
atmosphere within cleared as the sky without
darkened, and the domestic industries went forward
apace.

It was during one of the deceptive withdrawals
of the lowering storm-cloud, revealing great expanses of blue sky, when the sunshine was a-flicker
once more over the landscape, albeit somewhat wan
and tremulous, and a wind had sprung up, faint and
short of breath, and disposed to lulls and sighs, but
still setting mists and clouds astir, that Julia went
forth upon an errand some distance up the Cove.
It had chanced that a hen, with the preposterous
hopefulness of the species, had gone to " setting "
in the orchard upon an unremunerative assemblage
of fallen apples, in default of more appropriate

material; for, in ignorance of the fowl's intention, Adelicia had fried the last eggs for breakfast. Her momentary dismay was dispelled by the recollection that Mrs. Larrabee had promised her a " settin' of special an percise tur-r-key aigs," and, equipping Julia with a basket, she sent her forth to claim this pledge.

But in lieu of the hospitable welcome and the eager fulfillment of the promise, the reminder of which Mrs. Larrabee would have regarded in the light of a courtesy and a favor, Julia encountered at the door of the queer little house Henrietta Timson, her snuffbrush, her small unlighted eyes, her narrow discontented face, and her little brief authority oppressively in evidence.

" Waal, I do declar'," she said, regarding Julia sourly, when the errand was made known. " I dunno what Sist' Lar'bee means," — for Mrs. Timson was unfailing in the appellation of church-membership, and enjoyed no closer relation to Mrs. Larrabee. " She done gone off a-pleasurin' an' a-jauntin', an' lef' me hyar with this whole house-ful ter 'tend ter, an' ter work fur, an' ter feed, an' ter mend, an' the neighbors ter pervide with aigs — an' tur-r-key aigs at that ! "

Julia Tems's experience of life had been crude and scanty and monotonous. She had lived the successive uneventful years since her infancy at the little cabin down in the Cove in the humble domestic routine, without education of any sort, except perchance such as might be gleaned from the sermon of a stray circuit rider; without the opportunity of observation; with the simplest, most untutored, most limited association. It was to be doubted if she knew a score of people in the world. But this was her first encounter with discourtesy.

She flushed scarlet under the shade of her brown sunbonnet, not with anger, but with shame: she was ashamed for Mrs. Timson. She hardly felt the affront to herself at first; the flout at the proprieties in the abstract nullified for the moment all personal consideration. She was not conscious of a retrograde movement, for her instinct was to terminate the interview. She found herself murmuring, "It's jes' ez well, — jes' ez well," in an apologetic cadence which would have befitted Mrs. Timson's voice, and moving backward continuously, in her eager haste to be gone. Rather than prolong the ordeal for a moment she could with philosophy have beheld every hen that had ever owned the Tems sway in the grotesque catastrophe of patiently seeking to hatch apples.

But Henrietta Timson had hardly anticipated routing the invader so promptly. Noting Julia's eagerness to be gone, she perversely thwarted it by stepping briskly down out of the door, remembering to put her hand to her side, with a suffering look and an affected limp.

"I 'lowed ez I hed *hed* tribulation, but I never seen none sech ez now. Sist' Lar'bee gone, — tuck one o' my chil'n with her!" She shook her head with a dolorous accusation that might have become her if "Sist' Lar'bee " had been a kidnapper, and if the hero of the rickets had gone for aught but to insure being properly fed and provided for. "Jasper Lar'bee 's disappeared; an' old man Haight I do b'lieve hev gone deranged, — sets an' cusses the Lost Time mine all day; an' Jerushy's husband 's drunk, — 'pears like a rat-hole, ye can't fill him up; an' — hev ye seen Jasper Lar'bee down yer ways ? "

" Not fur a long time," faltered Julia, still retreating a few steps at intervals down the rocky, ledgy dooryard.

" Waal, I 'll tell him ez ye war hyar, an' 'lowed it 'peared like a long time sence ye seen him," said Mrs. Timson perversely, with the air of taking a message. "An' " — her small eyes narrowed — "ef I find enny tur-r-key aigs, I 'll let ye know."

She looked with a sour smile after the girl's light figure, for Julia was now fairly routed.

" I 'll let ye know, too," she muttered, " ez we ain't got none o' Mis' Lar'bee's slack-twisted ways hyar now, — givin' away a settin' of tur-r-key aigs, I say ! Ef I find enny tur-r-key aigs, I 'll send 'em down ter the store ter trade. I be mos' out o' snuff now."

Then she meditated swiftly upon her theory that Mrs. Larrabee had reasons of her own for all her good works; that they were subtle investments, as it were, sure of a return in better kind, and quadrupled in value. She could evolve no view in which the promised " settin' of tur-r-key aigs " could figure as assets save for a general conciliatory purpose; and then she remembered that Cap'n Lucy was a widower. A sneering smile stole over her face, arrested suddenly by a grave afterthought; if for this reason the family were worth conciliating for Mrs. Larrabee's sake, surely more for her own. "Lord knows, I need a house, an' home, an' land, an' horse critters, an' cows, an' sheep, an' hawgs — he hev jes' two childern, an' them growed, an' that niece gal could be turned out" (she hastily went over the list of Cap'n Lucy's earthly gear, omitting only that important possession, himself) — "a sight more 'n Mis' Lar'bee do, ennyhows."

With a sudden change of heart, she ran to the road, holding her hand to the level of her eyes to shade them from the glare of the sun; but look as she might, there was not a flitting vestige to be seen of the dark brickdust red, the color of the dress which Julia wore. She called again and again without response. She thought the girl must surely have heard; then she reassured herself by the reflection that the wind was blowing a gale, and doubtless the sound of her voice went far afield.

Its shrill pipe might have been easily enough distinguishable to ears that would heed, although the surges of the wind beat loud on every rock and slope. Julia took angry note as she went swiftly on and on, her skirts flying, her bonnet blown back, her heart hot with wrath against Mrs. Timson, against herself, against Adelicia who had sent her on so ill starred an errand. Her eyes and her gesture were singularly like Cap'n Lucy's, as, threading the narrow path above the precipice, she paused and flung the empty basket into the wilderness below, and then walked on less swiftly, her tense nerves relaxed by this ebullition of rage. Like Cap'n Lucy, too, she felt the better for it, albeit she realized as he never would have done that the basket would be sorely missed at home. With the riddance she somehow discharged her mind of the thought of the Larrabee threshold, of her inhospitable reception there, of the whole ignoble episode. She looked out with a sort of enjoyment at the muster of the clouds, the gathering of rank after rank; ever and again her unaffrighted eyes followed the swift yellow lightnings darting through the gray masses, and she seemed to be just opposite them as she stood on the verge of the precipice on the mountain side. Lower down on the wooded slope across the narrow valley, she could see the track of the wind, which never touched those silent, vaporous congregations, motionless, or coming with contrary currents from opposite directions. The trees below bent and sprang back into place, and she could hear the sibilant shouting of the leaves. It was like a myriad of shrill tiny voices, but they combined into a massive chorus. The growths hard by were adding a refrain; the wind was winning new territory as it came up the mountain. She could see far away a cloud torn into fringes, and presently the rain was falling. It was coming nearer and nearer; she would meet it

long before she could reach home. She quickened
her steps at the thought. Sometimes the growths
intervened on both sides of the path, and shut out
the observation of the coming storm. Whenever
she emerged, she noted the darkening aspect. More
than once the thunder shook the very mountains.
Suddenly, a searching, terrible illumination, the
rising of the tumultuous wind, a frightful succession
of peals, brought her to a pause. She hardly dared
to face a storm like this, shelterless, and the store
at the Lost Time mine was close at hand. Nevertheless she hesitated for a moment. Cap'n Lucy's
well-worn jest as to the "perfessional widower"
was hardly so funny to her as to him. She stood,
disconcerted, conscious, averse, in the teeth of the
storm, her dress fluttering, her bonnet tossed back
from her shining coiled hair, her eyes bright and
wide and wistful, and the breath almost blown back
from her lips. Then she noted suddenly the portal
of the Lost Time mine. She did not pause to
reflect; to dread the long, darkening, solitary afternoon in its dim recesses; to remember the terrors
of its traditions, and what ghastly presence she
might meet, and what sepulchral voices she might
hear, in the awful isolations of the coming storm,
when all the laws that govern the outside world
seemed set at naught; for if ever the supernatural
should break bounds, it might be at a place like
this. She ran against the wind as swiftly as she
might; skirted the water on the stones in the
channel at the mouth of the cave, now more deeply

submerged than their wont, for the stream was rising visibly, its underground tributaries already fed by the rains falling elsewhere; felt with a shiver the chill of the place, as the high, grim, rough-hewn rocks towered above her head; climbed up on the inner ledges; and as the first floodlike outbreak of the torrents came down with a crash of thunder, and a glare of lightning, and a wild shrieking of swirling winds, she sat down, high and dry, and drew a breath of relief.

The next instant her heart gave a great plunge, and then seemed to stand still. She was not alone. A man in a further recess appeared suddenly, approaching cautiously. He evidently had not seen her. Her entrance into the place had preceded his appearance only by a few seconds. He was watching the rain with intense interest. She would have said that he had been apprised of it by the rise of the water within. He bestowed an eager, careful, calculating scrutiny upon the stream below the high shadowy point where he stood; then he looked toward the portal where the descending sheets of rain cut off all glimpse of the world without. He was turning away, with the furtive, skulking, cautious air that had characterized his approach, when his eyes fell upon her. He dropped out of sight as if he had been shot.

She sat there, silent, trembling, her eyes fixed upon the spot where he had disappeared, her heart beating wildly. She heard the flow of the stream below, its volume and momentum continually increasing, and the foaming turmoil where the currents met the dash of the rain at the outlet of the mine; now and again she was conscious that lightning flashed through the gray and white descending torrents without, and lit up this dreary subterranean recess with its uncanny glare for a space, till distance annulled its power, and she heard the thunder roar. But she did not withdraw her eyes, and she wondered if he had known her in that short moment as she had recognized him. For it was Jack Espey.

It seemed so long while she sat there, waiting for some sign, or token, or further intimation, that she might have thought the apparition a mere illusion, had she ever heard enough of the tricks of the imagination to learn to doubt her senses. She was trembling still, although her voice was calm enough as at last she called his name.

" Jack Espey! " the echoes cried out, as promptly as if it were a familiar sound and long ago conned. They fell to silence gradually. She did not call again, but, with her slow and composed manner, she waited for him to answer.

When he finally approached, apparently ascending an incline from depths below, he met her intent gaze fixed upon him; but she seemed to him as impassive and as unmoved of aspect as if this were a daily occurrence in her life.

" I war in hopes ye didn't know me, Julia," he said, dully sad, as he came up near her.

He stood leaning his elbow on one of the shelves

of rock, looking up at her, mechanically shielding himself behind the jagged ledges from observation without, although it might seem naught could stand in the storm that raged beyond.

His plight was forlorn. His clothes were worn and torn, and miry with clay; it adhered in flakes and smears to his long boots, incongruously spurred. His face was lined and white. His hat was pushed far back on his black hair, as of yore, and his long-lashed grayish-blue eyes had an appealing look which she had not seen before.

" What fur ye wished I would n't know ye ? "

He looked hard at her. " 'Kase it 's dangersome. I 'm a man hunted fur my life, I reckon. It 's dangersome fur me, an' fur ye too, ter know I be hyar."

" It 's jes' ez well I ain't one of the skeery kind, then," said Julia hardily. " I be powerful glad I seen ye hyar."

She seemed curiously unfamiliar to him in some sort. So alert had his faculties become in the suspense of jeopardy that this slight point perturbed him, until he bethought himself that he had hitherto heard her speak so seldom, and had observed her so little, that the very inflections of her voice were strange. It was of a different timbre from Adelicia's. It did not vibrate. It had a conclusive, flutelike quality, without a trailing sequence of resonance.

" Waal, I 'lowed ez mos' ennybody mought be sorry ter see me in sech a fix as this," he said dolorously.

The deliberate, impassive Julia was almost in haste to avert this apparent misconstruction. " Oh, I war glad ter view ye, 'kase a heap o' folks 'lowed ye could n't hev got away 'thout yer horse, him bein' kilt, an' ez ye war a-lyin' in the laurel somewhar, dead, yit."

She turned her head, and looked steadily at him. Her deep, dark, translucent eyes were full of shoaling lights of variant blue, like the heart of some great sapphire. The long, curling lashes flung a fibrous shadow on her cheek; its texture, as the light fell upon it, was so fine, so soft, its tints so fair, its curve so delicate. Her lips, chiseled like some triumph of ideal beauty, but that no sculpture could express their mobile sweetness, parted suddenly in her rare and brilliant smile.

Many a man, under its glamours, might have taken heart of grace to be glad that he was alive; but Espey's face hardened.

" 'T would be jes' ez well, jes' ez well, lying dead in the laur'l," he said bitterly. Then, with an afterthought, " Let them folks stay 'feared. They won't spile thar health quakin' an' shudderin' 'bout me," he added cynically. As he marked her expression change, her smile vanish, he realized the necessity to please, to propitiate. He knew her so slightly; his temper must not be too savage and surly with so complete a stranger, and perhaps earn her antagonism, especially since he and his refuge were at her mercy.

" Course," he went on, with a clumsy effort at

amends, " I don't mean Ad'licia. Ye knowed we-uns war keepin' comp'ny ? "

She nodded gravely.

" I know Ad'licia hev quaked an' shuddered 'bout me a heap mo' 'n I be wuth," he added.

Was the day darker outside, or how was quenched that subtle brightness of aspect that had made the girl's face radiant ? It was beautiful still, that statuesque contour, but as chill and unresponsive as if indeed its every line had been wrought with a chisel. The smooth hair, with its sheen of silken fineness, caught the light on its coiled and plaited chestnut-tinted strands. One hand rested on her brown sun-bonnet, laid on the ledge of the gray rock, and she leaned her weight upon it. Her head and her fair complexion — so fair that it transmitted to the surface an outline of the blue veins in her temple and throat, and even her eyelids — and the roseate fluctuations in her cheek were very distinct against the yellow clay of the bank of earth behind her. Her little rough low-quarter shoes and the brown stockings showed a trifle beneath the skirt of the brick-dust-colored homespun dress she wore, as they were placed on a boulder that stood out of the tawny rushing stream below.

He noted the change. He could not account for it other than as a vicarious resentment.

" I ain't faultin' Ad'licia," he said, more emphatically. " She war tormented powerful 'bout me, war n't she ? "

" A-fust," said Julia veraciously. Her voice was

as inexpressive as her eyes. "But Ad'licia is one ez always hopes fur the best."

He drew back with a sudden recoil. "Waal, now, by the Lord!" he cried furiously, "she's welcome ter her hope! Settin' thar in the house, warm, an' dry, an' fed, an' clean,"— he looked down with a sort of repulsion upon his miry garments, — "a-hopin' fur the bes', an' makin' herself mighty comfort'ble an' contented, an' *me* hyar, freezin' in this cold hole, an' mighty nigh starvin', in rags an' mis'ry, an' sick, an' sorry, an' lonesome enough ter die, an' shet out o' the light! My God, ef I war n't 'feared o' my life, I 'd let the off'cer take me! The State hain't got no sech term o' imprisonment ez this!"

Julia was leaning forward, each line of her impassive face replete with meaning, reflecting his every sentiment, but with the complement of sympathy and acquiescence and responsive anger in his anger.

He turned suddenly, lifting his arm with a scornful gesture toward the low vault with its dank, earthy odor, the ledges of barren, inhospitable rock, the cold stream rushing forth from the darkness within, seen in an appalling blackness adown the tunnel, against which his white-lined face looked whiter, his form taller in his closely belted garb and with his long boots drawn up to the knees. He waved his arm as if to include it all. "An' Ad'licia, — she hopes for the bes'."

He broke out into a harsh laugh, which the echoes

repeated so promptly, and with apparently so ma-
lignant an intent, that he checked it hastily, and the
sound died on his colorless lips ; but far down the
black tunnel something uncanny seemed to fall to
laughing suddenly, and as suddenly to break off ;
and again a further voice still was lifted in weird
mirth, and the laughter failed midway.

He waited for silence, and then he leaned against
a higher ledge near which she was sitting, and,
resting his elbow on it, looked at her once more,
wondering how he might best revert to his object of
propitiation. He was remembering that Adelicia
had told him how prone was Julia to notice slights,
and how quick to take offense. He felt hardly
equal to the effort of repairing the damage of his
outbreak against her relative, so spent was his
scanty strength by the violence of his anger and his
agitation. He could only look at her silently, more
forlorn, more pallid, more appealing, than before.

"I ought n't ter think hard o' Ad'licia," he said
at last. "Nobody else would, I know. Would
they ? " he added.

For, with Julia's silent habit, conversation was
somewhat difficult without a direct appeal. It was
a direct appeal. She liked to remember that afterward.

"Waal," she said, slowly and judicially, as if
weighing matters submitted for arbitrament, "I 'low
Ad'licia treated ye right mean, fust an' las'."

"Why ? " he rejoined, in genuine interest, his
face resuming its normal expression before flight

and hardship and darkness and loneliness and fear
and privation had so marked it.

"'Kase," she went on in that soft, unfamiliar
voice that the echoes seemed hardly to follow, so
complete, so indivisible, was every flutelike tone,
"she oughter married ye whenst ye axed her —
ef she liked ye."

A faint surprise was dawning in his eyes.

"Cap'n Lucy would n't gin his cornsent," he said
succinctly.

"I reckon he 'lowed 't war his jewty ter say no.
But ef Ad'licia hed married ye ennyhows, do ye
reckon dad would hev let that leetle fice o' the law,
'Dolphus Ross, jail *his* nephew-in-law 'kase a man
he fought in Tanglefoot Cove *mought* die ef he
did n't hev the industry ter git well? Naw, sir:
ye 'd hev hed dad an' Luther fur backers, an' they
air toler'ble stiff backers, fur enny man. Dad
would hev fixed a way out'n it fur ye, fur sure,
count o' Ad'licia. She war a turr'ble fool not ter
marry ye, an' I tole her so."

The surprise, the doubt, and at last the conviction successively expressed in Espey's face might
have been easily discriminated by one skilled in
reading the human physiognomy. But Julia possessed no such craft, and when he spoke she appreciated no change in his manner, albeit it was not
guarded; for he did not conceive it necessary to
closely screen the discovery of a secret of which
he perceived that Julia was herself unconscious.

"Julia," he said appealingly, "ye see how I be

hunted an' harried, an' nobody keers fur me. Jes'
let the folks shudder an' quake fur a while longer
'thout knowin' what 's kem o' me. Don't tell nobody ez ye hev seen me hyar."

She was gazing out at the steely lines of the rain
curtain, so dense as to be like a veritable fabric, as
it swayed in the wind at the rugged mouth of the
mine, and its foaming white fringes that seemed to
trail upon the brown water where the continuous
downfall splashed into its currents. The peculiarly
clear, colorless light of a gray day, which, in its
adequacy for all the purposes of mere vision, would
seem to point the munificence and splendid lavishness of the sun's bestowals in the interests of beauty
and growths and the gladdening of the heart of
man, was upon her face, which responded with a
sort of subdued glister like marble. Her eyes and
the shadowy long black lashes were meditatively
downcast. She was evidently reviewing the course
of action which she had just sketched for him, for
Adelicia, for Cap'n Lucy. He did not hold her
undivided attention, and he realized that it was
only a mechanical assent as she nodded, her face
still reflective, absorbed.

"Not even Cap'n Lucy," he urged eagerly.
" Not Jasper Lar'bee " — He paused suddenly.

The word seemed to arrest, to enchain, her elusive attention. The delicate roseate tints of her
fair complexion deepened from throat to brow;
her cheek was vividly red. She was remembering
the Larrabee threshold, the greeting she had en-

countered there, the grotesque indignity of Henrietta Timson's affronts. But hers was a reticent habit, and she had a reserved nature. She only said, conclusively, slowly, " Ye may be sure I won't tell Jasper Lar'bee."

Somehow Espey felt a sense of loss; and he had so little to lose, poor fellow, that albeit her affection was unsought, uncared for, unsuspected till a moment ago, the doubt of it afflicted him as if his heart were cruelly rifled. That flush at Larrabee's name! To him it was conclusive. He had no other indication by which to judge. He had mistaken her sympathy, her idle talk; she was wont to talk so seldom that it was not surprising that he hardly knew how to take her words; he knew so little of her and her mental processes. She cared for Larrabee, not for him. Nobody cared for him. And Adelicia was hoping for the best.

" This be a mighty pore shelter an' home an' hope," he said, grimly looking about him. " I hed prayed I mought crope inter a hole ter hide or die, like a hunted fox or bar or painter be 'lowed ter do sometimes. That did n't 'pear ter me much fur a man ter ax of the Lord."

He stood off from the rock for an instant, his big white wool hat in one hand, the other in his leather belt where that formidable array of weapons still gleamed. His head was thrown back from the loose collar of his blue-checked shirt; his straight hair was tossed from his brow; his gray eyes, scornfully bitter, surveyed the dripping walls, — so dark that in the recesses here and there clusters of bats hung head downward, dimly descried, awaiting the night, — the rugged obtrusion of rock through the clay, the chill, chill flowing of the brown water in the channel below, as ceaseless, as cold, as heedless, as relentless, as in the days of yore when it broke its allotted bounds, rose into alien hewn-out caverns, and flooded the mine, wrecking the humble industry of man, wresting away with its grasping currents two struggling human lives, and carrying not even a gruesome memory or token of its deeds upon its sleek waves out into the sunshine, and the free air, and the genial warmth of the upper world.

"'T ain't much I hev axed, — this hole ter starve an' die in, — but mebbe it's too much!" Then, turning, with an eye alight, and a furious flush that made him look all at once well and strong and alert and reckless again, "But tell whar I be hid out — tell — tell who ye want! Tell ennybody — everybody! Cap'n Lucy! the sher'ff! Taft! Jasper Lar'bee!"

And what miracle was this! The silent, impassive, reserved, reticent Julia fixed her eyes upon him for a moment, amazed, troubled, and then, as she suddenly comprehended, full of a keen but tender reproach. And until that moment he had not known how beautiful those much-vaunted eyes could be. The next they were full of tears, and Julia, leaning back against the wall behind her, had burst into sobs.

"Tell! Why, Jack Espey, how kin ye think I could be made to tell whar ye be hid out?" She turned her head to look at him again with hurt and indignant amazement. "I'd die first! Powder an' lead"—she hesitated for hyperbole that might express this impossibility—"all the powder and lead the men shot away in the war times could n't git a word from me o' what I hev fund out this evenin'!"

"I know it!" he protested, coming up close to her, as she sat on the ledge. "I ought n't ter hev said that, but ye see, Julia, I feel so s'picious, sometimes; I be so hunted an' harried, an' nobody keers fur me or whar I be—'ceptin' the sher'ff." He lifted his eyebrows, with a fleering laugh at his own forlorn estate.

"I keer," said Julia stoutly. "I won't tell nobody whar ye be hid out,—not even dad, nor Luther, nor nobody, 'ceptin' Ad'licia."

He gasped in haste for utterance. He caught at her hand as if he were drowning,—as if she might be gone before he could stay her for a word.

"Not Ad'licia! Oh my Lord, no! Jes' leave her a-hopin' fur the bes'!" He had hardly realized how deeply he had resented Adelicia's optimistic resignation to his fate. His sarcastic laugh was broken off halfway in his eager resumption of his argument. "Ad'licia mought feel obligated ter tell Cap'n Lucy, an' 'bide by his word. With her a-hopin' fur the bes', an' Cap'n Lucy's foolin' long o' his jewty ter his orphin niece, I 'll git the sher'ff's bracelets locked round my wrists ; an' the jail ain't ez sightly a place ez this beautisome spot. I be a man fur myself, an' I can't ondertake ter cut out all my cloth with Cap'n Lucy's scissors. Ad'licia 's contented. Leff her be ! She 'll hope fur the bes' with a twenty horse power."

He did not remember Mrs. Larrabee's astute remark in the advice she had given him to the effect that " perlitin' round the t'other gal would n't go so hard with him," if she were really a " gyardin lily " for beauty. He only felt vaguely that he had not heretofore appreciated the radiance of the face that Julia bent upon him ; he did not understand that it was the moment, the unrealized thought, which so embellished it, as she said cogitatingly, " Naw, 't won't do ter tell Ad'licia. I won't tell her."

" See ter it that ye don't," he sternly urged her. And once more he was impressed with the idea that he really had not before known how singularly beautiful she was.

" Ye see, Julia," he said, lowering his voice confidentially, " I can't git away, 'kase I got no horse ; an' ef I hed one, I hev got no money, an' I 'd jes' be tuk somewhar, now that the folks hev got sot onto the trail of me. So I 'lowed I 'd hide hyarabout till I git news from Tanglefoot ez that man hev got better. Ye see I be hopin' fur the bes', too," he added, with a pathetic smile. " It 's all I kin do."

" How do ye git suthin' ter eat ? " she asked suddenly.

Espey looked embarrassed. "Oh, I makes out," he said evasively. "I gits out at night sometimes."

She assumed that he hunted or trapped at night for provisions. He noted that she did not argue nor contend, as Adelicia was wont to do. She accepted his arrangements as intrinsically the best.

"I could fetch ye suthin' wunst in a while," she suggested.

He looked aghast at the idea.

"Don't ye do that, Julia," he said warningly. "It mought git ye or Cap'n Lucy liable ter the law. Don't ye do it. I'll make out somehows." Then seeing her reluctance, "Ef I need ennything, or want ter git communication with folks outside, I'll let ye know. I'll — I'll put this hyar pipe in a nick in them rocks, jes' west, clost inter the freestone spring nigh yer dad's house."

She listened, breathless, and beamed with delight at the feasibility of this plan.

"An' whenever I pass hyar," she said, with wide, illumined eyes and a flickering flush of excitement, — "an' I'll kem frequent, — I'll drap wild flowers in the road. An' ye will see 'em, an' know I hev been by an' been a-studyin' 'bout you-uns. An' that will be plumb comp'ny fur ye. "

"'T will that!" he cried. His eyes were soft and bright and dewy. Somehow it seemed to bind him — that chain of flowers — to the fair world without, which had been slipping away, away forever.

He turned, and looked out toward the rocky egress of the cave as if he almost expected to see already a cardinal flower flaming in the sun on the gray rock.

There was no sun. The rain fell, dense still, — dense enough, doubtless, to preclude all observation from without; but from among the shadows within his practiced eyes descried through the shifting, shimmering veil, now white and gray in shoaling effects, all blown aslant by the wind, a canvas-covered wagon lumbering by, albeit for the rush of the stream and the fall of the torrent she could not hear the slow creak of its wheels. His heart was a-flutter, although he knew that the danger of observation was past, as the swaying white hood had disappeared.

"That's 'Renzo Taft," he remarked. "He's gittin' back late from the cross-roads. I reckon the storm cotch him an' kep' him."

He hesitated. Then, with a sort of falter of humiliation, "I reckon I'd better go back ter my hidin' place, Julia. The rain's slackenin', so somebody passin' mought view me. Ye jes' set hyar right quiet an' wait fur the rain ter hold up."

He turned away; then looked back over his shoulder.

"Good-by," he said.

The girl's luminous eyes dwelt smilingly upon him.

"Good-by," she answered softly.

He took his way along the ledges above the

treacherous stream to that blacker recess where the way deflected and the light failed ; he turned once more.

"I 'll be a-watchin' fur them flowers," he said.

Her smile itself was like a bloom ; he, unaware, treasured the recollection. He seemed to reflect it in some sort. He was smiling himself, as he went down into those sunless depths.

He could not forbear partly retracing his way once, and looking at her as she sat, quite still, gazing out with her eyes of summer and sunshine upon the rain, and the dreary, sad, tear-stained aspect of the world without, whence sounded the sobbing of the troubled wind.

When he came yet another time, the rain had ceased, and she was gone.

XIV.

Lorenzo Taft's arrival at his home, that afternoon, might have seemed to the casual observer
an event of the simplest significance. It is true, a
country trader, on his return from a bout of barter
at that emporium the cross-roads store, seldom
casts about him so vigilant an eye, or sustains so
controlled and weighty a manner, or wears a countenance of such discernment, its alert sagacity
hardly at variance with certain predatory suggestions, — on the contrary, finding in them its complement of expression. But these points might
only have argued ill for the profits of the bargainer
with whom he had dealt. As the great lumbering
canvas-hooded wagon came to a halt in the space
beneath the loft of the log barn, under partial
shelter, at least, and he began to unharness and
turn out the two mules, the anxious glances he cast
toward the house might have betokened impatient
expectation of assistance in unloading the ponderous
vehicle, and carrying into the store the cumbrous
additions to its stock represented in saddles, cutlery,
sugar, bolts of calico, stacks of hats, — the integrity of all more or less endangered by the weather.
But no one emerged from the house, and after
feeding the mules he turned hastily, took his way

in great strides through the rain across the yard, which was half submerged in puddles and running water, and unlocked the door. As he entered, big, burly, and dripping with rain, prophetically at odds with the falling out of the yet unknown events, he gazed about the dim interior with a dissatisfied, questioning eye. All was much as usual, save dimmer and drearier for the storm without. Here the unseen rain asserted its presence by the fusillade on the roof and the plashing from the eaves. The wind rushed furiously in recurrent blasts against the windowless walls. Since the denizens within could not mark how it bent the greatest tree, they might thus judge of its force, and quake beneath its tempestuous buffets. Now and again the writhen boughs of the elm just outside beat as in frantic appeal on the clapboards of the roof. The chimney piped a tuneless, fifelike note, and occasional drops fell a-sputtering into the dull blaze of the fire. Cornelia Taft herself was dull and spiritless of mien, as she sat on a low stool on the hearth knitting a blue yarn stocking. The room, lurking in a state of semi-obscurity, seemed the dreariest possible expression of a dwelling; only as the fitful blaze flared and fell were distortions of its simple furniture distinguishable, — the table with its blue ware, the bed and its gaudy quilt, the spinning-wheel, and the old warping-bars, where now merely skeins of cobwebs were wont to hang from peg to peg, since Cornelia Taft's precocity did not extend to weaving. A black cat sat blinking her yellow eyes before the fire. She had so conversational an aspect that it might seem that Taft had interrupted some conference, — of a dismal nature, doubtless, for there were traces of recent tears on the little girl's face, and a most depressed expression.

"Whar 's Copley? Whar 's yer uncle Cop?" he demanded, looking hastily about the shadowy place.

She paused to roll up her work methodically, and thrust the knitting-needles through the ball of yarn.

"He ain't hyar," she said, lifting reproachful eyes; "an' he ain't been hyar since ye been gone."

He stared down at her in silent surprise.

"Ye jes' went off an' lef' me an' Joe hyar by ourse'fs, an' we been mos' skeered ter death," she added, with a sob.

A sudden apprehension crossed Taft's face.

"I lef' Cop hyar. Ain't he been in ter git his vittles?"

She shook her head.

"Did ye call him in the store?"

She nodded.

"Mebbe he war in the barn."

"I blowed the hawn fur him; he ain't eat a mite sence ye been gone."

Taft turned hastily toward the door, his florid face paling. Then he turned back. "Whar 's Joe?"

"He hev runned away!" cried Sis, with a burst of sobs. "Las' night we-uns hearn sech a cur'ous hurrah — somewhar — I dunno — sech cur'ous talk an' hollerin' 'way down in the groun' — an' — an' — diggin' — an'" —

He had paused, looking amazed at her. Then his face changed, with a sort of aghast certainty upon it. "Jes' some boys diggin' in the Lost Time mine," he urged, however, plausibly.

"But — but"— she protested — "Joe, *he* say, they — they air — *dead*."

She looked at him, hoping for some sufficient adult denial of this terrible fantasy; but his face betokened only its confirmation, and she fell to shivering and sobbing afresh.

"Whenst it got so turrible in the middle o' the night, Joe, he looked out'n the winder upsteers, an' the moon hed riz. An' he clomb down by the tree. He 'lowed he would n't bide no mo' an' listen. So he jes' skun the cat out'n the winder. He war 'feared."

And once more she covered her face with her hands and wept. Nevertheless, between her fingers, as the tears trickled down them, she furtively surveyed him.

"Wunst," she said tentatively, "I 'lowed 't war revenuers. An' then I wisht 't war. I hed ruther hev hearn *them* 'n — 'n — dead ones."

His countenance did not change a muscle.

She was now alarmed by her own temerity. In the long ordeal of solitude and fright she had lost control of her small nerves, or she would not have overstepped her habitual caution so far. " Revenuers arter what ? " he demanded. His incidental, unconcerned manner reassured her.

" Arter the ' wild-cat,' I reckon," she hazarded.

He affected to consider the suggestion.

" Some boys *mought* be talkin' 'bout startin' a still down thar in the Lost Time mine. I 'll roust 'em out mighty quick, ef they do ! Ef thar 's enny whiskey sold round hyar, I 'm countin' on doin' it out'n my store, sure. I got a license ter sell."

She looked at him narrowly, suspiciously, hardly more credulous than he himself.

" I won't hev *my* profits sp'iled. Whiskey 's the best trade I got," he added, as he turned about. " Waal, I 'lowed Copley would be in hyar ter holp me tote the truck in ; but, howsever, set a rock afore the door ter hold it open, Sis, whilst I make a start, ennyhow."

His show of industry as he toiled across the rainy yard, now with a keg, now with a box, on his shoulder, of anxiety for the safety of his goods, his sedulous care in displaying them to the best advantage on the shelves to lure customers, might have deceived a wiser head than Cornelia Taft's. Her long-cherished suspicions were gradually dispelled, as she ran hither and thither, carrying the lighter packages in her arms, eagerly helping to bestow them, making place for them when she could do no more. It was not until she had gone back briskly to her task of preparing an early supper that he ventured to descend from the store to the room below, and take his way along the dark tunnel to the still in the recess of the mine. He paused surprised at the disordered and careless disarray about the entrance to the tunnel: some of the boards of the partition were on the ground, others aslant, none as they were habitually adjusted. With a steady hand he rectified this, and went forward forthwith, his lantern swinging in his grasp. Once he paused to listen: no voice, no stir; only the heavy windless silence. As he progressed, the faint tinkling of the running water smote his ear, and presently he had crossed it. No sound came from about the still; there was no suffusion of red light on the terra-cotta walls that sometimes glowed at the terminus of the tunnel when the furnace door stood open. He could hardly be said to have had a premonition. He was prepared for disaster by the previous events; but he could scarcely realize its magnitude, its conclusiveness, when the timid flare of the lantern illumined the dreary walls of the moonshiners' haunt, the dead cold furnace, the tubs of mash, — on the margin of one of which a rat was boldly feeding, scarcely pausing to look around with furtive, sinister bright eyes, — and his two lieutenants, whom he had left to guard Larrabee, bound and gagged upon the floor.

The craft which characterized Lorenzo Taft was hardly predicable of so massive an organization. It was an endowment of foxlike ingenuity, sinuous, lithe, suggestive of darting swiftness and of

doubled tracks. The expression of blunt dismay
on his big jowl dropping visibly beneath his broad
yellow beard, the widening stare in his round blue
eyes as he gazed about the dismal place, his heavy,
lumbering motion as he carefully set the lantern
down upon the cold masonry of the fireless furnace,
gave no intimation of the speed with which his
mind had canvassed the situation, accepted the inevitable, and fixed upon his future course. It was
hardly a moment before he was on one knee beside
the prostrate form of the elder moonshiner, and
had drawn from over his head the grain sack that
had served both to obscure his countenance and
more completely secure his gag. The glimmer of
the lantern, like a slow rill of light trickling feebly
through the darkness, illumined the expression of
eager appeal in the haggard, wild face and eyes of
Copley. An instant longer was too long to wait,
yet wait he must! Taft jerked his thumb over his
shoulder at the other prostrate form, convulsed
now in a frenzied effort to attract the attention of
the new-comer, whose footsteps had brought the
only hope of speedy deliverence.

" Drunk agin ? " he asked, in a low voice.

Copley made shift to nod his head affirmatively.
Then again that frantic plea for release illumined
his eyes and contorted his anxious features.

Taft, regardless, rose, with the swinging motion
which was characteristic of him, and, with the
lantern swaying in his hand, made his way to
the opposite side of the furnace, where the young

drunkard lay — very sober now, in good truth — cramped in every hard-bound limb, racked with the tortures of thirst, and half famished. Taft had partly unbound the ropes from about the furnace and cut them in twain, thus dissevering the companions in misery ; he swiftly knotted those that held the elder moonshiner, while the ends of Dan Sykes's bonds lay loose along the floor.

" Why, Dan," he cried roughly, " what sort'n caper is this ? "

The prostrate young fellow made an effort to rise, so strong that the already loosened cords relaxed ; and as Taft emphasized his demand by a sharp kick in the ribs, and an urgent exhortation to the young sot to " quit this damned fooling," the sack which Sykes had worn some twenty hours as hood and gag, and which, since his wakening from his long drunken sleep, he had strained in every fibre by his mad lurches of fright and efforts for freedom, rolled off, his pinioned arms were at liberty, and it seemed he had naught to do but to sit up and untie his craftily bound feet and legs.

" Ye demented gopher ! " cried Taft angrily, as Sykes sat up stupidly, blinking in the gleam of the lantern. " What ails ye ? Drunk agin ? "

If his bursting skull were admissible testimony, — but he shook his head stoutly in pious negation. Taft kicked him once more in the side with a scornful boot.

" Then the worse fool you-uns ! Look-a-hyar ! " he cried furiously, as he caught the young man by the collar and pulled him to his staggering feet, cutting with one or two quick passes with the knife the ropes about his legs. " Look-a-hyar, ye gallus-bird, what ye hev done in yer drunken tantrums! Murder! murder! or mighty nigh it!"

He swung the lantern round, so that its flickering gleams might rest on the figure of Copley, whose genuine bonds so closely resembled the plight which Sykes had thought his own. His bloodshot eyes distended, as he groped bending toward it in the darkness.

" Who 's that? Lar'bee? " he said.

" Lar'bee! " exclaimed Taft scornfully. " Lar'bee 's been out'n the still ever since yestiddy evenin'."

It was Sykes's drunken recollection that Larrabee was here when Taft departed ; but alack! in a cranium which is occupied by a headache of such magnitude, memory has scarce a corner to be reckoned on. Nevertheless he blurted out : —

" Ye tole me ter watch him," — he set his teeth in a sort of snarl, and glanced up under his eyebrows with a leer still slightly spirituous, — " ter gyard him like a dog. ' Hold fast! ' ye said, ' hold fast ! ' "

Taft suddenly shifted the lantern, to throw its full glare upon his own serious, grim, threatening face as he loomed up in the shadows.

" Sykes," he said, " this is a bad business fur you, an' ye 'll swing fur it, I 'm a-thinkin'. Nobody never set sech a besotted cur ez ye ter watch nobody.   I let Lar'bee out myse'f.   Ye an' Copley war lef' hyar ter keep sober an' run the still; an' what do ye do?   Ye murder him!"

As he lowered his big, booming, dramatic voice, the young fellow's blood ran cold.

"Ye murder him, an' tie him up like that, an' then do yerse'f up sorter fancy with bags an' a rope.   Ye 'll hev closer dealin's with a rope yit; I kin spy out that in the day that 's kemin'."   His eyes gleamed with a sinister smile.

Sykes's knees shook.

"Oh, my Lord!" he exclaimed wildly.   "Air — air he dead?   'T war n't me!   God A'mighty knows 't war n't me!"   The ready tears rushed to his eyes.   "'T war Lar'bee!   'T war Lar'bee!"

"Shucks!"   Taft turned wearily away.   "Ain't I tole ye I seen Lar'bee set out 'fore I did? Blackenin' Lar'bee won't save ye, Dan!   *Drink — drink!*   I tole ye drink would ruinate ye; always brings a man to a bad e-end.   Pity ye hed n't put some water in the jug beforehand, stiddier all them tears in the dregs o' yer spree."   He shook his head.   "So it is!   So it is!"

"Oh, is he dead, — air ye sure he is dead?" cried the young fellow in a heart-rending voice of appeal, flinging himself upon his knees beside the still, stark, motionless form of the elder moonshiner.

Taft swung the lantern slightly, and its lurid gleams played over the haggard, cadaverous face, ghastly with fatigue and the pallor of anxiety.

The boy drew back, with a shudder of repulsion. "Oh, I never went ter do it! I never went ter do it! I war drunk! crazy drunk! devil drunk! Oh" —

"They say," Taft interrupted suddenly, — "leastwise the lawyers do, — ez a man bein' drunk in c'mittin' a crime ought n't ter influence a jury, — the law makes no allowance; but," with an encouraging nod, "they say, too, ez it *do* influence the jury *every time*. An' the court can't holp it. The jury *will* allow suthin' fur a man bein' drunk."

The white face of the boy, imposed against the darkness with all the contour of youth, had hardly a characteristic that was not expressive of age, so pinched, so lined, so drawn, so bloodless, was every sharpened feature. The natural horror of his supposed deed, his simple, superficial repentance of the involuntary crime, were suddenly expunged; his whole being was controlled by a single impulse; a passion of fear possessed him. Jury, crime, lawyer, — these words looking to a legal arraignment first brought to his horror-stricken mind the idea of a responsibility other than moral for his deed. What slight independence of thought he had, what poor capacity for sifting and judging and weighing the probabilities his easily influenced mind might have exerted as he more and more recovered from his recent inebriation, became nullified upon the instant. He did not look once again back to the past, but to the future, wild, quaking, frenzied, as Taft elected to foretell the event.

"That 's why," Taft coolly said, nodding sagely, and inclining his head toward the breathless, frantic, almost petrified creature, "I 'd leave it ter men."

Sykes recoiled, with a shudder.

"Yes," reiterated Taft, weightily and slowly. "The jury would take yer drunk inter account; an' on the witness-stand I 'd testify ez ye war gin over ter the failin'."

The young fellow's gray, stony face did not change as Taft ceased to speak. Taft felt its fixed look upon him as he stood, his head bent, and his big hat thrust back on his yellow hair; one hand was laid meditatively on his long beard, as he gazed down on the prostrate figure of Copley; with the other hand he held the lantern, whose spare white glimmers of light thrown out into the surrounding obscurity seemed very meagre in the darksome place, which was never cheerful at best, but without the roar and heat of the furnace, the keen, brilliant glinting from the crevice of the door when closed or the red, suffusive flare when it was swung ajar, the still-room was the dreariest presentment of subterranean gloom.

"Yes," Taft continued thoughtfully, "I 'd ruther leave it ter men — ter the courts, ye know — 'n ter hev the folks round hyar ez war frien'ly ter Copley ondertake ter settle ye fur it; they 'd — Hey?" he interrupted himself.

For the young fellow had reached out his arm and laid his hand with a vise-like grip upon Taft's wrist. His head was thrust forward; he seemed about to speak, but his parted lips, drawn tight across his large, prominent teeth, emitted not a sound, although his wild, dilated, bloodshot eyes looked an eager protest. His voice had failed in framing the obnoxious words, which, however, Taft spoke patly enough.

"Why, ye know, they would — they would. Jedge Lynch is the only court fur this kentry. What sati'faction is it ter the folks hyarabout, ter hev a man kerried ter jail, thirty mile away, ter stan' his trial in the courthouse year arter nex', mebbe, an' then arter all 's come an' gone cheat hemp at las'? Yes, that's yer bes' chance; set out fur Colbury straight, an' s'render yerse'f thar."

He paused, apparently thinking deeply.

"Ef ye hed enny kin, though, in enny out'n-the-way place, my advices ter ye would be ter cut an' run, an' bide along o' them; fur this hyar air a mighty bad job, an' it's goin' ter go hard with the man ez done it."

Once more the pallid, evasive light flickered in feeble vibrations across the long, motionless, rope-bound figure, and the stark face curiously distorted and painfully repulsive with the gag in its stretched jaws.

"Ye ain't got no kin in no'th Georgy?" Taft demanded.

"Naw," replied the boy huskily.

The suggestion seemed to have restored his voice, albeit muffled and shaken; into his eyes,

staring, wide and bloodshot, into the gloom, was
creeping a definiteness of expression, as if he beheld, instead of the vacant black darkness, some
scene projected there as a possibility and painted
by his expectation. His grip on Taft's arm had
relaxed. It had been close and hard, and Taft
rubbed the wrist a trifle with the hand that still
held the lantern, setting the feeble glimmer
a-swinging swiftly about the dark walls.

"That's a pity, — that's a tur'ble pity," Taft
averred gloomily; then, with an air of rousing
himself, "Waal, ye'll jes' hev ter leave it ter men.
That's the bes' ye kin do." He was turning
briskly toward the tunnel. "I'll ondertake ter
gin ye the matter of a two hours' start of the folks
'bout hyar by not tellin' 'bout old Copley till then.
But ye hed bes' ride with speed, fur they'll be hot
shod on yer tracks, sure."

As he went forward with his swinging, elastic
stride, swaying the lantern back and forth, according to his wont, to illumine the path, his manner,
his words, his expression, so tallied with the situation he had invented and the rôle he had played
that even the most discerning might have descried
no discrepancy in point of fact. The young moonshiner, barely sobered and wholly frightened, was
easily to be deluded by a verisimilitude far less
complete. He followed, his clumsy feet stumbling
and stepping awry, as if his gait were still subject
to spirituous influences from which his brain was
freed. His cramped limbs yet felt the numbness

of their long constraint and the pain of his bonds, for Larrabee's ropes had not been adjusted with due regard to the free circulation of the blood. His progress was far slower than his host's, who paused from time to time and waited to be overtaken. On these occasions it soon became apparent that there was something in his mind on which he had begun to ponder deeply; for whereas at first he had visibly hastened to join Taft on seeing him whirl around, the lantern describing in the distance a wheel of pallid white light against the dense darkness of the tunnel, he now continued to plod heavily, slower and slower, even when the light settled to a shining focus, again motionless. Taft lifted it once as Sykes approached, throwing its force full upon the swollen, mottled, absorbed face, the fixed introspective eyes, the heavy slouching shoulders and bent head. At that moment of careful reconnoitre a genuine expression was on Taft's face, keen, furtive, triumphant; it passed unobserved. He whirled around again, leading the way with the lantern, and it was with a perfectly cloaked satisfaction that he began to observe the young fellow's convulsive haste to depart as they neared the exit from the tunnel, his flimsy pretense of heed to his elder's advice, and finally his heedlessness altogether, no longer able to maintain attention or its semblance.

He was gone at last, and Taft, returning to his prostrate comrade in the still, dismissed him from his mind, and thenceforward from his life, with a single comment. "That drunken shoat hev got an uncle in north Texas," he said, as he placed the lantern on the cold brick-work of the dead and fireless furnace. "I knowed that, so I fixed it so ez he 'd light out fur them furrin parts d'rec'ly. He ain't dawdlin', I 'm thinkin'."

Then, as he addressed himself to removing the gag and cutting the bonds of the elder distiller, his brow darkened.

"That cuss Lar'bee's work, hey ?" he demanded gruffly ; and as the liberated Copley gasped out an assent Taft growled a deep oath, his face scarlet, his hands trembling with rage, his anger unleashed, and his whole nature for the nonce unmasked.

"That kems from sparin' powder an' lead," he declared vindictively. "Why n't ye or Sykes shoot him ?"

"He war too suddint," gasped Copley. "Ye never see a painter so suddint an' sharp."

"An' why n't ye be suddint, too ?" retorted Taft aggressively.

Copley might have protested that in his own interest he had been as "suddint" as he could, and had done his best. He evidently felt, however, much in fault, and as, in silence, he ruefully rubbed his numb limbs, just free from their ligatures, tingling painfully with the renewal of the circulation of the blood, he gazed about, crestfallen and humbled, and even grief-stricken, at the scene of his wonted labors. It was but faintly revealed by the lantern on the masonry of the furnace, — the dimly white focus with divergent filaments of rays weaving only a tenuous web of light in the darkness which encompassed all. The great burly forms of tubs and barrels were but vaguely glimpsed as brownish suggestions in the blackness; a yellow gleam from the copper still gave the effect of an independent illumination rather than the resources of reflection, so dull and unresponsive was all else upon which the lantern cast its glimmer. Taft sat, according to his habit, upon the side of a barrel, his legs crossed, his elbow on one knee, his head bowed upon his hand, his big hat intercepting all view of his face. Copley gave a long sigh, as his spiritless glance noted the dejection of his friend; but his grooved and wrinkled face seemed as incapable of expressiveness as before, and, with its tanned tints and blunt, ill-cut features, resembled some unskillful carving in wood or a root. His thoughts swerved presently, almost with the moment of re-attaining his liberty, from the immediate disaster to the details of his drudgery which so habitually occupied his every waking faculty.

"That thar mash must be plumb ripe by this time," he remarked, his eyes fixed upon a spot in the darkness where presumably the tub in question was situated. "'T war nigh ripe whenst Lar'bee jumped up demented, it 'peared like, an' tuk arter we-uns."

Taft lifted a red face and a scowling brow. With an air of reckless desperation he strode to the tub, and the next moment Copley heard the splash as the contents were poured out down the shaft.

"Laws-a-massy, 'Renzo!" with the decisive ring of anger in his voice and all the arrogations of the expert, "why n't ye let me examinate it? Ye ain't got my 'speriunce; ye ain't ekal ter jedge like me. Why n't ye" —

"Ye miser'ble mole!" Taft retorted angrily. "Ye may be a jedge o' fermentin' an' stillin' an' sech like, but ye hev got powerful leetle gumption 'bout'n the signs o' the times. Thar ye sit, a-yawpin' away 'bout yer mash, ripe or raw, an' I 'm lookin' fur the shootin' irons o' the marshal's men under my nose every time I turn my head."

He suited the action to the word at the moment, looking down with a sudden squint which gave a frightfully realistic suggestion of the muzzle of a weapon held at his very teeth.

"The thing's busted!" Taft cried desperately. "It 's done! Kin ye onderstan' that? We-uns hev got ter the jumpin'-off place!"

The bewildered Copley looked vaguely at the verge of the deep shaft, perilously near.

"That Lar'bee 's loose now, full o' gredges fur bein' helt hyar," Taft continued. "We-uns oughter shot him, or let him shoot himself. An' the dep'ty sher'ff 's on his track, 'lowin' ez Espey be Lar'bee an' s'picionin' moonshinin'. The dep'ty sher'ff ain't got nuthin' ter do with sech ez moonshinin' hisse'f, but he air tryin' ter find Lar'bee, an' settle his gredges with him; so he 'll

gin the revenue dogs the word 'bout Lar'bee
an' distillin', an' whenst Lar'bee 's tuk he 'll take
a heap o' pleasure in guidin' 'em hyar, I 'll be
bound. He mought even turn informer hisse'f, ter
git even."

He sunk down suddenly on the barrel.

" It 's powerful hard on me ! " he cried. " I hev
treated them boys like they war my own sons."
He had forgotten, in this arrogation of age and paternal feeling, his recent youthfulness of matrimonial pretensions. " I hev tuk 'em in," — he did not
say in what sense, — " an' divided fair with 'em ;
an' they hev gotten mo' money out'n me than they 'd
ever elsewise view in thar whole lifetime. An' I
hev been keerful an' kep' the place secret an' quiet.
I hev tuk good heed ter all p'ints. An' we-uns
mought hev gone on peaceful an' convenient till the
crack o' doom, ef it hed n't been fur them. Oh,
thar never war sech a place ! " He looked round
with the eyes of gloating admiration on the gruesome, shadowy den about him, so singularly suited
to his vocation. " An' even the danger 'bout'n the
hotel is done with, an' the lan' percessioned by
now, I reckon, an' thar won't be no mo' packs o'
strangers in the Cove ; an' yit — an' yit — all fur
nuthin' ! "

He took off his hat, and rubbed his corrugated
brow with his hand with a gesture of desperation.

It is a singular trait of what might perhaps be
called sentimental economy that every individual
in this world should be the object of the hero wor-

ship of some other. It may be submitted that there are no conditions so sterile as to induce a dearth of this perfectly disinterested, unrewarded admiration and acceptation of some embodied ideal. It is familiar enough in the higher walks of life and with worthy objects. But there may be a champion among beggars. It is a potent agent. Its purblind flatteries have advanced many a dullard to a foremost place. The plainest face has some devotee of its beauty; and even the most unpromising infant is a miracle of grace and genius to a doting grandmother. Hardly a hero of the world's history is more dignified on his elevated plane than was Lorenzo Taft in the eyes of his humble coadjutor. His wiliness was wisdom; his dictatorial aggressiveness, the preëminence of a natural captaincy; his self-seeking a cogent prudence; and his natural courage — with which, indeed, he was well endowed — the finest flower of the extravaganza of valor.

Copley looked at him now with the respectful sympathy which one might well feel in witnessing the fall of a very great man. He scarcely remembered his own interests, inextricably involved. Every inflection of the mellow, sonorous voice raised to a declamatory pitch found a vibrating acquiescence in chords of responsive emotion. Every unconscious gesture of the massive and imposing figure — as histrionically appropriate as if acquired by labor and tuition, since it was indeed the nature that art simulates — was marked with appreciative eyes. A rat in a trap is hardly esteemed a fit object for sympathy by civilized communities, but consider the aspect and magnitude of the catastrophe to his friends and neighbors, consider the emotional melodrama within the small circuit of the wires!

"Don't take it so tur'ble hard, 'Renzo," expostulated Copley, still seated on the floor.

For Taft was standing motionless, his eyes staring and fixed, his hat far back on his head, exposing his set, drawn face with its teeth hard clenched, one hand mechanically clutching his flowing yellow beard, the other continually closing and unclosing on the handle of a pistol which he had half drawn from his pocket, — a habit of his in moments of mental perplexity, as if he instinctively appealed to this summary arbiter to decide on questions far enough removed from its jurisdiction.

"Don't be so tur'ble desolated; some way out'n it, sure ez ye air born," urged Copley in a consolatory wheeze.

The sound of his voice seemed to rouse Taft. He caught himself with a start and turned hastily away, looking about as if in search of something. He took the lantern presently to aid him in this, and when it came back, glimmering through the dusk, he carried a box of tools in the other hand.

"Thar's one way out'n it, sure," he said in a muffled, changed voice, "though it's gone powerful hard with me ter git my own cornsent ter take it."

He placed the lantern upon the furnace, and, as he went vigorously to work, the astounded Copley, still upon the ground, began to perceive that he was taking the apparatus carefully apart; he was disconnecting the worm from the neck, when his amazed coadjutor found his voice.

" Hold on, 'Renzo," he remonstrated; " ye ain't a-goin' ter take the contraption down, surely " —

" Ruther hev the revenuers do it? " said Taft, showing his teeth in a sarcastic smile as he looked up. " They 'll make wuss slarter with the worm 'n I will."   Then, pausing, with a frown of rancorous reminiscence, " I hed a still o' bigger capacity 'n this one over yander in Persimmon Cove, an' they cut it up in slivers, an' the worm war lef' in pieces no longer 'n that," measuring with both hands, " an' the furnace all tore up.   I never seen sech a sight ez whenst I croped back ter view the wreck.   I 'lowed I 'd never git forehanded enough ter start ter manufacture sperits agin in this worl'."

He stood idly gazing down these vistas of memory grimly enough for a moment; then, turning back to the still, " I 'll make a try ter save the property this time, so when the storm blows over we kin git started agin another way an' another day. I 'll fix it so ez when Lar'bee tells, his words will be cast back in his teeth fit ter knock 'em all down his own throat.   He 'll be sorry enough, sure 's ye air born.   They 'll be hard swallowin'."

The natural fortitude of Taft's character, the elastic quality of his strength, his big, bluff mental methods, combined to support him in this ordeal to a degree which contrasted advantageously with the weak, almost supine grief that Copley manifested. Perhaps, too, Taft's dinner was a material element which gave cohesion and decision to his mental resolves. Now, Copley, half starved, nervous, wild with anxiety, dread for the future, regret for the past, doubt of the present, would angrily protest, even while he aided in dismantling the apparatus; and then, after a word or two of argument, would admit its necessity, its urgency, and again lament it as futile. He almost wept when the object of his solicitude, which he had served as if it were a fetich, was finally dismembered, and he found only a partial consolation in being himself permitted to pack it, secure from injury, in boxes which Taft brought down from the store. This scanty satisfaction was short-lived, for, despite his objection, Taft poured out upon the ground the liquor which remained after the shipment of the two barrels to the cross-roads. The tubs were cut into pieces in true " revenuer " fashion, the mash was poured out, the furnace was demolished out of all semblance to its former proportions and uses, before Taft began to lay the train to blow the place up, and thus effectually silence its testimony forever.

" S'pos'n' — s'pos'n' " — Copley shivered — " s'pos'n' somebody war in the Lost Time mine down thar " —

Taft paused, with a lot of tow in his hands which he was arranging for a fuse; he glanced around, the lantern swinging on his arm, as if waiting for the sequel to the unfinished sentence; then, as

Copley remained vaguely staring as if at a vision of possible laborers in the Lost Time mine, " Skeer 'em powerful, I reckon," he said casually, and bent once more to his work.

" But — but " — Copley recommenced, in a tone so urgent that Taft once more desisted to listen, with an inquiring look on his half-turned face — " but — but — s'pos'n' the — a — 'splosion o' the powder war — war ter bring down the rocks an' the timbers in some o' them tunnels an' open shafts, an' somebody war in thar, hey ? hey ? " with eager insistence.

" Shut 'em in thar fur good an' all, I reckon, — git buried a leetle before thar time, that 's all," said Taft coolly, and went on with his work as before.

Perhaps some vague premonition, perhaps an intuition of subterranean proximity to an unsuspected wanderer in the Lost Time mine, perhaps only a morbid aversion to the whole project, induced by the lack of that conscience-fortifying force, dinner, actuated Copley, but for the third time he sought to disaffect Taft's mind toward it.

" Mebbe somebody mought be passin' an' hear the 'splosion ; mought n't they 'low 't war cur'us ? What would they make of it ? "

Taft did not now pause in his work; he answered still bending down to the ground laying the train.

" Yearthquake," he said composedly, " or else jes' some o' the rottin' timbers o' the mine settlin' an' givin' way.　Besides," he added, straightening himself up, " nobody 's passin' at this time o' night, nohow."

" Night ! " exclaimed Copley. " Is it night ? "

" Midnight," replied Taft laconically.

He stood silent, thinking, a moment, and resting after the labor of cautiously adjusting the charges of powder; and then, so quiet it all was, not the stir of a breath, not the whisper of a word, not the silken rustle of a ribbon of flame in the demolished furnace, he heard, what he had never before heard so far as here in the still-room, the reiterated strokes of a pick echoing down the tunnel, and cleaving the ground with the regularity of a practiced workman. He said not a word to Copley; he walked along the tunnel toward the sound, a chill thrill stealing over him despite the fact that his temerity was a trifle more pronounced than usual because he was about to leave the place forever. The strokes continued, now growing louder, now more muffled, always accurately timed; and suddenly the faint clamors of that high, queer, false-ringing voice that seemed to seek out and shock every nerve within him. He recoiled with fright and an unreasoning anger. He turned himself about, and swiftly changed the position of a can filled with powder which was to aid in the demolition of the place, arranging it in a niche in the earth close to the wall whence the sound came.

" I make ye my partin' compliments," he said, with a sarcastic smile and a mocking wave of the hand to the gruesome unknown. The next moment his expression changed to a frightened gravity, and he ran through the black tunnel as if he consciously had the devil at his heels, pausing not until he was safe in the cellar beneath the store.

The paroxysm, if so it might be called, passed in a moment, and he was laughing as he stood at the aperture of the tunnel, holding the lantern, red-faced and a trifle shamefaced, when Copley, left far behind, came hobbling up slowly and painfully. Taft was quite restored; it was with his own assured, definite manner and elastic stride that he presently took his way along the tunnel again and applied the match to the fuse. He evidently accomplished his work thoroughly, for he had no doubts of its efficacy when he returned and stood leaning against a pile of boxes, waiting quite carelessly as here and there tiny stellular lights sprang up along that darksome way that was not wont to blossom out such constellations.

Stars? No; lines of fire, vermicular, writhing, growing, serpentine, swiftly gliding, armed with venom, with destruction under their forked tongues; for suddenly a flare, a frightful clap as of thunder, a wrench as if the foundations of the earth were torn asunder, and the two men were thrown to the ground and the lantern extinguished in the jar.

The reverberations were slow to die away; only gradually quiet came. A stillness ensued, stifling with dust, and with such strong sense of alternation with that moment of deafening detonation that the pulses quivered with expectancy, and the slightest movement set the nerves to jarring. Taft had groped for a light, and as the faint coruscation of a match, then the steadier gleam of the lantern, pierced the darkness, the nearest results of the explosion were open to view. The timbers roofing the tunnel had been shaken down, and close at hand masses of earth had fallen with them and lay banked at the very door. If Taft had been warned in a dream, he could hardly have made his defense more perfect. He and his one trusted adherent worked there the rest of the night. The old original timbers of the house, partly rotten and time-stained, were replaced as formerly, leaving no trace that there had ever been an entrance into the abandoned mine; and when at last Taft clambered through the aperture of the counter into the store, he left the door broadly flaring after him.

"Trust Sis ter notice it," he remarked. "She 'll git used ter it in ten minits, an' it 'll 'pear like she always knowed 't war thar."

The still was conveyed some miles away and buried in a marked spot, and thus the business of moonshining was abandoned at the moment when the project of the summer hotel, from which it had so much to fear, was pretermitted amidst its varied entanglements, and the Cove, which certainly could not have comfortably contained both, was left without either for the nonce.

XV.

As Julia entered her father's house, quite fresh and dry after the tumults of the storm, each of the group gathered about the fireside was too insistently preoccupied at the moment to notice the discrepancy between her spotless attire and the aspects of the weather, except indeed Luther. The details of their attire she marked at once, and dimpled at the sight. These rain-lashed victims of the processioning had hustled themselves into their cast-off gear; and albeit the fashions of the day were not exigent in the Cove, very forlorn appeared these ancient garments, having long ago seen the best of their never very good days. Cap'n Lucy's brown coat was like a russet old crinkled leaf, as it clung, out of shape and ruffled by unskillful folding, about him; Luther wore one of his own of former years, far too small now for his burly shoulders that threatened to burst out of it at every seam, and his long arms that protruded their blue shirt sleeves only half covered from the elbow. He met her glance with a resentful glare, as if he could imagine now no cause for mirth, which was untimely in its best estate. His Sunday coat graced the form of Jasper Larrabee, who sat on the other side of the fire, and who albeit not of the processioning party, had been

caught in the rain in coming hither. Although
as tall as Luther, he was much more slender, and
he seemed to have shrunk, somehow, in the ampli-
tude of his host's big blue coat. He gave Julia
a formal greeting, and was apparently much perturbed by the untoward state of mind in which he
found Cap'n Lucy. And indeed Cap'n Lucy's
face seemed to have adopted sundry wrinkles from
his coat, so old, so awry, so crinkled, so suggestive
of better days, had it suddenly become. Julia was
reminded all at once of the business interests at
stake.

"How did the percessionin' turn out, dad?" she
inquired, as she stood with her hand on the back of
a chair, and looked across the fire at him.

If any eyes might watch Fortune's wheel undis-
mayed, whether it swing high or low, one might
deem them these surely, with perpetual summer
blooming there, as if there were no frosts, no
winter's chill, no waning of time or love or life.
What cared she for land or its lack?

The forelegs of Cap'n Lucy's chair came to the
floor with an irascible thump. He turned and
surveyed the room; then, looking at her, "Air yer
eyesight good?" he demanded.

"Toler'ble," she admitted.

"D' ye see that thar contraption?" he continued, leaning forward, and pointing with great *em-
pressement* at a spinning-wheel in the corner.

"I see it," she said, meeting his keen return
glance.

·" D' ye know what it 's made fur?" he inquired, dropping his voice, and with an air of being about to impart valuable information.

" Fur spinnin'," she answered wonderingly.

" Oh, ye know, do ye?   Then — mind it."

And thus he settled the woman question, in his own house at least, and repudiated feminine interest and inquisitiveness in his business affairs, and spurned feminine consolation and rebuke as far as he could, — poor Cap'n Lucy!

Larrabee had that sense of being ill at ease which always characterizes a stranger whose unhappy privilege it is to assist at a family quarrel. He was divided by the effort to look as if he understood nothing of ill temper in the colloquy, and the doubt as to whether he did not appear to side with one or the other, — to relish Julia's relegation to the spinning-wheel, or to resent Cap'n Lucy's strong measures; or perhaps he might seem lightly scornful of both.

He gazed steadily out of the open door, where a great lustrous copper-tinted sky glassed itself in myriads of gleaming copper-tinted ponds made in every depression by the recent rains ; between were the purplish-black mountains cut sharply on the horizon.   He heard a mocking-bird singing, and what a medley the frogs did pipe!   Then rushed out into the midst the whir of Julia's spinning-wheel, which made all other songs of the evening only its incidental burden.   She sat near the door, her figure imposed upon those bright hues of sky and water as if she were painted on some lustrous metal. Their reflection was now and again on her hair; she might have seemed surrounded by some glorious aureola. Not that he definitely discerned this. He only felt that she was fairer than all women else, and that the evening gleamed. The bird's song struck some chord in his heart that silently vibrated, and the whir of her wheel was like a hymn of the fireside. He wished that he had never left it for Taft and his gang, and the hope of making money for a home of his own, since his mother's hospitality had well-nigh left him homeless. The thought roused him to a recollection of his errand.

"I kem hyar ter git yer advices, Cap'n Lucy," he began.

Cap'n Lucy turned upon him a silent but snarling face. He needed all his " advices " for himself.

"I ain't got nuthin' ter hide from you-uns," Larrabee continued, after a pause for the expected reply. " Ye know all I do," — a fleeting recollection of the still came over him, — " that I 'm able ter tell," he added; for the idea of betraying the secrets ·involving Taft and the other moonshiners had never entered his mind.

Cap'n Lucy's scornful chin was tossed upward.

"We-uns feel toler'ble compliminted," he averred, " ter hev it 'lowed ez we-uns knows *all* you-uns do, fur that's a heap, ez ye air aimin' ter tell."

"I mean — I went ter say, Cap'n Lucy" —

Jasper Larrabee's words, in their haste, tripped one over the other, as they sought to set their meaning in better array.

"He jes' means, uncle Lucy, ez it ain't no *new* thing," Adelicia interposed to expound, touched by the anxious contrition of the younger man, who was leaning eagerly forward, his elbow on his knee, toward the elder, and to allay the contrariety of spirit of "uncle Lucy."

"An' meddlin' ain't no new thing, nuther, with you-uns, Ad'licia," snarled Cap'n Lucy, much overwrought. "I wish ter Gawd, with all the raisin' an' trainin' I hev hed ter gin ye, I could hev larnt ye ter hold yer jaw wunst in a while whenst desir'ble, an' show sech manners ez — ez T'bithy thar kin." He pointed at the cat on the hearth, and gave a high, fleering laugh, in which the sarcastic vexation overmastered every suggestion of mirth.

A slight movement of Tabitha's ears might have intimated that she marked the mention of her name. Otherwise she passed it with indifference. With her skimpy, shabby attire, — her fur seemed never to flourish, — her meek air of disaffection with the ways of this world, her look of adverse criticism as her yellow eyes followed the movements of the family, her thankless but resigned reception of all favors as being less than she had a right to expect, her ladylike but persistent exactions of her prerogatives, gave her, somehow, the style of a reduced gentlewoman, and the quietude and gentle indifference and air of superiority of the manners on which Cap'n Lucy had remarked were very genteel as far as they went.

Adélicia seemed heedless of the mentor thus pointed out. She noisily gathered up her work, somewhat cumbrous of paraphernalia, since it consisted of a small cedar tub, a large wooden bowl, and a heavy sack of the reddest of apples which she was paring for drying, and carried it all around the fireplace to seat herself between the two parties to this controversy.

"Now, uncle Lucy, ye jes' got ter gin Jasper yer advices, an' holp him out'n whatever snap he hev got inter."

Her deep gray eyes smiled upon the young man, as the firelight flashed upon her glittering knife and the red fruit in her hand, although her delicate oval face was grave enough. Ever and again she raised her head, as she worked, to toss back the tendrils of her auburn hair which were prone to fall forward as she bent over the task. There was a moment's silence as Jasper vainly sought to collect his ideas.

"Tell on, Jasper," she exhorted him. "I 'm by ter pertect ye now. An' ennyhows, uncle Lucy's bark is a long shakes wuss 'n his bite."

She smiled encouragingly upon the suppliant for advice ; her own face was all unmarred by the perception that matters had gone much amiss with the processioning of the land, for uncle Lucy was a man often difficult to please, and sometimes only a crumple in his rose leaf was enough to make him condemn the queen of flowers as a mere vegetable, much overrated. The girl's aspect was all the brighter as she wore a saffron-tinted calico blouse and apron with her brown homespun skirt, and she seemed, with her lighted gray eyes, her fair, colorless face, and her ruddy auburn hair, a property of the genial firelight, flickering and flaring on the bright spot of color which she made in the brown shadows where she sat and pared the red apples. She reverted in a moment to that proclivity to argue with Cap'n Lucy which was so marked in their conversation.

"An' who is the young men ter depend on in thar troubles, uncle Lucy, ef not the old ones?" she demanded.

"On the young gals, 'pears like," promptly retorted "uncle Lucy," pertinently and perversely.

Then he caught himself suddenly. In the impossibility, under the circumstances, to concentrate his mind exclusively on his own affairs, his interest in correlated matters was reasserted. It occurred to him that it behooved him to foster any predilection that Adelicia might show for any personable man other than the fugitive Espey. He could see naught but perplexity and complication of many sorts to ensue for himself and his household should Espey return; and although Cap'n Lucy selfishly hoped and believed that this was, in the nature of things, impossible, still he had reluctantly learned by bitter experience the fallibility of his own judg-

ment. It seemed to him a flagrant instance of in-
constancy on Adelicia's part, but Cap'n Lucy gave
that no heed. Few men truly resent a woman's
cruelty to another man. Adelicia might have
brought all the youth in the county to despair, for
all hard-hearted Cap'n Lucy would have cared.
And thus her appeal for Jasper Larrabee was not
altogether disregarded.

"Goin' ter set thar an' chaw on it *all* day,
Jasper?" he demanded acridly. "Why n't ye spit
it out?"

"Why," said Larrabee, "it's 'bout this hyar
Jack Espey."

The apple dropped from Adelicia's hand, and
rolled unheeded across the hearth; the spinning-
wheel was suddenly silent, and Julia, all glorified in
the deeply yellow glare about her, sat holding it
still with one hand on its rim. Cap'n Lucy's head
was canted to one side, as if he were prepared to
deliberate impartially on some difficult proposition.

"This Jack Espey, — I met up with him at the
cross-roads store, an' struck up a likin' fur him, an'
brung him home an' tuk him in, an' he hev been
thar with me fur months an' months — an' — an'
he never tole me ez he hed enny cause ter shirk
the law."

"He war 'feared ter, I reckon, Jasper," said
Adelicia.

"He never meant no harm, Jasper," the silent
Julia broke in from where she sat in her dull red
dress against the tawnily gilded glories of the western sky.

Beyond a mechanical " Hesh up, Ad'licia," Cap'n Lucy gave them no heed, but Luther glanced sharply from one to the other.

Jasper Larrabee replied in some sort: " Then he never treated me with the same confidence I done him. An', Cap'n Lucy," he continued, " ye yerse'f seen the e-end o' it. He purtended ter the sher'ff ter be *me*, an' tuk advantage o' my mother's callin' him 'sonny,' an' wore my name, an' went with 'em a-sarchin' fur hisse'f; an' whenst he got skeered, thinkin' ez they knowed him, he resisted arrest, an' kem nigh ter takin' the off'cer's life, whilst purtendin' ter be *me*, in my name ! "

" He never meant no harm," faltered Adelicia, aghast at this showing against her absent lover.

" None in the worl'; he never went ter harm nuthin'," protested Julia's flutelike tones.

" Did ye kem hyar ter git my advices fur Jack Espey ? " demanded Cap'n Lucy sourly. " He needs 'em, I know, but " —

" Naw, Cap'n Tems. I kem ter git 'em fur myse'f, fur I dunno which way ter turn. You-uns hyar saw the e-end o' it, — the night the dep'ty kem a-sarchin' fur Jasper Lar'bee, who he 'lowed he hed flung over the bluffs, an' I went along at his summons, knowin' 't war Espey ez hed got away from him, purtendin' ter be *me*."

Cap'n Lucy nodded.

" Now I have hearn that dep'ty air in the Cove agin."

Cap'n Lucy remembered the dark, facetious,

malicious face that the officer had borne as a spectator of the processioning of the land. He nodded again. " I hev seen him hyar ter-day."

" Ef I war knowed ter him ez Lar'bee, whenst he finds out 't war Espey ez escaped that night, I mought be 'rested fur harborin' a fugitive, ez holpin' out the murder arter the fac' — an' — an' my mother — Espey gin me no chance, no ch'ice! Would n't ye 'low ez ennybody — *ennybody* — would hev tole me that, Cap'n Lucy, ter gin me the ch'ice o' dangerin' myse'f afore he tuk so much from me an' mine ? "

Cap'n Lucy changed countenance. This was a new view of the matter. He had not judged from Larrabee's standpoint; for he himself had had full knowledge of the circumstances and the fact that they were withheld from Espey's entertainer. This was made suddenly manifest.

" Why, Jasper," expostulated Adelicia, her eyes full of tears, her vibrant tones tremulous with emotion, " he 'lowed ter we-uns ez he war sure the man would n't die o' the gunshot wound, bein' powerful big an' hearty; but he tuk out an' run, bein' turr'ble 'feared o' the law, and arrest an' lyin' in jail fur a long time, waitin', an' uncle Lucy said " —

She paused suddenly, for Jasper Larrabee had leaned forward in his chair, scanning the faces about him with a blank amazement so significant that it palsied the words on her tongue.

" Espey tole *you-uns !* An' Espey tole yer *uncle Lucy !* Why, then ye all knowed him ter be a runaway, an' ye knowed ez he war a-playin' his deceits on nobody but me an' my mother ez hed got him quartered on us, an' mebbe war liable ter the law fur it."

Adelicia, trembling, leaned back in her chair. Cap'n Lucy cast an infuriated glance upon her, and then, with a hasty, nervous hand, rubbed his brow back and forth, as if to stimulate his brain that offered no solution of the difficulty. Jasper Larrabee still sat leaning forward, his clear-cut face full of keen thought, a flush on his pale cheek, a fire kindling in his brown eyes, and a sarcastic smile curving his angry lips.

"My Gawd!" he exclaimed, "it is a cur'ous thing ez my mother ain't got a frien' in this worl'! She says she don't work fur thanks, an' I 'll take my livin' oath she don't git 'em. That thar door o' the widder's cabin on the Notch hev stood open ter the frien'less day an' night since I kin remember. Her table 's spread for the hongry. Her h'a'th 's the home o' them ez. hev no welcome elsewise an' elsewhere. An' her nigh neighbor an' old frien' sees a s'pected murderer quarter himself thar, an' bring s'picion an' trouble *ennyhow*, an' danger mebbe, on her an' hern. Ye mought hev advised Espey ter gin her her ch'ice, or leave. Ye mought hev done ez much ez that! My mother 's a old 'oman; an' she 's a proud 'oman, though ye mought n't think it, an' the bare idee o' sech talk ez that, — of s'picion, an' arrest, an' jail, — it would kill her! it would kill her!"

Cap'n Lucy sat almost stunned, as under an arraignment. He pulled mechanically at his pipe, but his head was sunk on his breast, and his face was gray and set. The circumstances so graphically placed before him seemed to have no relation to those of his recollection; they wore a new guise. He had known all his life instances of collision in which powder and lead had played more or less a tragic part; but the rôle of the law had always been subsidiary and inadequate in the background of the scene, sometimes represented only by an out-witted officer, and the jollity of details of hair-breadth escapes. This construction of crime was beyond his purview of facts. He did not know, or he did not remember, that aught that others than the principal could do subsequent to a crime might render them liable as accessory after the fact. Espey had, in a fight, shot his antagonist,—such things were of frequent occurrence in Cap'n Lucy's memory. He never expected to see or to hear of the beagles of the law on the trail of the fugitive; his care, and his only care, was to prevent his niece from marrying an expatriated man while expatriated.

He thought now with a grievous sense of fault of old " Widder Lar'bee," — her softness, her kindness, her life of care for others ; and then he thought of Rodolphus Ross and his crude brutality, his imperviousness to any sanctions, his rough inter-pretation of fun, his eagerness to shield his own lapses of official vigilance, his grudges against the supposed Larrabee, and his threats. What mischief might a chance word work!

The dusky red of the last of the evening glow was creeping across the floor. All the metallic yellow glare was tarnished in the sky. Instead were strata of vaporous gray and slate tints alternating with lines of many-hued crimson, graduated till the ethereal hue of faintest rose ended the ascending scale of color. Still the frogs chorused and still the bird sang, but shadows had fallen, and they were not all of the night. Something of melancholy intimations drew his eyes to the purple heights without as Jasper Larrabee spoke.

"Waal, I'm her friend, ef she ain't got nare nother." And then, as if he felt he were arrogating unduly to his purpose, "An' I s'pose I'm a friend o' my own, too, an' I know *I* ain't got nare nother. I kem hyar ter-night fur yer advices, Cap'n Tems; but ez ye don't 'pear ter have none ter gimme, I b'lieve I'll take my own. I'll settle this thing for myse'f. I'll find Jack Espey! I'll track him out. I'll run him down. I'll arrest him myse'f, an' I'll deliver him ter the law. An' let the door o' the jail that he opened fur me be shut an' barred on him!" There was a concentrated fury in his face as he said this. "I won't hide no mo' like a beast o' the yearth in a den in the ground, consortin' with wuss 'n wolves an' bar an' painters. I won't skulk homeless like a harnt no mo' through the woods. I won't shirk the sher'ff no mo' fur Jack Espey's crimes, an' 'kase I done him nuthin' but good an' kindness! I 'll find him, — the yearth can't kiver him so I can't find him, — an' I 'll deliver him ter the law!'"

He stood for one moment more, and then he strode across the room to the door, his shadow blotting out the last red light of the day, leaving the circle about the fire gazing wistfully and aggrieved after him, except Luther, who was picking up the borrowed coat which Larrabee had tossed aside as he passed.

Outside the night had fallen suddenly. The west was clouded, despite the lingering red strata, and the twilight curtailed. He looked through purple tissues of mists that appeared to have the consistency of a veil, to where yellow lights already gleamed through the shadows. They came from the shanties of the workmen beneath the cliffs, on which the ruins of the hotel had at last ceased to smoke. He hardly knew whither to turn. What pressure for explanations, what unbearable inquisitive insistence, would meet him at home, where Henrietta Timson reigned in the stead of his mother, he could well forecast; to venture near the Lost Time mine, within reach of Taft, was, he knew, as much as his life was worth. He hesitated now and again, as he went aimlessly up the road; regretting his outbreak at the Tems cabin; coveting its shelter, its fireside, the companionship of the home group; half minded to return thither; but resentment because of their half-hearted friendship, as he deemed it, pride and anger and shame, conspired to withhold him.   Once again, as he ascended the mountain, he turned and looked down at the cluster of orange-tinted lights from the workmen's shanties that clung so close together in the depths of the purple valley, and he hesitated anew.   White mists were abroad on their stealthy ways; a brooding stillness held the clouds; the mountains loomed sombre, melancholy, against them, indistinguishable and blent with them toward the west, save when the far-away lightnings of the past storm fluctuated through their dense gray folds, and showed the differing immovable outline of the purple heights. In the invisible pools below these transient flashes were glassed, shining through the gloom.   The reflection of stars failed midway, because of the mist. There were few as yet in the sky, but as he lifted his eyes he beheld again, immeasurably splendid in the purple dusk, that sudden kindling of ethereal, palpitating, white fire which he had marked once before, — that new and supernal star, strange to all familiar ways of night hitherto, shining serene, aloof, infinitely fair above the melancholy piping mountain wilds and the troublous toils of the world.

XVI.

Jasper Larrabee stood transfixed, gazing at
that tremulous, luminous astral presence with a
strange superstitious thrill at his heart. It hardly
seemed merely a star, so alien to his mind was its
aspect in the erst untenanted spaces whence it
blazed, so freighted with occult significance. Had
the moment been charged with some wonderful
apotheosis, some amplification of its pure white
lustre into the benignant splendors of a vision of
angels, the transformation could scarcely have ex-
ceeded the capacities of that breathless, insistent
expectation which the ignorant mountaineer lifted
toward it. For his was a simple faith, and his
untaught mind had learned no doubts. And had
never these nights of ours communion with celestial pursuivants? Did never the flutter of an
angel's wing illumine far perspectives that darkle
heavily over the earth? Was this rare fluid,
which we call the air, so dense; were its sensitive
searching vibrations, known as waves of light and
sound, so dull, that it should feel naught, reveal
naught, when the angel of the Lord flashed through
the stars and the wind, through blossoming woods
or bleak snows of deserts, and into the haunts and
the homes of men?

So many had come! He did not know that they were alien to the nineteenth century, and that the most spiritual-minded of to-day would account for their sudden vision as from prosaic natural causes, — as mental aberration, or the distortions of a diseased fancy, or the meaningless phantasmagoria of somnolent cerebration. To him it seemed that they had been with man from the very beginning; and why should their presence here be stranger than his own? Their very numbers served to coerce credibility. So many had come! To kings, to wanderers in the wilderness, to prophets, to shepherds, in dreams and in the broad daylight, they came : to stand with a gleaming sword before the gates of Paradise, and to sing in the starry advent of a new day, — On earth peace, good will toward men ; to bring the immortal lilies of the Annunciation, and to tread the ways of the fiery furnace; to touch the bursting bonds of saints in prison, and to roll away the stone from the sepulchre of all the world; to minister to the Christ alike in the shadows of Gethsemane and amongst the splendors of the Mount of the Transfiguration!

Larrabee was trembling in every limb, as the scenes trooped out before him in the vivid actuality of his recollections of the pages of the much-thumbed volume which he had left behind him when he had fled from the still in the Lost Time mine. He sank down upon the rocky verge of the precipice, amongst the clinging verdure of its jagged crevices. Some sweet-scented herb sent out its delicate incense under the pressure of his hands. A drowsy twitter of half-awakened nestlings came from the feathery boughs of a cedar-tree that a niche in the cliff hard by half nourished, half starved. The melancholy antiphony of the voices of the wilderness rose and fell in alternating strains, and at long intervals in a vague undiscriminated susurrus the night seemed to sigh.

He heard naught; he heeded naught. His unwinking gaze was fixed upon the wondrous star in the heavens, with that thronging association of angelic ministrants so definitely in his mind that he might have thought to see an amaranthine crown expanding from the rayonnant sidereal points, or the outline of a nearing pinion stretched strongly to cleave the ether. For so many had come!

But no! His imagination could compass no such apotheosis. The star remained a star. The exaltation of that moment of wild, vague, and breathless expectation exhaled slowly. A poignant sense of loss succeeded it. The prosaic details of the actual outer life pressed once more on his realization. He looked about him on the sombre wilderness, the black surly mountains, the itinerant mists, heedless whither, the steely glimmer here and there of the ponds where the water made shift to catch the reflection of the sky amidst the dun shadows, and sighed drearily with the sighing night.

He was penniless, shelterless, his life at the

mercy of any chance that might favor his crafty
enemy, his confidence betrayed by the fugitive
whom he had succored, his liberty endangered,
already a criminal in the eyes of the law, — an
outcast, in truth, within a league of his home.
From the nullity of the begloomed landscape the
glance naturally rebounded, and the very obscura-
tion of the earth lent glister and definiteness to
the wonderful precision of the march of the constellations, as, phalanx after phalanx, they de-
ployed, each in its allotted space and sequence,
toward the west.   And again his eyes dwelt upon
that new splendor in the midst of them.   How
strange that it should suddenly blossom whitely
forth among these old, old stars that had lighted
the bosky ways of the garden of Eden!   How
strange that the sight of it should be vouchsafed
to him — and why!

His pulses were tumultuously astir.   All at
once the thought that had been slowly framing
itself in his mind took definite form.   He wondered if it could be a sign for him, and of what!

In the arrogations of poor humanity of the
higher things, in the infinite breadth of the claim
of an immortal soul, vast incongruities meet.   The
extreme might seem reached in the ignorant mountaineer, the moonshiner obnoxious to the law, the
poverty-stricken laborer, seeing with the wild
preëmptions of fancy this star, all newly and miraculously alight in the sky, as charged with some
mysterious relation to his infinitesimally petty and

restricted life. But once admit the idea of an immortal spirit, heir of all knowledge, made a little lower than the angels, to be crowned with glory and honor, the climax of development, and even the splendors of the star are as naught.

Larrabee had no cultivated sense of comparison. His tenacious nature laid hold upon the idea of an intimate personal intention, a sign in the heavens, with a blunt and stalwart appropriation.

He rose swiftly to his feet. So different a spirit animated him that it seemed a different path from that which he had trod as he had plodded slowly up the mountain, with hesitating steps and frequent uncertain pauses. Now he went deftly down the rugged and far darker way, brushing amongst bushes and vines, and be-showered with the perfumed drops that his hasty transit shook from their boughs; swiftly slipping through the shifting mists that now hid the sky, and again revealed the glister of that great star amidst a myriad others at the vanishing point of a perspective of seemingly precipitous white ascents, as the uncertain light cleft the glimmering vapors. He looked up to it, as it were, through a defile between these impalpable white cliffs, from the dark abysses of the night; and then the gauzy medium interposed, and without the faint light of the stars the night was black again. His pace did not slacken. He went forward as confidently in the darkness as if he were led by the definite capacity of sight, trusting to that instinct of woodcraft almost as keen as sense itself.

Sometimes, indeed, his foot struck against a branch, torn by the wind from the trees and left to wither in the rugged path ; or the splash of a pool beneath his inadvertent step broke the silence of his journey, as these unaccustomed incidents of the way asserted their presence as obstacles. He never hesitated, nor doubted, nor deviated. He seemed led through the darkness by his will. He was aware in some mysterious sort of the looming propinquity of great trees or the locality of jagged rocks ; he avoided the verge of cliffs and abysses with that keen, accurate discernment of an unascertained faculty, as a somnambulist might have done. As far as his recognized intelligence was concerned, he was down in the Cove before he knew it, for the way was still sloping, the footing rocky and uneven. A long slanting burnished gleam of orange light appearing suddenly before him, revealing the white mists, and making the darkness a definite visible blackness rather than merely charged with a sense of sightlessness, he deemed only one of those transient lines of lightning reflected in the temporary ponds that he had marked earlier in the evening. It did not flicker, however, and die away. As he stared forward, he perceived, beyond a darkly lustrous interval, a parallel line of yellow brilliance, — another, and still another ; and he became aware that he was amongst the workmen's shanties, the lights of which were mirrored in the water. Presently illusory shimmering squares were visible in the mists which marked the open doors. A croaking frog by the waterside ceased suddenly, as, with more decided step, Larrabee skirted the pool and approached. He felt rather than saw the shadowy creature's leap from before his foot, again an elastic spring along the margin, and a splash as the frog jumped into the water, and the long lines of gilded light were broken into a thousand concentric shoaling curves. Voices sounded close at hand, and then the whole little settlement became vaguely visible, — the cabins further apart than they had seemed at the distance; a banjo was strumming at the most remote, and as Larrabee walked up to the nearest, boldly, in the avenue of light that the open door blazed out in the darkness, he saw within the man whom he sought, bending his frowning brow over a paper in his hand. In the other hand Kenniston held a cigar, which at long intervals he put between his lips; then he pulled energetically at it as if merely to keep it alight, and with no definite experience or expectation of nicotian solace. The county surveyor, on the contrary, on the other side of the table, puffed his pipe systematically, his eyes half closed, his grizzled bearded face showing in repose amongst the wreaths of smoke, his conscience discharged of every detail of the great science of mensuration which he sought to apply to the various parcels of land owned or claimed by his fellow-man. He had answered so much at random the occasional remarks of his host on the subject of the processioning that it became very apparent to Kenniston that he did not propose to work at his vocation out

of office hours, as it were.   From the consideration
of futility as well as decorum, Kenniston had relapsed into silently comparing the calls of the deed
with the notes he had made of the day's work, and
only unconsciously did an interjection of irritation
and disgust escape him.

"I ain't responsible for any disputed p'int, Mr.
Kenniston," said the surveyor, sibilantly sucking
his pipestem, his eyes quite closed, his feet upon
the fender of the little stove.   "Ye kin hev a jury
o' good and lawful men ter examinate an' decide
upon it; my business is ter run the line 'cordin'
ter the calls an' the compass.   That's all!"

Kenniston looked up, a sarcastic comment in his
eyes; the mere possibility of submitting the question of the boundary of his land to the wild will of
a jury of mountaineers, qualified by the surveyor,
according to the law of processioning land, and met
in those tangled precipitous woods to discriminate
in matters mathematical and to settle questions of
topographical fact, seemed to him so happy a travesty of the theory of law and justice that he could
not forbear a scornful smile at his own probable
plight when he should come forth from such unique
adjudication of his interests.

"There's no disputed '*p'int*,'" he said, laughing
satirically.   "It's the whole confounded line from
the Big Hollow Boulder to Wild Duck Falls!"

"'Cordin' ter the calls an' the compass," muttered
the surveyor, fast succumbing to the unholy fascina-
tions of a dream in which he found that in seeking

to ascertain the area of a triangular body of land he achieved the petrifying result of transforming it to a square. Reason revolted; he woke with a snort, filliped off the ash from his pipe, adjusted himself anew in his chair, looked very wide awake, to be overtaken again by the same irreconcilable process and result.

In the diversion of Kenniston's attention he had lost the run of his ideas; he paused, puffed his cigar into a glow, pushed his chair slightly back from the table, glanced with lowering disaffection at the slumbering surveyor, and then mechanically about him at his surroundings.

The house was the roughest of shells, and hardly compact enough to withstand the floods of rain that had descended upon it to-day. In one corner the floor was still damp, the eaves outside dripped. Beyond a cot, a table, and a few chairs there was no furniture save Kenniston's valise, his gun in its case, which was never opened, and a monkey stove, an object of aversion to its æsthetic owner; for, despite its utility, its outline and atmosphere were a continual affront to him, and it suffered grossly from the comparison with the great open fires of the mountaineers' hearths, the incense of hickory and ash and pine, the flash and flame and sparkle of those humble illumined interiors.

The shadowy figure of a man standing in the doorway Kenniston did not immediately notice. Beyond a slight start, a mere matter of nerve (for he could hardly be surprised by aught that the

mountaineers could say or do), he did not betray
the unexpectedness of the apparition. He smoked
silently, eying the intruder without salutation, as
if he sought to shift the discourtesy of the lack of
formality upon one who merely paused at the door
of his domicile and surveyed its occupant; it was
his rule not to encourage the mountaineers to come
about, and he felt at liberty, with so untutored a
folk, to depart from the decrees of decorum in such
small matters, which were, however, exigent even
with them. In this instance no offense seemed to
be taken, no intentional lack perceived. Larrabee
stood, his smiling dark eyes scanning Kenniston
with a steadiness which apparently had other actu-
ation than mere curiosity, his pale clear-cut face, his
auburn hair, his alert strong pose, distinct in the
crude white light of the unshaded kerosene lamp.
Whether it were the natural commendation of a
face and figure regularly handsome by the line and
rule by which Kenniston was wont to apportion
beauty; whether the exaltation of the discovery of
the star, the spiritual audacity of the arrogation
of a personal intimation in its manifestation, had
touched Larrabee's expression with something
strange, something aloof from the day, the time,
and the people, Kenniston's jaded interest was
stirred.

" Did you want to see me ? " he demanded, at
length. " Then come in."

Larrabee remained at the threshold, but he
leaned against the wall, his big brown hat on the

back of his head, as it rested against the rich veined amber and creamy tints of the yellow pine wood.

"Air you-uns the stranger-man ez hev been hyarabouts, buildin' the hotel an' sech?" he asked slowly.

Kenniston's eye became intent, hardening as he nodded. His thoughts flew instantly to that fair edifice and the collapse of all his plans, with the quick inference that here was information to come touching the incendiary. He felt his blood leap; by his pulsing veins he knew how it was burning into his face. He had that desire toward justice which should animate every civilized man, but although he sought to hold himself impartial, calm, circumspect to receive what might be a false accusation, it would have fared ill with Larrabee's enemy had he an old score to settle thus.

As he remained silent Kenniston spoke, with a view of urging forward the disclosure. "Have I ever seen you here before?"

Larrabee shook his head. "I hev never viewed you-uns ez I knows on." Then, after a pause, "Air you-uns a book-l'arned man?"

"Reasonably so," Kenniston said, with a slight laugh. He leaned his elbows on the table, holding his chin in his hand, which was half obscured by his full beard, and while he looked impatiently at his visitor his white teeth gnawed his underlip.

Larrabee hesitated. "Hev ye met up with the stars in yer readin'?" he finally blurted out.

A sudden look of blank disappointment crossed Kenniston's face.

"Stars ! " he echoed in dismay. " Why, I thought you had come to give me some information about the cur that set fire to my house."

(It was a different kind of brute, but the fact of Bruin's agency was relegated to the state of things not revealed, which we denominate mystery.)

It was Larrabee's turn for impatience, and an affronted sense of interruption.

" I dunno nuthin' 'bout who burnt yer hotel " — He paused suddenly, the conviction all at once fully fledged in his mind that it was the deed of the moonshiners, to rid the Cove of its prospect of troublesome invaders. The recollection of Espey's threat rang in his ears as if the very vibrations of the words were audible upon the air: " Burn him out ! Burn his shanty every time he gits it started ! "

Larrabee suffered the sense of a nervous shock, so great was the revulsion from the subject that had engrossed him ; for this reminiscence of all things he had least expected to meet here. He could hardly cope with it in the free outer air. It belonged so essentially to that other life of his, that underground world where he bore so different an identity, that it seemed to have thoughts and intentions and a conscience peculiar to itself. He had realized the dangers of the isolation in which he stood amongst those of his association, but he had thought himself safe here. Kenniston knew him neither by name nor face, and he was a stranger to all the workmen; since their advent into the Cove he had been held a prisoner in the Lost Time mine. Even a chance encounter with Rodolphus Ross he did not dread, for the officer had not been apprised of his identity on the night he had summoned him to search for the escaped Espey masquerading under the name of Larrabee.

The abrupt pause, the introverted look, the sudden recollection advertised in unmistakable characters upon his unguarded face, did not escape Kenniston's observation, now keen and all on the alert. For his heart was in this reprisal. If he had had naught to gain and much to risk, indeed much of certain loss, he would have pursued this injury to its ultimate and bitterest requital. All that was manly in him — his courage, his pugnacity, his tenaciousness, his self-respect, his vehement, insistent, vigorous personality, that could neither make nor keep covenant with concession, compromise, or defeat — rose to the occasion. He had cursed in his heart the lukewarmness of the authorities, who had opined that the mountaineers were mighty rough folks, mighty hard to catch, lived in a mighty difficult country, and who had offered him the half-veiled advice that they were mighty bad to run against, in lieu of the formulated and disciplined suspicions which he had expected, the canvassing of possible " fire-bugs," involving as sequence warrants for arrest, indictments, and other fierce and formidable engines of the law, set to work with full intent and expectation.

Here was a clue, — the first; and fortunately it had fallen into his own hands. However, it behooved him to be cautious, or the suggestion might be of as little ultimate value as if it were already given to the turbulent, ill-advised, precipitate deputy, or to his unsanguine, dubious, dilatory principal, with his wise saws about the lack of prudence involved in running against mountain folks, who were mighty hard to catch in the wilds of their difficult country.

Now and again the family of Cap'n Lucy had had an intimation of how pleasant Mr. Kenniston could be when he chose. It was reserved for Jasper Larrabee to experience the fascination of the full and ripened flavor, the bouquet, so to speak, of his geniality and good will. A second rapid covert survey from that altered point of view which one is apt to adopt when a personal interest looms in the background convinced Kenniston that his visitor was no fool. Although he intended to drop the subject for the present, he did not quit it abruptly.

"I was in hopes you could name some suspicious characters, or had heard some threatening talk, or " —

Once more he saw from his visitor's face that, inadvertently, he had again struck the nail on the head. His secret self-applause aided his self-denial in relinquishing so promising a line of investiga-

tion. The man must be made to talk freely, to dis-
close ; his confidence must be secured.

"I have had heavy losses in this matter, and the
officers seem of mighty little account. Every now
and then I hope I 'll hear of something some other
way. I 'm afraid to build again unless I know the
fire-bug is somewhere else, or discover what I 've
done to set people against *me*."

Larrabee's face was at once softened and troubled. "Burn his shanty every time he gits it
started," quoth Espey. And he that would work
ill to one man would work ill to another : witness
his own plight. His conscience began to stir. If,
he thought, the whiskey tax were not in itself so
tyrannical, so impracticable and obnoxious a thing,
he might have admitted for the nonce that moonshining was in itself wrong.

Kenniston's eyes were studying his unconscious
countenance. "Well," he said suddenly, "since
it 's nothing about my affairs, what can I do for
you ? Won't you have a chair ? "

Larrabee shook his head silently. He stood for
a few moments undecided. It might seem that his
enthusiasm, so ruthlessly dragged down to earth,
might hardly make shift to rise again ; but it was
strong of wing, as behooves that ethereal essence, and
in his ignorant assumptions he thought that he had
seen a sign in the heavens, a sign for him. The
fervor of all that he had half doubting believed, and
half believing doubted, fired his pulses once more.
He cared naught for Espey and his troublous usur-

pations, the officer of the law, the moonshiner and his deadly feud, the incendiary, the necessity of heed to his words. He cared for naught under the moon. Once more his face had that illumined, exalted expression. As he leaned suddenly forward, with a keen anxiety, and said, " Air ye 'quainted with the stars by name, bein' a book-l'arned man? " Kenniston had a swift doubt of his sanity.

" Yes," he replied. And after a pause he asked the counter-question, " Are you interested in the stars ? "

But Larrabee, still under the influence of the strong excitement that possessed him, did not answer directly.

" I kin read, but I hain't got but one book. The teacher what l'arned me ter read 'lowed ez the stars air named ; they air numbered in a book. Hev ye l'arned sech? "

" Oh yes ; I have studied astronomy," replied Kenniston capably. " I know their names."

" I know *them ;* I dunno thar names," said Larrabee, making a definite distinction. " That 's the reason I kem ter you-uns, hearin' ez ye air a book-l'arned man."

He turned his head and looked out into the night as he stood on the threshold. The mists had gone their ways. The clouds were far in the west. Above all, the clear, sombre field of the sky was thickly bespangled with stars, chill, keenly glittering, for below the night was very dark.

" Thar 's a new one," he declared excitedly, " a

new one never viewed afore! I seen it kindle up a matter of three week ago, three week an' better, an' it's thar now!"

Kenniston sat in silent amazement, looking steadily at him.

"Kem out!" Larrabee insisted, in tones strangely urgent. "Kem out an' see!"

Some subtle monition apprised Kenniston that there was something in the man's disclosure withheld; that it was not merely to bring his book-learning to bear upon the array of the stars that he was asked to step out of his door at this hour of the night. How often he had heard, as the climax of a feud, of a man in these mountains being summoned on some pretext out of his door to meet a murderous bullet fired by an enemy hidden in the dark! He was momentarily ashamed of this recollection as he glanced at the surveyor asleep close at hand; as he heard the rhythmic beat of feet on the shaking, ill-laid floor, and the patting of hands as some jovial young blade danced a "break-down" in one of the workmen's shanties to the strumming of the banjo, finding this far more congenial an occupation than shoving the jack plane.

Nevertheless, he had enemies, virulent, unscrupulous, powerful, as his short stay here might seem to attest, and what strange, fantastic vagary was this touching a new star! He would not refuse; that would impugn his courage even to himself, and he held it dear; and as he looked at Larrabee's face with its ever-smiling eyes, despite the intimation of

something withheld, of trafficking with a mere subterfuge, he doubted as causeless his prudence. Moreover, this was a man of whom he must keep track,
of whom he must know more. He was looking
about the room as he rose. "Wait a minute," he
said. "I have a strong glass here that may be of
use."

The door of the maligned monkey stove standing
ajar emitted a ruddy glow of embers upon the yellow pine walls of the room, and toned down the
white glare of the kerosene lamp. A deep, restful
red hue might have attracted the eye from the farther side amongst the shadows, as Kenniston tossed
a rug aside upon a chair to obscure a quick search
through his valise. A pernicious habit, that of
carrying his pistols at the bottom of his luggage,
amongst his clean shirts, and he promised himself
this should be the end of it. At the moment that
he thrust the revolver into his pistol-pocket he
picked up the field-glass from the cot. "Here it
is," he said, and he followed his guest out of the
door and into the dusky night.

It was still all vibrant with the twanging drone
of the cicada and the windy note of the booming
frogs. The air, damp and of clarified freshness,
was pervaded with indeterminate fragrance, the
blent perfume of some flower and the pungent aroma
of weed and shrub and the balsamic fir. A cluster
of great trees rose just outside of the little shell,
and though many a star shone down in the inter-
stices of the black fibrous foliage, Larrabee led the

way out beyond them and into an open space. It was nearer the other cottages instead of farther away, as Kenniston had half expected. The suspicion, the half-dormant fear, the doubt in his mind, were giving place anew to his determination to keep his hand on this man, to win his confidence or to surprise his secret. All those genial arts of ingratiation at his command were once more brought into play. It was he who introduced the subject of their mission, as they paused on a slight eminence, with a clear view of the great fields of heaven before them.

"Now which is the star that you want to know more about?" he demanded, lifting the glass with a free gesture, and adjusting it to his eye.

"Don't ye see nuthin' oncommon?" the mountaineer asked, in a tense voice.

The strained tone struck Kenniston's attention, and he lowered the glass and looked through the baffling darkness at his companion, whose form could only be discriminated by some fine sense from the surrounding darkness by an effect of solidity, given one could hardly say how.

Kenniston, the glass swaying useless in his hand, gazed upward once more.

"No, I can't say I do," he replied wonderingly.

Larrabee suddenly came up close to him, taking him by the arm.

"Now, hyar, todes the east, an' yit a leetle todes the north, sorter slanchwise todes Big Injun Mounting, setting a mite ter the west from that, an' plumb west from Chilhowee, a bright, bright star, — with," he added, in a surprised tone, as if he had not before discerned this, " a sorter silver shine onto it."

Kenniston laughed slyly in his sleeve. One can hardly better appreciate the immense distance that mechanical appliance has brought man from his normal state of natural, unassisted faculties than in the effort to point out, with such accuracy as to enable another to distinguish, an object in those fair and foreign fields of heaven, by the unaided means of the index finger. A suffusion of self-gratulatory pride is apt to overspread the consciousness, the unit assuming the credit of all that the genius of invention has achieved in the generic name of mankind. Kenniston had not even a slight expectation of being able to distinguish the particular star, but the affectation of effort, in his own interests, in some sort constrained his will. He looked about the skies with that vague sense of recollection which animates one who turns the leaves of a volume written in a half-forgotten language. He had not been the familiar of the stars. His choicest ambitions had lifted him no further than a reasonably safe height for an attic, or those fantastic simulations of turrets, with which the new architecture apes *haud passibus æquis* the old. He had naught in common with the full-pulsed aspiring audacity of those architects of eld who builded in the plain of Shinar; his was but a low-studded Babel. He had not cared for a higher outlook, and his building had no definite designs touching heaven. It had been so long since he had regarded the upper atmosphere other than barometrically that he hardly made shift to see the Swan arch her snowy neck from those great lakes of ether, whose indented shores seemed marked and foliage-fringed by the wooded summits of the Great Smoky Mountains. The assertive brilliance of Lyra he noted near the meridian, with the harp-strings all vibrant, doubtless, with that music of the spheres which we are told by the scientist is no longer a mere figment of poesy. The Cor Caroli gleamed pure and splendid amongst the mists of a struggling recollection. And where was Scorpio? — how low in the sky, how far to the southwest, how near to its setting! Through a water-gap of Chilhowee, cloven to the very heart of the range, he marked the gleaming coils. Of strangely melancholy intimations were the stars, seen so far through the steep wooded defile, dark and rugged on either hand; but he only remembered the relation of its early setting and the season, for it was near the end of September. How little building weather the year might spare him yet! How heavy the rains of to-day, and the west still harbored portents! Unless he relinquished all and left the field, baffled and beaten, he must have the incendiary behind the bars. To jail a suspect, at all events, would intimidate the lawless population, and point the moral of " Hands off! "

" I don't see it," he said, reverting to the prosecution of his intention to win the mountaineer's secret information as to the origin of the fire. "I'm sorry I can't see it, Mr. — Excuse me, what did you say your name is?"

His visitor had not said, but all thrown off his guard the young man replied promptly, "Lar'bee, — Jasper Lar'bee. Ef ye look jes' a leetle ter the right of that thar batch o' stars ez 'pears some similar ter a kyart-wheel" — He raised once more the futile inefficiency of his index finger.

But Kenniston was not looking. This name, — he placed it at once. In the short interview which he had had with the deputy sheriff touching the incendiary, without whose apprehension he feared to recommence the building, it had recurred repeatedly to Rodolphus Ross's lips coupled with many an imprecation. Kenniston had paid scant heed at the time to the story of the search for Espey, of the pretended arrest, of the escape of the supposed Larrabee and the inference of some crime which his flight fostered. It had all happened during his absence from the Cove, and shortly before the beginning of the building of the hotel. He could not conceive of any reasons for connecting one with the other; but this man indubitably knew something of the crime; his long and mysterious disappearance had baffled all the devices of the officers, and surely it was a strange subterfuge which had brought him hither. Strange to the minds of others as well, for sundry figures were detached now and again from the illumined thresholds near at hand; presently the foreman had joined the two, and several of the workmen approached, all pausing at intervals and craning their necks up toward the sky, having noticed the intent scrutiny of it, and expectant of some *lusus naturæ*, — comet, or aurora borealis, or other phenomenon, — the observation of which might serve to break the monotony. The resonant tone of the banjo now and again sounded loud in the damp air, as the musician who carried it under his arm jostled against one of the other men. Their attitudes and faces expressed an alert curiosity, for they were not altogether indistinguishable, the two star-gazers having insensibly changed their positions, and come within the line of light falling from one of the open doors.

"Some ter the right o' that batch o' stars ez be some similar ter a kyart-wheel," repeated Larrabee urgently.

" I don't know which you mean," replied Kenniston, drawing himself back to the subject with difficulty.

"Don't ye view one ez ye never viewed afore ? " demanded Jasper breathlessly. "Ef ye know 'em, ye air 'bleeged ter see that thar one air strange ! "

" Mr. Jackson," — Kenniston turned to the foreman, — "do you see anything unusual in that sky ? "

The foreman answered with a prompt and business-like negative, and then appealed in turn to one of the workmen. None of them could perceive aught amiss, although they all turned about and critically surveyed the majesty of the heavens.

"It's a new star," protested Larrabee, unconsciously adopting the scientific term of description. "I seen it kindle up myself 'bout three weeks ago."

There was an astounded silence; then a resonance broke out abruptly as the young musician smote his bullet head with the banjo, apparently inadvertently, but with the view of intimating to his fellows that all was not accurately adjusted in the cranium of their queer visitor.

Kenniston hesitated for a moment. There lay in his mind the residuum, so to speak, of an impression that new stars or temporary stars are not of infrequent occurrence in the economy of worlds, rating time by the long astral lengths. He could not say at once, — such scant commerce he had had with the stars of late years, to be sure! His mind had reverted instantly to the question upon what pretext he should seek to detain the man. He only saw rather than noted the workmen slowly turning aside, the long lane of yellow light streaming through the door, the lustrous mirror-like suggestions in the darkness hard by where the pools lurked and the frogs were still croaking, the outlines of the clustering roofs of the other little buildings, shadowy in the deeper shadow, the dense woods surrounding all, and above the great amphitheatre of the mountains on every side. The voice of the foreman recalled him : —

"That's a queer customer. First crank I've seen here."

"Where is he?" cried Kenniston, with a start, the freedom of the criticism notifying him of the absence of its subject. "Stop him! Call him! Hold on to him!"

But the effort was vain. Larrabee had departed as suddenly, as tracklessly, as if the night had swallowed him up.

XVII.

It was a buoyant, elated spirit that Jasper Larrabee bore as he slipped swiftly away through the darkness and the woods, unaware of the sudden vehement search for him, unhearing the hue and cry. He had put his discovery to the test, — the most searching that he could devise. And not the man learned in letters, who even knew the stars by name, not the clear-headed, prosperous, efficient foreman, not the humbler handicraftsmen, could see that gracious, splendid stellular presence still shining, — shining down into the wilderness, doubtless with some message, some token, some personal relation, that would be in due season made known. He had no uncertainties; he had said to himself that if it were invisible to others he would accept it as a revelation to himself. For had he not seen it even as it first kindled in the blank spaces of the midnight sky?

He felt with a sort of surprise that his limbs were trembling as he went, his breath was short; more than once he paused, with a reeling sense as if he should fall, and he beheld the summit line of demarkation where the dark woods touched the clear sky describe a long curve upward, and once more sink to its place. He had not known the physical exhaustion that ensues upon strong and long-continued mental excitement. Beyond the moment's impatient realization he gave it no heed. He was glad, glad beyond all power of analysis, expectant, breathless, his eyes continually fixed upon the star, unmindful whither his failing feet carried him. He passed without a thought the door of the store of the Lost Time mine, from which so lately he had escaped as it were with his life in his hand. He might have seen, if he had chosen, the twinkle of Cornelia Taft's fire through the chinking, as she nodded on the hearth and vainly waited for her father's return to supper. He heard naught, — no voice from the woods, no stir of leaf, no sigh of wind, no lapsing of the alien sheets of water, not even the full rush of the stream from the portal of the Lost Time mine, loud, sinister, seemingly charged with cavernous echoes from those hidden haunted recesses whence it came, wild, turbulent, with thrice its normal volume hurling out into the black night. Only once he paused. The unseen air and the invisible moisture were at their jugglery again, weaving from nothingness wondrous symmetries of scrolls tenuous to the eye, marvelous winged suggestions endowed with the faculty of flight and airy poise, graces of fabric, tissues, fold on fold of impalpable pearl-tinted consistencies; and now a floating film passed before the star, and again it shone out more splendid still, and anon dimly through the gathering haze, and so was lost to sight.

Larrabee stood for a time spellbound, still gazing up into heaven. But winds were astir in the region of the clouds. Heavy purple masses, with here and there flocculent white drifts in their midst, and showing lines of white at their verges, were spreading over the sky; the temperature had fallen suddenly; he was shivering. Vagrant gusts seemed to issue from defiles of the mountain, and he heard the awakening of the pines. Out of sight of the star his flagging energies failed. The definite realization of his fatigue, his hunger, his faintness, pressed upon his aroused senses. He could hardly support his tottering limbs to the door of the Lost Time mine, and drag himself up on the rocks, out of the reach of the water, to rest, as he waited till the clouds should pass, till the sight of the star should be renewed to his longing gaze. Even in its eclipse, in a certain yearning sense of bereavement, in his disappointment, he had a patience and calm acquiescence begotten of confidence. For he should see it again. Was it not his own, his very own, charged with some unimagined significance to him? He shifted his posture once, reckoning upon its position in the sky, that it might not fail his sight the moment the baffling clouds should withdraw. He was conscious of a high degree of happiness despite his tremulous thrills of suspense. He gazed upward, as he reclined on the ledge of rock, with smiling eyes and a heart full of deep content. He had gone far enough within to have an upward view through the jagged portal of rough-hewn rocks. Beyond their edges the sky seemed of lighter tint, so black it was within. He could mark here how the clouds made sail, how swiftly the wind sped them. He watched a section of a branch close at hand sway in sight, and swing back on the wind, and once more wave, nodding, plumelike, into view. He heard the sharp bark of a fox outside in the woods; it roused far-away baying of drowsy hounds, and again all was still, but for the reverberation of the water loud against the echoing walls of the darksome place. The sound affected his nerves; he was dizzy for a moment. Then something cold, clammy, suddenly struck him in the face. His heart seemed to stand still with the recollection of the spectral terrors of the place. The soft chill buffet came again and again, and the air was vaguely fanned about his brow before he recognized the noiseless flight of bats on their way to the outer darkness. He lay back upon the ledge, finding a solace in the mere posture of rest in his extreme fatigue, and once more watched the jagged black portal and the purple clouds with their hoary drifts, as in endless unbroken folds they rolled before the serene white splendors of that wondrous star. Again and again he would lift himself upon his elbow, fancying that the cloud textures waxed thin, and that presently, when they should fall away from before it, he would behold anew the sidereal incandescent glory that meant so much, that should mean more to him. Not once did his faith fail him. Not once did he doubt that the white fires of this star, which none else could see, were miraculously kindled and charged with some deep significance for him, with the vouchsafed will of God. For were not stars messengers in the olden time? Had he not read of one, supremely blessed and brilliant, which had led men, the wisest men, to the cradled Christ? As he lay back in the dense darkness, with the gathering clouds outside, and the air freighted with the sense of black noiseless invisible wings of creatures of ill favor and ill omen, he seemed to have a vision of that guiding star, — not a chill splendid crystalline glitter like his own, high, high in the sky, but low down in the dark east, and of a soft supernal silver sheen in the purple shadowy mist above the shadowy purple hills of Judea, that stretched out in ever-lengthening perspectives, as it fared on and slowly on its mystic way, for Bethlehem might still be far to seek.

And suddenly, with a start, Larrabee became aware that it was a real light at which he was gazing far down in the Lost Time mine. He had slept he knew not how long, nor in what danger, for the lantern whose starry lustre shone so far in the dark cavernous depths was swinging in the hands of one of two men who must have passed him as he lay dreaming and unconscious. He hardly dared move at first, so far those slanting, divergent rays extended from the white focus into the darkness. He lay still, struggling for a moment with the idea of the traditional spectres of the place,

whose grisly renown had served to make it so
solitary. It was the lantern which proved so re-
doubtable an exorcist. The sight of the little
mundane contrivance appealed to his logical faculty
as no mere theory of the impossibility of spectres
could have done. He lifted himself cautiously on
his elbow, and gazed down the vistas of the gloomy
place with a suspicious, inquisitive worldly pulse
beating in every vein. These were men in truth;
and what was their mission here? One of them
was singularly gesticulatory of manner. The
other slouched heavily. It was the latter who had
just lighted the lantern, for he was evidently
throwing away a match, an article which the Lost
Time store had made common in the Cove. Suddenly they were joined by a third figure, somehow
detached from the darkness, for Larrabee could
hardly have said whence he had approached, and
who turned with a light, lithe motion, swinging to
his shoulder an implement which the thickset man
had handed him. It was a pick. How often Larrabee had heard its vibrations ring through these
storied depths while he threaded the dark tunnel
to the still, and shivered at the thought of the two
dead miners digging and digging the graves these
thirty years for their bones which only the waters
had buried!

The lantern swayed, the shadows all flickered,
the group was on the move. Larrabee sprang hastily to his feet to follow.

He could not easily judge how far the feeble

glimmer led them, so rugged and winding was the way. Once, as the mouth of a submerged shaft yawned suddenly before his unprescient feet, he hesitated, half deterred; he was fain to skulk with the skulking shadows, lest the light should reveal his presence, and thus the dangers which his precursors braved menaced him doubly. He marveled that they dared the possibilities of the place, as he noted that the half-fallen timbers in a cross-cut through which they passed barely supported the masses of earth which any jar might dislodge. Everywhere was the sound of water working its secret will still on the ruins that it had made, and its tone added to the awe of the place, and the desolation, and the darkness, and the eerie effect of the bats that flew after the lantern and smote blindly against it.

The light was set down presently, and as the men seemed stirring about their work Larrabee ventured to approach nearer behind a pile of broken rock in the darkness, and mopped the cold perspiration from his brow. He caught his breath at the sight of the faces which the lantern revealed.

For they were all recruited from his mother's hearth. Some crazy folly, doubtless, of old man Haight had drawn him here. He had been one of the miners before that catastrophe which had closed the work forever; Larrabee remembered in what deep, blood-curdling tones he was wont to curse the Lost Time mine. And his daughter Jerusha's husband, — it had always been a marvel where and how he obtained the whiskey he so indubitably consumed ; perhaps, in consideration of his age and infirmities, Mrs. Larrabee furnished a too ample allowance of liquor to old man Haight, who, for services rendered in this wild enterprise, furnished his son-in-law.

" We-uns hev been toler'ble good customers o' the Lost Time still," Larrabee muttered sarcastically.

And there was Jack Espey ! The sanity of *his* presence here was easily demonstrable ; nowhere else could he so safely be. How he had chanced to coöperate in this strange work with the dotard and the sot was soon explained.

" Gimme a holt o' that thar grub," he said gruffly, with a look of poignant hunger on his thin face.

Old Haight, with a deprecatory expression and shaking hand, made haste to give him a small basket, of the queer shape and aspect which bespoke the work of the Indians of Quallatown. The young man voraciously thrust his hand into its narrow mouth, and as he drew forth its meagre contents gave vent to his disappointment.

" My Lord !" he exclaimed, " is that all? An' ye expec' me ter kem hyar night arter night — from — from " — the effort of his heavy flight of imagination showed in his face — " from 'way over yander whar I live now, an' holp ye dig an' sech, an' gin me sech forage ter work on ez that !" He pointed contemptuously at the food, albeit his mouth was full.

"Now, now, Jack, now, bubby, lemme tell you," expostulated the old man, his jaw quivering painfully as he spoke, and his wrinkled face showing, in the glimmer of the lantern, at once grotesque and piteous, encircled as it was by the brilliant hues of a little shawl of Mrs. Larrabee's, in which his head was tied up for protection against the weather, and which was surmounted by his hat. "Ye dunno how durned hard it war ter git that much. This hyar Henrietty Timson hev got us down on half rations, mighty short commons. 'T ain't like 't war whenst you-uns lived with us, Jack. Oh my! Oh my, no!" and he shook his queerly upholstered head as he sat quaking and shivering on a ledge of the rock. He impressed Larrabee as much out of place, — so habituated was he to the sight of the old man in the chimney corner, — as the oven, or pot, or crane, or any other naturalized appurtenance of the fireside might have been. He let his veinous old shaking hands fall on his knees with a gesture deeply significant of grief. "I wisht ter Gawd," he cried, "ez S'briny war hyar!"

He pronounced her name as if she were a sort of minor providence, as indeed she had been to him.

"Leetle as ye hed, ye mought hev brung it sooner," grumbled Jack, stuffing the half of a very fat, very heavy biscuit into his mouth.

"Law, Jack," cried the old man, "we-uns air plumb 'feared ter leave the house sooner, — even arter all war bedded up for the night. That thar 'oman hev got her pryin' nose in every mortal thing; 'pears ter me the longest, sharpest nose I even seen," he added injuriously, and with sudden sprightly interest, " ain't it, Tawm? "

His fellow-sufferer from its pointed inquisitiveness had seemed about to fall asleep in a heavy, shapeless lump, but he roused himself at this to add his testimony with some sincere acridity.

"Longes' an' sharpes' *I* ever seen," he protested thickly, " an' I hev known 'em p'inted an' drawn out to *de*-straction." His snore followed so promptly that one might have doubted whether he had spoken at all; his remark presented the phenomenon of a waking parenthesis, as it were, in the midst of the somnolent text.

" I tell ye, it 's good fur S'briny ter go, ter let we-uns savor how we miss her," said the old man. "Sech a house, Jack, sech quar'lin' an' scufflin' an' tormentin', f'om mornin' till night, — crowdin' *Me* up on the h'a'thstone, an' shovin' *my* cheer, an' talkin' 'bout useless cumberers, whenst I hev been treated with sech *re*-spec' by S'briny Lar'bee ez ef I hed been her own dad, stiddier jes' her husband's step-dad, — sech *re*-spec' an' hot vittles, an' the fus' sarved, an' the bes' o' everything! " His old face flushed with the recollection of the recent indignities offered him. " The pa'son tells ye ter lean on the Lord. Ef ye ain't got the grace ter do that, S'briny Lar'bee 's a mighty good help! "

For the life of him, Jasper Larrabee could not harden his heart.

"Her pet tur-rkey air dead," old man Haight presently observed disconnectedly.

"Glad of it," said Jack callously. "I never seen a beast so pompered, an' fairly hanker ter git stepped on, forever flusterin' 'roun' the floor underfoot."

"*She* 'll be powerful sorry. She sot a heap o' store by it, an' doctored it cornsider'ble. She 'lowed it hed the quinsy." Then after a pause, "Whenst I gits my money back," said the old man meditatively, "I be goin' ter buy S'briny Lar'bee suthin' ez will s'prise her, — I dunno what. I studies on it some mighty nigh every day. A spry young filly, mebbe, or a good cow an' calf, — I dunno. I 'd gin her the money, ef she would n't be sure ter fool it away on them wuthless triflin' cattle of chil'n an' folks she contrives fur all the time. I 'd gin S'briny half o' the cold cash, an' ennyhow I lay off ter spend half fur a presint fur her."

Espey, his energies recruited by food, and perhaps willing to postpone the evil hour of shoveling and digging, looked up with a satiric eye and a rallying laugh.

"Whar 's my sheer, ef ye be goin' ter gin Mis' Lar'bee haffen the money? Ye 'lowed Tawm hed hed his pay in whiskey," — he cast a side glance at the bloated slumbering face and collapsed figure in the shadow, — "an' he 's hed a plenty, too, fur he 's nuthin' but a cag o' liquor set a-goin' on two legs; but I 'm durned ef I 'll take my pay out in Mis' Timson's sour yeast an' raw dough." He twirled the empty basket over contemptuously. "Ye 'lowed that night, three weeks ago, whenst I — ye — whenst we run on one another, an' s'prised one another, ez ye 'd pay me solid silver ef I would n't tell nobody, but holp ye; now did n't ye?"

Espey's tone was so obviously that of one who speaks in flagrant jest that Larrabee perceived he gave the unknown enterprise no serious support or credence, and that he was only utilizing some preposterous delusion of the old man touching his work in the Lost Time mine to secure food to sustain him while he evaded the pursuit of the law.

"Ye 'low ez 't ain't enough money!" screamed the old man shrilly, and Larrabee recognized the clamors of the queer cracked voice which he had been wont to shudderingly mark in the tunnel that led to the still. "Ain't I done tole ye what I ain't never tole no other livin' man — I don't count Tawm — it air eighty-seben dollars! Yes, sir, nigh on ter a hundred, what I hed done sold my cabin an' lan' fur on Big Injun Mounting whenst I kem over hyar ter settle, — eighty-seben dollars in hard silver" — He broke off abruptly. Then, in the deep, hollow, blood-curdling tone which Larrabee had so often heard about the fireside, he cursed the Lost Time mine. His excitement was painful to witness, as Larrabee, still looking round the pile of broken rock, noted his feverish illumined eyes, the flush on his withered parchment-like cheek, the aimlessness and the quaking of his fluttering nerveless hand. Espey was gazing at him calmly, his face lighted by the lantern placed on the ground between them, and evidently believing that not a syllable he uttered had any foundation in fact.

"'T war the day o' the floodin' o' the mine," old Haight mouthed and gesticulated vehemently. "Every durned thing went wrong that day! I war hyar a-workin'. I hed worked in mines over in Car'liny, an' war ekal ter all. I war toler'ble young an' nimble, — knowed ter be ez nimble ez a painter! An' one o' them durned buzzards workin' of the windlass drapped the whole contrivance, winch, rope, bucket, man, an' all, down inter the bottom o' the shaft ; an' they could n't make the man answer, an' 'lowed he war kilt. An' I — the devil's own fool — mus' ups an' volunteer ter go down an' git the windlass an' let 'em hoist it out, an' then let down the bucket agin an' fetch up the man — (I furgits his name, dad-burn him ! — Tom, Jim, Pete, cuss him, whatever he be !) An' ez they war a sort o' harnessin' me up with ropes under my arms an' around my middle, I felt my leetle bag o' money a-poppin' 'bout in my pocket, an' 'peared ter me it mought pop out down in that deep onhandy shaft. An' I handed it ter the foreman ter keep fur me in his pocket, — he war a clever trusted man ; I never tole the t'others, kase they war toler'ble hard cases, an' some men would kill a man fur a dollar an' a half; an' bless Gawd — eighty-seben dollars ! An' down I goes ! I hed about teched bottom when — hell broke loose ! I 'lowed I hearn thunder : 't war the water on a plumb tear, breakin' down the walls an' cavortin' like a herd o' wild cattle through the mine. Sech screechin's! The men ez helt the rope drapped it on my head an' run fur thar lives!'"

With open mouth and shaking jaw, he rose up, and gazed eagerly about, while Espey wearily yawned and passed his hands across his eyes.

"It bust through about thar." He pointed about in real or fancied recognition of the course of the flood. "But over yander — the whole thing hev fell down an' caved in sence then, mighty nigh — 't war higher 'n the level o' the overflow, an' I stayed down thar in the shaft dry ez a bone. I stayed two days along o' that dead man. I furgits his name," he broke off in peevish irritation.

He sat down, readjusted his plaid shawl about his head, surmounted it again with his big broad hat, and recommenced : —

" Wall, they 'lowed at fust they 'd work the mine agin, — did n't know what the damage war ; an' ez they war pokin' 'bout, somebody 'membered me, an' when they fished me out'n the shaft I hed these hyar jiggets." He held up his shaking hands, and looked in exasperation from one to the other. " Some calls it the palsy, but the doctor, he 'lowed it kem from the narvous shock. An' the foreman, he hed done hed ter git drowned with my leetle bag o' money in his pocket." He rose to his feet, with a sudden steady blazing fire in his eyes. " But it 's silver, — eighty — seben — dollars ! " He pronounced the words as if they expressed the wealth of the Indies. " They air silver, — silver metal.

Water can't hurt 'em, an' the leetle leather bag kep' 'em from scatterin'. The foreman 's got 'em in his pocket. Mebbe he hain't got no pocket by this time, but he hain't got rid o' all his bones. The money 'll be nigh his bones, an' I be goin' ter foller the wash o' that flood, afore the walls fell in on it, till I find 'em."

There was something pathetic to Jasper Larrabee's sympathetic gaze in the record of the gradual failure of the old man's mental powers registered on the walls. He could easily distinguish, of course, the difference in the work wrought by numbers and with the expectation of valuable ore and this unique subterranean burrowing with only the object of old Haight's search in prospect. But at first accepted methods of mining had been held in regard with a due consideration of safety. The excavations had been carefully timbered, the débris of the ancient lumber serving for the purpose; the nature of the earth and rock all capably recognized either in the avoidance of obstacles or the seizure of advantage; the exact location of an old cross-cut definitely ascertained and intersected by the new tunnel, and utilized to further him on the way to some objective point, doubtless once definite in his mind, but now hazy and intermittent, or possibly lost altogether, for here and there, evidently at random, great vaults had been hollowed out and abandoned, and for a long time every precaution or thought of safety had been discarded. His plan and its feasibility were gone, and only his inadequate intention remained.

Larrabee started violently as the walls rang suddenly with the weird old voice, which, with its keen, false intonation, had so often struck terror to the stout hearts of the moonshiners of the Lost Time still. It was a voice of insistent command. He was urging his comrades to the work, and presently the regular strokes of the pick wielded by the stalwart "Tawm" set the echoes of the place to a hollow, melancholy iteration dreary to hear, and dismally blent with the rush of the cruel torrent. Espey's stroke seemed, in comparison, incidental and ineffective; but albeit both men worked apparently with a will, it was evidently quite at random, obeying implicitly now and again a gesture or command given in pursuance of some weak, wavering intention, and changed in a moment.

The accident which had put the secret into Larrabee's hands seemed to him now so natural that he marveled that it had not been earlier revealed. But doubtless the vocation of the lost miners had served to connect the stroke of the pick with their gruesome fate, and thus the very fact of the sound, which must otherwise have betrayed the enterprise, aided the spectral traditions and the consequent avoidance of the place to preserve it. Would Espey have dared, he asked himself, to venture within, had he not feared the living more than the dead? And but for his own recognition of the humble lantern and its necessarily human uses he would, for fear of the spectral miners, hardly have tracked the old miner to his new lead.

And suddenly, with the very thought, notwithstanding the perfectly natural solution of the mystery, he was solicitous as to the means of departure. He could not wait to follow that feeble lantern far enough in the background to insure his invisibility. He would not issue upon them now and advertise his discovery, and dismay the old dotard with his hopeless scheme. "I don't want to torment the pore old man," he said. He felt a keen thrill of savage joy to have discovered Espey's lair, but he would need some thought to secretly entrap him. "Fur ye air a mighty slick shirk, brother Jack," he said, with scorn. He was feeling some matches in his pockets, and judging of their number. Should they fail him before he reached the outer air, he could step aside and wait till the men should pass with the lantern. Its glimmer served now as long as the passage was comparatively straight; when it turned, himself out of the possibility of view, he struck the first match. The way was shorter than he had fancied. His store was not yet exhausted when he felt the warmer temperature from without, and saw the jagged outline of the portal and heard the melancholy dash of the rain; for it was once more "falling weather," and the sky was cloaked and gray.

As he hesitated outside, his mind intent upon Espey and the incidents of his career since he had been among them, there came to him the thought of the barn in which his whilom friend had been wont to spend so many idle and meditative hours.

A good refuge, to be sure, for a fugitive from the law. The idea of comforts allured him as he recollected the great fragrant elastic masses of hay. A hiding-place as well. Here even Henrietta Timson would hardly find him, for the rotting ladder, from which many a rung was missing, afforded scant footing for a barn swallow, or a flying squirrel, or an athlete like himself or his friend. Sleep would recruit his energies, quiet solace his mind, a vacant interval of time clarify his intentions and fortify his resolves. He started up the mountain briskly; the thought of home, even in this humble, secret, half-outcast guise, warmed his heart. He did not feel the rain dash in his face. A prescience of October was unheeded in the melancholy cadences of the midnight wind. He hardly noted the deep gloom of the Cove, where an owl was wailing at intervals, and whence all the orange-tinted lights had vanished. As the chill of the failing season struck him, he shivered, but unconsciously. He had forged on past the Lost Time store almost to the crest of the ridge, where the homeward way diverged, when suddenly a dull subterranean thunder shook the air, and the earth seemed to tremble. He paused in astonishment.

"Why, they air a-blastin' down thar in the Lost Time mine. Espey ought n't ter let two bereft folks tech sech ez that; 't ain't safe."

Then he reflected that Espey himself had doubtless superintended the charges with due regard to their safety and his own. Nevertheless, he shook his head as he stood looking over his shoulder into the blank, unresponsive darkness. He heard no more, and presently he turned again and went his homeward way in the dark persistent dripping of the early autumn rain.

XVIII.

THE anomaly of administering upon one's own estate Lorenzo Taft was permitted in some sort to experience. A definite realization of finality attended his meditations, at he sat bending over the embers in the great fireplace of the store, in the rain-clouded morning that rose upon the conclusion of his labors of removing the still and destroying all its approaches. His vocation was gone, and naught remained. He had no more affinity than a fox or a wolf for a law-abiding occupation. The possible profits that might stick to his hands in the process of the conversion of the goods upon the shelves from the wholesale ratio to the retail failed to allure him, for the store had never been aught but a "blind." The furrow was no thoroughfare. That wild gambling with the chances of the sun and wind and the rain in its season, and often out of its season, known as farming, and doubtless permitted by the law only because it insures its own punishment, was risky enough to jump with his humor, but the stakes were hopelessly inadequate. He could not look forward, and the glance backward over the shoulder needs a good conscience to commend the prospect.

Now and again he lifted his heavy boot and

kicked the embers together fiercely, as if at great odds with his thoughts and his own counsels. Like many another, he undervalued his success, its hairbreadth jeopardies and its difficulty of attainment, now that it was fairly secured. It seemed to him a slight thing, the device of his quick wits to insure his safety, and his satisfaction in its triumphant exploitation had already evanesced. Had it been possible to reëstablish the status of yesterday, doubtless he would have hardily risked the discovery of the still, the disclosure of Larrabee, the capture of Espey, Dan Sykes's drunken tongue, and, as a result of these, the "shootin'-irons" of the "revenuers" and the sentence of the federal court. But gunpowder as a factor in a scheme admits of no second thoughts.

He even upbraided his own acumen that, in the emergency, he had sought with an eye single the safety of himself, his one remaining comrade, and the apparatus, regardless of all considerations of enmity. But now that judgment was satisfied and escape certain, vengeance clamored.

Whenever he thought of Larrabee outside, triumphant, free, enjoying an absolute immunity from the law by reason of the destruction of the moonshiners' lair, which rendered the discovery of his complicity impossible, Taft frowned heavily and swore beneath his breath, and kicked the unoffending embers into a new adjustment, so bitter was the fact that his own safety made Larrabee's protection complete. Even poor Dan Sykes's exile — and doubtless the young sot was well on the way to Texas by this time — was as necessarily a measure taken in Larrabee's behalf as if it were the dearest desire of Taft's heart to shield and screen him. The realization that, despite himself, Larrabee shared his security cheapened it. Less and less he realized its value. A turbulent pulse began to stir within his veins. His heavy cheek was red and pendulous beneath his yellow beard. Occasionally he dropped his lower jaw with an expression of angry dismay, so ill had the event fallen out with his liking. The sight of Copley wandering about the half-darkened house, lighted only by the fire and the pallid grayness from the door ajar opening upon the rainy outside world, as uneasy as a homeless cat, able to settle to nothing, his face a palimpsest of care and trouble and failure, overwritten again and again above the half-obliterated script of years agone, irritated him vaguely. Taft eyed him loweringly, as the two children in the opposite room besieged him for the detail of the adventures and dramatic " taking off " of a certain " black b'ar," a vanquished enemy of his earlier days, which he recounted as aimlessly as if the story were elicited by a wooden crank ; but responding to a spirited encore, he plucked up heart of grace to add new and fresh particulars. His worn and not unkindly face did not ill become the armchair and the propinquity of the juvenile heads. His serenity, as the two resorted from contradiction to blows, smartly administered across

him to his own great jeopardy, bespoke a grand-
fatherly tolerance, nearly related to affection, for
the combatants. Without more masterful leading
than his own mind could originate or his own pro-
pensities could furnish, he might spend the rest of
his life at the plough-handles, and ask no better
society, and hope for naught beyond his coarse
garb and his coarser fare. He was growing old,
and this might be a better prospect than the still
could promise, with always the possibility of a federal prisoner's cell at the vanishing point of the
long perspective.

Taft could preëmpt no such demesne of mild
content. His rankling regret for all that he had
done, and done so well, in that it served his enemy
perforce as one with himself, deepened as he began
to realize that in escaping so great and imminent a
danger none sustained appreciable injury but himself. He alone seemed at the end. He could not
for years, perhaps, safely rehabilitate the still. A
new place must be sought, a new trade established,
new dangers guarded against; and complicated by
his relations with Larrabee, at large and at enmity,
a removal unobserved and a reëstablishment without pursuit seemed impossible. He dwelt with futile persistence on the peculiar adaptability of his
hiding-place, now demolished forever. Nowhere
else could he have commanded such advantages of
seclusion. Surely nowhere else could his dangerous
vocation have been so safely plied. He enumerated
the varied precautions that he had observed, the

dangers that he had successfully balked. All the chances of the world outside had run in his favor; even the mysterious burning of the hotel was strangely calculated to aid his design in preventing the advent into the Cove of summer sojourners, that might lead to the discovery of his lair. Doubtless, too, by this time, in addition, Kenniston's plans were definitely and forever baffled by the untoward result of processioning the land. And as the thought of it recurred to him he started suddenly, the color deepened in his face, and he beheld the events of which he had elected to play the motive power in a new and baleful light.

Certainly there was no flaw in his reasoning that stormy night when he had betaken himself in company with the wind and the rain, high up into the solitudes of the "bald" of the mountain. A wild night, with none else abroad save perchance a stray marauder of the furry gentry. Only the mists dogged his steps, and only the lightnings searched out his path. The gigantic boulder that seemed immovable, grim, gaunt, forbidding, the agency of giant powder set astir easily enough; and although the charge, accurately calculated for the purpose, was not sufficient to fracture the great mass, its equilibrium on the steep slope was destroyed. A wild turbulent dance it had as it hurled down the slope from the spot where the ebbing seas of centuries agone had left it stranded. A thunderous crashing voice it lifted as it went, and the thunder of the clouds seemed to reply. In the pallid dawn of the rainy day, Taft had crept back through the wet clouds of the summits and the spent winds lingering in the dank woods, to behold it lying there in this alien stop, as immovable of aspect as of yore, with great trees uprooted by the tempest athwart the rocky ledges about its path, and every trace of the action of powder effaced by the persistent rain. It marked a new corner for the beginning of Kenniston's survey; on a line with the old, it is true, but full five furlongs distant. It was a northwesterly line to be run out thence; the greater divergence would occur in the Cove, which fact Taft had learned as Kenniston made a swift plat of his irregularly shaped land with his cane on the floor of Cap'n Lucy's cabin porch. A simple scheme enough, this, — that the one available site for the hotel should be thrown within the lines of Cap'n Lucy, who would not bargain, sell, or convey, and thus the ill-omened caravansary crowded out of the space it was expected to occupy; for as yet Bruin's intervention as incendiary was among the uncovenanted things, and since the unlucky threat to burn the building had originated among the moonshiners Taft feared discovery should he apply the torch himself. A simple scheme, well planned and carried out with full effect, — and how should its completion so ill please its projector?

The fact that Cap'n Lucy should profit by it Taft had heretofore hardly heeded, since this was the necessary incident of his own greater profit.

Now, however, that treachery, as he esteemed it, had riddled the whole finespun web and brought it to naught, a turmoil of rage possessed him. It seemed some curious chicanery of fate that he alone should sustain loss, and that to others should accrue all the advantage of his subtle weavings of chance and fact, as if the threads still held fast. Cap'n Lucy was in possession, doubtless, of many hundred acres of Kenniston's land. He suddenly grudged them to Cap'n Lucy as he had never bethought himself to grudge them to Kenniston. Jealousy is an intimate passion, and insistently of the soil. The neighbor, the associate, the friend's friend, — it makes no far casts. Kenniston was beyond its restricted bounds.

Cap'n Lucy's causticity, his arrogance, his insulting courage which belittled the possibilities of another man's wrath, his intrenchment in the subservience of his household, and his preëminence in the esteem of his small world did not serve to commend him to his unwilling benefactor, who stood in immediate contemplation of his own loss. And as the radiant face of Julia appeared in the dim midst of Taft's recollection, he rose to his feet, his resolution taken in the instant. He had not forgotten the look in Larrabee's eyes when Espey had demanded of him whom he had been " a-courtin' at Tems's." Now, with Espey gone, and Larrabee foot-loose and free, it might chance that these hundreds of acres of which he had bereft Kenniston would one day fall into Larrabee's possession as

his wife's inheritance, when Cap'n Lucy should go
to his account, — which Taft doubted not would
be a long one.

"I 'll be dad-burned," he cried, "ef I 'll stand
by an' see Kenniston choused fur old Lucy or
Lar'bee, air one!"

Few human motives are simple. The travesty of
restitution served to cloak even to himself jealousy
and grudging and revenge, and that mad impulse
to hurl down and wreak woe upon those who had
chanced to prosper in the dispensations which he
had ordered himself, and which had wrought perversely to his injury. He had, however, nothing
of the appearance or the manner of a subtle villain
when he was on horseback in the slanting lines of
rain, that mutiplied till they hid the mountains
near at hand, and erased the Cove, and nullified all
the conditions of the familiar world. On the contrary, his bluff, bold, open aspect was of a reassur-
ing geniality, notwithstanding its overbearing intimations, and served to identify him to Kenniston,
as he lounged in his unsubstantial domicile, and
looked out ruefully at the dull day with the gray
rain and the grayer mist and the ochreous pools of
water, seeing naught else till this massive equestrian
figure materialized in its vaporous midst and
seemed to ride straight out of it. Taft flung himself from his saddle with a decision which implied
a mission; and despite Kenniston's intention to
discourage the visits of the mountaineers, he could
not, with so assured a guest, have withheld the

customary greeting of hospitality without more definite rudeness than he had expected to adventure.

The new-comer was the more welcome since Kenniston's companion in keeping the monkey stove warm was Rodolphus Ross, who had come to the Cove for the purpose of examining the scene of the fire, and ferreting out the incendiary. He had, under the guise of questioning Kenniston on the subject, inflicted his society upon his restive host for the better part of an hour, now and then desisting from the discussion to work away at the damper of the monkey stove, which he patronizingly denominated a "smart little trick," albeit by reason of the heavy air and ill adjustment and the lack of adequate draught it was doing itself no credit. Ross experimented with an ardor and uninformed energy which threatened the total wreck of its constitution. The clatter of the metal was hardly more grating upon Kenniston's educated nerves than were his guest's speech and bearing. There was something in the exaggeration of the deputy's urban boorishness, the plaid of his ill-fitting garments, the hilarity of his vulgar townish impudence, that daunted a charitable acceptation of his foibles. So distasteful to Kenniston's cultured taste was the degree of sophistication acquired by the deputy sheriff, and with many a misconception adapted to his personality, that the absence of it seemed dignity in the mountaineer, and Taft's unvarnished address the unpolished substratum of good manners.

"How 's ducks in the hills?" Ross greeted him,

dropping the small poker, and looking up with bright dark eyes, the two prominent front teeth visible beneath the short upper lip.   There was a moment of rabbit-like expectancy of expression ; then his lips widened to a laugh as the burly stranger turned his serious, impressive face toward him.

" Air you-uns speakin' ter me, sir ? " demanded Taft, in a grave, direct manner, his steady eye full upon him.

The airy deputy shifted ground for once. " Good day fur ducks," he modified his speech.

" Cornsider'ble fallin' weather," admitted Taft incidentally, and, seating himself in the chair indicated by Kenniston, he proceeded to take part in the conversation, his big booming voice rendering interruption impossible save as he listed.

" I hev viewed you-uns afore at old Cap'n Lucy Tems's house," he said to Kenniston, crossing his legs, and eying the steam casually as it rose from the damp boots under the persuasive heat of the stove. " Yes, sir, Taft is my name."

" I remember you very well," said Kenniston affably. " Won't you light your pipe ? " He pushed a match holder and tobacco pouch across the table to him.

Taft, without comment, filled his pipe from an inexhaustible supply of tobacco that seemed always loose in his pocket ; it was far stronger than that of his host, as the rank odor which rose on the air presently demonstrated. Rodolphus Ross had looked at him with a grin of hopeful anticipation, which shrunk at once when he recognized and adapted to his own needs the uses of the lucifer match.

"Yes, sir," Taft resumed, "I war toler'ble sorry ter hear 'bout'n yer hotel bein' burnt. I did n't view it at the time." He puffed the coals into a glow, and pulled away comfortably.

"Meanes' people on yearth, these hyar mountaineers!" cried Ross. "They jes' so durned ignorant they don't know sin from salvation, nor law from lying."

"Then they ain't 'sponsible," remarked Taft coolly. He pressed down the burning tobacco in the bowl with a callous forefinger indurated by long practice to crowding his pipe, and resumed: "I 'lowed it mought gin ye a start ef I war ter tell ye I hearn sev'ral men talkin' 'bout burnin' it, — long time ago, 'fore it war begun."

Kenniston was leaning back in his chair, much at his ease, noting with a sort of languid interest the intimations of force and ferocity in his visitor's face: the keen sagacity, rather as of the instinctive endowment of one of the lower orders of creation than an enlightened intelligence; the beaklike nose; the contradictory geniality of the full blue eye and broad floridity. He brought his tilted chair suddenly to the floor, leaned forward on the table, with a slight exclusive gesture toward Rodolphus Ross, which, although it escaped that worthy, caused Taft a sharp regret for his precipitancy.

The deputy sheriff was all a-clamor.

"Why, now, my big bull o' Bashan, ye hev got ter make that statement under oath with full partic'lars, — names, dates, and place!" He rose up on the opposite side of the monkey stove, with the lifter in his hand, with which he gesticulated imperatively.

Kenniston could hardly repress his impatience.

"Of course, Mr. Ross, of course, — all in due season," he said irritably.

"But abuse the authorities, in season an' out, an' 'low the devil will ketch the officer, in due course o' jestice, 'fore the officer 'll ketch the malefactor. I ain't a-goin' ter lose you, Mr. Durham, ye bet high on that!" he added, turning to Taft.

"Mr. Taft expects to swear to the facts, of course," said Kenniston. He paused abruptly, meditating a remonstrance with the tumultuous brute; but Ross's very vulgarity, his clamorous brutality, the impossibility of reaching through his hardened exterior any sensitiveness, or pride, or sense of decorum, or whatever sanction may control the heart of a man who is a gentleman in jeans, gave him an advantage over a man of breeding which no culture could compass. Kenniston could not cope with him; his training had prepared him for no such encounter.

Only Taft's great sonorous voice could overbear the deputy's words, which sounded in his first utterance with the disjointed effect of Christmas firecrackers enlivening the booming of Christmas guns.

"I'll make oath ter statements ez ter date an'

person, but not place, — I hev no call ter drag other folks inter sech. I dunno ez they fired the hotel; I only heard 'em threat it."

" But why? " demanded Kenniston eagerly.

" Deviltry, — deviltry, o' course," protested Ross. He had contrived to smirch his face in the careless handling of the poker of the monkey stove, which added a certain grotesque effect to his appearance, if one were in the mood to be amused by it.

Kenniston's mood was far from such influences.

" I must ask you to be quiet, sir," he said, with acridity.

" Ye must? " sneered Rodolphus Ross. " An' who war that ez 'lowed ef the local force war so ' torpid,' — *torpid*, ye hed it, — ye 'd hev up private detectives from Bretonville ter settle the hash o' these kentry varmints? "

He threw up his eyebrows almost to the smirches obliquely laid across his forehead, laughed with a gleam of white teeth and an intent widening of the dark eyes, the whole facial expression gone in an instant.

" Waal, we ain't ' torpid' no longer. ' Wake up, snakes ! ' Now, old buck, answer my questions, an' tell me why they war n't willin' ter let Mr. Kenniston build his hotel in the Cove."

Kenniston folded his arms as he tilted himself back in his chair, and resigned the conversation to its unique leadership. The ceaseless motion of the falling lines of rain gave a spurious effect of motion to the great monastic forms of the mountains cowled with mists and robed in dreary hue, seeming continually in sad processional along the horizon. The ochreous pools near at hand had lost all capacity for reflection, although the dark green branches of the firs here and there bent above them, and the gray rain dripping from the fibrous fringes upon the unquiet tremulous surface took its color, and was seen no more. His returning glance met Taft's eye as he was about to speak, and somehow in that momentary contact a quiet understanding was established between them.

"The reason, I reckon, they did n't want Mr. Kenniston ter build his hotel hyar war 'kase 't would bring too many strangers round."

"An' what 's the objection to strangers?" asked Kenniston anxiously. It was not merely a retrospective interest that the question served. He asked for the future.

"Waal, I reckon they hed some moonshinin' or sech on hand," returned Taft coolly.

"Thar, now! what did I tell ye?" vociferated Rodolphus Ross, appealing to Kenniston. "An' I 'll bet this hyar Larrabee war one of 'em."

Taft nodded, and Kenniston meditatively eyed the dull flashes from the stove, recollecting the strange conversation of Larrabee here, and his sudden significant betrayal of secret knowledge of the origin of the fire when it was mentioned.

"Strangers air powerful onhealthy fur the moonshinin' business," said Taft, as a sort of corollary of his former statement.

"Speak from experience?" sneered Rodolphus Ross.

"I do so," declared Taft unequivocally. Then turning to Kenniston, "I sarved a prison term fur illicit distillin' whenst I war a young man. I 'lowed, like all these other young muskrats, ez I could do what I pleased with my own corn an' apples. But whenst I traveled all through six or seben States goin' to the North, an' seen this big kentry an' sech, I knowed I war n't ekal ter runnin' agin its laws; an' whether thar's reason in 'em or no, I ondertook ter keep 'em arterward."

This unexpected confession disconcerted Ross in some sort. He silently eyed Taft, whose criminal experience seemed rather an error of an unripe judgment than the turpitude of law-breaking, and his candor in admitting it bluntly did not detract from the serious impression he had evidently made upon Kenniston. With Ross nothing was serious long. There was a sudden breaking up of the gloss of intentness in his round dark eyes, and as they shifted they fell upon the poker of the stove, and he once more thrust it through the bars and rattled it smartly.

"I oughter say," said Taft, meditatively sucking his pipestem, "that 't war Espey ez fust 'lowed ter burn ye out. 'Burn his shanty!' he say."

A picture as definite as if it were the reality of pigments and canvas glowed suddenly before his contemplation, — the red walls of his den a-flicker in the flare of the furnace fire, the burnished gleam

of the copper, the burly forms of the tubs of mash,
familiars of the brown gloom, and the circle of
faces, definite with those sharply marked shadows
and striking high lights that a strong artificial glow
elicits from the darkness. For his life he could
not repress a long-drawn sigh, and then he shifted
his position and cleared his throat raucously. But
the picture, like many another masterpiece of the
painter Memory, was not on general exhibition.
For all its close detail and strong salience and brilliant reality of hue, it was invisible to Kenniston.
As to the regretful sigh, fat men are often wont to
sigh for very fatness, and it passed without significance.

After a meditative pause, " Did it ever occur to
you that this Larrabee is a crank," asked Kenniston, " what you call, and very aptly, touched-in-the-
head ? "

" Who ? Larrabee ? " exclaimed Taft vehemently, all alert once more, his eyes on fire, his
angry breath quick. " He's smart ez the very
devil ! Don't you let him pull the wool over yer
eyes with the lunacy purtense."

Rodolphus Ross gave a final rasping clatter of
the poker between the bars ; then flung it, resounding, down upon the floor. He rose to his feet,
stamping with first one and then the other to shake
out his trousers from their persistent kneed effect,
and, turning to Taft, he said, with an off-hand
manner, " Now, look-a-hyar, Prize Beef, when did ye
an' this sca'ce buzzard Lar'bee meet the last time ? "

The " Prize Beef " apparently perceived no sort of offense in this form of address.

" I ain't viewed him in — I dunno when. I 'lowed he hed lef' the kentry till he war up at my store, a few nights ago. I war n't thar, but my leetle gal, she seen him."

The sly, predatory look was in Rodolphus Ross's eyes. He lifted his knee and smote it as if he had discovered a very apt coincidence.

Taft hesitated; then he said, " Ye 'd better go up yander an' talk ter my leetle darter 'bout'n it." He hesitated once more. He feared that Copley might be inadequate to the situation, but, with his ever alert suspicions, he would doubtless fly at the very sight of a stranger; and as to Sis, he could rely upon Rodolphus Ross's address and manner to arouse the enmity of old Mrs. Jiniway's disciple in etiquette, and he knew of old that Sis was wont to give her adversary no quarter. A dozen of such as Rodolphus Ross would hardly be a handful for Sis. He would learn naught from her which he wanted to know. " Take my mare out thar, bein' ready saddled," he said hospitably. " I 'll wait hyar till ye kem back."

Contrariety was the breath of the deputy's life. The congeniality of his vocation lay much in the opposition of his duties to the desires of those of his fellow-men with whom he was brought into offi- cial contact. He earnestly wished to negative Taft's suggestion, but the possibility of getting at closer quarters with Larrabee, of once more finding

his trail, which had seemed to disappear from the
face of the earth, was stronger for the moment.
His enmity had not grown cold ; it was the more
vehement the more it was baffled. He lingered a
moment ; then, turning up his collar, and pulling
down the broad rim of his hat all around to afford
eaves to conduct the rain from his head, he plunged
out into the steady torrents with a discordant yawp
that made the little shanty ring.

Taft gazed thoughtfully after him as he vaulted
into the saddle and rode off with a good deal of
unnecessary heel-and-toe exercise in the region of
the animal's ribs. The restive mare apparently
resented the ungentle treatment, for the last that
was seen of mount and rider was a profile rampant
against the blank white expanse of the closing
mists ere they were enveloped in the opaque multitudinous folds.

"They tell me that Gawd made man," said
Taft at last. "'Pears ter me ez the Almighty
slighted *that* job, sure."

Kenniston was a man of painfully orderly
instincts. He could not satisfactorily resume
the conversation without gathering up the poker,
the lifter, and other appurtenances of the stove
which Ross had scattered about the little zinc
square on which it sat, replacing them, rearrang-
ing the writing materials, newspapers, tobacco, and
cigars on the table, and stirring the fire to brightness and a possibility of burning. As he threw
himself into his chair he marked how the encroach-

ing mists had invested the house. Not half a
dozen paces of the path remained visible from the
door; even upon the threshold the vapor hung in
vague white wreaths, to vanish in the heat, and be
replaced by white clouds floating in with a rolling
motion, — never disappearing utterly, but venturing no further. On the roof and in the invisibili-
ties of the white mists outside they could hear the
chilly rain still steadily falling. The seeming
isolation gave a certain confidential character to
the conversation even before its developments war-
ranted this.

"How did the percessionin' turn out?" Taft
demanded.

"The rain stopped it," returned Kenniston,
gloomily eying the thickening mists, while Taft
critically but covertly observed him.

"Satisfied ez fur ez it went, I s'pose?" Taft
flicked off the ashes from his pipe, and pressed
down the remainder of its contents with that sala-
mander of a forefinger.

"No," said Kenniston irritably. "It is a great
surprise to me."

"Mr. Kenniston," said Taft, with that blunt
directness which so commended him to the experienced man and so warped his judgment, "that
thar Big Hollow Boulder, the beginning o' yer
survey, hev been bodaciously moved."

Kenniston lifted his head suddenly, the excitement of the moment showing red in his face. A
half-scornful incredulity was in his eyes, almost on

his lips. He was about to speak; then paused
doubtfully. The testimony of his recollections of
Cap'n Lucy's significant insistence on the phrase
" Big Hollow Boulder " and a thousand satiric allusions to the stationary functions of a monument of
boundary overwhelmed him for the moment; for
their incongruity with a culpable knowledge or
agency in the fact was more than inexplicable;
it was mysterious. There needed no dexterous
jugglery with phrase and fact, however, to account
for Luther's furtive, hang-dog manner and averted
eye.

"It seems impossible! But I will not believe
that old man Lucy had anything to do with moving it," Kenniston began. He suddenly caught
his lip and bit it hard. It was evident from his
flaunting remarks that the old mountaineer had
not been similarly generous to his neighbor.

"A heap o' land," suggested the politic Taft.
" But then I s'pose ter run yer eastern line out
would show whar yer corner is ? " He asked the
question eagerly.

" Oh no. Calls for permanent natural objects
usually control calls for distance. I suppose that
rule would hold fast in this instance. My eastern line can only run to the boulder, which is presumably immovable."

Taft's countenance fell. He had thought that
the further survey of the eastern boundary would
serve to reëstablish the corner where the boulder
should be ; on the contrary, Cap'n Lucy was invested

with many hundred acres for which he had given no equivalent in goods, or money, or even occupancy.

"I saw that something was mighty wrong with the line that the surveyor was running; and so did Cap'n Lucy, for that matter," said Kenniston, revolving the events of the processioning. "He looked dumfounded when he saw Wild Duck Falls in his boundary, and the hotel, — or rather the place where the hotel ought to be."

Taft caught a quick inspiration. "That's it, — them boys is a-moonshinin' fur true. They must hev moved the boulder ter crowd ye out of a buildin' site. An' then they burnt the hotel."

"Well, they've got me pretty badly crowded, — I'll say that for them."

Kenniston was looking out of the door, with that sullen sense of injury and hopelessness which oppresses a city man in the country in bad weather. The world had slipped away, somehow; he was left to the vague unresponsiveness of the inexpressive white mists; the rain would probably continue forever; the day was of a longevity known to no other that had ever dawned; without the prompting of his watch he could not have said if it were morning or afternoon. The roof leaked; the boots of his uncouth visitors tracked up the floor with red clay mud. A saddle in one corner gave out an obtrusive odor of leather, and the monkey stove, despite all this dankness, filled the room with that baking, dry, afflicting aroma common to all its kindred. His pugnacity was abated under these untoward conditions; his enthusiasms were overwhelmed beneath the depression of the rain. He thought wistfully of Bretonville, and of a cosy corner in the reading-room of a certain club, and of his office, and sighed as his mind reverted to the jeopardy of the present, the futility of the money and thought he had spent here, and the froward tangle which must needs be untwisted if these unpromising assets were to be utilized at all.

"Mus' hev been Lar'bee an' Espey a-moonshinin'." Taft once more sought to prompt that inimical sense of injury. "An' moved the boulder bodaciously, — the corner landmark."

"A felony," said Kenniston thoughtfully.

The patter of the rain came heavily through the silence, and in that bleak whiteness without they heard far away the wind rousing from its lair in furthest defiles. The terrors of its voice did not shake the mists; only the sound touched a responsive chord of feeling, and the day was the drearier for the broken stillness.

"A felony," he said, and fell a-musing. He vaguely repudiated the idea, and then bethought himself, contradictorily, of the strange subterfuge with which he had been summoned to the door. For no harm, surely, he argued. There was a certain fascination in the thought of the new star that the mountaineer had brought to his contemplation. Not a bad face, this star-gazer's, and with a coloring which had always commended itself to his artistic sense. A good face and finely cut, he would have said but for that association of ideas, "a felony," that sudden conscious expression as of some guilty knowledge of the burning of the hotel. He could not believe it of his star-gazer, with his elated upward look! He remembered afterward that he thought then that the dankness of the weather, in relaxing all manner of tension, had slackened his rigid standards and his taut personal exactions. He was morally limp, doubtless, as well as physically; but he shrunk from the phrase in this application, and he considered that the most definite sensation of that most indefinite day was the relief he experienced when Rodolphus Ross came plunging out of the mists.

In high dudgeon the deputy was with the events and results of his mission, and he had wreaked his resentment on the unoffending animal which he rode. The mare's sides showed the marks of his stinging lash, and she had retaliated as well as she could by perversely refusing to pause where he wished to dismount to avoid the pools. A false start or two dragged him through water knee-deep, and as he came into the house his eyes were flashing with his various anger, and his lip curled scornfully.

"I tell ye," he said to Taft, with his fractious mirthfulness, "thar 's money in that brat o' yourn, that Cornelia Taft! Buy her a muzzle an' a chain an' jine a show, an' she 'll draw a crowd ez the Leetle She-B'ar o' Persimmon Cove! Bless my boots! I 'm glad I 'm all hyar. The leetle b'ar like ter tore me ter fringes!'" he exclaimed metaphorically. He canted his head mockingly to one side as he threw himself into a chair beside the stove, seized the poker, and administered a rousing shake. "I tell you what," he said, eying Taft gloweringly, "I 'd keep her nails an' teeth well pruned, my friend."

For Miss Cornelia Taft and Rodolphus Ross had failed signally to hit it off amicably. Copley had watched the interview through the open door of the store with varying emotions of anxiety: first, lest Ross was a "revenuer" or a spy; then, lest, as an officer of the state law, he had some charge against them; again, lest he cause Sis some apprehension; and lastly, lest the temerity of the doughty Sis bring woe and wreck upon the devoted household. Joe cowered in a corner of the fireplace, leaning against the great jamb, essaying only a few of the writhings and twistings of his anatomy which he affected, and sometimes sitting still altogether, so did the interest of the colloquy overmaster the tendency of his muscles.

"Hello, youngsters!" was Ross's affable greeting as he tramped in when Joe opened the door. He flung himself into a chair before the fire, then turned and surveyed Cornelia, whose prim, pale, precise face looked more unfriendly and forbidding and negative than usual, as she sat, her hands demurely crossed on her lap, on the opposite side of the fireplace.

" My Lord! is this all? I 'lowed yer dad hed
a heap bigger gal 'n you. Some similar ter a
shrunk-up gran'mammy; ye look like ye mought
hev lasted sence the flood. How 's yer fambly,
ma'am ? "

The juvenile heart resents a scoff. Cornelia
Taft's faculties were limited, but she gathered herself for revenge.

" Waal, then," he demanded, as she sat stiffly
silent and insulted, " how 's rats ? "

" I could n't jedge," she piped up suddenly.
" We-uns hain't hed a terrier happen in hyar afore
now fur a consider'ble time."

He was fairly silenced for the nonce. Elated by
the execution of her sally, and not propitiated by
his subsequent effort to ignore this passage at arms,
she took full advantage of the opportunity to harass
him which was presented when he announced himself an officer of the law, and demanded to know
when and where she had seen Larrabee the last
time. No perverse adult witness could have more
dexterously baffled him with indefinite statements ;
and when he appealed from her to Joe, whose
clumsy efforts to remember were hopelessly inadequate, her open glee was peculiarly tantalizing to
Ross ; for none can so resent a jest as a confirmed
joker. Then it was that he made his fatal false
step.

" Look-a-hyar, Small Female, leetle ez ye be,
I 'll arrest you-uns an' kerry ye off ter jail, ef ye
don't spry up an' answer my question."

And then it was that Sis, bracing her small back, defied the majesty of the State of Tennessee as exemplified in Rodolphus Ross. So it came to open war. She was animated, too, by a partisan spirit for Larrabee. She remembered, with her infrequent approval, how he had conducted himself on the occasion in question ; how quiet, how gentle, he was, how observant of the graces of her house-keeping, how commendatory of her dominion over Joe. Their conversation had since been often in her mind ; she had rehearsed it, as she sat in the gloaming on her stool before the flickering fire, with the history of the Biblical worthies of which it was redundant. With no one else could she talk of these things. With quick adulation she had transformed Larrabee into a hero, and she longed to see him again. Her tongue, being feminine, could not be held altogether, but she told Ross naught which he desired to hear. She sounded the praises of Larrabee on many a key, and " disremembered " persistently whether it was Friday or Monday, or last week or week before, when she had seen him.

" Waal, what war he a-doin' of hyar, ennyhows ? " queried Ross.

" Talkin'."

" 'Bout what, gal ? "

" 'Bout no gal," Miss Taft responded, with a flash of the eye.

" Waal, then," — even he was fain to concede, in the hope of finding some thoroughfare in thus beating about the bush, — " 'bout what boy ? "

She hesitated. She had not intended to cheapen the subject of her interest and enthusiasm by mention in this queer symposium. The talk with Larrabee had been in the nature of a confidence, as in the admiring canvass of mutual friends; she had a sense as if it were not the thing for general public and unworthy conversation. Nevertheless, her affinity for the subject constrained her. There was a light in her face, a placid softening of feature. Her flabby little colorless cheek mustered up a dimple.

"'Bout Sam'l," she said, with a smile.

"Sam'l who?" he demanded keenly.

Sis hesitated, suddenly posed. "I — I disremember his — his — surname," she admitted.

"Did ye see him with Lar'bee?" he asked, his big pertinacious eyes on her face, expectant of immediate developments.

"I — I ain't never seen *him*. I — I reckon" — it seemed too terrible to contemplate — "I reckon he mus' be — daid." She had never before looked upon it in this light, and her heart sank.

"Friend o' Lar'bee's?" he persisted.

"I reckon so; he hed read 'bout him."

"Read 'bout him? Whar? In the 'Colb'ry Gazette'?" He lowered his voice respectfully, for to him personal mention in the 'Colbury Gazette' meant fame.

"Naw. In the Bible, o' course," said Sis, stiffly reproving.

He stared at her in blank amaze for a moment;

then he smote his leg a sounding thwack, and burst into a howl of derisive laughter.

"Ye an' Lar'bee hed a pray'r-meetin', did ye? An', my son," he continued through his nose with a sanctimonious whine, turning to Joe, "did ye lead the saints in supplication, or raise the hyme-chune?"

Joe responded with a fat chuckle of delighted laughter, rejoiced to see his Mentor, the professor of many novel and distasteful arts of household economy, put to ridicule and out of countenance.

It was only for a moment. She turned acridly against the domestic insurgent.

"*He* tuned up arterward. Joe done *his* quirin' arter Lar'bee war gone, an' the wind riz, an' the rain kem down. He wisht an' wisht Lar'bee hed bided. He fairly blated fur skeer!"

"I never!" protested Joe in pouting indignation. "*I* war n't 'feared o' the wind an' rain, nare one! 'T war the racket them dead ones kep' up in the Los' Time mine diggin' thar graves. This hyar house air right over the mine."

Ross's great shifting wild eyes widened as he looked from one to the other.

"Thar *ain't* no dead ones diggin' thar graves!" cried Sis didactically. She must needs spend too many lonely hours here for that suggestion to be a welcome one. "Them ez dig ain't dead. Dad say jes' some boys, he reckon, a-moonshinin' or sech of a night in the Lost Time mine."

Rodolphus Ross rose to his feet. He was elated,

confident. He snapped his fingers noisily in the air as he took two or three of the sideway paces usually preliminary to a clog dance, which accomplishment he had acquired by viewing what he termed a " minstrel show." He had long suspected Larrabee of moonshining, and here was the *locus in quo.* He had said that Larrabee's trail had seemed to disappear from the face of the earth; with what literal reason he had not dreamed. Notwithstanding his haste, however, he must needs tarry for a fleer.

" Gran'mammy Taft," he said, leering at the little girl, with her prim, antique aspect, " I never thunk ter find ye hobnobbin' with moonshiners."

" Lar'bee ain't no moonshiner," she protested, with swift alarm.

He joyed in her evident flutter.

" Ah, gran'mammy Taft, ye kin consider yerse'f under arrest fur aidin' an' abettin' in moonshinin', ye an' all yer fambly."

" Ye ain't no revenuer!" cried Sis, moving back a step, however. " Ye ain't 'lowed ter *purtend* ter be one, nuther. I hearn o' a man in Persimmon Cove ez *purtended* ter be a off'cer o' the law, an' got 'rested hisse'f. An' I would hev thunk ennyways ez ye hed hed enough o' arrestin' folks fur fun, sence that time ye flung Lar'bee over the bluffs, an' nigh kilt him. Ef ye be so sharp set ter 'rest ennybody, go find Jack Espey an' 'rest him."

Ross was out of countenance. Nevertheless —

"How many j'ints hev her tongue got?" he demanded of Joe, with a feint of serious interest.

But Joe had deserted to the enemy. He thought
that Sis was in the ascendant, and Ross's threat at
once angered and terrified him. He received with
pouting silence the officer's aside, while Sis went on
triumphantly : —

" Dad say my granny Jiniway air kin somehows
ter the high sher'ff's wife; an' whenst I go ter
Colb'ry nex' week with dad, I be goin' ter go ter
her house an' ax the high sher'ff ef he 'lows his
dep'ties ter arrest people fur joke, an' *purtend* ter
be revenue off'cers, an' skeer leetle gals by arrestin'
'em, an' 'lowin' he'll take the whole fambly fur
moonshinin'. My granny Jiniway's third cousin
air the high sher'ff's wife ! "

In the face of this genealogical detail, it was
with a somewhat subdued spirit that Ross mounted
the mare and set forth on his return ; for the high
sheriff was a man with a most attenuated sense of
humor, a literal interpretation of the duties of his
office, and notwithstanding the fact that Ross's
willingness to ride long distances, in all manner of
weather, relieved him of this the most irksome of
duties to an inert temperament, he had begun to
look doubtfully upon him, particularly since the
untoward result of the facetious arrest of the supposed Larrabee, and Ross felt that his tenure was
not altogether secure. As he passed the portal of
the Lost Time mine, the thought of his quest recurred to his mind, and the important clue which he

deemed he had obtained from the little girl's conversation. He no longer considered it important, for from the rough-hewn portal of the cavern poured forth the compressed stream of the divers subterranean currents, gathered together and hurled forth in a great spout, and with a plunging force that astonished him, remembering as he did the far tamer flow of the earlier season. He ascribed the change to the persistent autumn rains flooding some watercourse that doubtless pierced the hidden chambers. It filled the outlet within a few feet of the summit of the arch. Any entrance here was impossible; as for another opening to the mine, he looked about him upon the limitless tangled wilderness of wood and rock, the shifting beclouding mists, the endless skeins of the rain, and he swore between his big front teeth an oath which, despite the grotesque humor of its phraseology, had within it all the bitter profanity of his baffling disappointment. And in default of aught else on which to wreak his anger, he cruelly lashed Taft's mare; and so he went down to join the others at Kenniston's quarters amongst the shanties of the workmen in the Cove.

XIX.

Tʜᴀᴛ night, the rain, beating out its strong
staccato rhythm on the old clapboards roofing the
barn, made scant impression on Jasper Larrabee's
senses; he slept soundly amongst the great elastic
billows of the hay. As by degrees the downpour
slackened, the comparative silence affected his
half-dormant consciousness as sound had failed to
do. He roused slightly from time to time, and
presently was broad awake, to hear only the melancholy drip from the eaves and the chorus of
far-away frogs beginning to pipe anew along the
pools. He did not welcome his other self, that
mysterious essence of thought and will that was
torn with hopes and fed on regrets, and was prone
to hold troublous disputations with yet another
inner self, which on its part was always keen to
find out every fault, to upbraid each cherished sin,
and had an ugly trick of unmasking and setting
in a strong unflattering light motives which might
otherwise seem to be above suspicion. The humbler obvious entity known as Jasper Larrabee
would, he often thought, be happier without so
definite a development of either of these endow-
ments, his mind or his conscience; for thus he
learned from their functions to differentiate them.

When this Jasper Larrabee was well fed, he was
hearty and happy. The sun shone on him, and
he sang till the woods rang. When he went down
into the sunless depths of the Lost Time mine,
every strong muscle rejoiced in the work, and his
steady nerve, which is called courage, gave a zest
to danger, whether the menace were of the law, or
of the wild beast in the wilderness, or of the civilized savage amongst his own associates. If it had
not been for his mind forever asking "Why?"
and his conscience grimly protesting "Because,"
what a thriving, well-balanced physical organization
Jasper Larrabee might have been! He knew
others who were little more than body, who asked
no questions and heard no answers ; he held them
far the happier for it, and he did not realize how
much the duller. And so he hated the "Why?"
and flinched from the "Because." And here they
were in company, these choice spirits, in the suddenly silent midnight, with only the melancholy
drip at long intervals from the eaves, the vague
piping of frogs sounding afar off and failing again,
and that strange preponderating sense of the proximity of the mountains although enshrouded and
invisible in the mist. The sibilant rustle of the hay
was loud in the stillness as he shifted his posture.
He shifted it often, being anxious and restless,
for his brace of companions were more censorious
even than their wont as to that limited cheerful
physique which he accounted Jasper Larrabee.
He had had naught to eat but a few handfuls of

grapes from the vines that clambered over the gable of the barn, and some unpalatable raw eggs found among the hay; and this fact of hunger gave a mighty grip to the poignancy of " Because." He had had naught to do all the long rainy day but to lie in the hay and look out through the crevices of the logs at the queer acorn-like roof of his mother's house, that had welcomed so many, and had no place now for him or for her. He watched with all the grief of an exile the children coming and going, and the gaunt Mrs. Timson wielding an unbridled authority, making the most of her usurpations; he heard, with the indignant objection that naturally appertains to the heir to the throne, her raucous raised voice in objurgation or command. Again and again these sounds came from the opaque blankness of the mist; for often the clouds obscured the little house altogether, and crowded through the crevices of the barn, and shifted back and forth. For the reason of the continuous fog he had delayed to inform the officer of the law and deliver Espey to him. Doubtless, in the idleness of his solitary day in the mine, Espey would be alert and hear an approach, and might escape through some aperture of the cavern other than the main entrance; the thick mists would then conceal him indubitably, and further his flight without the slightest scruple as to responsibility as accessory after the fact. Larrabee was waiting for the darkness that he might take Espey the more certainly, while his vigilance was relaxed in working at the forlorn enterprise of old

Haight and his lieutenant " Tawm " in the mine. But in waiting Larrabee had fallen asleep, and the iteration of the steady rainfall was somnolent in its effects, and the hours drowsed by. He knew that it was past midnight before he noted the slant of a late-risen moon, golden, lustrous, dreamlike, softly shining through the crevices of the logs in one corner of the ramshackle old place. The sky was clearing, then. He rose hastily to his feet, and leaned out of the window. Clear! It was of a deeply limpid and definite blue, with white and gray clouds, moon-illumined, drawing back swiftly from vast expanses of this lucid ether all a-sparkle with the whiteness of the stars. With the dank earth so dark below, and the dully glamourous light of the moon in her last quarter, it seemed to him that he had never seen the stars so splendidly white. The next moment a sudden pang of suspense, of fear, that was like a bodily throe had wrested away his breath. He hardly realized that he had moved; he only knew that he had sprung down the rotting rungs of the old ladder and through the barn below, because he was standing outside the door upon the ground, gazing up, bareheaded, wild-eyed, in a frenzy of doubt, of anxiety, of a sort of unreasoning terror, at the skies. For the star — his star — was gone! It had vanished! Again and again, with the strong pulse of hope, he swept the heavens with eager search. Afterward he thought he remembered a dull leaden-hued minute object in the place of that splendid silver shin-

ing that had made his heart so glad. It had vanished, — its message withheld, its mystery unre-
vealed, like an illusion, like a fagged-out enthusiasm,
like the futile words of a prayer without the fervor
of faith. He could not believe it. Again and
again he sought a new posture, a new hope. He
followed its closer neighbors along the steeps of
the mountain as they journeyed toward the west in
the sky above. The tint of the heavens was changing presently, — a lighter blue. The golden moon
grew of a pearl-like lustre. The stars waxed faint.
The clouds were red. And here was the gray day
hard upon him, and in the earth naught of value,
for in the sky he had lost a star. How strong,
how resistless of advance, was the riding up of the
great sun! Get ye away, illusions, and glamours,
and dreamers of dreams! Such a definite visible
world! How full of fixed facts! He saw, as he
stood, the shanties of the workmen in the Cove,
where the mists were hustling off in great haste,
as if too tenuous, too unsubstantial, too inutile, to
hold ground in the face of the strong practicalities
dawning over the horizon. The smoke was curling
up from the chimney of Cap'n Lucy's cabin,
where breakfast was cooking. The cows were at
the bars. All the woods were lustrous with moisture, and splendidly a-glint with the yellow sunbeams striking aslant through them. The distant
mountains were blue and amethyst and violet and
purple, — a rhapsody of color. Here and there, as
if the rain had painted them, boughs of sumach and

sourwood were scarlet in the woods ; the sweet-gum showed flecks of purple leaves, and the hickory had occasional flares of yellow. The goldenrod had burst into bloom, and with this seal of the autumnal season stamped upon the land came Julia along the road, her bonnet hanging on her shoulders, her head bare, her face like spring itself, her hands full of flowers that she scattered as she sang. How her fresh young voice rang against the turmoil of the current from the Lost Time mine, like some sudden burst of joy from out the fretted tides of a troubled life ! As she tossed the flowers, and glanced over her shoulder to see where they fell, Larrabee crossed the log laid from one deeply gullied bank to the other side of the road, to serve foot passengers when the water was high in wet weather. She paused, and looked at him with a frown. The unwonted corrugations in her fair young brow changed her inexpressive face almost out of recognition. He stood in silent deprecation for a moment. His heart was sore. His life was full of trouble of many sorts and degrees. That æsthetic loss, that sense of bereavement because of his vanished star, outrankled them all.

Courage is of the nature of an essence ; one may not judge how it will pull the beam, nor is it dispensed by dry measure. Something seemingly inadequate, a breath of wind, a change of mind, or the chilling of the fervors of some futile and foolish enthusiasm, and behold the volatile element is dispersed through the air. The strain on Larrabee's nerves had been great.   His sensibilities had waxed tender.   He faltered before the definite bending of those delicately marked brows.

"Ye air out betimes, Julia?" he ventured propitiatingly, as she stoutly maintained silence. "What be ye a-doin' of with them flowers?"

"Sowin' 'em," said Julia instantly.   "I expec' 'em ter bloom thar in the road ter mo' purpose 'n they ever did afore."

He cast a glance of wonderment at her.   But her unfriendly manner, her cold eye, disconcerted him afresh, and nullified his surprise at her words.

"Air you-uns mad at me down at yer house?" he demanded eagerly.

"What fur?" she asked, with a keen, belligerent look that was mightily like Cap'n Lucy.

"'Bout my speakin' so free 'bout Espey, an' Cap'n Lucy not warnin' me an' my mother, knowin' him ter be sought fur murder?"

"Oh!" she cried, with airy causticity.   "I hed furgot it."

He felt the covert fleer of this speedy dismissal. But with him pride was at a low ebb.   He silently looked at her as she held a cardinal flower to her red lips, while her long-lashed blue eyes scanned the dewy bunch of jewel-weed and mountain snow and wild asters that filled her hands.   The wind swayed her dark blue skirt as she stood on a great fragment of rock beside the running stream.   It gave a certain volant effect to her pose, her flower-laden hands, her singular beauty; she seemed the

very genius of the flowering season, its perfect per-
sonification.

"Waal, I 'm glad o' that," he said humbly. "I
need all my friends, an' all the comfort I kin git."

He paused, daunted in a measure by her unresponsiveness. But she was always silent, always
undemonstrative, and perhaps her manner in this
instance went for less than its worth.

"Julia," he said, "I hev hed a powerful strange
'sperience lately. An' it hev cast me down mightily. Not religious,— though I expected suthin'
leadin' an' speritual out'n it. I viewed a new star
in the sky."

She was looking at the flowers on the soggy road
as if she cared for no other radiance than their
gleam of earthy hue, albeit an evanescent glow.

"Nobody but me viewed it," he went on after a
moment of unfruitful expectation. "I tried other
folks, an' they seen nuthin'. An' by that I 'lowed
it hed some charge fur me, some leadin'. Stars hev
been messengers afore this." He interposed this
affirmation of precedent for proof. His senses were
keen. He had not failed to note the ring of incredulity in Kenniston's voice. He paused, thinking
again of the wise men of the East, and the blessed
path to the cradled Christ as the Star guided them.
He sighed deeply as he plucked off the yellow plumes
of a wayside spray of goldenrod. The fragments
floated away on the stream, and he drearily lifted his
haggard eyes to the broad whiteness of the day bright-
ening over all the purple mountains and bronze-

green valleys; here all miracles exhaled with the mists of the night and the evanescence of the stars. The atmosphere of the practical, the prosaic, the recognized and thrice-tried forces of nature was paramount. Naught seemed to exist that man in his ignorant cognoscence had not explored. But he had expected no miracle; he had sought no wonderful worldly gifts or graces. True, the will of God is much to know, but he had thought that with so signal an intimation a leading might be vouchsafed. Had not other men followed a star to Christ? And was there naught for him, no little thing for him to do? Did that gracious supernal stellular presence shine on him, and him alone, only to amaze, to baffle, to dismay him, — to find his life but poorly furnished, and to leave it empty?

"I got no leadin' out'n it," he said drearily. "It jes' disappeared somehows. I dunno ef ez suddint ez it kem or no, bein' ez several nights war rainy and clouded over. It's gone!"

Something in his dreary tone smote upon Julia's preoccupied faculties. Whether she harbored rancor against him for Jack Espey's sake, whether she resented his criticism of her father, whether she repelled the intrusion of the consciousness of any other emotion than the paramount emotion which possessed her, and love crowded out and trampled on pity, she spoke with a keen fling of satire.

"Waal, ef yer star hev petered out, ye hed better go an' get Ad'licia ter hearten ye up by tellin' ye ter take notice how many stars thar be lef'. Ye'll be lighted full well on occasion."

He flushed at the taunt, but love is of long patience.

"Air ye mad at Ad'licia?" he queried, interested in aught that touched Julia.

"Naw — yes" — She hesitated, interested herself. "That is, I can't holp bein' mad with the idjit fur bein' *sech* a idjit."

"How is she a idjit?" demanded Larrabee.

"Fur not marryin' Jack Espey whenst she hed the chance. Dad an' Luther would hev stood off Ross an' sech cattle, or gin bond fur him an' patched up things somehow. Ye know they would. Ef I hed been in her place, now, an' ef he hed axed *me*" —

She paused abruptly, with a sort of appalled recognition of the sentiment that animated her. A sudden illumination had broken in upon her; her heart throbbed tumultuously with pleasure, or was it pain? For she loved Jack Espey; and he — oh, was it true that he loved Adelicia still? She hardly heeded or realized her self-betrayal. She did not see — so little did she care — the pallid dismay, the heartbreak, on Jasper Larrabee's face. He could not deceive himself, — it was too patent. He turned away with a bitter sense of resentment, another grudge toward Jack Espey for thus slyly and completely supplanting him. At that moment his eye fell upon the jagged rock about the entrance of the Lost Time mine, and he drew back in amazement.

"Why, where does all this water come from?" he

exclaimed sharply. He wondered that he had not marked it before, despite his preoccupation. For the flow of the stream was quadrupled, its momentum every instant greater. Naught could enter now. The interior must be flooded anew. As he gazed at it, wide-eyed and dumfounded, a sudden enlightenment as to the phenomenon broke upon him. The blasting which he had heard, — he remembered it now ; doubtless the concussion had brought down some mass of rock or earth, damming an underground current, and forcing its waters into the channel of the stream which partially emptied here, while the residue backed up and filled the spaces. He thought that Espey and the old man and " Tawm " had possibly made good their escape before it happened ; but if not — and Taft — He remembered how close were the ghostly voices when he had last heard the false, cracked tones of command ring through the tunnel. Those ill-timbered galleries would fall to a certainty. He turned pale at the very thought of a living burial in the den of the still-room.

He did not hesitate. Without a word he sprang upon the log, crossed the water, and sped away like the wind, leaving Julia gazing in astonishment after him. He thought his worst fears were realized, when he reached the store of the Lost Time mine. His hasty question elicited from the children only the fact of the absence of Taft and Copley. He ran down into the cellar, to find the obliteration of the traces of the old door, which he recognized only as an added precaution since his departure. Doubtless some other method of entering the tunnel had been devised. An axe hacking through the chinking served to reveal the ruin of the tunnel, and to admit a strong and pervasive odor of gunpowder.

Lorenzo Taft's plans were very perfectly calculated and adjusted to the probabilities. There had been no rift in his judgment. Nowhere could he find fault or flaw in his reasoning. A lucky chance had fired the hotel, and freed his hands from the smirch of the firebrand and the possible penalties of arson. The moving of the great monument of boundary had thrown the only available site for the hotel on the Kenniston tract well within Cap'n Lucy's lines when the land was processioned, and thus the summer swallow must needs alight elsewhere, and the commercial interests of moonshining would thereby be promoted. Each detail had fallen out exactly as he had planned. Success seemed the essential sequence. Only Espey's frantic fear of arrest had precipitated all the untoward events which had advanced parallel after parallel, and forced him to his last defenses. And these one might think were most sagacious and adequate. The foolish drunken boy, whose tongue might work mischief, was within the hour hustled out of the country. Every trace of the forbidden vocation was demolished beyond the possibility of detection. If Larrabee should seek revenge by informing, he could prove naught, not even his own complicity. It would seem but the groundless accusation of malice. And Taft had even taken time by the forelock by avowing his former illegal practices, his prison record, his familiarity with the motives and manœuvres of moonshiners, and insidiously casting suspicion on Larrabee, ascribing to him an adequate motive for moving the Big Hollow Boulder, in the eyes of the law a felony.

No possible flaw in his reasoning from the premises from which he argued. He had guarded himself logically, boldly, with great perspicacity, from enmity, from revenge. It never for one moment occurred to him to devise protection from good will!

Kenniston and Ross, even in the excitement of the emergency, and the tumultuous tide of Larrabee's eager explanations when he suddenly burst in upon them as they sat smoking together after breakfast, could but take heed of the subtler subcurrent of significance in his disclosure. More than once they exchanged glances charged with a meaning deeper than he wot of.

"Thar 's a shaft," he cried, "an old air-shaft, a-nigh that thar tunnel! Ef ye 'll rig up a windlass, or let yer men put me down with a rope, I 'll find Taft, an' the t'others too, ef they be thar yit."

"You 'll drown yourself, or fall, or suffocate with gas," Kenniston said tentatively, looking about for his hat, and pausing to cast a keen glance at Larrabee.

"I 'll resk it — I 'll resk it — fur him and Espey too — an' I dunno what my mother would do ef old grand-daddy Haight war ter kem ter sech an e-end!

Oh, I 'll resk it! An' Taft, he ain't a bad man when all 's said. Taft 's mighty clever sometimes."

' "I think he's the worst man I ever saw," said Kenniston, as he flung away his cigar.

A call for volunteers and the offer of a reward by Kenniston secured no companion to Larrabee in his venture when the workmen looked down into the dark shaft,. with its crumbling sides, and sound of tumbling waters, and chill dank foul breath. They only manifested their good will in their alacrity in adjusting and adapting such appliances as they could to insure Larrabee's safety as far as possible. Kenniston doubted at the time whether he ought to permit the jeopardy; being assured, however, that the effort would be made at all events, but without the advantage of the heavy cables and pulleys which had been used in building the hotel, and which his compliance offered, he yielded. Afterward he was disposed to take great credit to himself for several devices which facilitated the enterprise, and from his knowledge of mechanical resources he doubtless insured its success; he bore the honors of the rescue, — which Larrabee at the peril of his life achieved, — with all the unblushing effrontery of an officer whose command has won a battle.

He was in a glow of enthusiasm for the nonce, and he continued the rôle of benefactor with more genuine pleasure than had lately fallen to his jaded susceptibility. He placed eighty-seven silver dollars in a worn leather bag, a tobacco pouch of one of the workmen, to be given to old Haight when he should be sufficiently recovered, with the pious fiction that his own money had been found in the shaft. "This will keep the old mole from burrowing again," he said.

His abounding good nature was very thorough when once aroused. His heart was touched by Espey's forlorn plight, as he lay panting on the grass, and the pallor of his young face marked by the dread of life that had just succeeded the dread of death.

"Can't you make out to let up on Espey, somehow?" he said aside to Rodolphus Ross, whose clumsy pranks of delight at the successful outcome of this most exciting episode were like the extravagant joviality of a gamboling Newfoundland dog, and not unpleasing to his interlocutor from their common bond of sympathy.

"Who? Espey?" He paused, turning his lighted dark eyes on Kenniston, his peaked hat shading his elevated eyebrows and surprised face. "I ain't hyar arter Espey no more. I 'm arter the fire-bug, ye know. That thar man ez Espey shot in Tanglefoot Cove hev got well o' the pip, or the gapes, or whatever the weak-kneed chicken took from the bullet; an' this hyar warrant fur arrest hev been kerried round in my pocket till it 's mighty nigh wore out." He took the ragged paper from his pocket and shook out its tatters, and laughed and grimaced in the very face of its august authority. "Go on, boy, go on! I

wouldn't put the county ter charges ter board ye ! "
he said to Espey.

A supply of whiskey was on hand, for the ostensible purpose of reviving the victims of the Lost Time mine, as they were drawn up one by one from those treacherous depths, limp and pallid and fainting. But the quantity was sufficient to enable the company of rescuers subsequently to refresh themselves, and Kenniston genially treated the crowd. Some of the men now and then began to coil up the ropes, and again fell to discussing the jeopardy and the disastrous possibilities ; and much hilarity and gratulation prevailed amongst the group in the dewy woods, still filled with the slant of the early morning sunshine, when Espey slipped away from it. His heart was still sore, as if it had forgotten to beat except with a dull throb of pain, unrealizing his change of fortune except to sullenly rebel against all the unnecessary woe that had fallen to his lot. As he went along the road, he scarcely noted a flower here and there on the soggy ground. The dash and fret of the stream from the portal of the Lost Time mine caught his attention. He marked its added volume, and, with his familiarity with the terrible subterranean chambers, he could picture to himself the obstacles which lay in its course, and which the blasting from the tunnel or the still-room had brought down. He trembled and grew cold with the thought of his jeopardy. He mechanially cursed anew Taft's name, as he had done again and again since his voice, his "partin' compliments," had been audible before the charge in the tunnel had been fired. He shuddered again as he recalled the sound of the water backing up ever higher and higher through those black dungeons, lisping and hissing its insidious threat through all the long night. How woeful it had been — with the wild terror of his companions to contemplate, till he was as wild with the terror of them as of his own fate — to look momently to meet death here, without a soul on earth to truly care, to anguish for him as he was anguished — He paused, the tenor of his thought breaking abruptly. Had he seen it before, or had he only fancied that cardinal flower lying in the sun on the gray rock by the water? Was it not thus that he should know that Julia had passed and had thought of him, — was not this their covenant? He doubtfully picked up the delicate spray — another; still, it might be an accident, a coincidence. A cluster of jewel-weeds lay caught in the bark of the log that served as footbridge, and swayed and glowed in the sun; it was in his hand when he reached the further bank. As far as one might hope to command a glimpse from the mine, the fragile tokens were scattered. They were full of dew; their breath allured him. They trembled as with some shy, timorous thought in his trembling hand. The color had come into his face ; a light was in his eyes ; his tired, troubled pulses were beating fast, strong, with a new rhythm. And as Julia, still loitering homeward, her head bare, her hands empty, heard a footstep behind her and turned, she saw him, all her garnered blossoms in his grasp, and all his heart in his eyes.

Kenniston, still elated, but somewhat tired out with the morning's excitements, upon reaching his quarters among the workmen's shanties, found Cap'n Lucy there awaiting an audience, and all unaware of the progress of events of so much moment elsewhere to-day. A rousing "cock-a-doodle-doo" might be a fair summary of Cap'n Lucy's discourse. His perplexities had vanished with the tangled twists of the rain, and he set forth boldly and with much detail his discovery of the moving of the boulder, the corner monument of boundary, his anxiety and doubt as to his proper course, and his realization that the surveyor's line had thrown much land which he knew was Kenniston's within his own domain.

A man of tact was Cap'n Lucy in his own way. He so glossed over his suspicions of Kenniston that albeit the latter detected them rather through the correlated circumstances than through the veneer of that section of his mind which it pleased Cap'n Lucy to present, he did not look upon them seriously. He was a stranger; the old man was densely ignorant, and his experience of life and comparative knowledge of men were limited indeed; and in truth it was apparently impossible to deduce from the facts any other interest than

Kenniston's to be served by the moving of the boulder. Thus he silently forgave Cap'n Lucy for his suspected suspicions.

And Cap'n Lucy was heartily ashamed of them now.

" I know it air moved bodaciously — Big Hollow Boulder — corner mark — monimint o' boundary; an' now what air ye an' me goin' ter do 'bout that thar dad-burned line what's gone an' coiled itself like the plumb old Scorpion o' the Pit?"

"Procession the land again, and prosecute the man who moved the boulder," said Kenniston coolly.

And indeed justice had hardily overtaken Lorenzo Taft, for Kenniston's unwonted leniency did not hold out to include his offending. It seemed to him a very pretty play of cause and effect that so close upon the heels of Taft's accusations of Larrabee, and his subtle and successful hoodwinking of the practiced man of business, who made a point of knowing men, Taft should be hurrying to Colbury and the county jail, under the escort of the jubilant Rodolphus Ross and a posse of two or three stout fellows, to answer these very charges of arson and of feloniously moving a corner monument of boundary, — all because of Larrabee's voluntarily putting his life in jeopardy for his sake.

Nevertheless, Kenniston listened mildly enough to Adelicia's earnest intercessions for Taft that evening, when he sat as of yore with the family circle around Cap'n Lucy's fireside; he seemed to find a certain fascination in the incongruities of her ingenious palliations and extenuations of his crime.

" He mought n't hev been acquainted with the boulder ez a monimint o' boundary," she urged ; and when the fallacy of this was demonstrated, " He mought hev been sorry an' wanted to put it back, but it war too heavy an' the hill war too high."

Whereupon Kenniston burst into satiric laughter.

" He 's sorry enough now, I 'll warrant you ; and he 'll be sorrier still before I 'm through with him."

But although Adelicia's expertness in excuses for other people failed in this instance, Kenniston's purposes were frustrated by a wholesale jail delivery which occurred at Colbury shortly after, and Taft was among the jail-birds who took flight thence. He was never heard of again in the Cove. The thought of him at large and at enmity served to postpone the building of the hotel for a time. The plans for a great public edifice in Bretonville absorbed Kenniston in the immediate future, and finally he grew indifferent to the project of the mountain resort, and it was definitely abandoned.

Larrabee profited by Kenniston's advice, and availed himself of the " amnesty " proffered by the government to moonshiners about that time, and thenceforward the still knew him no more. The manufacture of " brush whiskey " was never resumed at the Lost Time mine. The store there be-

came truly a centre of barter under the ministra-
tions of old Copley and the power behind the
throne, his niece, Cornelia Taft, who developed
much of her father's decision and definiteness and
shrewdness of character as she grew older, always
tempered by Mrs. Jiniway's precepts, to which she
rigidly adhered. She received much countenance,
and guidance too, in these early years, from Adelicia, who persisted in following the bent of her
own lenient inclination toward others, making the
most of their good qualities and light of their foibles. It was a certain solace in the bitter loss of
other illusions for which she was less charitable.
She never could be brought to believe that Julia
had not intentionally wiled her lover's heart away
from her. It was a relief when these strained relations were at an end, when Julia and Espey were
married, in defiance of Cap'n Lucy's opposition,
and had gone to Tanglefoot Cove. Cap'n Lucy
argued their much-mooted points of difference with
Adelicia less than before, and deferred in silence to
her. It was only when, in the winter evenings,
Jasper Larrabee was wont to come and read aloud,
as in the old days, that Cap'n Lucy rose to his normal temperature of contradiction, and controverted
sundry hard sayings difficult to be incorporated in
the life of a willful man, and contemned Jasper
Larrabee's learning, and accused him of ignorantly
perverting the Scriptures. Then it was that Adelicia's talents of optimism became transcendently apparent. She developed a wonderful craft of inter-

pretation. Leaning over one arm of Cap'n Lucy's chair, while Jasper Larrabee leaned over the other with his book and page to show, — Cap'n Lucy, flustered and red-faced, acrid and belligerent, vociferating between them, — Adelicia would demonstrate that this doubtless meant the other, or it was plain to see that the reference was not general, thus including Cap'n Lucy, but was made directly to the character under discussion; whereby Cap'n Lucy, perceiving that no added burden of meekness or other Christian grace was to be laid upon him as essential to salvation, would permit himself to be pacified. And Adelicia's gifts grew by much exercise. Even Cap'n Lucy, always acute, became reluctantly aware of this, in some sort. " Ad'licia hev got so durned smart she kin mighty nigh explain away the devil," he fretted, unaware that this feat had already been accomplished by other and more pretentious theologians than Adelicia. The gossips said, in the Cove, that it was in the process of trying to " ' square ' Cap'n Lucy to the Scriptur's, or ter square the Scriptur's ter Cap'n Lucy," that Adelicia and Jasper fell in love with each other. Certain it is the days came in which neither had aught to regret, and Adelicia's optimism was triumphantly justified.

Even his vanished star came to be a tender memory to Larrabee rather than a poignant bereavement. Sometimes thinking of that dread descent into the crumbling old shaft of the Lost Time mine, with the chill sound of the tumbling waters below, the thick foul air in his every breath, the desperate straining of the ropes that so shook his nerves, the fragments of rock falling about his head, and his heart fairly failing him for fear, he deemed he had found the " leading " he had asked and had followed it. For since he could do naught for Christ, whose humble humanity is merged in the majesty of the great King of heaven, he might do somewhat for man whom He died to save.

He did not know that his star remained for a time a faint telescopic object and interested the speculation of astronomers, whose outlook from their wisdom was also limited as his from his igno-rance.   They merely accounted it one of those mysterious, unwonted apparitions, a stranger to all the astral hierarchy, prettily called " guest-stars " in the ancient Chinese records, and they knew after a time that the " Ke-sing dissolved."   They did not dream that this celestial visitant could be charged with a moral mission ; for in all the discoveries and advances of science, what mystic lens might serve to reveal the amaranthine wreath and the nearing pinion ?